MAGENTA DAIRY

Robert Forte

MAGENTA DAIRY

ISBN 13: 978-1984158178

ISBN 10: 1984158171

Library of Congress Control Number: 2018934064

Fifth Wind Publishing LLC, Johnstown, PA

MAGENTA DAIRY

To Our Friends and Our Fans

MAGENTA DAIRY:

1. A government bureau drug enforcement code 2. A snafu 3. Any given situation seemingly in good order which quickly escalates to bad and to worse Example: The Alamo, The Titanic, The Hindenburg, and Rachel Stone Barbieri

CHAPTER ONE

The day seemed to be getting away from her. It was almost two o'clock in the afternoon and she still had not made the bed from the night before. She had finished all the breakfast dishes, kissed her husband Jonathan goodbye as he drove off to work, removed two steaks from the basement freezer hoping to have a nice evening dinner when her husband returned, and ran her brand new vacuum cleaner across every room upstairs including the upper hallway.

Carole Wainwright always felt like the perfect wife.

After completely dusting the entire living room and the dining room, she turned off the radio playing Patti Page's number one song on the hit parade, The Tennessee Waltz, and placed her ample cleaning supplies under the kitchen sink cabinet. Standing a little over five feet four, she was all suited up, as she liked to call it; her long black hair tied back in a ponytail, wearing her favorite old tight beige slacks, her favorite pair of black fringed slip on shoes without any socks, and one of her husband's old

1

button down dress shirts. This was her "uniform" for whenever she went about her housework, always making certain that the house was extremely neat, tidy, and impeccably clean.

It was her routine every day, Monday to Friday, without fail.

"A clean house becomes a happy home," her mother always told her and that advice had stuck in the forefront of her brain since she was nine years old.

For some unknown reason on this particular Friday afternoon she found herself dragging her feet and all her usual daily chores were moving forward much too slowly. She thought it might be a cold coming on or maybe just the fact it was one week after the holiday season and the stress of all that shopping, planning and celebrating was beginning to catch up with her. A normal house cleaning for Carole was usually completed just before noon.

But not today.

She sighed heavily, sat down on the living room sectional, and took a much needed break. She had gone all out this year, spending a big chunk of her household money to buy her husband an expensive gold watch for Christmas. He had seen a magazine photo of Gary Cooper wearing one at some Hollywood producer's house and tried to find it himself in several stores with no success.

She found the exact watch in the city after only two days of searching. She had become the perfect wife. After deciding together to throw a New Year's Eve Party, it was she who perfected every little detail, making certain their celebration with her husband's new employers was impressively fanciful. She wanted her party's welcoming in of the new year, 1951, to be the celebration everyone remembered and spoke about for years to come.

And thanks to her hard work, the New Year's party was exactly that. She had the evening catered, hired a professional bartender, bought black and silver party hats and noisemakers for everyone in attendance, and could tell days later her diligence had made it a memorable occasion.

Her husband was filled with pride and admiration for her and a job well done, inspiring her to think about possibly starting her own catering business. But that would be a few years down the road.

For now, it was all about her husband's success. It was part of their nuptial agreement. Jonathan Wainwright was an up and coming assistant DA for the city of Newark, New Jersey. Three years ago on their wedding night, he had told his beautiful wife that he would always provide everything she ever required or needed to run their household.

"I'll take care of all our expenses, honey, you take care of our home," he always told her.

Carole loved their arrangement.

Jonathan's job did keep him working late some nights in the city but she never complained about his absence or his late hours. She happily managed their household without regret, doing all the housecleaning, cooking, laundry and shopping. It was only the two of them happily living the American dream in Montclair, New Jersey. Any time anything else needed to be done to assist her husband up his ladder of success she was right there at his side offering him her love, her undying support, and a strong, guiding hand whenever he called upon her.

They were a good team.

She was his rock and nothing would or could make her falter. Everyday life was good for the Wainwrights. Although they had a great sex life, they hadn't made love the entire week. Jonathan was working extremely hard on a new case and had been coming home mentally tired and physically drained. He promised to make up for their lost time this coming weekend and she was looking forward to the next two days. She pictured them having a nice quiet dinner alone and then, as they always did, would stroll slowly upstairs to the bedroom with a chilled bottle of champagne, two glasses, and after getting completely naked, engage in a long night of lovemaking.

She suddenly remembered their unmade bed and quickly headed up the stairs.

She never noticed the brand new cream colored Cadillac coming slowly up the drive.

The car parked in front of the house, and a well-dressed man stepped out and rang the front doorbell.

Carole had no idea what was about to unfold in front of her regarding her husband's so-called ladder of success. It couldn't occur to her that it would be this day everyone at their New Year's Eve party would remember most and speak of in the months to come.

She ran down the stairs, thinking it might be another one of those door-to-door salesmen, like the handsome young man with the nervous smile who rang the bell and sold her the newest state-of-the-art vacuum with all the fancy attachments.

Carole opened the front door and was greeted by an older man in his late forties, dressed in an expensive dark blue suit and tie, carrying a leather briefcase. He politely tipped his hat and smiled at her as she looked past him briefly and took in the new Cadillac he was driving.

This was no salesman.

"Good afternoon," he said.

"Good afternoon. May I help you?" she asked.

The man stood there for a moment not speaking which gave her pause to wonder who this man could be and what brought him to her front door. He was a bit taller than she and she noticed he had large hands and very broad shoulders.

"You are Carole Wainwright. Yes?" he asked.

"I'm Mrs. Wainwright," she replied.

"You don't know me, Mrs. Wainwright. I am Frederick Lynn," he answered kicking his heels together slightly and nodding his head forward. "I am an attorney, an associate of your husband, Jonathan."

He handed her his business card and she saw his information was as he stated and also included a local phone number.

"What can I do for you, Mr. Lynn?" she asked.

"I am sorry, Mrs. Wainwright. I can tell by your face you are not expecting me at all? Are you?"

She smiled and shook her head no.

"Expecting you? No, I am not," she said completely taken by

surprise but beginning to feel comfortable with his demeanor and the fact that he knew her name and her husband's.

"Allow me to give you my sincerest apologies, Mrs. Wainwright. Your husband told me he was going to call you letting you know of my arrival. I am heading down to Trenton today and I have some legal papers your husband needs to go over this weekend."

"Legal papers?" she asked.

"Yes," he quickly responded and kept talking without skipping a beat. "Your husband asked me to stop by, drop them off, and make certain I hand them to you, personally. It's Carole with an E, yes?"

"Yes," she answered and glanced at herself in the hallway mirror for a second and leaned against the door.

"Are these papers in my name?" she asked.

"No. No," he quickly responded. "The papers have nothing to do with you personally, Mrs. Wainwright. They concern a new case he will be working on next week. It's evidently very sensitive material and he wanted to make sure I put them into your hands and not anyone else."

He stood waiting patiently and smiled again.

"A new case? Oh. I see," she added. "More work at home."

"Yes," he said. "I'm afraid so."

Carole began to feel completely at ease with the man and smiled back warmly.

"If this is not a good time, Mrs. Wainwright, I completely understand. I can come back tomorrow morning if you'd like," he announced politely. "When your husband is at home."

He took a step back and smiled again.

"No. No. It's all right. Please? Come in," she offered and leaned slightly once more against the door.

"Thank you," he replied and stepped inside. "This will only take a moment."

"I'm surprised Jonathan forgot to call me," she said turning her back to him and closing the door. "He must have gotten caught up in something or other."

5

"Possibly," he answered assuredly. "We lawyers are a busy bunch."

She thought his reply was rather odd.

For lawyer-speak it was a bit off the mark.

Carole turned and faced him and for a split second wondered why his right hand was now bunched up into a fist with several brass rings wrapped around his fingers. She looked up into his face and opened her mouth to speak but before she could utter a word or move he slammed his fist across the side of her face with tremendous force, breaking her opened jaw and knocking her completely unconscious.

Before blacking out a sharp pain shot up one side of her face and she felt her knees buckle beneath her. Carole's mind shut off completely and she fell against the wall, cutting her forehead as she slowly dropped down onto the carpeted floor like some tall rag doll, her head just missing the bottom wooden stair by a matter of inches.

He placed his hat on the half table under the foyer mirror and put the brass knuckles in his pants pocket. He stared down at Carole lying on the floor, quickly retrieved some rope from his briefcase, looped it tightly around both her wrists, and once he successfully knotted the rope as if she were some rodeo calf, dragged her down the hallway alongside the staircase. He looked up, threw the other end of the rope over the bannister and pulled her to her feet with both arms stretched above her head. He expertly tied the rope off between two rungs, calmly walked to the front door and locked it. He casually looked down the driveway to the street, saw no one moving about, took a deep breath, pulled down the fringed shade, turned, and walked calmly back to her.

He slowly looked her up and down, checked the knots of the rope, looked at her jaw and the small cut across her forehead, and satisfied with his inspection and his work, casually walked into the kitchen.

He glanced around, took a good-sized steak knife from the wooden butcher block sitting on the counter, walked back to the hallway with it, leaned comfortably against the opposite wall facing the staircase, folded his arms in front of him, and calmly waited.

About three or four minutes passed and Carole slowly came to and opened her eyes. Her head pounded with a pain she had never experienced before and when she tried to speak realized her jaw was broken. A small amount of blood ran down her right cheek from the scratch on her forehead and the blood began to pool slightly on the collar of her shirt.

"Hello again, Mrs. Wainwright," he said. "Can you hear me all right?"

"I hear you," she answered without moving her jaw.

He looked directly into her eyes and smiled.

"You and I need to have a little talk," he announced.

She tried to remain calm, worked through the pain and spoke as best she could.

"You don't work with my husband. Do you?" she uttered quietly.

He laughed slightly, tilted his head to one side, and looked directly into her eyes a second time.

"Yes and no, Mrs. Wainwright," he answered. "Yes and no. You see, I do, but I really don't."

His face and eyes began to terrify her but she still attempted to remain calm.

"I don't understand," she said quietly.

She glanced down and saw the knife in his hand and she could feel her heart pounding in her chest. He noticed her staring down at the knife and smiled up at her.

"I borrowed this little item from your kitchen. I hope you don't mind."

Carole stiffened and held her breath as he suddenly reached out with the knife and cut the rubber band from her ponytail. His face almost touched hers and he smelled of alcohol and cigarette smoke and she noticed a large mole behind his left ear. His face blocked her vision for a few moments, and she stiffened even tighter as he slowly ran his free hand through her hair until he was satisfied at how she now appeared.

She slowly let the air out of her lungs as he calmly stepped back and gazed at her as if she was a painting or some other piece of art work.

"Much better," he said, sounding like some deranged hair stylist.

Carole could feel her fear and adrenalin quickly flowing through her entire body. She silently cursed herself for being so gullible and stupidly allowing someone like this into her home so easily.

A million scenarios began to race through her mind as she wondered and feared the worst.

"Let me get right to the point of our discussion today, Mrs. Wainwright. I've never met your husband but in a very strange and somewhat odd fashion, your husband, Jonathan, and I, are clearly working together. Especially this afternoon. Of course he doesn't know that yet and whether we ever work together again, will clearly be up to you."

"Me?" she asked and tried to slowly struggle out of the rope around her wrists.

He gently moved a piece of her hair back behind her left ear.

"What do you want with me?" she questioned again trying to stay calm.

"All in good time, Mrs. Wainwright. All in good time. And please? Don't move your arms like that. I find it quite disturbing."

Her fear forced her to struggle with the ropes even more.

"You are not making any sense!" she cried. "Why are you here? What do you want from me?"

"Please? Mrs. Wainwright. Stop moving," he pleaded.

She kept struggling but the ropes were much too tight. He reached up with his left hand, grabbed the rope above her wrists, and gently tapped the flat side of the knife twice against the tip of her nose.

"Stop!" he commanded.

The word echoed through her head. She slowly stopped her struggle and felt her body begin to shake.

He ignored her nervousness and stared at the knife as he spoke.

"I will not ask you again, Mrs. Wainwright," he threatened. "Stop all this struggling! Please? I'm trying to have a simple conversation here and I need your undivided attention."

She stared at him, took a deep breath, and stopped moving

completely.

"Thank you," he politely added.

He smiled and looked her up and down.

"You are a very beautiful woman, Mrs. Wainwright. I can see you take very good care of yourself. You keep your house here very clean and neat. Your kitchen sparkles just like on those television commercials. So do your eyes. I like that in a woman. The eyes. They say the eyes are the mirrors of the soul. I believe that to be true. Don't you?"

He smiled again broadly and before she could answer he suddenly stabbed the knife into the side of the stairway, extremely close to her face, making her jump and flinch with fear.

He stepped up close to her face again, and slowly began running his hands over her breasts, sliding both hands down her stomach and back, placing his left hand between her legs and gently stroked the left cheek of her backside with his right hand.

Carole froze and stiffened from his hands touching her body and she wanted to scream and cry out for the entire world to hear, hoping someone would come to her aid and remove this monster who was pawing at her like some sex crazed madman. She stood motionless, knowing there was no one coming to save her except for herself. She saw the handle of the knife out of the corner of her eye and wondered how she could possibly get hold of it and defend herself by cutting him several times and forcing him out her front door forever.

"You are very sweet, Mrs. Wainwright," he whispered. "Very sweet. Your husband is a very lucky man to have a woman like you around. A very lucky man indeed."

She held her breath and shuddered from his touch. The pain from her jaw was excruciating but she didn't move as he had requested.

He leaned in closer, gently squeezed her throat, and whispered directly into her ear.

"There is a man, Mrs. Wainwright. His name is Rockwell. Say his name for me."

Her body began to shake.

"Say it!" he screamed.

"Rockwell," she whispered.

He grabbed the knife, stepped back from her, and as he spoke, slowly began cutting off the front buttons of her shirt, one by one.

"Very good, Mrs. Wainwright. Very good. This Mr. Rockwell thinks he is a bird. He thinks he is some big, black bird who can sing like the angels from up above. This man wants to sing for your husband and the District Attorney's office and he is going to do this in a few weeks."

Several buttons fell to the floor and Carole's breasts become exposed as her shirt began to open up.

"Mr. Rockwell wants to tell your husband all about some associates of mine and a certain enterprise they run. Quite successfully run I will tell you. It's a real money maker. This song, Mr. Rockwell wants to sing? Well believe me, this man is no Perry Como, but the song cannot and must not happen. Do you hear me?"

Carole took in another deep breath and nodded yes.

"This man Rockwell wants to sing in exchange for his freedom. He has been locked up for some time now and he is growing tired of his situation. If you can't do the time then don't do the crime. Right?"

The last button fell to the floor.

"Do you understand what it is I am asking you?" he asked.

Tears began to fall from Carole's eyes. He slowly reached inside the shirt and pulled back the front exposing both breasts. "I said do you understand what it is I am asking you?" he repeated.

Carole's body began shaking as she struggled to remain calm and still speak.

"Yes. I understand. What does this man, Rockwell, have to do with me?"

He stepped back and stared at her. Carole's body shook even more as the fear inside her became unstoppable. She gasped and her eyes widened with fear, wondering in her what he was about to do next.

"I'm sorry, Mrs. Wainwright. I know this must be quite difficult for you. Speaking to me in this manner and under these extremely trying circumstances."

He ran the palm of his right hand across her nipples. "I am sorry about your jaw," he said. "I am. I am also sensing you're feeling extremely frightened of me, Mrs. Wainwright? Maybe you are becoming just a little more tense right about now? A bit apprehensive with the situation?"

She looked directly into his eyes and nodded her head slightly.

"Yes. Very much, so," she whispered.

He looked away and continued rubbing her nipples with his palm.

"Don't be afraid. Relax yourself. I am not going to rape you. Or cut you up into little pieces with your kitchen knife. I'm not going to kill you either. Although? I could if I wanted to. If I had to. If I was told to. You know that? Right?"

She nodded her agreement slightly. He leaned in closer.

"The people I work for are very dangerous people, Mrs. Wainwright," he whispered. "Very dangerous and very powerful. Your husband is stepping into an arena where men like him do not belong and if he wants to survive? If he wants you to survive? He needs to step away. Turn a blind eye."

"You're not going to hurt him?" she asked as tears rolled down her face.

He stopped touching her and locked eyes with her again.

"No, no, no. Today, I am simply sending your husband, Jonathan, and all those powerful people he works with, a little message from the powerful people I work with. Think of me as your local delivery service. A local. Message. Delivery service."

"A message?" she asked.

"Yes," he replied.

He jammed the knife into the opposite wall, reached over quickly, and pulled her slacks and underwear down to her ankles. He stepped back again, looked her up and down slowly, and sighed.

"Very nice, Mrs. Wainwright. Very nice. You are a stunningly beautiful woman."

She tried to stare coldly at him but her fear was much too great. She

11

wanted to reach out and tear at his face until his own blood would blind him and she could escape from her entire ordeal but the rope around her wrists were too tightly bound and she knew she was at his mercy with no chance of escape or of fighting back. Her eyes welled more with tears and they began running down both sides of her face.

"You see, Mrs. Wainwright? It is like this. You? Hanging here, in your front hallway, appearing as you do right now? With everything you have? Everything you are all about? Hanging out for everyone to see? You? You, are my message. Your husband is going to come home later today. He is going to walk through that front door as he always does, only this time he is going to find you. Just like this. And when he does? He will ask you, sweetheart, who did this to you? And you will tell him all about my little visit here. With you."

He reached down and ran his hand lightly across her vagina.

"At first, he'll be angry. That's understandable. That's expected. Then, he will be sad. He will want to know what kind of a person does this to someone? Someone like you? His own wife. In his own home? And you, Mrs. Wainwright, will tell your husband. It was me."

He kissed her forehead and smiled at her once again. She could sense he was becoming aroused and prayed her ordeal would soon come to an end.

"You tell your husband to take a good, long, hard look at what I can do, to someone like you, whenever I please, if he does not do as my powerful friends have asked? Can you do that?"

"Yes," she whispered.

"What? I can't hear you, Mrs. Wainwright."

"Yes," she said in a louder voice.

He reached out and gently stroked her nipples again with the palm of his hand.

"Rockwell does not sing! You get that?"

"Yes," she said. "I get that!"

"I can't hear you!"

"Yes! I get that! Rockwell does not sing!"

12

He stepped in close almost nose to nose with her and whispered.

"That's right, Carole. Rockwell. Does not. Sing. To anyone."

He kissed the tip of her nose and stepped back.

"Are we clear?"

She stared at him and hoped he could see the hate in her eyes."Yes," she said. "We are clear.

He tilted his head again, looked directly into her eyes, and laughed.

"Remember this too, Mrs. Wainwright. This request? This warning I have brought to you? Don't take my kindness towards you today as a sign of weakness. My message is really a matter of life and death."

"Life and death?" she asked.

He suddenly stepped in closer again and jammed two fingers of his left hand into her vagina. Carole stiffened and stopped breathing for a moment as sheer terror encased her entire body.

His eyes only inches from hers.

"You have a nice vagina, Mrs. Wainwright," he whispered. "Does your husband like your vagina?"

She tried to speak but her fear kept her voice silent.

"Well? Does he?" he asked again and pressed his fingers deeper inside her. "Answer me!"

She nodded her head yes as best she could. Her breathing came back to her in short uncontrolled bursts.

"Yes," she said but could hardly hear her own voice.

"You tell your fucking husband if Rockwell sings, to him, or to anyone else in his high and mighty office? I will come back here. Right to you, Mrs. Wainwright. We will have another discussion very similar to the one we are having right now, but when I am done with this vagina of yours on our next little get together? And these lovely breasts of yours? And your soft, delicate, little throat? Your husband is not going to like what he sees. And neither will you! Do you understand me?"

Carole looked into his eyes and nodded yes.

"Say it?" he demanded in a whisper. "Say yes. I understand completely."

Carole began to sob.

"Say it!" he screamed, his words forcing her to lean her head back slightly.

"Yes," she answered as tears rolled down her cheeks and her body shook. "Yes. I understand completely."

He slid his two fingers out, stepped back, made certain he locked eyes with her once again, placed the two tips of the same fingers between his lips and lightly kissed them. He pointed his fingers at her and smiled.

"Sweet," he whispered.

He took the knife and walked back into the kitchen. Carole could hear water running. He washed the knife, placed it back into its proper place on the counter and dried his hands.

He came out of the kitchen, picked up the briefcase, and without looking at her walked slowly to the front door. He pulled back the shade and looked down the driveway.

"You better hope and pray, Mrs. Wainwright, that we never, ever, see each other again."

He put on his hat and looked back at her.

"Hope and pray. Hope. And pray."

Carole stared to the left, shaking uncontrollably as he laughed, unlocked the door, and casually stepped outside. He closed the front door and walked to his car. He suddenly heard Carole scream at the top of her lungs. He laughed, got into the Cadillac, revved up the engine, and drove down the driveway.   He got down to the street but before he could turn, two vehicles suddenly pulled up, one from the left and the other from the right, completely blocking his way. Three men in business suits, vests, and hats, and one woman, dressed in matching slacks and jacket and all pointing handguns quickly approached him. One man, much shorter than the rest, opened the driver's side door.

"I am Special Agent Edwards with the FBI. I will ask you, sir, to cautiously and carefully exit your vehicle, step to the rear, and place both of your hands on the trunk."

Totally taken by surprise, he stepped out and placed his hands on the trunk as requested.

"What is this all about, shorty? Did I run a red light somewhere?" he asked.

"This isn't about any red light," answered Agent Edwards, "And the name is Special Agent Edwards."

"Okay, Special Agent Edwards, you want introductions? My name is Frederick Lanai. I'm a lawyer and I know my rights."

"Frederick Lanai?" Agent Edwards repeated.

"Yes sir."

Agent Edwards removed a hand gun from the man's suit jacket and placed it on the trunk.

"I have a license for that," he added.

"I'm sure you do, Mr. Lanai," said Agent Edwards as he continued his search and tossed out the man's wallet, three business cards, a pack of Lucky Strike cigarettes, an expensive gold lighter, and the brass knuckles.

The female agent, Loretta Davis, opened the wallet and checked the I.D.

"This says he's Frederick Lanai," said Agent Davis. "He lives on Prospect Avenue in Woodbridge. No gun license."

"I must have left it at home," he replied. "What does the FBI want with me? What's this little shakedown all about? And who's this cute little twist?"

"I'm Agent Loretta Davis. Put your tongue back in your mouth before I twist it out of your face!"

"Spunky," he replied. "I like spunky."

Agent Edwards leaned in close to the man's face.

"This is no little shakedown. You, sir, are wanted for questioning in regards to the whereabouts of a certain murderer and drug trafficker by the name of Rachel Stone Barbieri."

"Never heard of her," he answered. "I'm not very good with names."

"I am and I know your name isn't Frederick Lanai," said Agent Edwards. "You're not even a lawyer. You are a small time con man and cleaner presently working for Ponce Delgado."

"Ponce Delgado? Now him? I do know. We used to hang together years ago but he's in prison now, up state," said the fake lawyer. "Delgado is somebody you should be talking to about murder and drug trafficking. Delgado is one bad hombre. Always was."

"Shut up and listen up," said Agent Edwards. "Before Delgado, you worked for a small time gangster here in Jersey named Carmine Scarola, and before him, you were scaring college kids over at Rutgers into buying watered down whiskey you stole from the New York docks. I know all about you, Mr. Lanai. Your real name is Henry Long. And you have been dodging the law for most of your life. But not today. Henry Long? Today? You are under arrest."

"This arrest will never stick," he said. "It's bogus and you know it."

"We will be the judge of that," said Agent Edwards.

Agent Edwards stepped back and nodded at one of the other agents.

"Cuff him. Get up to the house Loretta and check on Mrs. Wainwright."

"Yes sir," said Loretta and ran up the driveway.

Another agent, a thin man named Vannetti, quickly handcuffed Henry and turned him around.

"You have no right to place me under arrest?" he cried. "What's the god damn charge? I haven't done anything!"

"Just visiting an Assistant District Attorney's wife for what reason? Swapping dinner recipes?" asked Agent Edwards. "What are these for?"

Agent Edwards held the brass knuckles up to his face.

"Those? Me and the lady have a thing."

"A thing? I know your kind of thing, Henry. I know it very well. I saw first-hand what you did to Juror number seven, Susan Friar, over in Freehold. She lost an eye. And Lisa Kupchick, a single mother with a beautiful little boy. I saw her too. She will never have any more children because of your thing with the ladies."

"The broads I date like it rough," he said. "It's not against the law."

"You are telling me that you and Mrs. Wainwright are having a thing?" Agent Edwards asked.

"Yeah, that's right. And she likes to get a little wild. A little rough. Come on. You guys know how it is. The husband is away. She calls me. I come by. We're lovers for Christ's sake! Screwing around and doing a little rough and tumble with another man's wife is not illegal!"

"Screwing around? Rough and tumble? Is that what you were doing here?"

16

"Yeah. Among other things. That's exactly what we were doing."

"We'll see what she has to say about that. And we'll check her phone bill and see how many times she actually called you."

"Look? She don't want her husband to know about us. She's going to lie and make up some story to cover up her extracurricular activities with me. She's not going to tell you Feds the truth."

"Is she all right in there or did you hurt her?" asked Special Agent Edwards. "Did you leave her bloodied and beaten like you did with Dorothy Owens back in '49?"

"Dorothy who?" he asked.

"Or did you bust out her kneecaps like you did with Kitty Krumke?"

"That floozie fell down on her own. I had nothing to do with hurting that bitch."

"Did you kill her? Did you kill Mrs. Wainwright, Henry?"

"Kill her? No! Hey! I didn't kill anybody. I didn't! I swear! I didn't do nothing like that! I told you. We were only fooling around. Having a little fun."

"Is that so?"

"Yes. That is so! This is not right. You got to have a valid reason to arrest me. I told you! I know my rights!"

"You want a reason? I'll give you a reason. You are under arrest for insulting my intelligence and lying to the FBI," answered Edwards.

"That's no crime," he said.

"It is today," said Agent Edwards.

"Fuck you, short stuff!" he shouted and lunged at Agent Edwards.

Agent Edwards grabbed Henry's belt buckle with his left hand and punched him squarely in the crotch with his right fist. Henry doubled up in pain and the two other agents took hold of his arms to keep him from falling back down on his knees.

"Stand him up!" Special Agent Edwards ordered.

The agents pulled Henry up and leaned him against the car.

"You can't take me like this!" he cried.

"We are taking you, Henry. And? We are confiscating your car."

"I just bought this car!" he cried. "You bastards can't do this!"

"Today I can, Henry. Today I can do just about whatever I want in regards to you. Get him the hell out of here."

"Where are you taking me?" asked Henry.

17

"We will ask the questions from now on," said Agent Edwards.

"This is against the law!" he protested. "You have no legal cause to arrest me like this! I want a god damn lawyer! I think I need a doctor, too!"

The two agents quickly shuffled Henry to one of their cars and tossed him face down in the back seat. One agent got into the back seat with Henry while the other agent jumped in the driver's side as Henry kept up his protest.

"You bastards can't do this to me!" he cried.

Special Agent Edwards stood and watched as the car sped away.

Agent Edwards took a deep breath, got in the Cadillac and backed it slowly up the driveway. He stepped out, looked at the house, and walked up to the front door.

Mrs. Wainwright was sitting up on the hallway floor wrapped in a blanket and sobbing uncontrollably.

Agent Davis stepped out of the living room.

"He broke her jaw," said Agent Davis. "I called for an ambulance. It's on its way."

"Did he do anything else?" asked Agent Edwards.

"He stripped her down, fondled her, and penetrated her with two fingers."

"What was the warning this time?"

"Rockwell is supposed to be questioned next week by her husband, Jonathan Wainwright. He told her if Rockwell sings he would come back here and kill her."

Agent Edwards took a deep breath and shook his head.

He saw the rope hanging from the bannister.

"Jesus Christ," he gasped. "He tied her up with that?"

"Yes," she replied.

Agent Edwards took out his federal identification and held it up so Mrs. Wainwright could see it.

"I'm Special Agent Clovis Edwards with the FBI, Mrs. Wainwright. I am so sorry for the horrendous ordeal this man has put you through. We have apprehended him and he is under arrest."

"Thank you," said Mrs. Wainwright quietly.

"An ambulance is on the way."

Carole burst into tears and nodded yes.

"Thank you," she repeated.

Agent Edwards knelt down next to her.

18

"I'm so sorry we couldn't get to you sooner, Mrs. Wainwright. Our office only got the call he was coming here about a half hour ago from one of my undercover agents. But I want you to know, we did arrest him and he's never going to hurt anyone like this ever again. That much I can promise you."

Carole began crying again and no matter how hard she tried, she couldn't stop the flood of tears running down her face. Agent Edwards placed his hand on her shoulder trying his best to console her.

"Can we get you anything?" he asked.

"No," she sobbed. "He said he worked with my husband. That's why I let him in. He said he had some legal papers."

"You don't have to talk, Mrs. Wainwright. Just try to stay as comfortable as you possibly can until the ambulance gets here. We can take a statement from you later. First we will get you all taken care of and I will call your husband personally," he assured her.

"Thank you," she replied and with several heavy sighs began to calm down.

"You are going to be all right, Mrs. Wainwright. You are going to get through this and you are going to be all right."

Carole nodded but could not stop crying.

All Agent Edwards could do was hope his words would ring true. True for her and true for himself. He knew in his heart and in his mind, Mrs. Wainwright and her husband, Jonathan, and the New Jersey DA's office, were not going to be happy with the outcome he would have to give them concerning Ponce Delgado's message boy, Henry Long.

Agent Edwards would have to tell them that Henry Long, AKA Frederick Lanai, would never be prosecuted for his brutal attack upon Mrs. Wainwright.

Not ever.

The ambulance siren sounded in the distance.

CHAPTER TWO

I sat in my chair doing the best I could to listen to my latest prospective client's story but kept getting distracted with one other pressing thought running through my mind.

I needed to know where Rachel Stone Barbieri was hiding.

She was my woman in the yellow dress who had somehow managed to successfully get herself released from a federal prison pending her trial for drug trafficking, extortion, and murder.

"How the hell does something like that happen?" I kept asking myself.

I asked and kept asking that question over and over and over again.

When I saw her acting free as a bird, I thought my head was playing tricks on me. But once I realized it was really her I saw that day at the Beverly Hilton, I immediately began to suspect everyone I had come into contact with since our first meeting back at Barney's By The Sea.

Rachel Stone Barbieri was nowhere to be found and as hard as we searched for her, we kept coming up empty handed.

Someone got her released and I promised myself I would not rest until I got my answers to the how, the when, and the why, and returned Mrs. Rachel Stone Barbieri back in federal custody where she belonged. The only way that would happen was to work solely with people I could absolutely trust with my life.

Those people were my new secretary, Phil, Special Agent Edwards, and Detective Blaine.

Under the supervision of J Edgar Hoover, we worked diligently for six weeks straight, day and night, going over every single detail we could think of, including the premise that Hoover himself might be involved with her enterprise and her escape.

We also decided when we referenced Rachel Stone Barbieri we always used the code Magenta or Magenta Dairy just in case there were people out there possibly listening to any of our inner circle conversations.

Happily we discovered Hoover was not involved with Rachel's disappearance.

Our investigation revealed that Rachel Stone Barbieri had a federal judge in her pocket.

His name was Lizunkis and his office was a stone's throw from where she was being held. Lizunkis signed her official release papers together with an FBI mole who just happened to be working right alongside J. Edgar Hoover for over a year and a half. Both men worked their Barbieri magic without drawing any suspicion to themselves until weeks after she was released. The mole was responsible for not only orchestrating her transition to freedom, making it appear to be the decision of Hoover himself, but singlehandedly destroyed every piece of documentation the FBI had on Rachel Stone Barbieri before he was finally discovered and arrested.

His name was Richard L. Sundell. He was handsome, a Harvard graduate, class of '48, spoke several languages fluently, typed sixty words a minute, and was recommended for his position as an office assistant with the FBI by the governor of New Jersey, Alfred E. Driscoll. The governor was a man similar to Hoover who was big on fighting crime. Driscoll had cleaned up most of the New York docks, closed down a national book-making network, unified all law enforcement in New Jersey under one leader, and gave the District Attorney the power to supersede local county prosecutors, specifically in cases dealing with drug trafficking.

Richard's wealthy father and the governor also happened to be old friends.

When I made my initial call directly to Hoover using the code given to us, Magenta Dairy, Richard attempted to intercept the call but was totally in the dark and did not know the proper reply or its meaning. After eliminating all our suspects, Richard was the only remaining person having the means, the motive, and the opportunity.

Hoover was in shock and politically embarrassed, as was the governor.

Under intense interrogation, Richard told us he was in love with Rachel and she was in love with him. Once she had made good on her escape, she told the sap they would meet again in Acapulco, on New Year's Eve.

Acapulco was where they had first met.

Where they had first made love.

Their meeting and love affair began at the Hotel El Mirador, about three months before her arrest, and Rachel, obviously had made a lasting impression on this young college graduate who was about to begin working for the number one G-Man at the FBI. She told Richard that she in fact, herself, was an FBI undercover agent attempting to expose Hoover as a Communist and a man drunk with power who was attempting to orchestrate a Russian takeover of the United States government with the help of Mexico.

Sir Richard the Dope bought her story hook, line, and sinker.

She was good.

Convincingly good.

Dangerously good.

She asked for his help and after a little sexual persuasion, Richard had convinced himself that Rachel Stone Barbieri was indeed a woman dedicated to saving our republic from the Russians and Mexico, and together they would conspire and bring down Hoover and expose him for the man he really was.

She also told him she had fallen madly in love with him. When she was arrested, he went to see her secretly, and once again, she convinced Richard that Hoover now knew what she was up to and had to be stopped.

She told him the charges against her were all false and her only option was escape. Then and only then, could they fight the good fight for god and country, and really be together as the two lovers were destined to be.

And again, Rachel Stone Barbieri was good at getting what was wanted and needed.

She was very good.

Dangerously good.

And once again, the sap bought her nonsense, got her out, and eagerly waited for the new year to arrive, only to be arrested himself by our small team and whisked away to interrogation.

Hoover, hoping Barbieri might actually show, even if only to silence Richard, sent him down to Mexico with Special Agent Edwards and five other Special Agents to set up a sting for her arrest.

The New Year came and went but Rachel Stone Barbieri never arrived.

We were not surprised in the least but Richard was devastated once he finally realized the truth.

Back in the States and after many hours of explaining who the real Rachel Stone Barbieri was, Richard finally came to see that he was only one of many men being used by the charms of Mrs. Barbieri, and immediately began filling the FBI in on every detail he could remember about her.

The things we do for love.

Richard's father and the governor of New Jersey were beside themselves over the kid's behavior and as a professional courtesy from Hoover, allowed Richard one last weekend with his family before his incarceration.

23

On that Sunday morning his body was found hanging from a water pipe in the family estate's basement.

His death was ruled a suicide but I had my doubts.

We all did.

Rachel Stone Barbieri's M.O. was getting men to do what she wanted and needed and once that was accomplished, her next action was murder.

The elderly Judge Lizunkis, had been found dead in his bedroom the day of Richard's arrest. He apparently had a massive heart attack while taking his morning shower. He was sixty-eight years old with a long history of heart disease.

Or so we were told by the doctor who did his autopsy.

We all had our doubts on his passing too.

Our small group was dedicated to one thing and one thing only, the discovery, arrest, and conviction of Rachel Stone Barbieri, but unfortunately found ourselves back at square one. J. Edgar Hoover had to explain his failure to find this woman to several committees and late one night was ordered by President Truman, personally, to put a special task force together to find and apprehend Rachel Stone Barbieri at all costs. Hoover told Truman he had a team in place and promised the President and the committees swift and timely action.

Special Agent Loretta Davis, Agent Correlli, and his new partner, Agent Adrian Younger, were added to the team. Seven months went by and not one word, one sighting, or one solid lead manifested itself. It was as if Rachel Stone Barbieri had simply vanished from the face of the earth. All we could do was wait and hope something would turn up and point us in the right direction.

On a somewhat warm late January afternoon, in my new office space in Santa Monica, the something we were all hoping for miraculously walked into my office.

It was the something we needed but at the time had no idea of the unsurmountable cost we would be forced to pay.

Most clients hire a private eye because the police won't help them and they don't know where else to turn, or they're being blackmailed by some sleazy type who thinks they have them over a barrel, or maybe they know something that is true and don't know what to do with that kind of information.

Sometimes the job I do can also be dangerous but that kind of situation is rare. Most of my time working as a private eye is either sitting in my car drinking hot coffee and eating cold sandwiches watching some stranger come and go about his daily routine, or sitting at my desk making a ton of phone calls looking for answers to unasked questions, or taking a batch of unflattering photos of people doing things to each other which will never be published in any national newspaper or magazine.

This client's reason for wanting to hire me was completely different from any of my other experiences in my work.

I had to admit, it was an odd request.

I didn't know it at the time, but taking this man's case would eventually lead me and Hoover's special task force to the exact location of Rachel Stone Barbieri.

The client's name was Roberto Santoro. He was Cuban, seventy-three years old, gray-haired, well-dressed, and obvious dealing with some serious illness causing him to cough frequently as he related his reasons for coming to my office.

Phil offered him our usual donut and freshly brewed cup of coffee but he graciously declined.

Mr. Santoro was an old time gangster and had made a small fortune working several rackets for the infamous mobster, Mickey Cohen. Back in the day, he had his hands in a lot of illegal opportunities as he liked to call them, and for the last fifteen years of his life, felt he had made amends with his unsavory past and got himself involved in big money land deals.

Legal land deals. All of them on the up and up.

At one point, a few of his real estate investments had him crossing paths with Rachel's late father, Jonas Stone. When he mentioned that name it made sense to me that if you were doing any type of business in that world you were bound to run into a mogul like Stone or someone working for him.

I chalked it up to coincidence at first and didn't give the Stone angle another thought.

"Back in the day," Santoro said, "A guy like me, if you were relatively smart and faithfully loyal, could make a good amount of dough supplying the rich and the not so rich with extra-curricular activities, you know, like gambling, booze, or prostitution. I openly admit to you, I did my share of supplying all three and for the most part, business was good. It was very good. But things change. The times change. You get a little older. A little slower. And before you realize it, the way you knew how things were done, no longer applied. The balance of power in the so called underworld seems to change now on a monthly basis. There is no more loyalty. Not like the old days. Too many greedy hands reaching out now for their piece of the pie if you know what I mean?"

"I understand," I replied. "We all seem to be in a constant state of change nowadays."

"Yes, we are. Aren't we? Hard to tell the good guys from the bad guys any more. Yes?"

"Yes," I agreed.

He looked around the office as if we hadn't yet spoken a word to each other, coughed slightly, took a standard white business envelope from his suit jacket pocket, and placed it on my desk.

"I know Barney Hubbs. I have been to his restaurant many times back in the day. Barney saved my life once," he said.

"Barney is my best friend," I said. "He never mentioned you to me and I never heard this story."

"I asked him to keep a tight lip."

"Barney is good at that."

"Loyalty," he added.

"Yes," I agreed.

"One night, very late, Barney found me bleeding badly in the parking lot of his restaurant. It was back in '41. It was August. I was running

26

a weekly numbers game and some young little snot nose shot and robbed me and Barney drove me to this doctor he knew. The kind of doctor who didn't always report gunshot wounds to the police."

"Doctor Caldwell," I said.

"Yeah, that was him. Doctor Caldwell. I heard the doc got killed in some car crash."

"He did," I said. "He died on Memorial Day in '44."

"He was a good man."

"He was," I agreed. "A good man and a good doctor."

"Right after the war ended, I was having drinks at Barney's By The Sea and Barney told me about you. Said you were a good man, too. A stand-up kind of guy. A man that could be trusted."

"I'm a lot of things," I said and wondered where the man's words were leading.

"Good things," he added. "That's what I heard from Barney. Good things about you, Mr. Atwater."

"I always walk the straight and narrow. Always have."

The old man smiled and looked me in the eye.

"There's fifteen thousand dollars cash in that envelope, Mr. Atwater," he said. "If you agree to work with me? It's yours. All of it."

"Fifteen thousand dollars? For doing a good thing?" I asked.

He laughed and began coughing again. I could tell he liked my subtle way of saying I wasn't for sale if what he wanted me to do was in any way, illegal.

"I don't want you to kill anybody if that's what you're thinking," he said. "I'm dying. Lung cancer. These god damn doctors I see, tell me I got a month, three months, maybe even a year depending on how aggressive this thing I'm carrying decides to be with me."

He sat back in his chair and tried to catch his breath.

"I have a daughter, Mr. Atwater. Her name is Diana. She was just a little baby when her mother and I divorced. Her mother, Louise, was thirty-two when we split and I was fifty. We were a hot item for about a year and she got pregnant. Louise was a cocktail waitress, a beautiful woman inside and out, a good Irish girl, very loving, loyal, but she never could appreciate my chosen profession or the people I did most of my business with. Truth be told it scared her half to death. She took Diana and moved to Florida. Coral Gables. It's near Miami."

"The place with that unique swimming pool?" I asked. "The Venetian?"

"That's the place," he said. "Huge pool. Been operating since the twenties."

He reached in his pants pocket, took out a silver key, and placed it on the desk.

"You got something I can write on?" he asked.

I gave him a pen and a piece of paper and he began writing.

"There's an old large estate house down in the Florida Keys. This is the address."

He slid the paper to me. I picked it up and quickly began reading.

"I own it. I bought it for cash back in '34. There is a good sized warehouse in the back of the property. We used it for storage when I ran rum and cigars out of Cuba. There's an older woman living there now. Her name is Maria. There's a trunk in the attic of that warehouse and that key opens it. I want the entire estate, the house and the warehouse, and that old trunk, to go to my little girl."

"I'm not a lawyer, Mr. Santoro."

"I don't want a lawyer. I want someone I can trust. Someone who will see that this is done right. The way I want it done."

He started to cough in a heavier manner and struggled to suppress it .

"Would you like some water?" I asked.

"No, thank you. This will pass."

He sat back and caught his breath.

"I appreciate your offer, Mr. Santoro, but I would advise you to simply draw up a will stating your wishes and sign the deed to the estate over to your daughter."

"The deed has already been signed over."

He began to cough and pulled a white handkerchief from his suit pocket and coughed into it. The handkerchief became spotted with blood.

"I apologize for this damn disease of mine."

"It's all right," I said.

"I don't trust lawyers, Mr. Atwater. Or the law. Especially when it comes to people like myself that have had such a checkered past. Things have a way of getting changed around to somebody else's way of thinking. Or somebody else's pockets. I don't want that to happen to my little girl. She deserves better."

I decided to be blunt.

"Are you going to tell me what's in the trunk, Mr. Santoro?" I asked.

He didn't hesitate or blink an eye.

"Two million dollars," he said matter-of-factly. "All cash money. And it's all clean money. Squeaky clean money. It's the real estate money I made doing things the honest way and developing most of Los Angeles over the years. It is money I even paid taxes on. Making sure it was clean. Leaving it to my only kid is my one last good deed before I leave this life. I need to make certain I have the right person who will see she gets it. All of it. Every dollar. Without any legal mumbo-jumbo getting in the way. Can I trust you, Mr. Atwater? To do this for me? For my little girl? If you say yes? That envelope there on the desk is all yours."

His coughing became more acute but managed to suppress it as he calmly awaited my reply.

"What do you say, Mr. Atwater?" he added. "Will you help me?"

"What about the older woman?" I asked. "This Maria person?"

"She and I, and now you, are the only three people that even know the trunk exists."

"Does she know what's in it?"

"No. All she knows is that the house, the property, and the trunk, are going to my daughter and nobody else. Ever."

"If I find your daughter and bring her there, there won't be any problems with Maria?"

29

"No. Maria is my sister. She used to have a little gambling problem way back when but I got that and her all straightened out and I've let her live there for years. She takes care of the place. Rents the house to some business man who also allows her to live on the property. She has the deed with Diana's name on it and has been waiting for Diana to arrive for over twenty years. You won't have any problems. Not with her. That? I can promise you. Find my daughter, Mr. Atwater. Do this for me. Do this for her. I don't have the strength or I would be in Florida right now, looking for her myself."

I gazed at him across my desk and after a short amount of silence the old man looked at me and smiled again.

"Is that a yes I see in your eyes?" he asked.

For a quick second I thought of the Clifford girls, Sandra and Elizabeth, and how their father never gave his daughters an opportunity like the one this guy Santoro was offering. I knew what my decision had to be and the old mobster read me like an opened book.

"Yes," I announced. "I'll see to it that Diana gets everything you ask. Do you have an address for her?"

"This is the last one I can remember," he said and took up the pen and scribbled the address on the same piece of paper I had given him.

He stood up and reached out his hand. I rose to my feet and we shook hands.

"Thank you, Mr. Atwater," he said. "That address. It's over ten years old. I had a guy I paid weekly money to who goes by the name of Willie "The Nose" Kendall, keeping his eyes and ears on Diana and Louise over the years, but he stopped sending me written reports and phone calls about three weeks back and now it has me worried. I've been stuck dealing with doctors and this damn disease and we have completely lost touch. All I have on Willie "The Nose" is this photo of him with Louise and my little girl at some trailer park called The Trade Winds and this beat up old business card."

Roberto pulled out the photo and handed it to me. It was a small old black and white photo with a white border all around it. It showed

Willie standing next to Louise with Diana, who was about ten in the picture. The Trade Winds Trailer park sign was behind them with several palm trees lined up in a row.

"You can keep the photo," Roberto said as he took out his wallet, thumbed through it and took out a weathered light blue business card and handed it to me. The card read: The Glass Palace and had a phone number.

"What's the Glass Palace," I asked.

Santoro chuckled.

"Back in the day, the Glass Palace was the biggest and the best whore house in Florida. Al Capone and his boys used to stop in quite often. Some big name politicians, too. I don't know what it is now."

"How can I get in touch with you?" I asked.

He laughed for the third time and stuffed his handkerchief in his pocket.

"You won't have to. There's not going to be any me to get in touch with, Mr. Atwater. I'm living on borrowed time as it is. Just see to my Diana. Tell her I'm sorry for not being involved with her life and tell her I love her. I always have and I always will."

"I will, Mr. Santoro," I said and we shook hands one last time.

"Thank you," he said. "Tell Barney I said hello. And goodbye."

"I will," I said.

He gave me a quick smile and a nod, turned and walked out. I sat at my desk and began thinking how I would begin my search.

Phil appeared in the doorway.

"Mr. Santoro just left. Do we have a new client?" she asked.

"Yes, we do," I answered.

I removed five one hundred dollar bills and held up the envelope.

"Put the rest of this in the filing cabinet for now. Under Santoro. Roberto Santoro."

"Will do," she replied.

Phil entered my office, grabbed up the envelope, and saw how much cash it still held.

"Holy crap," she said. "Who do we have to kill?"

"Hopefully, nobody," I said. "I have to go to Florida for this one."

"Florida? Can I go too?" she asked.

"No," I said. "I need you here, managing the office and answering the phone. I should be back in a week or two, maybe three. You definitely need to stay in communication with me on a daily basis."

"A daily basis?" she asked.

"Yes," I said. "Daily."

"Is that really necessary, Patrick?" she asked.

I ignored her question and kept talking.

"I'll call you here. Once at five PM your time."

"You don't have to be so precise," she said.

"Yes I do and I will."

"You worry entirely too much," she said.

"I need to worry, Phil," I said. "We all need to worry."

"Barbieri?" she asked.

"Yes. Barbieri. She is still number one on our hit parade and until we take her down we all have to keep our guards up. And when I say all of us that includes you, doll."

"The woman doesn't even know me."

"That doesn't matter. She will use you to get to me. Or to anyone else. Do you understand?"

"I get it."

"Good," I said. "That's why it is so important for you to stay sharp and focused, Phil, and if you get any news on her you call my hotel immediately. When you hear? I want to hear?"

Phil saluted me.

"Yes, my general," she said. "Do I really have to use the code? Can't I just say her name?"

"No. If it is in regards to her? Always use the code. Barbieri has eyes and ears everywhere and she has the kind of money to work those eyes and ears. We have to be extremely careful. I mean that. This is serious business we're locked into."

32

"Magenta Dairy, right?" she asked.

"For now? Right. She is our Magenta Dairy until we put the cuffs on her."

"Or if she dies," Phil added.

"Or that too," I agreed. "I put a little stopper in your desk drawer."

"I saw it. I don't think I'll have to use it," she replied.

"Look, Phil, I know you might not have to use it but it's better to have one than to need one."

"You're the boss," she said.

"Do you know how to use it?" I asked.

"Yes. I know how to use it. I'm probably a better shot than you are."

"That may be," I agreed. "Get on the horn and book me on the next flight to Miami starting anytime tomorrow and please find me a room at some nice hotel. Nothing too swanky. I'll need to get over to my apartment and put some clothes together. And give Detective Blaine a call and tell him where I'm off to."

"What about Special Agent Edwards?" Phil asked.

"He's in Upstate New York or New Jersey right now running down some leads on Barbieri. He will call us if he has any news. You just be careful and stay on your toes until I get back. Okay?"

"Okay. I will," she said.

"Good," I replied.

Phil smiled and walked out of the office.

I stared down at the two addresses on the piece of paper Santoro left, picked up the silver key, and put it in my pocket. I put the photo and the tattered blue card and put them safely in my wallet.

I always felt I had failed miserably with Mrs. Clifford and her two girls and decided I was not going to fail this time with my promise to Santoro. This time I would keep my promise no matter where it took me or what I might have to do to insure its success.

Failure would not be an option.

Not on this case.

CHAPTER THREE

The way to the cabin was a one lane dirt road several miles back from the main highway and luckily there was only a light amount of snow covering the area. The man in the black 1950 Chevrolet was instructed to look for three large boulders sitting alongside the southern entrance leading to the cabin or he would surely miss it.

He did miss it.

Twice.

He had driven through the night from the Canadian border. In his coat, which was folded on the passenger side seat, a small vial of cocaine had kept him wide awake the entire trip. He didn't smoke or drink and his ten year drug habit always kept him focused on his work.

At least that is what he told himself.

He had learned way back how to keep his anger in check and the frustration of getting lost just before arriving at his destination did not make him waver. He remained calm and quietly whistled the old Irish lullaby, Too Ra Loo Ra Loo Ra, as he suddenly saw the three boulders, plain as day.

"Aye," he announced out loud with his Irish accent. "I see you all now, you three bloody rock bastards."

There were no houses to be seen for miles and the terrain on both sides of the highway was thickly covered with tall pine-laden forest. He made the turn, and the drive up to the cabin was over a mile and a half long.

He sighed heavily, took another quick pinch of the white powder into each nostril and regained his calm once again.

The Chevrolet finally came to a small round driveway made of cobble stone and he parked in front of the two door wooden garage sitting twenty feet from the small two-story house. Both buildings were painted white and appeared to blend into the surrounding untouched snow.

The man got out of the car and stretched his arms and rolled his neck. He was well built, over six feet tall, with steel blue eyes and short graying hair. He wore a black suit and tie and left his vial and overcoat sitting on the front seat. His ride from the Canadian border to this isolated cabin in Pennsylvania took him over eleven hours and he hoped he could get a hot shower, a steaming hot cup of coffee, and maybe something to eat once he went inside. His shoes crunched in the snow as he approached the front door and casually rang the bell. His instincts told him someone was inside and he noticed the thin trail of smoke coming from the stone chimney.

His line of work and choice of drug kept him cognizant of his surroundings at all times.

A young beautiful dark-haired woman, Joanne Parrish, just three weeks shy of her thirtieth birthday, dressed warmly in slacks, boots, and a red flannel shirt, opened the door.

"Good afternoon, lass. I'm Terrence," he announced.

"Hello Terrence. I'm Joanne," she said. "Please? Come in."

Terrence entered the small foyer and Joanne closed the door behind him. The blaze in the fireplace warmed the entire house.

"You can wait in the living room and I will tell her you are here," she said.

"Thank you, Joanne," he replied and stepped into the living room.

Joanne turned and walked down the hallway. Terrence walked to the stone fireplace and stood warming himself by the fire.

A few moments passed and he heard a familiar voice.

"Terrence Bruce, as I live and breathe," the voice said.

Terrence turned and smiled at his old friend.

"Well now, look at you," he replied. "Rachel Stone Barbieri, all grown up and smiling through this bitter winter cold."

Rachel had short hair, dyed ash blonde, and wore dark brown slacks and a pale yellow sweater. She stretched out her arms, walked to Terrence, and gave him a big, warm, welcoming hug.

"Thank you for coming," she said.

"Did you think I would say no?" he asked.

"I'm glad you are here."

"As am I," he replied.

"You must be exhausted from the drive," she said.

"Just the opposite. I enjoy driving. Day or night. It makes no never mind to me. If anything it keeps my mind clear."

"Can I get you something?" she asked.

"A hot cup of coffee and a bit of a nosh would be sweet," he replied.

"Of course," she said and turned her attention to the foyer. "Joanie?"

Joanne entered the room.

"Yes Rachel," she said.

"Would you please bring Mr. Bruce some black coffee and a corned beef sandwich. Put it on that new rye bread we have. He likes a lot of mustard."

"A lot of mustard. Of course," Joanne said.

Joanne nodded to Terrence, smiled, and walked out.

"Please. Sit," she offered.

Terrence sat on the couch and Rachel settled into one of the large leather easy chairs directly across from him.

"You're looking well, Terrence. The years have been quite kind to you."

"My work keeps me young. And I try to stay in shape. This is a quaint little hideaway you have here. I missed those bloody boulders out by the road twice before coming up the drive."

Rachel laughed.

"It can be tricky. I do like my privacy. The more privacy these days the better."

"You remembered I like my corned beef with mustard," he said. "Thanks for having it on hand as they say."

"Men like you, Terrence, never change," she said. "How long has it been? Twenty years at least?"

"Twenty-four," he said. "Lindbergh had landed in Paris. You wanted to leave London and go see the plane. Your father said no and you had yourself a huge hissy fit and stomped your little feet all the way up those white marble stairs."

"My god, I remember that. I was angry with him for days afterwards."

"Spoiled little brat you were."

"Still am," she replied.

Terrence sighed heavily.

"I miss the old man," he said.

"Me too," she added.

"Your family enterprise has made you rather popular in several circles, I hear tell."

"Some good. Some not so good," she replied. "The last thing I want right now is to be popular with anyone. Except for you, of course."

"Of course," he agreed.

37

Terrence looked Rachel over.

"I understand your present situation completely," he said. "I do."

"Do you?" she asked.

"People in my circles, darling, don't contact the likes of me unless their situation calls for my particular services. Your father was very discriminating about the people he gave my name to. I'm certain your present situation is no different. I do like the hair."

"Thank you. It suits me and my present situation," she said. "For right now, anyway."

Joanne entered carrying a tray with a large black cup of coffee and a corned beef sandwich on rye smothered with mustard. She placed the tray on the coffee table and Terrence took a quick sip.

"Ah, thank you, ladies, this is just what the doctor ordered." he said.

He picked up one half of the sandwich and took a large bite.

"Delicious," he said. "Thank you."

"Enjoy," Joanne said and stood next to Rachel. "Do you need anything else?"

"No, Joanie. This is good for now. Thank you."

Joanne smiled, touched Rachel's shoulder, slid her palm down the arm of Rachel's sweater and lovingly squeezed her hand before walking out.

"Still playing on the girl's team, I see," Terrence replied with another big bite of corned beef in his mouth.

"At times," Rachel added. "I want to thank you for arriving so promptly."

"Your message said urgent. You have a client who needs me?"

"It isn't a client," she replied. "I need you. Are you ready to get to work?"

A large grin crossed his face.

"For you, lass? I am, always, ready for work," he said and picked up the other half of the sandwich.

"Can we discuss the business at hand while you eat?" she asked.

"We can. By all means," he said and sipped his coffee. "I'm all ears."

"I am going down to Cozumel in a few weeks."

"Cozumel? Will you be needing a ride, then?" he jokingly asked. "Is that why you've asked me to come all this way and see you?"

"No," she said and smiled slightly. "I have already arranged my transport, thank you. Cozumel is going to be my new base of operations."

"Cozumel? Are you certain you will be safe down there?" he asked.

"Quite safe," she answered. "It is already well armed and Mexico's President Muchado has given me his word not to interfere with my business as long as I keep a low profile and we do not draw any unwanted attention. This, I and my new associates, will do."

"New associates?" he asked.

"Out with the old. In with the new, Terrence. You know how this business goes."

"Yes, I do," he said. "If I may ask?"

"You are family, Terrence. Ask me anything?"

"Are you certain these new associates of yours can be trusted?"

"Of course they can't be trusted. As long as I keep making them money and keeping my distance I will be all right. There is a big discussion presently of Cuba possibly becoming their new base of operations but negotiations are still not completed as yet."

"If Cuba is chosen, don't go there. Too volatile and you'll never be protected properly."

"I know that, Terrence. Cozumel will suffice me nicely."

"Asking a president of Mexico to look elsewhere must require a hefty tariff in regards to your importing and exporting. Yes?" he asked.

"It's substantial but still a small price to pay for doing business unheeded."

Terrence nodded silently.

"It sounds like you have almost everything in working order. I still haven't heard the urgency part of your request."

"I do have everything in working order, Terrence, but I also have a few Americans doing their damn best to get in my way."

"Some FBI pebbles in your shoes?" he asked.

"Yes," she replied. "Too many pebbles to my liking."

"Aye," said Terrence, now realizing why he was there. "I never trusted any of the bloody flag waving Americans working for the FBI. They speak peace and democracy but they also always want to keep a certain amount of control over everything and put their suspicious eyes on everyone, foreign and domestic. They think they are the almighty saviors now of this new world order we're all facing. But I don't have to go on to you about my feelings for the United States of America. So. All right then. To business. Which particular Americans are we speaking of and what's my time frame here?"

"I have a folder for you."

Terrence's eyes widened as he took another sip of coffee.

"A folder? You are following in your father's footsteps. Your father and his bloody folders made death appear so official, like some edict from the crown royals."

"It's rather extensive but you have always enjoyed the longer lists."

"Aye, I do. Yes. I do enjoy the extensive lists. I always have. The longer the list the fatter my account grows."

"I would like you to start at the front of my folder and work your way to the last. There is no urgency or any time restraints. Take all the necessary time you need. It took us quite a while to get all the photos and current addresses but I can assure you they are all accurate and up to date."

"Your dad was always extremely efficient in that area. I would expect you to be the same."

"I have been," she stated.

"That's always a plus. My expertise does require a certain bit of efficiency on my benefactor's part."

Rachel leaned in closer to Terrence.

"Terrence? This needs to have your special kind of signature work stamped on each and every one of these pebbles. I have to send a clear and concise message out not only to them but to everyone else in our circles."

"I understand completely, darling," he said. "The fear factor always holds sway with the less fortunate."

"Ponce Delgado made a vain attempt in regards to Rockwell and failed miserably. I can't afford to work with that level of incompetence any longer. This is why I have sent for you. I need your level of expertise. Your unique style of
professionalism. You know what I mean."

A smile crossed his face again as he finished the last bite of his sandwich.

"Aye, indeed I do, girl. You want these particular works to be graphic and personal."

"In extreme terms, Terrence." she said. "Extreme terms. It's imperative at this stage. I made a promise to these arrogant flag wavers and I need to make them realize that Rachel Stone Barbieri is a woman of her word and a woman you do not want to fuck with."

"I hear you, girl, loud and clear. Are we going with the usual rate?" he asked.

"For you? And for this? I'm offering double rate plus expenses. You get whatever it is you need. Whenever you need it."

"Who is my contact if things get dicey?" he asked.

Rachel took out a small pad and wrote a name and number down and handed it to Terrence.

"His name is Dix Haggis. That's his contact number. He can get you anything you require."

"He's a solicitor in the States?" he asked.

"One of the best and a loyal friend. Dix will be able to assist you no matter what part of the country you may be. You need it? He'll get it."

Terrence let out a whistle.

"You must have made one hell of a promise."

"I did," she said. "There's also a hundred thousand dollar bonus once the folder is completed."

"A bonus, too?" he said. "This is going to assist me greatly towards my future retirement plans, girl."

"You'll never retire. You like your work too much and you are too damn good at it."

"I am that and I do happen to enjoy myself greatly while I'm working," he said and smiled again. "Where's the folder?"

Rachel stood up, walked to the mantle above the fireplace, and took down a green folder. She handed it to Terrence and sat back down. Terrence opened the folder and whistled again as he went through the pages and the photographs.

"This is an impressive list of American flag wavers, girl. Especially this one fellah here near the end. This, Patrick Miles Atwater. Is he Irish?"

"Welsh. I'm told. Can you handle this, Terrence? There is no room for errors of any kind."

Terrence nodded his head yes.

"If I have free reign you will get your completed folder," he said.

"Of course. Folders always have a way of creating collateral damage to some degree. I understand that. Do whatever is necessary. Just get it done."

"I never let your father down and I won't be failing you, girl. You made these folks a promise. I'll make certain that promise of yours is kept. No matter who else may get hurt in the process. There will be no errors. My word on it."

A broad smile crossed Rachel's face and she let out a sigh of relief.

"Thank you, Terrence," she said. "Thank you."

"Graphic and personal," he said. "I will wrap this up quick and simple for you. It should get a lot of front page headlines, too."

"Even better," she added.

Terrence looked at the small stack of cash in the folder sleeve.

"Expense money? This is quite a generous sum."

"This has to happen, Terrence. There's more cash available if need be."

"Doubtful," he said and sipped his coffee. "I have all the necessary equipment at my disposal. I still have that special gift your father gave me. That should come in very handy in this given situation. Don't concern yourself, girl. You can go down to Cozumel with a cleared mind. As I said,

I will remove these pebbles for you and get this done as you have requested."

"There's one other thing," she added.

"Something else?" he asked.

"It's only a curiosity of mine as of right now, but I want to know what magenta means? It's some kind of FBI code."

"Magenta?" he asked. "Sounds colorful and rather cheeky for the FBI. These people here in your folder? They know its meaning?"

"Some will. Some won't. I want to know its meaning."

Terrence laughed and finished his coffee.

"Trust me, darling, whoever knows the meaning of magenta will be telling yours truly. You can bet your family's fortune on that."

Rachel smiled.

"That's what I love about you, Terrence. You are always extremely dependable. As my father used to say."

"I am a lot of things these days, girl. Dependable? I am that. For certain. Especially when it comes to my work ethic."

Terrence put the contents of the envelope in his suit jacket and stood up, placing the folder under his arm.

"Payments will be received as always then, I assume?" he asked.

"Of course. You haven't changed your account, have you?"

"No. I have not. My bank in London has always kept a discretionary eye on my account over these many years. I have no complaints there. Never have thanks to your father."

"Then payment in the usual manner," she said.

"Most appreciated," he said.

Rachel extended her hand and Terrence shook it.

"We are in agreement then, girl?" he said.

"We are in agreement. Yes," she said. "Can I get you anything else?"

"I would like to take a long hot shower if I might?" he asked.

"Of course," said Rachel. "Can I make arrangements for some company for you? If my memory serves me right, you have an affection for the darker female?"

"I do, yes, and thank you, but no. I will have to pass on that for now. Once I'm fed and showered, I like to get to the tasks at hand immediately."

"I understand," she said. "I have something else for you."

Rachel opened a drawer next to her and took out a large vial of cocaine.

"I am assuming you still dabble?" she asked.

"I do. Yes," he replied. "Now and again."

Rachel handed the vial to Terrence and he looked down at it and smiled.

"It's uncut," she said.

Terrence took a deep breath and tried to hide his growing excitement.

"May I?" he asked.

"By all means," she said. "It's yours to keep."

Terrence opened the vial, scooped up a small amount of cocaine with his fingernail and snorted it into one nostril. He rubbed the residue across his teeth and sat back on the couch.

"Oh my girl. This is quite an exceptional product you have here."

"The best of the best old friend," she said.

Terrence held up the vial.

"Thank you," he said and put the vial in his pocket.

"The bathroom is upstairs. I'll have Joanne bring you some fresh towels."

"Thank you, lass," he said and went up the stairs.

No more than twenty minutes had passed and Terrence came down the stairs feeling totally refreshed and ready to go.

Rachel handed Terrence his folder.

"You left this on the table," she said and walked him to the front door. Joanne came back to the foyer and stood next to Rachel.

"Terrence is leaving us, Joanne," Rachel said.

"So soon?" Joanne asked.

"Duty calls, lass. Duty calls."

Joanne opened the front door. Terrence looked at Rachel.

"Be careful down in Cozumel, girl" he said. "I never trusted the bloody Mexicans either. No matter how much money changes hands it's never enough with those in power. Watch yourself."

"I will," said Rachel and kissed Terrence on the cheek. "Good seeing you."

Terrence laughed.

"What's funny?" she asked.

"Most people I meet never say that to me. Especially the ones I'm hired to meet. Good day to you, ladies. A real pleasure doing business with you."

Terrence smiled at Rachel and Joanne and walked out to his car.

Joanne and Rachel watched Terrence get in his car and wave as he drove away.

"How was the meeting?" asked Joanne.

"It was productive with all things considered," Rachel answered and closed the door.

"He's still on the nose candy?" Joanne asked.

"Definitely."

"Can he do everything you've asked of him?" Joanne asked.

"Terrence is very good at what he does," said Rachel. "He is one of the best, if not the best. If you want someone to go away and you have the money to pay for his services that person is going away."

Rachel stared at Joanne with some unease.

"What is it?" asked Joanne.

"I am concerned the years are beginning to catch up with Terrence. And his drug use is not any help. To him or to me."

"Meaning?" Joanne asked.

Rachel moved closer to Joanne.

"Meaning, once Terrence has completed this request of mine, I'll need you to close out his account in London."

Joanne kissed Rachel deeply. Joanne gently pressed Rachel's body against the front door and held her hands.

"And?" asked Joanne in a whisper before kissing Rachel's neck.

"And then I want you to make him go away. Go away for good."

Joanne reared back and looked into Rachel's eyes.

"You want me to kill Terrence Bruce? What if he suspects me coming for him?" Joanne asked.

Rachel responded in turn and kissed Joanne on her neck.

"He won't suspect you. I'll tell him you're bringing him his bonus money and some more nose candy. Terrence is good but you're much better. Younger and better. Much better. And definitely much prettier to look at."

Rachel and Joanne kissed again deeply.

"Do you want his death to be graphic and personal?"

Joanne kissed Rachel lightly and nibbled at her bottom lip.

"No. I want it to be quick. Painless. My family owes him at least that much."

"I can do quick and painless."

"Yes you can," whispered Rachel.

Joanne smiled and kissed Rachel passionately once again.

"Shall we go upstairs and continue what we started earlier this morning?" Joanne asked.

"No," Rachel replied. "I want you right here. Right now."

Rachel and Joanne kissed again and slowly descended to the floor, wrapped tightly in each other's arms.

CHAPTER FOUR

The flight from Los Angeles to Miami was tedious and uneventful. The stewardesses were kind and professional and I spent most of my air time staring out the window wondering where Rachel Stone Barbieri might be at this very moment. I ran several possibilities of what I might do to her if and when we were ever to meet face to face again.

Killing her immediately was not one of the options although the thought did pop up every now and again. First I thought I would kill her slowly, one bullet at a time in multiple places throughout her body until she either bled to death or begged me to end her life. In each and every scenario, no matter how they played out, the one constant was to never give Rachel Stone Barbieri even one second to attempt to get the upper hand.

That wasn't going to happen, no matter how our next meeting transpired.

Phil was able to get me on a non-stop flight to Miami at nine in the morning through National Airlines. Once airborne, my mind made me think of my last flight bringing Detective Munoz's body back from Aruba, the funeral that followed, and watching the pain in the faces of his widow, Sara, and their son, Roberto. Sometime around one o'clock the airline hostesses began offering sandwiches and drinks. I ordered my usual Johnny Walker Black but had to settle for a Dewar's White Label. I sat by the window slowly sipping my drink while the large passenger next to me, an insurance salesman named Douglas Sands, quickly downed four gin and tonics and proceeded to sleep soundly the remainder of the flight.

When I finally arrived and stepped off the plane the humidity was heavy even for the month of January. It was my first time in Miami and I began to feel like a stranger in a strange land.

I knew a quick and easy remedy for those feelings.

I had learned many years back if a private eye needed information about some new place or a person of interest he hadn't met and weren't quite sure where to go, you could always get the straight talk from just about any local cabbie, bartender, or hard-working waitress. The real trick was to know who to talk to, how to ask the right questions without arousing suspicions, and it was always a plus having a little throw around cash handy.

I came to Florida well prepared.

I thought once I was settled I would first run down the whereabouts of this Willie "The Nose" Kendall. I figured if it turned out he was someone I could talk to, he could give me the full skinny on Diana and her mother, Louise. I grabbed my one suitcase, hailed the only available cab, and immediately began to "work my magic," as they say in the trade.

I started my investigation by asking the cabbie, a tall thin man with a warm smile named Charlie Lindman, what was the Hotel Bancroft like?

Charlie turned out to be an excellent choice. The man loved to talk and knew Miami inside and out.

"The Hotel Bancroft is a real sweet place," said Charlie. "Miami has an entire row of good hotels all up and down Collins Avenue and every one faces the ocean beach on one side and the bay on the other. You are one lucky man if you have a room at the Bancroft."

"Why so," I asked.

"For one thing, it's one of the best hotels in town, and for another, the place is packed this time of year with more women than you could shake a stick at. The food and the service is first rate, they got a real fancy bar overlooking the bay side pool called The Treasure Cove, and this time of the season all those pretty little northern dames swarm down here to Miami to escape the cold winter and snow. Most of them are young, attractive, single women, with a lot of spending cash, all trying to get themselves tanned before they head back home, if you get my drift? Yes sir, you are one lucky man. Are you here for business or for pleasure?"

"Business," I said.

"What is your business?" he asked. "If you don't mind the question?"

"I'm a private investigator, Charlie," I announced.

"Private investigator?" he repeated. "We don't get many private investigators down here. We mostly just get insurance salesmen or those pretty girls I was telling you about."

Charlie made the turn onto Collins Avenue and looked at me through his rear-view mirror. I could tell he was hesitating to say something so I smiled and figured I would put some more cards on the table and get him to say what was on his mind.

"My name is Atwater. Patrick Atwater. I work the Los Angeles area mainly. I came here to try to locate a client's daughter. If you got something you want to say to me, Charlie, you can spit it out."

Charlie smiled.

"You read people really good," Charlie said.

"It's part of the job, Charlie," I replied.

Charlie reached back and handed me a small white business card.

"I try to make myself available to certain people coming into town. You look like you might possibly need a tour guide," he said. "Someone who could show you around if need be? For a couple of days maybe?"

"That is a possibility, Charlie," I replied, letting him know I definitely could use someone in that capacity. I also knew there would be a price for those services but it was a price I was willing to pay. I wanted to get this business with Santoro and his daughter, Diana, wrapped up quickly as possible.

I took his card and read it over.

"That's my private number, not the cab company. If you want some professional female company or you just need me to take you somewhere off the beaten path? Give me a jingle. I know all types in this town, if you get my drift?"

I smiled, put his card in my pocket, and nodded.

"Thanks, Charlie. That's good to know. What's the uh, cost for these services of yours?"

"I'm sure we can come up with a workable figure," he said and smiled. "Fifty will get you the entire week."

"Fair enough, Charlie," I said and smiled back. "Fair enough."

"Here's the Hotel Bancroft, Mr. Atwater," he said. "Call me if you need anything."

"I will do that, Charlie. And thanks again."

"Enjoy Miami," he said.

I paid the fare, threw Charlie a nice tip, and walked inside.

The hotel had an old twenties feel with several small couches and high backed chairs all with their own individual small cocktail tables. Several guests were taking advantage of the hotel's hospitality area and one long legged waitress worked the entire area. Straight ahead was the long front desk and to the left were three elevators and a wide hallway leading straight to the Treasure Cove bar.

I checked in, told the front desk man, a nattily dressed individual named Conklin, I wouldn't be requiring a bellman, got my key, and took the second elevator up to my hotel room. Phil had me on the fourth floor facing the beach and the ocean view reminded me of my new office space in Santa Monica.

This ocean view had mine beat by a country mile. The beach was packed with umbrellas, swimmers, mothers and fathers with children of all ages, and lots of pretty young women.

Tons of those pretty girls working on those tans Charlie spoke about.

It was almost seven o'clock and I thought I would check out the Treasure Cove and maybe grab a bite before making my promised call to Phil.

The bar was a large oval shape that jutted out from one wall and stretched almost to the middle of the room. Red leather booths lined the bay windows and the ones on the opposite side sat two steps up from the rest of the floor. The place was fairly busy. There were two male bartenders, a maitre'd named Tony, and four cocktail waitresses working the room. I found an empty leather stool between a young couple sharing some large coconut drink together using two straws and three young, attractive women dressed in shorts, sandals, and casual tops and chatting away about Bette Davis' latest performance in All About Eve.

I saw the movie but kept my distance from the girls and their conversation.

I looked around and could see Charlie was right about the Bancroft. The hotel was sweet. It wasn't like the Beverly back home but I began to feel just as comfortable here on the east coast as I did on the west.

That feeling of being a stranger in a strange land was quickly dissipating.

I no sooner sat down and the bartender, an older man named Vernon, according to his red plastic name tag, plopped a small bar napkin down in front of me that read The Hotel Bancroft in big red letters.

"Good evening and welcome to the Hotel Bancroft, sir," he said. "What can I get for you?"

"Johnnie Walker Black," I answered. "On the rocks. Make it a double."

"Yes sir," he said politely.

Vernon smiled and after a quick nod, made my drink and placed it in front of me.

"Do you have a room key, sir," he asked.

"A room key?" I answered. "Yes I do," and held it out for Vernon to see.

Vernon wrote the number down on a small pad.

"Very good sir," he said and walked away.

I thought there was no time like the present to keep asking questions and caught Vernon's eye and motioned him back. As he approached I took out the blue card given to me by Santoro and placed it on the bar.

"Yes sir?" he asked.

"Do you know this place, Vernon?" I asked

Vernon read the card and laughed.

"I do know this place, sir. But it's not what it used to be, sir. Not today anyway."

"I already know what it used to be. I'm looking for a man who might still be connected with the place. What can you tell me about this joint today?" I asked.

Vernon leaned in and lowered his voice.

"You know the Glass Palace was a high class whore house. Yes?" he asked.

"So I was told," I said. "All types all the time."

"That's right, sir. The Glass Palace was top of the line. It got closed down by the local police and the local politicians just before the war. It was mob owned then by some gangster family out of Atlantic City and as far as I know, they still own it. Only today the Glass Palace is a posh and very private gambling club. Very hush hush, very high class, and the people who come to gamble at the Glass Palace are all extremely wealthy. The only way people like you or myself can get in there is if you are invited by one of the members or you happen to know the entrance password, which changes on a day to day basis. The men all have to wear suits and ties and the ladies must be dressed to the nines. Diamonds and pearls if you know what I mean? No shorts or casual dress allowed there like these three over here."

Vernon tilted his head at three girls in the bar lounge, referring to their outfits.

"People go there to be seen by their wealthy friends and to gamble large amounts of cash money. And? Unfortunately, there are no more high-end hookers, pal. Not at the Glass Palace. Sorry."

I laughed and leaned in closer to Vernon.

"I'm not looking for hookers, Vernon. I told you I'm looking for a guy that might work there or know some people that do. Name of Kendall. Willie "The Nose" Kendall. Have you ever heard of him?"

"Kendall?" he repeated. "Willie "The Nose" Kendall?"

"That's what they call him," I said.

"No," Vernon replied. "I can't say I have."

Vernon leaned in close and lowered his voice a second time.

"Is this guy mob connected?"

"I don't know for sure if he is or he isn't," I said.

"His name sure sounds like it. Don't those gangsters all have nicknames? You know? Johnny "Short Eyes" Vesco, Vito "The Butcher" Tunucci?"

"And Willie "The Nose" Kendall," I added.

"Exactly," said Vernon as he cleaned out an ash tray and turned back to me. "Do you have a nickname, sir?"

His question made me smile.

"I do not," I said and extended my hand. "The name is Atwater. Patrick Atwater. Los Angeles, California."

Vernon shook my hand.

"Vernon Koster," he said. "I too, do not have a nickname."

"Good to know," I said with a grin.

"You're not an insurance man, are you?" he asked.

"No, Vernon. I'm a PI," I said. "Here trying to find a client's daughter."

"And she's somehow connected with this Willie "The Nose" and the Glass Palace?"

"I'm sure about him but not sure about the other. Have you ever been to the Glass Palace?"

"Me? The Glass Palace is much too rich for my blood. I'm a lowly bartender with a love for the sand and the surf. I am no high stakes gambler. But I do know some very wealthy people that frequent the club every now and then."

"You do?" I asked.

"I do," he said. "Yes."

Bingo.

I could almost hear the roulette wheels spinning and the craps table dice rolling across the felt. I slid a crisp twenty across the bar.

"I've got a very nice suit and tie, Vernon. Do you think you could get me an invite from one of those members you were talking about or possibly let me know what the entrance password might be for tonight?"

Vernon smiled and looked at the twenty.

"That's a very good possibility, Mr. Atwater," he said. "A very good possibility."

Vernon looked around and put the twenty in his pocket.

"Actually, Mr. Atwater, it's a real possibility," he added. "Give me a couple of hours and I'll see what I can do for you."

"I have your word?" I asked.

Vernon looked around and stared back at me with a grin.

"Yes, sir. You have my word."

"Thanks," I said and raised my glass to him and took a swig. "You know my room number."

"Yes, sir," he said.

Satisfied with my conversation with Vernon, I finished my drink, grabbed a quick meal, and headed up to my room. On my way to the elevators, I told Conklin at the desk to have the hotel operator connect me with Los Angeles.

"Right away, sir," said Conklin.

The wait took about twenty minutes.

I had taken a shower, gotten halfway dressed except for my shoes and shirt when the phone finally rang.

"Hello," I said.

"This is the hotel operator, I have your call to Los Angeles, Mr. Atwater," she said.

"Thank you," I replied and Phil's voice came on the line.

"Hello, Patrick," Phil began. "Have you gotten bit by any alligators yet?"

"No alligators. Not yet," I said. "How are you doing?"

"I'm fine. I took a few calls today. Told everyone you were working a case and could be reached sometime next week."

"No word on Magenta?" I asked.

"Detective Blaine told me he hasn't heard a peep and Agent Edwards is following up on one possible lead but didn't give me any information on who or what it is. He wants you to call him sometime this weekend."

"I will. Did he leave a number?"

Phil gave me the number and I wrote it down.

"Did Agent Edwards have anything else to say?" I asked.

"Agent Edwards and I only spoke for a few moments. He told me to tell you to stay safe and sounded like he was in a rush so I didn't stay on the line too long."

"The job does keep him moving. Is that it?" I asked.

"Sorry," she replied. "I wish I had better news but I don't. How was the flight and the Hotel Bancroft? Are they taking good care of you?"

"The flight was fine and as far as the hotel goes, you picked a good one, kid."

"That's good to hear. Are you making any progress?" she asked.

"You know me. I already got one lead so far."

"Cabbie, bartender, or hooker?" she asked.

"Bartender," I said. "And it's not hooker. It's waitress."

"Oh, sorry," she apologized.

"You keep your guard up and I'll ring you again tomorrow. Same time."

"Long distance calls are going to add up and cost you a pretty penny."

"No they won't and we can afford it on this case. The calls aren't just for magenta's sake or for Magenta's whereabouts. I want to know that you're okay working all alone back there."

55

"I've got my trusty fire power close by. Don't worry. You be careful too and watch out for those alligators."

"I will," I said. "Until tomorrow, kiddo."

"Bye. And good hunting."

I said goodbye, hung up the phone, and laid out my suit.

Someone knocked on my door and I instinctively grabbed my .38 and held it behind my back as I opened the door. A uniformed bellboy leaned forward politely and handed me a small envelope with my name and room number written on it.

"This is for you, Mr. Atwater," the bellboy said.

I tipped him fifty cents, shut the door, and opened the envelope.

The paper had one word hand written in black ink.

It read: Saratoga.

I smiled, picked up the phone, and dialed Charlie.

"Charlie? This is Patrick Atwater? Are you available this evening?" I asked.

"Absolutely," he replied excitingly.

"Pick me up in an hour," I said.

"I'll be waiting out front. I've got a black Dodge Coronet. Four door."

"See you then," I said and hung up the phone.

I continued to get dressed and thought again about Phil. I didn't like the fact of her being at the office alone. I decided to get a hold of Betty and Jake the next day and ask them to keep tabs on her.

I realized Rachel Stone Barbieri had seeped into my brain making me paranoid and I also knew my friends were not safe and Rachel would never leave my thoughts until we had her and her associates in custody and locked away for good.

Easier said than done was the thought of my evening as I got down to the lobby, walked out, and jumped in the back seat of Charlie's Dodge Coronet.

The ride to the Glass Palace was a little over twenty minutes.

Charlie kept the Dodge immaculately clean inside and out and the fifty bucks I handed him gave me carte blanche access to anywhere I needed to go.

Cabbies. bartenders, and waitresses.

Worth their weight in gold.

The private club sat off the main road a good two hundred feet back and looked like one of those large southern mansions from Gone With The Wind. Every vehicle drove up in an orderly line and was greeted by two black men in tuxedos. The two men would wait until the arrivals were cleared for entrance by four very large burly-looking men also in tuxedos and one of the five young valets in black vests and white shirts would drive the vehicle to a specific parking area around the corner of the building. There was another spot for limos, private cars, and cabs, and the drivers waiting there would all congregate to smoke cigarettes and shoot the breeze.

"I'll be waiting over there for you," said Charlie. "By the limos."

Charlie was no stranger to the Glass Palace. He told me he had driven quite a few people here in the past and he had a sense as to who the people were that ran these kind of clubs. I gave Charlie a quick nod and stepped from the back seat of the Dodge. The two black greeters gave me welcoming smiles and the four burly men standing at the front door gave me their best and hardest stares as I walked up to the front entrance steps as casually as I could.

I did my best to act and sound like a regular who knew all the rules.

"Saratoga," I said and slowly looked each man in the eye.

There was a small hesitation from all four men before one finally spoke out.

"Welcome to the Glass Palace, sir," the man said and opened the door. "Enjoy your evening."

"Thank you, gentlemen," I replied.

I stepped inside and immediately gave the place the once over. There were several white marble columns forming a large circle around the main room. There were two long bars, one on the left and the other on the

57

right. There were floor to ceiling mirrored walls behind the bars, giving the place the illusion of being much bigger, but I had the feeling it assisted management with keeping close eyes on the clientele. There were nine crap tables, eleven poker tables, and at the very back of the room were three roulette tables. To play roulette you had to walk up four wide carpeted stairs. I noticed the stairs height gave certain observers a clear look at the entire floor. There were at least a dozen or so of these men, all wearing black tuxedos and all watching the action and the floor. The noise level in the room was almost deafening with the talk and the excitement of people either losing their hard earned money or once in a while claiming a win.

People exchanged cash for chips at a small caged-in counter near the rear of the building on the right under the stairway. The public rest rooms were there also, with fancy gold lights above the entrances reading Ladies and Gentlemen.

As per my usual, I opted for the bar on the left and found an empty seat. I quickly realized no one was paying for their drinks. Every libation was poured and offered freely by the professionally dressed bartenders. The only time cash came out was to tip them, your cocktail waitress, or the men in charge of the tables. I ordered my usual Johnnie Walker and kept checking out the operation.

I tried to imagine what the joint might have looked like back in the day when Al Capone and company would come in to party with the girls. The men were most likely fed watered down liquor and then led upstairs to some private room where money would change hands and whatever the girls were offering would quickly take place.

Not my kind of scene but I'm certain it was a money maker.

The main floor was packed and busy and at times I noticed several people being escorted up the rear stairway on the right to what I assumed were private rooms where the bigger spenders, the whales as they are called in the trade, were offered certain amenities not usually offered to the average club member. My bartender walked slowly past me, checking to see if anyone at the bar needed anything.

I took another shot at finding another lead.

"Excuse me?" I asked.

"Yes sir?" said the bartender, a stocky wrestler type with a name tag reading Kevin.

"Has Willie "The Nose" been in tonight?"

"Willie "The Nose"?" he replied and his face went cold. "I haven't seen him."

The bartender quickly turned away and walked down the bar to light the cigarette of an older attractive woman. I noticed him saying something to the woman, and she instantly looked right at me. I turned, trying not to get caught staring at her but I was fairly certain we had made eye contact. The bartender came back and leaned over the bar.

"The lady at the bar would like to speak with you," he said, and winked at me.

I looked at her and she nodded yes.

I picked up my drink and walked over to her.

"Hello," I said.

"Good evening, handsome," she replied.

"You wanted to speak with me?" I asked.

"I do," she said and looked me over like she was shopping for a man take-out order.

I cut right to the chase.

"Is this about Willie?" I asked.

"Yes," she said.

She was tall and thin, clearly over forty but still very attractive, with chocolate brown hair, light blue eyes, very well dressed and sporting enough diamonds from her neck down to the fingers on both hands to open up her own jewelry shop.

"I'm Shannon," she announced, and offered her hand. "Shannon Lorde."

We shook hands politely and I parked myself on the empty stool next her.

"My name is Atwater. Patrick Atwater."

"Nice to meet you, Mr. Atwater," she said as she crushed out her cigarette. "You're not from around here? Are you?"

"No. I'm not."

"Are you a cop?" she asked.

"A cop? No. I'm not that either."

"My apologies for asking you that," she said. "A girl likes to know who she's talking to. Especially if you're a girl talking to a handsome stranger in the Glass Palace."

I figured I would stick with the task at hand and try to skip the small talk.

"What can you tell me about Willie "The Nose" Kendall, Shannon?" I asked.

She turned and faced me.

"I can tell you a whole bunch about Willie "The Nose" Kendall, Mr. Atwater, but when a man like yourself comes here to the Glass Palace asking questions about certain club members or men with the kind of reputation as Mr. Kendall, it's a house requirement to offer some small compensation for any and all reliable information."

I felt the pinch and I have to admit it surprised me coming from a woman who looked like she did.

"Is that what you have, Shannon, any and all reliable information?" I asked and grinned slightly.

She sipped her drink and leaned in closer.

"About Willie "The Nose" Kendall? Absolutely, honey. But you have to be careful around this place. When I tell you what I know you'll understand what I'm trying to say to you right now."

I looked around the room and noticed two men watching us.

"Lots of eyes and ears in here?" I asked. "Is that it?"

"Too many," she replied. "And yes. That's exactly it."

She sat up straight and sipped her drink.

I took the hint and figured most of her jewelry must be fake if she's putting the squeeze on me and placed a twenty on the bar by her drink.

"Okay, Shannon. A small compensation. What can you tell me?" I said.

Shannon took a quick look around and leaned in closer to me.

"Willie "The Nose" Kendall is as shady as they come and has been hanging around this place for as long as I can remember, and I've lived here for ten years. He was never a club member but he was as they say, very well connected with the owner of this establishment."

She slid my twenty closer to her, folded it in half, and held it in her hands. She smiled, turned again, and nodded to the roulette table on the far right.

"Do you see that older gentleman standing by the roulette table? The bald headed man sporting the goatee? The one way in the back wearing the tuxedo?"

I glanced up and saw the man watching the players and the croupiers with his arms folded in front of him.

"I see him," I said and took a sip of my Scotch. "Is he the owner?"

"No. His name is Joe Collins but everyone around here calls him the Butler. They call him that because whenever there is a problem in this place? You know, people getting too drunk or upset because they're losing too much money or they become a little too loud or argumentative, or they talk about people they shouldn't be talking about, if you get the picture?"

"I get the picture," I said.

"The Butler is the man who steps in and cleans all that kind of stuff up," she explained. "He does it quietly, quickly, and most efficiently. Almost enthusiastically as if he enjoys hurting people. You don't want to ever mess with that man. Not with the Butler."

I wasn't quite certain why she was telling me about the Butler and thought maybe I was putting a little scare into her.

I tried to ease her mind.

"I'm not here to cause any problems, Shannon? I'm just looking for some information."

"On Willie?" she said.

"Yeah. On Willie. That's the whole of it."

She took another sip of her drink and looked at me.

"You seem to be a straight shooter, Mr. Atwater but your timing is what shook me a little."

"My timing?" I asked.

"If you don't mind me asking? What is it you want with Willie Kendall?"

"I just need to speak with him. Have a little conversation. Like the one we're having right now."

"Willie knows something?" she asked. "Something about the Glass Palace?"

"Something like that. Yes. I'm still listening. And I'm still waiting for that reliable information you mentioned."

She finished her drink with a final gulp and motioned to the bartender to bring us two more. She took out another cigarette and faced me.

"Do you have a light?" she asked.

I smiled, grabbed some matches sitting on the bar, lit her cigarette, and Shannon leaned in closer and finally began to earn her twenty bucks.

"Three weeks ago Willie "The Nose" Kendall walked in here and caused a major upheaval."

"Three weeks?' I asked.

"To the day," she said.

Now I fully understood her timing statement.

"What did he do?" I asked.

"It was real late. Almost two in the morning. There was hardly anybody in here. There was only the one bartender and one cocktail waitress. All the other help had gone home for the night. I was still here at the bar having a nice conversation with an older gentleman. I forget his name. Willie was by himself, gambling up there at that same table next to the Butler. Willie was drinking but he wasn't drunk. I've seen him drunk. I could tell something was clearly on his mind and it wasn't good. Then Luis arrived with a couple of his boys and as Luis got to those stairs, Willie suddenly pulls out a gun and starts firing right at Luis, saying he was going to kill him. Called him a son of a bitch."

"Who's this guy, Luis?" I asked.

"Luis Verdun. He's the owner of this club and most of southern Florida, or so I am told. Luis and I used to date a few years back but he doesn't call me anymore. But, he does allow me to come in here, play a little poker now and then, drink for free, and hang around as much as I like."

Shannon let out a deep sigh.

"Did Luis break your heart?" I asked.

My question made Shannon laugh.

"You men," she added. "You always get what you want from a lady and then in no time you're all moving on to someone else. Usually someone younger. Or someone prettier."

Shannon stared over at two beautiful women in their early twenties, sitting at the end of the bar and laughing with two men in tuxedos. I figured Shannon was beginning to realize the meaning of the old phrase, nothing lasts forever.

I felt a little sorry for her but I had bigger fish to fry and kept pressing.

"So what happened with all the gunfire, Shannon?"

"Willie got off three shots. Two missed but the third one caught Luis in his shoulder. The Butler walked straight up to Willie and clocked him real good with some black leather thing he had in his pocket. Willie went down for the count and Luis's boys dragged him upstairs with Luis holding his wound and moving right up the stairs behind him. A few minutes went by and the Butler came back and gave each of us a hundred dollar bill to forget what we saw and then told us all we had to leave. I still got my hundred. It's back at my apartment. I can show it to you if you'd like?"

"Another time maybe," I said.

The bartender delivered our second round and walked away. Shannon stared me up and down for a few seconds and sipped her drink.

"What happened to Willie?" I asked.

"I don't know. I haven't seen Willie since that night. Nobody has and nobody really cares. He was not a very nice man."

"What was Willie's beef with this guy, Luis?"

"I don't know that either," she said and took another sip. "Not for certain."

"Maybe I should ask Luis?" I said. "Is he up those stairs right now?"

Suddenly Shannon's face went white.

"Luis is probably up there. See the dark glass? When he is here? He's always watching someone from up there. He's probably watching us right now. Trust me, Mr. Atwater. You don't want to involve yourself with the likes of Luis Verdun. He's the kind of man you don't go asking a lot of questions. Especially questions now about Willie "The Nose" Kendall or why Willie tried to put a bullet in Luis' head instead putting it in his shoulder."

"I'll take my chances, Shannon. Nice talking with you."

I stood up and she quickly placed her hand on my shoulder.

"Watch yourself," she warned. "I'm serious. Luis Verdun might be great in the sack with us women but once he has his pants back on he's one ruthless son of a bitch."

"And you, Shannon, are absolutely beautiful. Thanks for the offer and the conversation."

"My pleasure. Hope to see you again some time, Mr. Atwater."

"Maybe," I said. "Maybe."

I put another twenty on the bar next to her drink and gave her a wink and a smile.

Shannon smiled back, grabbed up the twenty, and I headed for the stairs.

I could sense I was being watched as I crossed the floor and by the time I reached the Butler I had two other men close behind me, with another one standing to the Butler's right. I decided to be polite and direct.

"Are you the one they call the Butler?" I asked.

"I'm the Butler," he replied. "What can I do for you?"

"My name is Atwater and I would like a word with your boss."

The Butler looked me over and nodded to the other men to relax and back up.

"And who is my boss?" he asked.

"Luis Verdun. I'm a private eye from Los Angeles and I'm looking for a certain woman."

"A certain woman," he repeated. "You didn't find Shannon to be your taste?"

I tried to play it dumb.

"Who?" I asked.

"The woman you were speaking with at the bar," he said.

"It's not like that. I'm looking for a client's daughter."

"A daughter? Does she work here?" he asked.

"I don't know."

"Does she know Mr. Verdun?"

"I don't know that either."

"And the name?" he asked.

"I told you that. It's Atwater."

"Not your name, gumshoe. This client's daughter you are looking for."

"I will tell you her name if you put me in front of Mr. Verdun. I only want a few minutes of his time."

"Mr. Verdun is a very busy man."

"I only need a few minutes," I repeated. "I've come a long way."

"Are you armed, Mr. Atwater?"

"I am. Yes. I've got a .38 in my jacket. I'm not looking to shoot anybody. I'm just looking for some information. For my client."

"The girl's name?" he repeated.

I watched for any reaction on his face.

"Her name is Diana Santoro. She has a mother named Louise. Does that name ring a bell?"

"No. It does not," he said.

I detected a slight blink on the Butler's face, especially when I said Diane's last name but I could also tell he was well schooled in the art of deception.

His type always is.

"I have no beef with Verdun. I don't even know the man. I'm just trying to do my job and get some information in regards to my client."

I could tell the Butler gave my response the once over in his mind and he allowed me the benefit of the doubt and nodded yes.

"Wait here, please?" he said and disappeared up the stairs.

A man at one of the crap tables sent a roar up from the crowd and I was certain he must have made his number. His next roll brought out an even louder groan. I turned and saw a large individual giving me the once over but I pretended not to notice. A few moments passed and the Butler was suddenly standing on the bottom stair motioning to me.

I smiled and walked over to him.

"Mister Verdun will see you," he announced. "This way, please."

I followed the Butler up the stairs and he opened a large wooden door on the left.

"I'll take that .38, please?" he said. "It will be returned to you after your conversation with Mr. Verdun has ended."

"Do I have your word on that?" I asked.

"You have my word," he said and held out his hand.

I smiled again, handed over the .38, and the Butler motioned me inside.

I walked in and realized I was standing in Luis Verdun's spacious office. It was big enough to park six cars quite comfortably and the entire room smelled of lilac. I assumed it was Luis' choice of after shave.

Luis was a large man with dark hair that had tinges of gray here and there. He stood holding a drink with his back to me, peering through the large double mirrored glass at the gambling floor below. He was well dressed in a dark blue pin striped suit and I could see his tie reflected in the glass. The tie had a large pink flamingo on it.

He spoke without looking at me.

"The Butler tells me you are a private eye from Los Angeles and your name is Atwater." he said.

"That's correct," I said.

He turned and put his drink on the desk. He opened a desk drawer and took out a German Luger hand gun and placed it on the desk.

"The Butler also told me you are armed."

"I was. The Butler is holding my piece until our little discussion here is over," I said. "I'm only looking for information, Mr. Verdun. I'm definitely not looking for any gun play with you or anyone here in your club."

"If you make any sudden moves or reach for some other weapon I will shoot you with this. Are we clear?"

"I am very clear," I said. "Like I said, I'm only looking for some information."

There was a twitchiness about him and I couldn't tell if he was on some sort of drug or simply paranoid around strangers. I decided to choose my words carefully for the duration of our little meeting.

"What did you and Shannon talk about down at the bar?" he asked.

I decided to be vaguely honest unless he pressed me. I didn't want any repercussions coming back onto Shannon just because we spoke a few words together.

"I asked Shannon about the club and she told me you owned the place. I figured you might know the person I'm looking for."

"This Diana person and her mother?" he asked.

"Diana Santoro. Yes," I answered.

Verdun didn't flinch and appeared to relax somewhat.

"I will be honest with you, Mr. Atwater. I don't know them," he said, and took his drink over to a small bar set up and put more ice in his glass.

I knew right then he was lying.

Men like Verdun never say they are going to be honest with you unless they have something to hide and I could tell this guy was hiding plenty.

"That's too bad," I lied. "I guess I'll have to look elsewhere."

I looked around the room waiting for his response and suddenly a framed photo on the wall by the wooden door caught my eye, making me hold my breath for a second or two. The photo I assumed was the official opening and ribbon cutting ceremony for the grand opening of the Glass Palace.

Luis was in the same blue suit and stupid flamingo tie and he was cutting a large blue ribbon with a pair of oversized scissors.

It wasn't the ribbon cutting that almost knocked me off my feet. Or the flamingo tie.

I took another deep breath and did my best to remain calm.

Luis casually poured more bourbon in his glass.

"I don't know who you are, Mr. Atwater."

"I told you. I'm a private eye looking for a client's daughter. That's all there is to it."

"The people who come here to the Glass Palace go right to the tables and spend their money. I like that. But people who come in here and start asking questions? I do not like that. That kind of behavior is unacceptable."

"My apologies to you, Mr. Verdun. And to the Glass Palace. I'm only trying to do my job. For my client."

I tried to act as humble as I could and hoped he would buy it. He was clearly testing my defenses and I let him believe he was winning our conversation.

He sipped his bourbon and smiled.

"I am going give you a free pass tonight, Mr. Atwater. Stay if you'd like. Gamble a little. Have a few drinks. But know this. In a few days, I will know everything there is to know about you. If you are who you say you are? You need not be concerned. But if I discover you are lying to me right now? Pretending to be someone you are not?"

"I'm not lying sir," I added.

"If you are lying to me? You will find yourself right back here in this office and our conversation will not be as comfortable as the one we are now having. Is that understood?"

"Understood," I said. "I can answer any questions you might have about me right now if you'd like? As I said. I have nothing to hide. Not from a man like yourself, Mr. Verdun."

I thought I would play the humble card even deeper and see where it got me. Inside I felt myself beginning to rattle like a broken barn door in a wind storm. I held my ground and stayed focused.

"Questioning you now will not be necessary, Mr. Atwater," he said. "After tonight, do not come here again unless you are invited. You won't be welcome. Is that understood?"

"Understood," I said. "If I have offended you or your clientele with my questions I apologize."

He walked back slowly to his desk, pushed a button under the desk, and looked at me.

"Good night, Mr. Atwater," he said and sipped his drink.

The Butler entered and stood in the doorway.

"The Butler will show you out," he said.

Verdun put his hand gun back in the desk and sipped his drink once again.

I turned towards the door and without Verdun or the Butler realizing, took a closer look at the photo on the wall.

I had been right.

There was no doubt in my mind as to what I had seen.

Standing a few feet to the left of Luis, in the photograph, smiling along with all the other people present, holding drinks in their hands, was Rachel Stone Barbieri.

I knew I was dodging a major bullet in my conversation with Verdun and now had maybe two days max to hopefully find Diana and get out of Miami. Once Verdun learned of my association with Barbieri, the bullets would be coming my way in spades and I was clearly outnumbered.

My gun was returned to me as promised and I walked down the stairs following the Butler. He stopped at the bottom and looked at me.

"You can get some playing chips over there," he pointed.

"Another time perhaps," I said. "I'm going to call it an evening."

"Very well," he replied and walked me to the front door.

As I walked past the bar I noticed Shannon was no longer sitting at her spot. The Butler opened the main entrance door.

"Have a good evening, Mr. Atwater," he said.

"Thank you," I replied, nodded my head, and walked out.

I passed the goons at the front steps without incident and figured I was good to go as I moved quickly and approached Charlie's car.

"How did you make out?" Charlie asked.

"Like stepping on a land mine, Charlie," I said. "Like stepping on a stinking land mine."

"I still got your back," he said as I got into the car.

"These boys play pretty rough, Charlie. You better take me back to the Bancroft."

"Are you sure?" he said as he drove away. "The night is still young and I don't work tomorrow. And I don't scare easy. You say the word and I'll take you wherever you need to go."

I admired Charlie's bravado but I needed to get back to the hotel and make some calls. It was time to call in some backup in case things turned ugly and it certainly looked like that was going to be the case.

Then, I reminded myself of the promise I made to Santoro.

"Do you have any friends over at the county morgue, Charlie?"

"I know an old high school buddy who works there. His name is Mike. He moves all the stiffs where they need to be."

"Ask Mike if a stiff with the name Willie Kendall came in down there in the last few weeks. Tall guy. Around sixty. Got a snot locker you can hang a hat on."

"I'll give him a holler for you," said Charlie. "Kendall you said?"

"Yeah. Willie Kendall."

Charlie wrote the name down on a small pad on the front seat.

70

"You got it."

"Thanks," I replied. "Pick me up tomorrow morning around nine. Okay?"

A big smile crossed Charlie's face.

"Yes sir," he said. "Nine o'clock it is."

Charlie stepped on the gas and drove away.

I figured the more I learned about Louis Verdun and his activities in Florida the more help I would certainly need if I was going to find Diana Santoro and still remain upright and breathing. I decided a good offense at this juncture would serve me better than a weak defense especially if Verdun was as ruthless as Shannon stated. My gut told me Shannon was right on all counts.

I also hoped Shannon was safe and not paying some price for talking to me.

I decided to look her up tomorrow too, and make certain she was all right.

CHAPTER FIVE

The call came in to Agent Edwards' hotel room around six forty-five am. Two bodies were brought in to the County Coroner's office in Newark, New Jersey and needed to be officially identified as soon as possible. The two deceased were **FBI** agents, one male and one female. Their federal ID's were found at the crime scene at the male's apartment in East Orange, and one was known to be a member of Agent Edwards' special Magenta Dairy squad.

That was all he was told.

It was more than enough information for Agent Edwards. A blanket of sadness wrapped around him and much as he tried to remain professional the tighter his sadness felt. Patrick Atwater was right. They were in a whole new war now and Rachel Stone Barbieri was one of the major players for the other side.

A very dark and ruthless side which was tugging at his very core as an FBI agent.

Special Agent Vincent Correlli had an apartment in East Orange. Agent Edwards had worked there many nights with him and his new female partner going over every lead they had on Rachel Stone Barbieri. The terrible news knocked him to the floor and he remembered the night they arrested Rachel in Nogales and her bitter warning to his team.

Her words echoed across his mind.

"It will never stick," she told us. "And each and every one of you? You are all dead men. My word on that."

Agent Edwards suddenly remembered her warning to Agent Loretta Davis too and reached over, picked up the phone, and called her.

She picked up on the first ring.

"This is Loretta," she said.

"Agent Edwards here, Loretta."

"Did we find Magenta?' she asked.

"No."

Agent Edwards tried to think of the right words to say but nothing was coming to his mind. Loretta sensed instantly something was terribly wrong.

"What is it?" she asked. "What's wrong?"

"It's bad," said Agent Edwards. "Vincent Correlli has been killed along with his new partner."

"Oh my god," exclaimed Loretta. "Adrian Younger? She's the new one."

"Yes."

"What the hell happened?" she asked.

"I don't know all the particulars yet. I just got word. This has to be Magenta's doing. I'm calling you as a warning. Watch yourself. I'm going to assign someone to work alongside you until we get a handle on this. I'm sending over Agent Gregory."

"I'll be careful. No sense placing someone else in harm's way."

"I understand but this is an order. I'm sending Agent Gregory to you before the day is out. He has field experience and will keep a watchful eye. Are we clear?"

"Yes sir," she said. "We are clear."

"Good. I'll be in touch and keep you updated."

"Thank you, sir."

"Stay safe," said Agent Edwards and hung up the phone.   Agent Edwards dressed quickly and drove to the coroner's office arriving just before seven-thirty. It was a cold day and the basement morgue felt even colder as stepped inside and descended the stairs.

The first policemen on the scene, Officer Doug McBride and Officer TB Lincoln, two men clearly shaken by what they had experienced, stood in the hallway waiting with the new detective now assigned to the case, a fifteen year tough as nails veteran named Detective Richard McCrory.

All three were standing silently smoking cigarettes and drinking coffee as Agent Edwards entered the hallway.

"Good morning, Officers. Detective McCrory. I am Special Agent Edwards with the FBI."

Each man shook hands with Agent Edwards.

"Are you taking over my case?" asked Detective McCrory.

"I am not," answered Agent Edwards. "I'm here to identify the deceased for the record and to ask you, sir, as a courtesy to the FBI and myself, to keep me posted daily on your investigation. I am more than willing to share any and all information I may have or receive regarding this case."

"Thank you," replied Detective McCrory. "The two deceased agents were on your special task force?"

"That is correct. Yes. These were good agents. Good people. We have reason to believe these murders were perpetrated by a professional killer hired by the individual my team has been searching for."

"Some type of payback to your team?" asked Detective McCrory.

"That is what we believe. Yes."

"Allow me to express my deepest sympathies for your loss," said Detective McCrory.

"Thank you, Detective. What can you tell me?" asked Agent Edwards.

Officer McBride chimed in first and read from his notes. His hand shook slightly and Agent Edwards could tell the officer was visibly affected much more than the other two men.

"We received a routine disturbance call from dispatch at four twenty-eight am by someone stating loud screaming was heard. We proceeded to the residence of one Vincent Correlli, in East Orange."

Hearing Agent Correlli's name prompted Agent Edwards to gasp uncontrollably and Officer McBride stopped talking.

"Are you all right?" asked Detective McCrory.

"I'm fine," answered Agent Edwards. "Please? Continue."

Officer McBride went back to his notes.

"Upon arrival Officer Lincoln and myself noticed Mr. Correlli's front door was wide open. We thought it might be a burglary in progress, drew our weapons, and quietly entered the residence."

"The whole place had been tossed," added Officer Lincoln. "Furniture was overturned. Dishes were broken all over the dining room floor. I proceeded to the kitchen area and Officer McBride went up the staircase."

Officer Lincoln stopped talking and took a deep breath.

"Go on, Officer Lincoln," urged Agent Edwards.

"I got to the top of the landing, took one step, slipped and slid to the floor on one knee," said Officer McBride. "I grabbed the railing to steady myself and realized there was this vast amount of blood on the upper hallway floor coming from the first bedroom. It was dark. I couldn't really see very well. Excuse me. But I need to use the rest room. I'm sorry."

Agent Edwards noticed the dried blood on Officer McBride's left pant leg as he walked swiftly to the men's room a few feet away.

Agent Edwards turned to Officer Lincoln.

"Officer Lincoln?" he asked. "Can you continue?"

"Yes sir," he responded and took a deep breath.

"I made certain the first floor was clear, noticed one of the chairs from the kitchen table was missing, and proceeded up the stairs to join

Officer McBride," said Officer Lincoln. "Mick pointed to the large blood stream on the floor and I cautiously entered the bedroom."

Officer Lincoln stopped speaking and stared at the floor as if he was seeing the scene all over again in his mind.

"What did you find, Officer?" asked Agent Edwards. "Officer Lincoln? Please continue."

Officer Lincoln took another deep breath and went on with his report.

"I turned on the bedroom light. There was so much blood. I never saw that much blood in my life. There were two naked bodies in the room. Both appeared deceased and both were covered in blood. Their clothes were thrown about all over the room. The man was handcuffed to the missing chair from the kitchen with his arms behind him. His feet had been nailed to the floor. His left eye was removed and was stuck to his chest. His penis and several of his toes had been severed. His throat was cut from ear to ear."

"And the woman?" asked Agent Edwards.

"The woman's ankles were tied to the legs of the bed with small pieces of rope and her wrists..."

Officer Lincoln had to stop to compose himself. He took a heavier deep breath, fought back his emotions, and continued.

"...her wrists were nailed to a wooden shelf hanging on the wall. She was spread eagled sideways on the bed. Her skin was shredded all over the front of her body. Someone had taken a sharp blade and kept running it down her torso. All the wounds were two inches apart exactly and they looked like columns on some accountant's entry sheet."

"These men didn't realize it at the time but the woman was still alive when the officers arrived," said Detective McCrory.

"What?" exclaimed Agent Edwards. "Still alive? No one checked for a pulse?"

"She wasn't breathing and as far as we could tell and with all that blood she appeared to us to be deceased," said Officer Lincoln. "But after we did a full check of the other rooms upstairs we heard her faintly gargling and gagging and we ran back to her."

"Did she say anything?" asked Agent Edwards.

"No. She just struggled and shook for a few seconds longer and then she just stopped moving all together," added Officer Lincoln. "She never uttered a word to us. Officer McBride checked for a pulse but she was gone. There was nothing we could have done to save her. Or him! Nothing!"

Officer McBride came out of the men's room and stood by his partner still clearly shaken.

"Are we done here, Agent Edwards?" asked Detective McCrory. "I need to get back to my crime scene and these men need to go off shift."

"Certainly, of course," said Agent Edwards. "Let me know if you find anything that could lead us to the people responsible for this."

"I certainly will," said Detective McCrory. "This wasn't done by any people I have ever encountered before. This was done by monsters. Sick, blood thirsty monsters. Have you ever seen anything like this before?"

"Never," said Agent Edwards. "But we will find them. And we'll stop them."

"Yes we will," agreed Detective McCrory.

Agent Edwards shook hands with all three men.

"Thank you, gentlemen," said Agent Edwards.

Agent Edwards nodded to Detective McCrory and watched the men walk away.

Agent Edwards took a deep breath and walked into the morgue.

The coroner, an older man named Baxter, had the two bodies laid out on the table, both covered with sheets.

"Mr. Baxter?" Agent Edwards asked.

"I'm Baxter. You must be Agent Edwards?"

"Yes, sir. I'm Edwards."

"Are you ready for this, Agent Edwards?" Baxter asked.

"I'm ready. Yes."

77

Baxter pulled back the sheet from Correlli's body first and Agent Edwards gasped loudly.

"Whoever did this knew exactly what he was doing. This wasn't rage. This was done slowly and concisely."

"Slow torture?"

"Slow torture and very slow death. Painful. Excruciating. These killings were done methodically and these two people suffered terribly."

Agent Edwards reeled back a step and gasped again.

"Are you all right?" asked Baxter.

"I'm fine," said Agent Edwards. "For the record, that is Vincent Correlli. Special Agent Vincent Correlli."

"Thank you," said Baxter and wrote something on his folder.

Baxter nodded and pulled back the sheet on the other body.

"And this one?" asked Baxter.

Agent Edwards' body shook slightly and a tear ran down one side of his face.

"Oh my god," said Agent Edwards.

"You know this woman?" Baxter asked.

"Yes. I know her."

Agent Edwards closed his eyes and put his right hand over his face.

"Do you need a moment?" asked Baxter.

Agent Edwards took a deep breath and blew the air out slowly. Tears fell from both eyes.

"My god," Agent Edwards said. "This is the work of a real sick son of a bitch. A real horrific monster."

"A monster very knowledgeable in regards to inflicting pain. For the record, Agent Edwards?" asked Baxter.

"For the record, Mr. Baxter, the deceased is Special Agent Adrian Younger. Agent Correlli's partner. She's fresh out of the academy. Only twenty-five years old."

"Were they lovers?" asked Baxter.

"Lovers? No. They were partners. Only partners. We have all been working together for some time on a specific case."

"Then I will have to assume whoever killed these people, also raped Miss Younger. According to my findings."

"Raped? Is this the work of one person? One man?"

"Quite possibly if he somehow subdued them both before torturing them. There were no defensive wounds of any kind. They were both bound and nailed before they were tortured and killed. I'll know more in a few weeks what might have been used to sedate them and let you know when I have my report completed."

"The arriving officers told me that Agent Younger was choking on something before she died."

"Yes she was," said Baxter.

Baxter bowed his head and looked down at the floor.

"What was it?" asked Agent Edwards.

"I discovered Agent Correlli's severed penis stuffed in her throat."

Agent Edwards reeled back further and took a sharp breath. More tears ran down his face.

"Agent Edwards?" Baxter asked.

"Yes?"

"Do you need a moment? Some water or something stronger? I keep some Irish Whiskey in my desk drawer."

Baxter headed for his desk but Agent Edwards stopped him.

"No. Nothing. I'm good. Thanks."

Baxter sighed and held out his folder.

"I'm sorry but I also have some papers for you to sign," said Baxter.

"I understand," said Agent Edwards.

Agent Edwards wiped his tears and signed the papers.

"I hope you catch this son of a bitch," said Baxter. "If you take him alive? You are more than welcome to bring him down here to any one of my tables and I will personally give him an anatomy course he will never forget."

Agent Edwards smiled slightly but his face still held the pain he was feeling for Agent Correlli and Agent Younger.

"I will see if I can get some federal approval on that."

"Thank you, Agent Edwards," said Baxter. "Nothing would make me happier. You will have my full report by the first week in February."

"Thank you, Mr. Baxter," said Agent Edwards.

"Do these agents have family? They will need to be contacted."

"I will see to that."

Agent Edwards took out a card and handed it to Baxter.

"Call me the minute you have that report," said Agent Edwards.

"I will," replied Baxter. "Again, I am very sorry for your loss."

"Thank you. They were good agents. Good people."

Agent Edwards took one last look at his fallen team members and stepped out into the hall. He leaned on a nearby gurney and took several deep breaths. Suddenly a loud voice echoed down the hallway.

"Special Agent Edwards!" the voice said.

Agent Edwards looked down the hall and saw a very upset and angry Assistant District Attorney, Jonathan Wainwright, heading straight for him.

"What are you doing in regards to my wife's assault?" he asked. "I was informed you had this man Long in custody and you let him go!"

"I did. That's correct," answered Agent Edwards.

"Well, sir that is unacceptable. I am not letting this creature walk away from prosecution over some technicality in the law. No sir! My wife can identify this man and is more than willing to testify in court, at his trial. I want this man arrested immediately. Do you hear me?"

Agent Edwards sighed deeply and looked at Wainwright.

"I hear you."

"I don't think you do. This monster needs to be held accountable!"

"Accountable?"

"Yes! I want this man arrested! Today! Right now."

"Calm down, Jonathan. You of all people should understand the FBI's position on this."

Jonathan stepped in closer to Agent Edwards.

"The FBI's position? After what this son of a bitch did to my wife? You are telling me about your position? That is not going to fly with me,

80

Agent Edwards, and it certainly will not fly with the office of the District Attorney of Newark, New Jersey! Now get out there! Do your god damn job and arrest this bastard!"

Agent Edwards took a second calming breath and lowered his voice.

"Henry Long is a low life bastard. And? Yes! He did a terrible injustice to your wife. I was there. I saw what he did. He is a horrible bastard. He is a horrible individual. But Henry Long happens to be part of a much bigger, ongoing, federal investigation which goes all the way up the federal food chain and lands right in Hoover's office. J Edgar Hoover's office. So take a breath, Jonathan. Go home. Hug your wife, tell her you love her and explain to her the situation we are in. We are trying to close down a world-wide drug organization that has just butchered and killed two of my agents. Their bodies are lying in this morgue as I speak. The FBI have their eyes on Henry Long! He is not going to hurt anyone ever again, and when the time is right, Henry Long will be prosecuted to the full letter of the law. My word from me to you on that!"

"Your word? The time is right?" exclaimed Jonathan. "What does that even mean?"

Agent Edwards took a deep breath and locked eyes with Jonathan.

"It means Henry Long thinks he's beaten us. We are hoping he reaches out to the people we need to get to and until he does, we will be watching his every move. We can't do that if he's locked up in some New Jersey jail because you are demanding justice for the attack he made on your wife. So back it up, Jonathan. Take a real deep breath. And calm yourself down on this. Please?"

Jonathan stared hard at Agent Edwards and his face began turning red with anger.

"No! I do not accept that!" ranted Jonathan. "I am sorry for your agents but life moves on and you and the FBI doing nothing in regards to my wife is not enough!"

Agent Edwards took another deep breath and tried to remain calm. Flashes of his two dead agents raced across his mind.

"Well it's all you're going to get today, Jonathan," added Edwards. "I'm sorry but this matter is in the hands of the FBI and that's the way it is and that's the way it's going to stay. So again! Please? Back away. Let this go. For now. And let me do my job."

"That's my point! You are not doing your job!"

"Yes I am!" said Agent Edwards.

The two men stared at each other.

"I will go over your head! I will go to Hoover myself if I have to!"

"Go ahead! Do it! You will get the same answer from him I'm trying to give you now. Let this go! Please! I'm trying to remain professional here, Jonathan, but you are beginning to try my patience!"

"This is not right! I want satisfaction! I demand satisfaction. He brutalized my wife!"

"Brutalized? You don't know the meaning of the word! Your satisfaction on this is not available. Get that through your thick skull! Not available! Not yet and not today, Jonathan! I'm sorry."

Jonathan pointed his finger at Agent Edwards.

"You make this happen, Edwards! You can talk to Hoover!"

"No!" snapped Agent Edwards. "I'm not going to do that!"

Jonathan softened his approach.

"Don't tie my hands. Not now! My wife has been traumatized. She's depressed. She doesn't eat. She does nothing but sit on the couch and stare out the front window. She's afraid this monster is going to show up again at our front door and do god knows what."

Agent Edwards looked at Wainwright and shook his head.

"I'm sorry. I can't help her. And I can't help you. I have to go."

Agent Edwards started walking away and Jonathan's anger level rose higher.

"Don't you dare walk away from me, you son of a bitch! Who the hell do you think you're talking to?" screamed Jonathan.

Jonathan hurried after Edwards and grabbed him by the arm.

"You can leave this building when I say so!" said Jonathan. "I have legal cause here!"

Agent Edwards turned and punched Jonathan squarely in the face, knocking him to the floor.

Agent Edwards pointed his finger at Jonathan lying on the floor holding his face in his hand.

"You don't have squat, Jonathan! This is a federal matter. It is going to stay a federal matter. If you persist any further from this moment on I will have your ass arrested for hindering a federal investigation. So shut your face! Go the hell home, be a concerned and loving husband, and console your wife! Tell her she has nothing to fear from Henry Long. The FBI is protecting her from this man and we will keep protecting her. You have our word! Now I am done talking to you about this!"

Agent Edwards turned away and walked down the hallway.

"We're not done, Agent Edwards. We are not done by a long shot! I'm putting all of this and you in front of a grand jury!" yelled Jonathan.

Agent Edwards walked out without answering.

Jonathan sat up and felt his bloodied nose for any signs of breakage. There wasn't any.

Jonathan looked to his right and saw the coroner standing in the doorway staring at him.

The coroner shook his head, walked away, and closed the door behind him.

CHAPTER SIX

Charlie arrived at the Hotel Bancroft precisely at nine a.m. as promised. I jumped into the back seat and handed him an address. Charlie looked it over and tossed it on the seat.

"You didn't need to write that down, Mr. Atwater," he said. "I know exactly where the Bell Haven Trailer Park is. My Aunt Millie retired there until her death last year. She was ninety-three. Smoked like a train and drank like a fish. Buried four husbands up in Albany before coming down this way. I miss that crazy woman every day. She cursed like a sailor too. She would have loved hanging around you."

"She sounds like my kind of woman," I added trying to make light of my situation.

"She never met a man she didn't like in one way or another," he said.

"Any word from your friend down at the county morgue?" I asked. "That guy named Mike?"

"No one with that description of yours is down there right now. If he gets someone in like you described he'll call me straight away," said Charlie. "Mike's the reliable sort."

"Good to know," I said and settled back in my seat.

I had placed calls in to Agent Edwards and Detective Blaine late last night but wasn't able to reach either one. I decided not to leave any more messages until we could actually speak to one another and figure out what should be done with Luis Verdun. I knew I had to have some plan of action in place before the end of the day or things would begin to turn badly.

"Don't turn around and look," said Charlie. "We have a tail on us."

"Is it a light blue Cadillac with two gorillas in the front seat?" I asked.

Charlie glanced into the rear view mirror.

"Yes. King and Kong about four cars back."

"I caught them out front of the hotel when you picked me up. I'm pretty sure they were part of that group working the door last night at the Glass Palace," I said.

"What do you want to do?" asked Charlie.

"I don't want to spend all day looking over our shoulders. Do you think you can lose them?" I asked. "Daylight doesn't give us much cover."

"I know these types," Charlie said. "Just sit back and watch my magical disappearing act."

Charlie made a quick right turn and drove along a service road adjacent to the beach on the bay side. There were several small houses along one side of the road and the other side had all types of vacationers, short and tall, but mostly pretty young college girls in bathing suits and sandals heading to the beach from all the different hotels. Charlie watched his rear view mirror until the goons in the Cadillac had to stop at a red light.

"This is too easy," Charlie announced and quickly backed into a driveway and parked alongside a dark blue Plymouth Coupe.

"Watch," said Charlie. "King and Kong are going to drive right past us because they will be ogling all the young broads here in their bathing suits strutting their stuff."

Sure enough the Cadillac came down the road and both men were looking in the other direction as they drove right by us.

"Women in bathing suits should run the world," Charlie said.

"Women are running the world, Charlie, no matter what they wear or don't wear. Don't ever doubt that."

We waited for a few more cars to go by and Charlie pulled out and headed in the opposite direction.

"Nicely done, Charlie, but we have to be careful with these guys. I'm afraid they may be playing for keeps."

Charlie reached in his glove compartment and pulled out an old revolver.

"So do I Mr. Atwater," he said. "So do I. Those goons don't scare me."

"Let's try and keep any confrontations to a minimum today. All right?"

"I'll try but I won't make any promises," said Charlie and put his revolver back in the glove compartment.

We got to the trailer park in about twenty-five minutes with no Cadillac to be seen. There was a big empty field next to the place and it had a large swimming pool surrounded by palm trees. It wasn't the Ritz but it did have a certain charm all its own. There were about thirty mobiles of all shapes and sizes with only one road leading in and out of the place like some large horseshoe.

"What's the number?" Charlie asked.

"Eleven," I said and Charlie stopped the car.

"There it is. Number eleven," said Charlie.

MAGENTA DAIRY

The place was a small single-wide mobile with an attached wooden porch and a metal roof. There were two chairs set outside, but the entire area looked like no one had lived there for some time.

"The place looks empty," Charlie said.

I got out, walked to the front door and gave it my best policeman's knock.

"Hello? Anybody home in there?" I yelled.

There was no response.

Then a voice from an old frail woman sounded from across the street.

"They're gone, mister," the old woman said. "Some men in a blue Cadillac took them away."

"Verdun's gorillas," I thought.

The old woman stepped closer and looked at Charlie sitting in the car.

"Took who away?" I asked.

"Louise and her daughter, Diana," she said.

"Was it a light blue Cadillac?" I asked.

"I think it was," she replied. "Yes. Now that you mention it, it was a light blue."

I looked at my watch.

"How long ago," I asked. "Did we just miss them?"

"Just missed them?" she repeated and looked at me as if I was crazy. "Louise and Diana have been gone for months. Just before Christmas it was. Yup. That's when it was. Just before Christmas."

"Did they go willingly?" I asked.

"Couldn't tell that for sure. There were three of them. Big galoots. The ladies weren't smiling but they weren't trying to run away neither."

"Did one of them wear a tie with a big flamingo on it?" I asked.

"Yes! He had dark hair and a real nice dark suit. Little spots of gray up top and by his ears. He reminded me a little of Victor Mature. You know? The actor. But older."

"It had to be Verdun and his men," I thought.

87

The old woman fluffed her hair.

"Nobody called the police about them leaving?" I asked.

"The police? I'm retired, sonny. Not my place to interfere in people's business. It looked to me like they was all just going for a ride somewhere."

"But they never came back?" I asked.

"Nope."

"And they've been gone since Christmas?"

"Yes sir. Are you with the police, young man?" she asked.

"No. I'm a Private Detective," I said. "My name is Atwater. Patrick Atwater."

The old woman smiled warmly and fluffed at her hair again.

"I'm Beverly. Beverly Toth."

"Nice to meet you, Beverly."

"I've been holding their mail for them ever since. Do you want to see inside their place? I got a key."

The old lady grinned from ear to ear.

"Please," I said. "Just a quick look if that's okay?"

"Sure. Be happy to oblige you."

The old woman reached in her house dress pocket and took out a key. She opened the door and stepped back.

"Louise and Diana are two of the nicest women you'd ever want to meet. I hope they're doing all right. The men that drove off with them didn't seem quite right to me. But like I said it weren't my business. You boys seem okay. Detectives, huh?"

"That's right," I said.

The old woman suddenly wrinkled up her face.

"Sweet Merry Christmas what's that smell?" she asked.

"I'll take a look," I said and stepped inside.

The place was well lit from the morning sun and there were four foul smelling eggs still sitting in a pan and rotting on the stove. An opened bottle of milk was on the counter and that too had seen better days. I opened the kitchen window and looked around. There were two suitcases opened on the small couch. Both with folded clothes, one had a hand mirror, and a pair of black high heels. It looked as if the women had plans to go to some place after their breakfast but were rudely interrupted by Verdun and his two goons. I looked in the bedrooms and both were picture perfect as far as being neat and tidy. The beds were made and the bathroom was immaculate.

I opened the small hallway closet and couldn't believe my eyes. Or my sense of smell.

Leaning back against the wall was a man's dead body standing straight up, wrapped tightly in thin clear plastic and bound with rope. I figured this was the body of Willie "The Nose" Kendall and took out the photo given to me by Santoro.

I compared the earlier photo with the body in the closet and surmised from the enormous nose on the dead man's face this was clearly the remains of Willie Kendall. He had a small bullet hole in the center of his forehead and it appeared his body had been there for a few weeks.

I put the photo in my pocket, stepped back, and walked outside.

"Do you have a phone, Beverly?" I asked.

"A phone?" she asked. "Yes, I have a phone."

"I want you to call the local police. Tell them there's a dead man in here."

The old woman's jaw dropped almost to the ground.

"A dead man? Oh sweet Jesus, Mary, and Joseph! Pray for us!"

"I'll try to put in a good word but for right now I need you to get to your phone and make that call. Please?"

The old woman nodded her head yes several times, turned, and ran to her trailer.

Charlie walked up to me.

"While you were inside? King and Kong did a quick drive by. They didn't stay long. Who's the dead guy?"

"I'm pretty sure it's Willie Kendall. They most likely put him here until they figured out what to do with him. Or tried to make it look like Diana and her mother did him in and ran off."

"I guess we've upset their plans somewhat," said Charlie.

"We did exactly that," I said.

"What's our next step?" Charlie asked.

"For now? We'll hang here and wait for the police," I said.

Charlie nodded.

"And King and Kong?"

"We'll be dealing with them soon enough and everyone else over at the Glass Palace until all this gets sorted out."

"You're not just a private eye. Are you?" asked Charlie.

"In this matter with Diana? I am just a gumshoe working a case. But I do have a few good friends with some pull if push comes to shove with this bunch. And trust me, Charlie. They are going to push and they're going to push hard."

"Where did these women go?" Charlie asked. "Dead maybe?"

"I don't think so. I hope not. One way or the other I am going to find out."

I knew now I had only one option if I was ever going to set my eyes on Diana Santoro and her mother Louise and that was to get back to the Glass Palace as soon as possible and force some straight answers out of Luis Verdun.

And I wasn't going there alone.

Three police cars arrived shortly along with the coroner, a heavy set chain smoker named Andrew Thomason, his young assistant and high school friend of Charlie's, Mike, and two police Detectives, Lennis Miller and Steve Brooks. I laid out the entire scenario to the two Detectives and after convincing them that time was of the essence in this matter, they agreed to accompany me with two patrol cars to the Glass Palace and pick up Luis Verdun and his goons for questioning.

I asked Charlie to stay behind and keep tabs on what the Coroner might discover in regards to Willie Kendall and meet me at the Bancroft around seven so we could compare notes.

He happily agreed.

On the ride to the Glass Place Detectives Miller and Brooks told me they have been secretly watching Luis Verdun ever since opening his gambling establishment but were never able to observe any illegal activity they could put their hands on.

Until now.

My police entourage arrived quickly and quietly at the Glass Palace. The joint wasn't officially open until two in the afternoon but a cleaning crew was there and the front door was wide open.

Running from our vehicles with guns drawn, we all entered the place.

Two women were running vacuums and three older men were cleaning the mirrors behind both bars.

"Luis Verdun? Where is he?" I asked the woman closest to me and she pointed to the upstairs office.

Detectives Miller and Brooks followed me up the stairs as the other police officers searched the entire downstairs area. I walked into Verdun's office and discovered the Butler sitting at Verdun's desk casually eating breakfast.

"Where is he?" I asked.

"Where's who?" he asked and sipped his coffee.

Detective Miller stepped up next to me.

"I am Detective Miller and this is Detective Brooks with the Dade County Police Department. We are looking for Luis Verdun. Answer this man's question."

"Luis is not here," answered the Butler and continued calmly eating his breakfast. "Do you gentlemen have a warrant to enter these premises?"

"We don't need a warrant," said Detective Miller. "We're here to pick up Luis Verdun for questioning. We're not here to toss the place."

"Questioning?" asked the Butler. "May I ask in what regard?"

Detective Brooks stepped up next to Detective Miller.

"In regards to the murder of Willie Kendall," answered Detective Bracken. "Where's Verdun?"

"I don't know where Mr. Verdun is and I refuse to answer any more questions without my attorney present."

I knew every minute counted now and I was not going to be stopped dead in our tracks by some legal mumbo jumbo. I decided to take matters into my own hands. I looked over at the two Detectives, leaned in close and lowered my voice.

"Would you two gentlemen please step outside for a few moments? The Butler and I have a little private matter we need to discuss at the moment."

Both Detectives grinned.

"A private matter?" asked Detective Miller.

"Yes." I replied.

"We would be happy to," replied Detective Miller and both Detectives smiled at the Butler and left the room.

I walked behind the desk with my gun still in my hand. As the Butler quickly opened the desk drawer and stuck in his right hand, I leaned in with my hip, closing it tightly on his wrist.

"Don't be stupid," I said.

"Step away. You're hurting my wrist."

"I'm going to step away from this drawer in a moment, Butler, and I better not see that luger of Verdun's in your hand or I'll splatter your brains all over this desk. Do we understand each other?"

"Yes," the Butler replied and I eased away from the drawer slowly.

"No need for any gun play." I said.

The Butler removed his hand and began rubbing his wrist as I pulled the luger from the drawer and stuck it in my belt.

"Listen up, Butler. I'm trying to help you here. The detectives out there have to go by the letter of the law. My hands aren't as tied. If you don't want to be arrested for murder, I suggest you start talking to me and talking quick. Verdun and his two goons in their fat blue Cadillac are definitely going down for the murder of Willie "The Nose" Kendall. We just discovered his body all wrapped up nice and neat at the home of Louise and Diana Santoro. So if you are as smart a guy as I think you are and you don't want to be put on the same bus your boss and his goons are going to be riding soon, you'll start telling me everything you know about Willie Kendall's death, where your boss and his two boys are, and what's the relationship with Diana Santoro, her mother, and this Glass Palace."

The Butler put his hand down on the arm of the chair, sat back, and looked up at me.

"I don't have to talk to you and I didn't kill anyone."

"What were you planning to do with this luger?" I asked. "Take me hostage and negotiate some kind of an escape?"

"I don't like cops. There's a rear entrance. I would have knocked you cold and been long gone before those detectives outside the door or the cops on the grounds even knew I was off the premises."

"And then what? Keep looking over your shoulder for the rest of your life? Now you're disappointing me, Butler. You're starting to sound like you are guilty of something."

"I'm not guilty of any murder."

"And I don't have any time to play word games with you. I need straight answers and I need them right now. You didn't kill anyone? Good. If what you just said is true then I can help you. Do you want these detectives outside to go away and leave you totally out of this? I can make that happen and you won't need any secret rear escape plan."

I could see in the Butler's face that he was beginning to contemplate his options.

There weren't many.

"Talk to me or talk to them," I said.

"All right. I'll tell you what you want to know," he said.

"For starters, where's Verdun?" I asked.

The Butler hesitated and I could see there was something resting heavily on his mind.

"You have one shot at this pal, and the time to speak up is right now. Tell me what I need to know and I'll make certain to keep you in the clear. My word on it."

The Butler took a deep breath and looked up at me.

"If Verdun knows I gave him up? He'll kill me."

"The conversation we are about to have? Never happened. As far as anyone else has to know, we came here looking for Verdun and his goons and you told us to take a hike. Fair enough?"

The Butler smiled slightly.

"Fair enough," he said.

"Good. Spill it. All of it," I said and put my gun away.

"I am the manager of the Glass Palace. I have been for years. If there is trouble on the floor? I handle it. When Verdun is not here? I am the man in charge. That is the extent of my position here. I am a first rate gambling hall manager. That is all I do. It's a job I take quite seriously and one I do quite efficiently. Luis Verdun on the other hand is a common thug, a ruthless gangster, and if something or someone gets in his way he simply makes it disappear. He is the kind of man you must always obey and always do what you are told or you face the inevitable consequences. Verdun has his hands in a number of legitimate businesses but he also has several illegal endeavors, some of them are highly illegal. I am not part of that. I am paid very well here to do my job and unfortunately at certain times I am also paid extremely well to keep my mouth shut or look the other way."

"I understand completely but there's no looking away on this one," I said. "Tell me about Willie Kendall and the night he shot Verdun."

"Willie is on Verdun's payroll. He pays him cash under the table and has been doing that for the last fifteen years or so. Verdun runs a very clean business here. But outside of the Glass Palace he deals in drugs and prostitution. Not the kind of prostitution like the old days. Those women back then knew their job and what was expected of them and they were always kept safe and protected. They were treated fairly, paid very well, looked after by doctors, and if they wanted to quit? They quit. No repercussions. The Glass Palace was a first class operation all the way, top to bottom. Everyone came to the Glass Palace. The good and the bad."

"And then what? Things changed?" I asked.

"Yes," he replied. "Florida began cleaning up the entire state. Turning it into the vacation destination of the country. The Glass Palace got closed down and all the girls moved on. But Verdun was not happy about that and decided to run an entirely different operation. He still deals in prostitution, but the girls who work for him now operate underground and each and every one of them gets treated like they are slaves. Once they are in they can never get out. If they don't do as they are told, they simply disappear or become drugged-out whores. He has a place down in the Keys where he ships his girls in and out. Sometimes there are ten or more in a group. They're all promised work in the motion picture business. That's his come on. They are all fairly young. Pretty. Totally naïve to what's really in store for them. He tells them how it is and when he has to he gets them hooked on the hard stuff and ships the girls off to god knows where. The word around here was Willie had some feelings for the mother Louise. She and her daughter worked here for a time as cocktail waitresses. Willie kept hitting on Louise but her heart belonged to Verdun. But then Louise suddenly dumped Verdun. Told him it was over. You don't tell a man like Luis Verdun he is no longer wanted in your bed. Luis wouldn't take no for an answer and kept following Louise wherever she went. Louise got hot and threatened to blow the whistle on Verdun's other operations. Verdun grabbed up Diana and her mother and Willie "The Nose" Kendall suddenly went missing.

"So Verdun killed Willie?" I asked.

"I would have to assume so. Yes. But I don't know for certain. I really don't know the how or the where. I just know Willie "The Nose" is gone and he's never coming back. Those were Verdun's words. Not mine."

"Is that where Diana and Louise are now? At this place in the Keys?" I asked.

"I don't know for sure. But that's where you'll find Verdun. Whenever the heat's on him? That's where he runs. He's the big man down there. Controls everything and everybody. Down in the Keys Luis Verdun is untouchable."

"Where is this place of Verdun's down in the Keys?"

"Going down there now would not be a smart move."

"If that's where he has Diana then I have no other choice but to go there."

"If you go down there it's highly unlikely you will survive the visit."

"I'll take my chances," I said. "Give me the exact address."

The Butler grabbed a pen and wrote the address down. I looked at it and almost fell over backwards.

"This is where Verdun operates?" I asked.

"For as long as I can remember," Butler answered.

The address was Roberto Santoro's place.

The very same exact address I was hoping to bring Diana to.

"This is Verdun's base of operations?" I repeated trying to believe my eyes.

"Yes," replied the Butler. "He has had it for years. Do you know this place?"

"I only know of it," I said. "I was told it belongs to someone else."

"I'm telling you, Verdun runs the Keys and most of southern Florida," said the Butler. "He has for years. If you're going to take him down there it will not be an easy thing to do."

"Have you ever been there?" I asked.

"Only once. He had a Christmas party there once for all the staff here at the club. He treated us all like kings and queens. He even gave me a brand new car as a Christmas gift. A blue Cadillac."

"The same car they took Willie in?"

"Verdun needed to borrow my car. I gave it to him."

I held up the addressed paper.

"You're certain this is where I'll find him?"

"He's there. He's safe there. If you are going in with a lot of police he will know you're coming for him long before you arrive. He has eyes and ears in many places."

"His eyes and ears won't stop me. We are coming for him. That's for sure."

"Then expect a lot of bloodshed and a lot of gunfire. He always has four men surrounding the place outside, two men inside, and they are all well trained and heavily armed."

"And his two big goons?" I asked.

"Always doing something for Verdun or with Verdun twenty-four seven," said the Butler.

The Butler smiled and nodded. I thought he was pushing me a little too hard. Trying to scare me off but I wasn't buying it. We took Hitler and Mussolini down and I knew in my heart I would find a way to take down Luis Verdun.

One way or another.

"If you were going to take Verdun down at this place in the Keys? How would you play it? What would you suggest?"

"If you don't have a small army handy?" he asked.

"I don't," I said.

"I would go in quietly with about ten good men, also well-armed and highly trained and come in from the west side."

"The west side?" I asked.

"Yes. By boat. An approach like that? Verdun would not suspect. The dock sits down below a hill and there are no lights. If you do manage to take him by surprise and you have enough fire power you might get lucky. If you come in by the main road entrance like you did here today? You and your men won't stand a chance."

Now it was my turn to weigh my options.

In my mind there was only one option beginning to form and it didn't involve any boat. I could tell the Butler was playing both sides and whoever came out on top would be the one he would place his money on. I let him think I was buying his suggestion.

"If Verdun calls here? Make sure you tell him our little agreed upon story."

"I will" said the Butler and picked up his coffee cup.

I politely stopped him from drinking and looked him square in the eyes.

"If you warn him that we're coming? You and this legal gambling establishment you run so efficiently will shut down forever and you will live out your days in prison. Do we have an agreed understanding?"

The Butler smiled, put down his coffee, and offered his hand.

"We most definitely have an agreed understanding, Mr. Atwater," he replied.

"Good," I said and shook his hand.

"Can you draw me a quick layout of the house?"

"I can."

The Butler drew a fast picture of the grounds and the first floor and handed it to me. I took a look at it and put it in my pocket.

"Stay healthy, Mr. Atwater."

"I'll do that," I said. "You do the same."

I grabbed a piece of the Butler's toast.

"Nice not talking to you," I said and walked out of the office.

I laid out everything to Detectives Miller and Brooks but either their hands were legally tied or they both decided going down to the Keys was definitely a suicide mission and told me if I was going after Verdun, I was on my own.

Their attitude did not sit well with me but I didn't have time to figure out why they were suddenly running scared.

The detectives had a police officer drive me back to my hotel.

On the ride to the Bancroft I ran some possible approaches in my head of how I could get to Verdun.

Each and every one of them spelled disaster.

I hoped Charlie might give me some new perspectives.

Charlie and I were having drinks at the bar as I was deciding our next move when an angry looking Shannon walked up to us.

I was happy to see she was still alive and breathing.

"Verdun killed Willie?" she asked.

"That appears to be the consensus," I replied.

"I knew it," she said. "Hell! Everybody knew it. Verdun skipped town?"

"He wasn't at the Glass Palace," I said.

Our bartender, Vernon poured us another round. Shannon passed and waved the bartender off.

"I know where Verdun is," she added. "He's in the Keys. He always goes back to the god damn Keys. Are you going to arrest him?"

"Charlie and I were just discussing that very subject," I said. "The word is Verdun is untouchable in the Keys. Too well protected."

Shannon laughed and reached into her purse.

"He just tells everyone he is. The people down there call his little gang of cutthroats the "escuadron de la mort", the squadron of death. He's got most people down there shaking with fear. Trust me Atwater, I know his entire crew and they're nothing but a bunch of drunken limp dick cowards. Luis Verdun barks at them and they all jump to his tune."

Shannon handed me a card.

"Here," she said. "You want to take Verdun? This is all you'll need."

I looked at the card but it was confusing to me.

"Who is this?" I asked.

"That's my sister Liz' card and her phone number. She lives down there. In the Keys."

"Your sister Liz? What can she tell me?"

"When it comes to the Keys? Liz can tell you plenty. And? She can help. She's been in the Keys most of her adult life. Verdun doesn't scare her. Or her friends."

I stared at the card wondering what her sister Liz could actually do to help me. Shannon suddenly pulled me out of my thoughts by grabbing me by my shoulders.

"Hey? Do you want to take Verdun or don't you?" she asked.

"Yes!" I said.

"My sister, Liz, can help you make that happen."

"I want Verdun," I said. "This card says she sells coconut heads to tourists."

"She does. Sculpts them herself too. But she's also retired military and she has a small "escuadron de la mort" of her own. You mess with my sister? Or you mess with her crew? They mess you right back."

"Is she Verdun's competition down there?" I asked.

"No! Liz and her girls just look out for each other."

"Her girls?" I asked.

Shannon ignored my question.

"Believe me, my sister and her friends, and most of the other law abiding citizens of Key West want Verdun and his henchmen gone and will be more than happy to assist you in his arrest or his demise. What do you say?"

I gave her question about three seconds of thought and smiled.

"Your sister is ex-military?"

"Yes she is. And her friends."

"They have fire power?"

"They have enough to take out a man like Verdun. And his goons. They just need the legal means to do so. You have that? Right?"

"Yes I do," I said. "In a roundabout way."

"Explain what you mean by roundabout?" she asked.

"It's complicated but I do have the authority. You and your sister will have to trust me on that."

Shannon gave my answer a few moments of silent consideration.

"All right. Let's say I trust you. Convince me."

"The FBI has my back," I said.

"The FBI?"

"Yes."

"All right then. If you are working hand in hand with the FBI then enough said. Consider yourself trusted."

"Good."

"So? What do you say?" Shannon asked.

"How far is it to Key West?" I asked.

"I can get you down there in two and a half hours, Mr. Atwater," said Charlie.

I knew I had to act fast and the gods suddenly seemed to be putting things in order and leaning them in my favor.

"Well, is that a yes or are you going to let Verdun get away with another murder?" Shannon asked.

I nodded yes.

"Not today. Give your sister a call and tell her we are on our way."

A big smile crossed Shannon's face.

"I could kiss you right now," she said.

"I'll take that kiss when we get back," I replied.

"There's a bar down there called Dottie's," she said.

"Dottie's? I know that joint," said Charlie. "It has a big electric palm tree out front?"

"That's the place," she said. "My sister owns it. The bartender's name is Patsy. I'll tell Liz you boys are on your way down to her. Liz will get you everything you need and I do mean everything."

"Do you want to come along?" I asked.

"Not my kind of party. I don't like guns. My sister is the fighter. I'm the lover type. Just get your asses down there and arrest that son of a bitch."

"We will," I said.

"Thank you," she said and kissed me on the cheek.

"Thank you," I added and finished off my drink.

Shannon smiled and looked at the bartender, Vernon.

"Where's your phone, honey?"

Vernon pointed Shannon to the phone booth back by the rest rooms.

"I'm going to give Liz a call right now," said Shannon. "She knows her stuff and so do her girls. Keep me in the loop?"

"I will," I replied and left a nice hefty tip on the bar for Vernon.

Charlie and I headed out to his car.

"I don't want to just drive you down there, I want to be part of the action too," said Charlie.

"Are you sure?" I said. "I paid you to drive me around. I can't ask you to step into harm's way."

"And what?" asked Charlie. "Let you and this Liz broad and her girls have all the fun? Fat chance, Mr. Atwater. I'm going all the way with you on this one so don't try to talk me out of it. With this guy Verdun you're going to need all the help you can muster."

"Okay Charlie. You want in? You're in."

"Thank you," said Charlie.

I had no idea what I was walking into but knew there was no turning back.

Not now.

Not ever.

Verdun had Willie killed, that was for sure and if he was ever going to be held accountable I knew the time was now and the person to make that happen had to be me. The added fact that Verdun had been running his illegal operations out of Roberto Santoro's place made my head spin. I wondered how he had managed to take over the property without Santoro knowing. Or if Santoro's sister, Maria, was part of that equation, or did Verdun have her killed too?

All of my questions needed answers but I knew they would have to wait for another day.

Now it was time to act.

If I had more time I would have called Agent Edwards and set up a whole different approach but the clock was ticking on this one and I hoped Diana and Louise were still breathing in the Florida air.

Only time would tell.

I sat in the passenger seat, put my head back, and closed my eyes.

"Are you going to sleep?" Charlie asked.

"No, Charlie," I said. "I need to think and I do my thinking much better with my eyes closed.

"You do your thinking, Mr. Atwater," said Charlie. "I'll do the driving."

"You know how to get us there?" I asked.

"I could get us to the Keys with my eyes closed," he said.

MAGENTA DAIRY

Charlie fired up the engine and the black Dodge Coronet pulled out of the Bancroft and headed south to the Florida Keys.

I knew I was the only person to stop Verdun and his goons and if it came down to a gun fight, so be it. I just hoped Liz and her girls were everything Shannon had promised me.

By Shannon's account the women all appeared to be quite able and highly capable.

I just hoped Shannon was right.

CHAPTER SEVEN

Joanne had slept the last three hours of the seven hour drive from Pennsylvania to Woodbridge, New Jersey. Her driver, Bobby Collucci, a young mob soldier working for the local Jersey crime syndicate, kept wondering who this beautiful, long-legged, dark haired woman in the back seat of his uncle Carmine's Cadillac could possibly be.

"What is her story?" he wondered. "Why is she being driven to New Jersey?"

She wore a black leather jacket and skin tight jeans and her skin appeared almost peach colored.

Bobby kept reminding himself what his strict orders were regarding this special beauty. He was told where and when to pick her up and where to drop her off.

That was it.

Any questions or small talk conversation was deemed inappropriate and Bobby knew the rules of his trade having seen the consequences dealt to other men who did not follow all the given rules to the letter.

His friend, Benny Perret lost two fingers of his left hand for trying to cop a cheap feel of some woman he thought was a street whore, discovering much too late she was a top ranking mobster's wife running a test of his loyalty and trust to the ever growing crime syndicate.

The attractive woman in the back seat had clearly caught Bobby's attention and as much as he wanted to know who she was and hopefully have her sleep with him, he knew well enough to keep his distance and wanton thoughts to himself.

The ride was long as it was silent.

Joanne had asked for his name when he first arrived at the cabin in the woods but never offered hers. The only other words she spoke was when she asked him once to stop somewhere so she could use a rest room.

That was the entire extent of their conversation.

"You don't talk to her unless she asks you a question," his uncle Carmine told him. "Do you understand?"

Bobby understood but his mind still raced with thoughts of who she might be and why she was being driven to Jersey.

Bobby also thought what she might look like totally naked lying next to him.

She carried no purse or luggage of any kind.

Bobby thought maybe she was some high classed hooker brought to New Jersey as company for some high ranking mobster but if she was, she would have been carrying a bag of some sort. He just couldn't quite figure this woman out no matter how hard he tried.

Bobby knew all about the house on Lockwood Avenue in Woodbridge.

He had driven his uncle Carmine there several times before. He was told by Carmine that the house was a mob-owned safe house, used specifically for important clandestine meetings or a place for transports, people hiding from the law, or brought secretly into New Jersey for some needed service.

He kept thinking she was a high classed hooker for sure and ran several scenes in his head of the two of the them lying naked somewhere and servicing each other for hours on end.

After all, she was a beautiful woman and Bobby loved beautiful women.

She was casually dressed but her clothes, other than the jeans, were obviously expensive.

Her nails were well manicured and she wore a perfume scent that made Bobby's mouth water every time he took a breath.

She was well-spoken, even though she had only uttered a few words to him the entire trip. She was quiet but polite and respectful, and she carried an air about her that Bobby just couldn't quite put his finger on.

Other than her beauty, Bobby was wrong on all counts concerning Joanne, but he knew better not to pry or ask any leading questions.

Drive the car.

Do what you are told.

Do your job.

Keep your mouth shut and your big Italian cock in your pants.

Bobby pulled up to 157 Lockwood, turned off the headlights, cut the engine and looked up into the rear view mirror.

"We are here, Miss," he announced and Joanne slowly opened her eyes and stretched out her arms and legs. Bobby could taste her scent as he sat in the front seat. He gently wet his lips and thought for one last time about what she might look like naked in his uncle's back seat and then quickly erased the thought from his brain.

Do your job.

Do your job.

Joanne looked out the car window at the small house and sighed.

"Thank you, Bobby," she said and handed him an envelope.

"These are your instructions for tomorrow," she added.

Joanne opened the car door, got out, walked slowly up the small sidewalk to the front porch and entered without even knocking.

A light came on from the front room.

Bobby sighed heavily and put the envelope in his pocket. He started up the engine and drove away still wondering who this beautiful woman could be and what she was doing here in a mob owned safe house in New Jersey. Maybe the contents in her envelope would give him some clues and maybe tomorrow they would make a better connection with each other.

Bobby pulled the car over and opened the note.

There was a pick-up time, an address, and simple instructions on how to drive around the block.

Nothing more.

No satisfying clues for Bobby. Just more mystery.

Bobby put the note on the seat and drove away.

The house Joanne was brought to, smelled of cigar smoke but she welcomed the muskiness of the little place and walked into the back bedroom and turned on another lamp. A single brown suitcase sat closed on the bed and Joanne opened it up and tossed the top half back.

A black skirt and a tan blouse sat at the top next to a black bra, pair of ladies underwear, some black knit stockings, and a pair of black heels. A blonde wig, still wrapped in plastic, was set on the right side and Joanne took it out, placed it on her right hand and shook it out. She put the wig on and gazed at herself in the mirror and made several adjustments to it until she was happy with the way it looked.

She opened the closet door and found a single pale yellow coat hanging on a hanger. She went back to the suitcase, removed all the clothes and placed them on the bed. She discovered a small makeup case, a toothbrush, a hairbrush, a bar of soap, and a small bottle of shampoo. She looked to the left and found ten packets of hundred dollar bills, each neatly wrapped with paper reading First National Bank.

Joanne found a large empty brown canvas bag with a shoulder strap and took that out and placed it on the floor.

She continued looking in the suitcase and pulled out a hand gun with gray tape wrapped around the handle. There was a box of ammo and a small metal silencer set in the left corner. Joanne casually attached the silencer, walked to the mirror and pointed the weapon as if she were going to fire it.

She put the gun on the dresser and went back to the suitcase.

Another item of clothing in the small suitcase was a light brown tam hat. Joanne put the hat aside and picked up a small green folder. She opened the folder and pulled out a photo of a basement apartment circled in black with an address.

Joanne found one other photo in the folder and held it out in front of her.

The photo was a black and white of Henry Long in a dark suit and tie leaning against a Cadillac.

Joanne smiled, tossed everything on the bed and walked to the bathroom.

The bathroom was done in all white tiles with several fluffy lime green towels hanging next to the toilet. A cheap white shower curtain hid the tub. She pulled back the curtain, ran the water in the tub, and began removing her clothes.

She submerged her naked body into the warm soapy water, put her head back, and closed her eyes.

Instructions had been set in motion but she couldn't dismiss her concerns.

She always liked to work alone.

She was much happier and always one hundred per cent successful working as a solitary unit without any unnecessary assistance from outside sources, and although this go around appeared simple on the surface and all bases seemed to be covered, there was still a slender thread of uneasiness permeating her mind.

Something kept nudging at her, telling her to be more focused now than ever before.

It was a gut feeling, and Joanne always paid close attention to her gut feelings in everything she did.

This time would not be any different and any questions she might still be harboring would quickly be answered in the next few hours.

She placed her hand between her legs and drifted off with tender thoughts of Rachel Stone Barbieri.

CHAPTER EIGHT

The drive down to Key West felt like a few minutes instead of the driving time Charlie had professed. I leaned back to think and fell fast asleep. I had slept soundly the entire ride until I felt Charlie tugging at my shoulder.

"We're here, Mr. Atwater," said Charlie.

I opened my eyes and sat straight up in my seat.

"Key West?" I asked.

"Yes sir."

"What time is it?" I asked.

"It's almost nine," said Charlie. "Welcome to Dottie's."

I gazed up at the large neon sign of a palm tree with the words Dottie's in pink running across the top. There were only four cars in the parking lot and I could hear the loud juke box playing Nat King Cole's "Mona Lisa."

"Are we close to Verdun's place?" I asked.

"I don't know," said Charlie. "I do know I have to tell you something before we go inside."

"Changed your mind about being part of the action?" I asked.

"Hell no! I'm still in where that's concerned. It's about this place."

"What about this place?" I asked.

"I should have said something sooner but this place? Dottie's? It isn't your normal neighborhood bar."

"What do you mean by not normal?" I asked.

"It's for girls only. Dottie's is what they call a lesbian bar."

"So that's why Shannon's sister, Liz has her little military group," I said. "They have to protect themselves from Verdun and any locals who don't care for their kind of lifestyle. Is that it?"

"That's exactly it," said Charlie.

"Makes much more sense to me now and I can't say I blame them for arming up."

"And there's something else."

"Something else?" I asked.

"I've never been in a queer bar before," said Charlie. "Men or ladies."

Charlie's concern made me laugh.

"Are you serious?" I asked.

"Dead serious," he answered.

"I don't think you have anything to be concerned about here, Charlie."

"Are you sure?" he asked. "I've heard stories."

"Stories?"

111

"Weird stories."

I shook my head and took a deep breath.

"They're just women, Charlie. They happen to like other women. So what? Whatever stories you've heard? Weird or otherwise? Are most likely stories from people with very small minds and brains. Trust me. You'll be fine."

"I feel funny and I don't know why but all of a sudden I'm getting really nervous."

I took one last shot at calming Charlie's mind and thought I would have some fun with him at the same time.

"Do they serve alcohol in here, Charlie?" I asked.

"Of course they do. I think they do. Don't they? It's a queer bar but it's still a bar. They sell alcohol."

"If they do? Then Dottie's is my kind of bar. Queer or otherwise."

"Your kind of bar?" Charlie asked.

"Yeah. Didn't I tell you, Charlie? I'm a lesbian, too."

"What? No! You can't be a lesbian. You're a guy. Right?"

"Yeah. But I'm a lesbian locked inside a man's body."

"What does that mean?" asked Charlie.

"Do you like women, Charlie?" I asked.

"Of course I do."

"Do you kiss them? Make love to them? Hang out. Dance and drink with them?"

"Yeah. Of course I do. Like all the other guys."

"Do you have a girlfriend, Charlie?"

"I don't have a girlfriend. I used to. She dumped me for some rich doctor."

"Well, when you did have a girlfriend? Did you have a lot of fun with her?"

"Of course."

"I have fun with women too. Fun is a good thing. And these girls here in Dottie's? I'm certain they like to have fun too. The only difference between us and them is their plumbing. Everything else they do is the same. Just like the rest of us human beings."

"You mean they're like one of the guys. Right?"

"Right," I replied. "Come on. Let's go talk to Liz and see what we can get going here."

Charlie and I stepped out of the Dodge and we went inside.

Dottie's was small with a few wooden booths across the front, several tables on one side and a small dance floor right next to the large juke box. A pair of ladies were dancing slowly to Nat King Cole. The bar sat straight ahead of us and took up most of the back wall. There were two rest rooms with a "Ladies" and a "Gentlemen" sign in neon pink over their doors. Sitting at the bar was another couple, also women, quietly sipping their drinks.

All eyes at the bar turned and gave us the once over as Charlie and I stood in the entrance way.

I caught the bartender's eye, nodded, and she waved us over.

"Good evening gents," she said.

"Good evening," I replied. "We're looking for Liz."

"We got word you were coming. Which one of you is Atwater?" she asked.

"I'm Atwater. This is Charlie."

"Hello, Charlie," she said and looked him up and down.

She extended her hand and had a strong grip for a thin woman.

"I'm Patricia Potter but everyone around here calls me Patsy," she said. "Can I get you gents something to drink?"

"Hot coffee if you have it," I said.

"I do," she replied. "Just made a fresh pot. Grab yourselves some seats and I'll let Liz know you're here."

"Thanks," I said and sat down at the bar with Charlie.

"I've been down here a few times but I was never actually inside the place. Not like this," said Charlie as he gave the place the once over. "It's kind of nice. But there is a different feel."

"Different how?" I asked.

"Women with women I guess. It's different. But it's nice. I kind of like it."

"Feeling a little less funny?" I asked.

"Yeah," said Charlie and a big smile crossed his face. "I am. A lot less funny."

I leaned over to Charlie and lowered my voice.

"Maybe you're a lesbian locked in a man's body too, Charlie," I kidded.

Charlie gave it a quick thought and chuckled.

"Maybe I am," he said and laughed.

Patsy walked out from a back room area with another woman I assumed was Liz. She was a sturdy female with a warm smile and nodded hellos to the other women at the bar as she walked up to us.

"Hello," she said and shook our hands. "I'm Liz Franklin. My sister Shannon tells me you have come down here to arrest Luis Verdun."

"That's right," I said. "He's wanted for the murder of Willie "The Nose" Kendall."

"He's responsible for more than just one murder. I can tell you that. Do you have a warrant for his arrest?" Liz asked.

"No. I'm going to make a citizen's arrest and bring him back to Miami to be questioned by the Dade County police department."

"Are you bringing him back dead or alive?" she asked.

"That's going be his choice. Not mine." I said.

"I like your style, Atwater. I understand you need our help in this arrest of yours?" she asked.

"That was the word I got from your sister, Shannon. Verdun has a few extra gunmen at his place and we're going to need some strong back-up. Shannon tells me you and your crew are the ticket I need."

"We are that and we can definitely help you," she said and nodded to Patsy as she brought us two cups of coffee and placed them on the bar in front of us. "Tell those lovers on the dance floor we have to close early tonight and they have to go."

"Sure Liz," said Patsy and walked away.

"My entire crew will be here in about ten minutes and we'll set up a game plan."

"How many are there in your crew?" I asked.

"There's nine of us including myself," said Liz. "All veterans and all good at what they do. Verdun won't go down easy but nine of us should do the trick."

"Eleven by my count," said Charlie and sipped his coffee. "Don't forget us men."

"We're both ex-military too," I said. "Marines."

"Happy to have you both aboard. Verdun has everyone down here shaking in their panties. He's been doing that for years. He operates out of intimidation. We don't scare so easy as the rest and Verdun knows it. Does he know you're coming for him?"

"I don't know that for certain but if I were in his shoes? I would be expecting somebody to come calling on him," I replied.

"Trust me. He already knows. That son of a bitch has eyes everywhere. You know what I mean?"

"I know exactly what you mean."

"Verdun sent two of his men over here a year or two ago," said one of the women at the bar. "They tried to shake Liz down and take over this place."

Liz nodded to the woman who spoke.

"That's Ronda and her girlfriend Myrtle. They're part of the team. This is Atwater and Charlie, girls."

"Nice to meet you, ladies," I said.

"Likewise," said Myrtle. "Nice to see someone with the stones to come down here and get rid of Luis Verdun once and for all. That man and his gangster asshole buddies need to go away."

Suddenly there was a loud altercation coming from the dance floor. One of the dancers, a large burly looking woman, stepped up close to Patsy's face.

"You can't kick us out," she cried. "It's not even nine o'clock! Bars in the Keys never close at this hour!"

"Unfortunately, Miss, Dottie's is closing early tonight," replied Patsy. "My apologies but I have to ask you both, again, to please leave."

"I'm not going anywhere and nobody in this dump is tossing me out of here."

"If you don't leave right now? I won't be tossing you out of here. I will be dragging you out. Am I making myself clear?"

"Very clear. And you ain't dragging me out of here, sweetheart! Not even on your best day!"

Patsy smiled slightly and in a matter of seconds knocked the woman cold with a few lightning fast karate punches to the woman's neck and face. Patsy grabbed the woman by her left arm and dragged her out the front door. The woman's dance partner quickly left some cash on the bar, grabbed up their purses and walked swiftly out the front door.

I knew then that Shannon had sent me to the right people.

"The lovers are gone and the front door is locked, Liz," said Patsy and sat down next to Charlie and smiled at him.

"Impressive," said Charlie.

"Thanks," said Patsy.

"We could have taken Verdun out the night they tried to take over this place," added Ronda. "I still say we should have done it back then."

"That night we sent Verdun's boys packing real quick like and Verdun and his men have left us alone ever since," added Liz.

"How far is Verdun's place from here?" I asked.

"It's just down the road. About two miles," said Liz. "It's a big place. Sits on several acres. There's a house and a large warehouse behind it and there's a decent sized dock."

"I was told Verdun would most likely be in the main house. I was given a drawing by someone who was actually there once."

I took out the paper given to me by the Butler and laid it out on the bar. Ronda, Myrtle, and Liz leaned in and looked at it.

"There's a long row of palm trees on both sides of the roadway in," said Liz. "It could provide good cover for us as we approach. Did you have a specific plan in mind?"

"I just want to go in and take him as easily and as quickly as we can," I responded.

The three women laughed.

"What's funny?" I asked.

"We can take him but I can't guarantee it will be easy or quick," Liz said. "We hear tell Verdun is running girls out of his place now so he most likely has extra gunners on the property. That good-sized warehouse in the back of the place? That's where those girls are kept. Verdun brings them in from Brazil, Columbia, and Cuba. They promise these girls work in the movie business and then ship them off to god knows where and for god knows what. It's all a big sham. The girls have no clue what's really waiting for them. Verdun is an animal and would probably use the girls as shields if he had to protect his sorry ass. This man needs to be stopped and we have been waiting for a night like this for a long, long time. A very long time. One of his girls slipped away from him one night and made it here to us. She told us Verdun always pretends to be some community minded citizen down here throwing lots of money around but that's all for show. He's built two schools and a small hospital which looks good to the real world but behind the scenes he's nothing but a filthy pig and a ruthless gangster."

"He's a low-class, evil womanizer," said Patsy. "First he charms but then he harms."

"He's a greasy, slick, mean son of a bitch," added Myrtle.

"All true," said Liz. "I'm sorry for this man he's killed but believe me when I tell you, Verdun has killed a lot of people over the years but no one has stood up to him until you came around. My sister tells me you're some private eye from Los Angeles."

"That's right. I think Verdun might be holding my client's daughter against her will."

"You do have the authority to arrest this son of a bitch?" asked Myrtle. "Right?"

"I do. My client sent me here looking for his daughter, which led me to Verdun. I asked two Dade County detectives to assist me but their story is it's not their jurisdiction. Is there any law down here?"

The girls laughed again.

"One sheriff," said Liz. "Name of Michael Bass. Verdun pays him to keep looking the other way when needed and Bass is always looking the other way. Doesn't he girls?"

The girls all nodded yes.

"Well we're not looking the other way tonight," said Patsy. "Right ladies?"

"Right!" the ladies answered.

"We are all able, we are all ready, and when the rest of the team gets here, we'll put a solid plan together and take these bastards down," said Liz.

"Sounds good to me," I said.

I no sooner took a sip of my coffee and five more women, all quite attractive and able bodied like the others, entered from the rear carrying large black duffle bags. They placed the bags on the floor and sat at the bar.

"This is the rest of the crew," said Liz. "This is Mr. Patrick Atwater and his friend Charlie. That's Mandy, Alice, Crystal, Sissy, and Joan. We call her Jojo."

Jojo sat next to Patsy, leaned over and offered her hand to Charlie.

"Jojo" she said. "Nice to meet you and to finally see some good looking men in this joint."

"Charlie Lindman," he said and shook Jojo's hand.

"Tonight we are going in and assisting Mr. Atwater in the arrest of Luis Verdun for murder," said Liz. "So let's all get focused on our task at hand, put our heads together, ladies and gentlemen, and get this operation started. Jojo?"

"Yes, Liz?"

"You're our forward observer for tonight. Grab our rubber raft and see what's shaking with Verdun. I want you to paddle over there and take a look see. Do your recon and meet us at the front entrance, here by these trees, in two hours."

"The front entrance by the trees?" she repeated.

"That's what I said," added Liz.

"Two hours. Got it," said Jojo and looked at her watch.

All the women looked at their watches.

Charlie raised his hand.

"You have a question, Charlie?" asked Liz.

"Can I go along with Jojo?" asked Charlie. "I was an FO and I could help her with the rowing."

"Nothing wrong with my arms, Charlie," said Jojo and flexed her left bicep.

The girls laughed.

"No one is questioning your strength, Jojo," said Liz. "I think it's a good idea to have an extra set of arms and eyes even if they have to belong to a man."

The girls all smiled at Liz' little joke.

Liz looked at me.

"Is it all right with you, Atwater if Charlie here tags along with Jojo?"

"It's fine with me," I said, nodding.

"All right. Grab some gear and take this Marine, Jojo."

"You're a Marine?" she asked and smiled broadly.

"Jojo?" yelled Liz. "Move it!"

"Yes ma'am," replied Jojo.

Jojo grabbed a small green bag and tossed it over her shoulder.

"Let's move, Marine," she said and headed for the back door. Charlie nodded and smiled at me and quickly followed her out.

"Huddle up everyone," Liz announced. "This is the layout. If Verdun knows we're coming he'll expect us to come in from his flank. Either here or here. I think we should use the palm trees here as our cover as Mr. Atwater suggested, and go right in the front entrance and quietly and quickly take out anything he might have placed in our way."

"I think it's the best way to go," I said. "They'll be looking for car headlights not people coming in on foot."

"Carrying rifles and grenades," said Liz.

The women all looked over the drawing again and I felt I had made the right decision in accepting Liz' help.

Going in after Verdun had to happen.

For Diane and her mother, Louise, I hoped my decision was the right one and one where we all went in and we all got back in one piece.

In two hours I would have my answer.

Suddenly a loud knock pounded on the front door that grabbed everyone's attention.

"If that's the same bitch coming back for more I will oblige her," said Patsy.

"Come on, Patsy," said Liz. "We all know who knocks like that."

The girls muttered their agreement in unison.

It was that familiar sounding police knock and Liz gave Patsy the okay to let whoever it was in. Patsy walked over, opened the door, and who I assumed was Mike Bass, the local law, strutted into the place like some school principal discovering his students smoking in the girl's room.

"Good evening, ladies. Hello, Liz," he said. "Closing up a little early tonight, aren't you?"

"It's my place," said Liz. "I can close up whenever I want."

Bass stepped up to the bar and gave me the once over.

"The grapevine tells me you have some male guests here in the Keys from up Miami way?"

"The grapevine?" asked Liz. "And who might that be, Sheriff?"

"That is police business, Liz," said Bass. "It's privileged information."

Bass looked at me and grinned.

"Is this one of them?" he asked.

"The name's Atwater," I said.

"I heard you're some private dick out of Los Angeles and you've been up at the Glass Palace asking a lot of questions. The kind of questions that can get a man like yourself into a heap of trouble down here if he isn't careful."

"Wait a minute, Mike," Liz butted in.

I quickly interrupted her and got off the stool.

"It's all right, Liz. I got this."

120

I walked up close to Bass and looked him straight in the eye.

"You're the local law here?" I asked. "Sheriff Bass? Right?"

"That's right," hissed Bass. "That's what my badge reads. I'm asking you, sir, to turn around now and place your hands behind you."

Liz and the girls all started protesting my possible arrest while Bass raised his voice and quickly quieted the women down.

"This is official police business!" announced Bass and took out his handcuffs. "Turn around Atwater and do as I have asked. I won't ask a second time."

"Not tonight, Sheriff," I said.

"Excuse me?" he said.

I grinned.

"I said not tonight. Tonight I'm going to be handling the official business."

"What does that mean?" he asked.

"I have a badge too, sir," I said.

"What are you talking about?" he asked.

I took out my federal ID badge and held it up in front of Bass' face.

"Do you see this? You are correct about one thing. I am a licensed private dick from Los Angeles. But I also carry this badge. This badge is different than yours but it also gives me more legal rights than your badge. This badge reads that I am a Special Agent working with the FBI under the specific direction of J. Edgar Hoover. I will assume you know who Mr. Hoover is. You, sir? Might be the local sheriff here in the Keys but as far as I have learned since my arrival in Florida, you're just some half-assed lawman who takes orders and bribery money from Luis Verdun. That sir, is against the law. Tonight Mr. Verdun is being arrested for murder. Verdun, his men, and now you too, sir."

Bass reached for his gun but Crystal and Alice quickly drew theirs as Patsy grabbed his wrist and quickly tossed his gun on the bar.

"Like I said, Sheriff, not tonight. Cuff him up, Patsy, and let's put him on ice somewhere until the conclusion of our evening. I don't want any warning phone calls going out to Verdun from this upstanding lawman."

"Yes sir!" said Patsy as a wide grin spread across her face. "Looks like his badge is a might bigger than yours, Bass."

"You really think you can arrest me and take down a man like Luis Verdun?" Bass asked as Patsy cuffed his wrists.

"We are arresting you and we are taking him down. So yes, we can and yes, we will."

"Then you are all dead. Each and every one of you."

"I've heard those words before only we aren't like you," I said. "We don't scare so easy."

"That badge won't save you! Not here! Not in the Keys!" Bass added. "Verdun will chew you all up and spit you all out."

"Not tonight," I added. "After tonight things are going to change down here in the Keys."

"You're dreaming, Atwater. Things only change down here if Luis Verdun says so and you and these faggot twats aren't going to stop him. He's too smart and he's too well protected."

"I beg to differ. And I'll stand side to side with these ladies any day before I ever fight with the kind of men like you and Luis Verdun."

"Put this needle dick in the back room," said Liz. "Just like Special Agent Atwater asked."

"You are all dead!" Bass yelled as Patsy and Mandy took him to the back room. "All of you! Dead, I tell you! Dead!"

Liz looked at me and smiled.

"Special FBI Agent, Marine, and an LA private eye?" said Liz. "I knew there was something different about you."

"Not your average dick," said Alice. "Right, Liz?"

"Not like we have here in the Keys," Liz replied. "That's for certain."

"Is that going to change our relationship for this evening?" I asked.

"Not in the least," Liz said. "Not in the least, sir."

"Shall we run over some possibilities on who should do what and when depending on what we find out there tonight? If this Bass knows I'm here than Verdun must also know and is most likely gearing up."

"We have enough fire power," added Crystal and held out two hand grenades.

"Maybe Verdun will skip," said Patsy. "He has that Steelcraft sitting on his dock."

"A Steelcraft?" I asked.

"Yes," said Liz. "It's a thirty-five footer. Two stateroom sedan with a fly bridge."

"A smuggler's boat," I said.

"You got that right."

"Is it fast?" I asked.

"Fast enough and sturdy enough for a long haul to Cuba or the Mexican coast if need be. If he's carrying enough fuel for the trip."

I could sense Verdun was already three steps ahead of me and holding all the cards in his favor. My mind began running scenarios and considering all our options.

"If Verdun does decide to skip on us, do you girls have something we can chase him down with?" I asked.

"You mean a boat of our own?" said Liz. "Something to go out on the ocean? At night?"

"Yes," I added.

"Unfortunately, no," said Patsy. "We don't."

"We can put out a call to the authorities if the boat isn't at the dock," I said.

"Can we get the Navy to pick him up?" Liz asked.

"Don't know for sure," I said. "First things first. Let's get our game plan down before we go making any phone calls."

"I agree," said Liz. "Huddle up, ladies. We have work to do and a short amount of time to get it done."

CHAPTER NINE

The ongoing case involving Henry Long and his possible connections to Rachel Stone Barbieri had more questions than answers. Special Agent Edwards specifically assigned this detail to Special Agent Loretta Davis and her new partner, Special Agent Richard Gregory. They were under orders only to observe all of Henry's comings and goings, take photos of anyone arriving to meet with him, but not to engage with him unless they were provoked or physically placed in harm's way.

Agent Davis understood the orders but observing suspects was not her style and Special Agent Edwards was quite cognizant of that fact. He hoped the addition of Agent Gregory constantly at her side might sway Agent Davis' usual tendencies in regards to working a case order.

The best laid plans of mice and men.

Agents Davis and Gregory, as ordered, had been observing and documenting for the last three weeks. They had witnessed and photographed Henry going to the movies at the Beacon Theater around the corner eight times, living consistently on Chinese food from the Golden Dragon Restaurant, consuming morning coffees with three sugared donuts from the corner grocery store, getting drunk from large amounts of take-home beer and stale hot dogs from the Green Lantern Bar, and smoking Lucky Strike cigarettes day and night as if chain smoking was an Olympic event.

Mr. Long did these things practically every day, at the same time, and always completely alone. It appeared to the FBI that Henry Long did not know one living soul in New Jersey, or on the planet Earth for that matter.

Both agents were slowly becoming bored with the assignment and slightly unnerved with each other.

Special Agent Davis was not happy about the new assignment at all. The days and nights of sitting in a government issued vehicle with little or no heat in the last week of a January winter in East Orange, New Jersey was beginning to eat at her and sitting was definitely not Loretta's choice by any means. Loretta was an undercover agent, that was her forte, she was a woman who enjoyed putting herself in the center of the action in spite of the danger or the unnerving possibility of her true identity being discovered by the people she had infiltrated.

On the other hand, Agent Gregory loved the assignment.

Agent Richard Gregory was a fifteen year veteran of the FBI and worked extensively in the field on numerous cases but had never had to draw his weapon or face any one-on-one dangers. For the last six years he had only pushed a pencil taking intelligence reports from undercover agents around the globe. He had never come across a report from any of Agent Davis' assignments but her bravado in the field and her exceptional good looks had been discussed many times over and over and by practically every agent in the bureau.

Agent Loretta Davis was legendary and one of the best agents ever placed in the field.

Bar none.

Agent Gregory was delighted with himself to be working with her. Although Agent Gregory was older than Loretta, she was the agent in charge so he manned the camera while she kept a sharp eye on Henry's front door.

Henry lived in a basement apartment on Grove Street, just around the corner from the movie theater. There was only one door in or out and it faced the street, so Agent Davis and Agent Gregory could park a good half a block away and still have an excellent view without drawing attention to themselves. Three days had passed without anyone going in or coming out and Agent Davis was beginning to truly tire of the assignment.

"I wonder what Henry does in there all day?" she asked aloud.

Agent Gregory always seemed to have an answer for everything.

"He most likely sleeps and then exercises," said Agent Gregory.

"Exercises?" she asked, totally surprised at his reply. "Why would Henry Long do that? Have you ever seen him? Does he look like a man who exercises?"

"Mr. Long has been in prison. Men with that mind set who are accustomed to being confined in small places with little to do usually exercise. You know. Simple exercises to pass the time. They do push-ups. Sit-ups. Jumping-jacks. Anything to stay in shape, pass the time, keep their minds occupied. He might also do a lot of reading."

"Reading?" she asked. "I can't believe that one. I've met Mr. Long. He doesn't strike me as the kind of man who has ever exercised or opened a book. He's a bully. A thug. He's a man who likes to hurt women. That's who Henry Long is."

Richard remained silent and a woman turning the corner suddenly caught his eye.

"Look," he said and pointed to the corner. "Speaking of women."

A long-legged bleached blonde woman wearing high heels and a short black skirt came around the corner.

It was Rachel's girl, Joanne.

She wore the pale yellow coat that had hung in the closet and carried the large dark brown cloth bag over her shoulder. She was chewing gum like some Jersey cow chomping on grass and walked right to Henry's entrance, walked down the stairs, and knocked loudly on the door. The agents could see she was tall and thin and wore a soft brown tam cap tilted slightly on her head.

Agent Davis and Agent Gregory picked up their respective binoculars to get and a closer look at the woman.

"I can only see the top of that hat she's wearing," said Agent Gregory.

"I've seen enough of her," said Agent Davis. "Let's get a few photos of her when she comes back out and she reaches the street light. I don't think she'll be in there very long."

"How long do you figure?" asked Agent Gregory.

"If I had to venture a guess I would say about twenty minutes, max."

"I agree," said Agent Gregory.

A few short moments of silence passed as the two agents stared at the apartment.

"She appears to be rather young and quite attractive," said Agent Gregory.

"In a slutty kind of way," said Agent Davis.

"A woman of the evening?" asked Agent Gregory. "Is that what you have surmised?"

"I don't think she's selling vacuum cleaners or Bibles."

"I agree," added Agent Gregory.

"I would say that her ugly bright red lipstick, her short but very worn little black skirt, and by the way she was cracking that gum in her mouth, I would have to concur, Agent Gregory, we have ourselves, at best, a third-rate street hooker for sure," said Agent Davis. "Write that down.

Date and time. Like I said, I got a good look at her. And for the record? I do like her coat and her hat."

"They are rather stylish," said Agent Gregory.

Agent Gregory grabbed a pen and began writing.

Agent Davis glanced over at Agent Gregory and smiled.

"So much for your reading, sleeping, and exercising profile. Henry Long is doing what most of you men always do and that's getting himself a little evening roll in the hay action."

"I would have to readily agree with you on that note, Agent Davis," said Agent Gregory. "Is hooker capitalized?"

"In her case? No."

Joanne suddenly came walking out of Henry's apartment just as casually as she entered and got to the top of the stairs and put her bag over her shoulder.

"Holy crap!" spurted Agent Davis. "Grab the camera! She's coming out already! I can't believe it!"

Agent Gregory quickly reached for the camera and pointed it towards the apartment.

"The negotiated price was too high, maybe?" asked Agent Gregory.

"I don't think that was the case. Maybe she was just delivering something."

"Drugs?" he asked. "A bottle of hooch perhaps?"

"Maybe," answered Agent Davis. "Both are good possibilities but I don't think those type of deliveries are her specialty."

Joanne stopped for a moment, looked around and strolled up Grove Street slowly and casually as if she had just left a library or a restaurant. Agent Gregory began clicking the camera.

"Are you getting any good shots?" asked Agent Davis.

"More than a few. I got her front and back this time," responded Agent Gregory as he clicked off several more shots before the woman finally turned the corner.

"I've heard the expression having a quickie but that wasn't even time for a half-quickie!" said Agent Davis and tossed her binoculars on the seat. "Had to be a delivery of some kind but what the hell could it have been?"

A few more brief silent moments passed. Agents Davis and Gregory stared down the street without saying another word.

"Something is not kosher!" she announced. "Something was not quite right about her but I'm just not seeing it yet! What the hell am I missing?"

Agent Gregory put the camera on the seat between them. Agent Davis picked up her binoculars once again.

"What are you thinking?" he asked. "What's not kosher about this hooker? Maybe she's a relative. Does he have any living relatives?"

Richard opened their file on Henry and started looking for the answer to his own question.

"It says here he has one brother. Older. Doing three to five upstate for burglary. His name is George."

"Shit!" exclaimed Agent Davis. "It's the damn coat!

What?" asked Agent Gregory. "The coat?"

"No street whore wears an expensive coat like that!" said Agent Davis. "Or makes a drug or a bottle of hooch delivery!"

"If she didn't make a delivery then what was she doing there?" asked Agent Gregory.

"Holy crap! It's a god damn hit! The bitch is a pro pretending to be a street whore! God damn it!"

Agent Davis quickly opened the car door, leaped out and began running towards the apartment.

"What are you doing?" he yelled. "We are not supposed to engage!"

Agent Davis ignored Agent Gregory's words and ran full speed towards the apartment. Agent Gregory sighed deeply, exited the car and followed Agent Davis as fast as his old legs would allow.

Agent Davis pulled her service revolver from inside her jacket and walked carefully down the stairs to Henry Long's front door.

The front door was wide open.

Agent Davis looked up as Agent Gregory leaned over the iron railing.

"Get around the corner and see if you can see that girl anywhere," she asked. "Do not engage! Observe only!"

"Understood!" yelled Agent Gregory, nodding his head excitedly and heading for the corner.

"FBI!" announced Agent Davis loudly and stepped inside.

Henry Long was lying face down on the floor in a pool of his own blood. Henry wore nothing except an old tattered gray bathrobe. There were two bullet holes as far as Agent Davis could tell. One was in the back of his head and the other was in the center of his back. Two spent shell casings laid on the floor by the doorway and Agent Davis surmised the blonde woman shot him immediately after entering the apartment. No gunshots were heard so if she was the killer she must have used a silencer on her weapon.

"Had to be a sanctioned hit," Agent Davis said out loud as she looked at the fresh blood on the floor. "This had to be our girl."

Agent Davis leaned down and felt Henry's neck. His body was still warm adding to her quick summation that the gum chewing blonde was clearly the shooter and most likely some hired pro.

Poor Henry never saw it coming.

"Shit!" Agent Davis exclaimed and stood up and looked around the apartment. There was some old Chinese cartons sitting open on the small kitchen counter and numerous empty beer containers strewn everywhere. Three ash trays were loaded with used cigarette butts. The entire apartment reeked of cigarette smoke.

Agent Gregory entered the apartment breathing hard from running and was taken aback slightly at seeing Henry's body lying face down on the floor.

"Oh my God!" said Agent Gregory. "Should I call an ambulance?"

"Too late for that," she replied.

Agent Gregory tried to catch his breath.

"Are you okay?" she asked.

"I will be in a minute or so," he replied, trying to get his breathing back to normal.

"The phony whore got away?" Loretta asked.

"I turned the corner as fast as I could but I didn't see her anywhere," he answered.

"She didn't get on a bus or get in a vehicle, maybe?"

"Nothing like that on the street," he said. "Not when I turned the corner."

"What did you see? Exactly?" she asked.

"Just an older couple buying movie tickets," he replied.

"Movie tickets?"

"Yes. At the Beacon. Around the corner. That new Victor Mature movie."

"Call this in. Stay with the body until I get back!" ordered Agent Davis.

Before Agent Gregory could answer, Agent Davis was out the door heading for the corner. Agent Gregory saw the black phone sitting on an end table next to the pull out sofa and picked up the receiver.

The movie marquee was showing Gambling House starring Victor Mature, Terry Moore, and William Bendix. Agent Davis showed her FBI identification to the young attractive woman in the booth selling tickets.

Her name tag read Maxine.

"I'm looking for someone, Maxine. A tall woman. Blonde. Had a tan tam on her head. Wore a pale yellow coat. Might have bought a ticket earlier today or just a few minutes ago? Had a big shoulder bag with her?"

"Sorry. I didn't see anyone like that but I just came on. I've only sold two tickets so far. A couple of older folks," she said.

"I need to go inside and look around?" she asked. "Can I do that?"

"Sure. The manager is at the candy counter. His name is Cedric. Little Irish fellah. You can't miss him."

"Thank you," said Agent Davis and went inside.

The film was just beginning and the older couple were headed quickly to their seats carrying two bags of popcorn and a Mary Jane. Cedric sat on a stool behind the candy counter casually reading a newspaper.

Agent Davis stepped up to the counter and showed her badge.

"Can I help you?" Cedric asked.

"Are you the manager? Cedric?" she asked.

"I am he," he said.

Agent Davis lowered her voice and stepped in closer.

"I'm Agent Loretta Davis with the FBI. I'm looking for a blonde woman. She's wearing a yellow coat. I think she may have come in here."

"Great legs and black high heels?" he responded.

"That's her," she said.

"She came in and went straight to the ladies room," he said and pointed to the ladies room sign above the door.

Agent Davis took a deep breath and smiled broadly.

"Thank you," said Agent Davis.

Cedric went back to reading his newspaper and noticed it was beginning to snow outside.

Agent Davis drew her weapon and walked to the ladies room. She took another deep breath and stepped inside.

The initial entrance room was a large carpeted lounge area with two small red couches facing each other and the rear wall had a small counter with three large mirrors above it. Several large movie posters dotted the other walls. The entire rest room appeared empty. Agent Davis suddenly heard a toilet flush and carefully stepped into the tiled area pointing her weapon.

One stall door opened and a young girl of no more than fourteen wearing a plaid skirt and black and white shoes with white socks stepped to the sink area. The girl paid no attention to Agent Davis as she washed her hands. Agent Davis placed her weapon behind her and patiently waited for the young girl to leave.

The two exchanged smiles and the young girl walked out.

Agent Davis went down the row pushing open every stall but found no one. She looked around and walked to the trash can and removed the top.

Inside she found a blonde wig.

Agent Davis quickly exited the ladies room and scanned the darkened theater seats hoping to see a glimpse of a yellow coat. A flash of bright light from the movie screen revealed a dark haired woman sitting alone about halfway down the aisle on the left side of the theater but there was no sign of the coat.

Cedric walked up to Agent Davis holding a flashlight in his hand.

"Have you found her?" he asked in a quiet voice. "Was she in there?"

"No. I think she's in the seating area about halfway down on the left side," whispered Agent Davis. "See the woman sitting down there? Sitting all alone?"

Cedric looked and quickly shook his head no.

"I don't recall seeing her but that can't be her. The woman I saw in the yellow coat was a blonde," he said.

"She was wearing a wig," said Agent Davis. "I found it in the ladies room trash. I'm fairly certain that woman down there is the one I'm looking for."

Cedric scanned the theater.

"She seems to be the only one sitting alone here tonight. She must have slipped by me while I was selling some popcorn. I'll go check her out," said Cedric.

"You can't do that" said Agent Davis. "I'm fairly certain she's armed and dangerous."

Cedric opened his jacket revealing a holstered handgun.

"I'm a Jersey lad who survived D Day, Miss and broads with guns in my theater don't scare me none," he said and nodded towards the left side of the theater. "Come with me over this way."

Agent Davis followed Cedric to the left side aisle and he stopped at the top and turned to her.

"You wait here beside the soda machine. I will ask her politely to come with me and you can grab her when I bring her up."

"What makes you so sure she'll do as you ask?" asked Agent Davis.

"Trust me," he said. "I've done this a hundred times. People don't like to create scenes in darkened movie theaters. They just don't."

"I'd rather go with you just the same," she suggested.

Cedric shook his head no.

"The both of us together will be too threatening. Let me use my Irish charm on her. She'll comply. You wait right over there. In the corner and out of sight. I'll bring her up to you. I promise."

"All right," said Agent Davis.

Agent Davis waited in the main foyer using the soda machine for cover as requested and Cedric smiled and walked down the aisle pointing his flashlight on the floor in front of him. Cedric got to the woman and noticed her yellow coat folded up on the seat beside her. He leaned in close to her and whispered.

"Excuse me, Miss. My name is Cedric. I am the manager here at the Beacon. There is a phone call for you. I think it might be an emergency call of some kind."

Joanne's gut feeling surged through her body and she looked up at Cedric with a fake cheerful smile.

"I don't know anyone here in East Orange," she lied hoping he would simply walk away.

Cedric pressed her harder and leaned in closer.

"They asked specifically for a woman wearing a yellow coat," he said and pointed at the seat beside her. "Maybe you're not the party they're looking for but I would appreciate you coming with me so I can clear my phone line."

Cedric smiled and sighed trying to act unconcerned.

Joanne remained focused as her gut feelings grew stronger.

"Please?" he added. "It will only take a minute or more of your time. I'll give you a free bag of popcorn for your trouble."

MAGENTA DAIRY

Joanne smiled and motioned Cedric to come closer. As he leaned in she quickly grabbed her silencer from under her coat, placed it under his chin, and fired one shot up into his skull.

Cedric fell face down onto the floor in front of her with only his feet remaining in the aisle.

Joanne casually got up, tucked the gun in her folded coat, and headed back to the front of the theater. She walked briskly up the darkened aisle as several shots of gunfire suddenly blazed across the movie screen.

Joanne entered the main foyer and Agent Davis stepped out from the soda machine and pressed her hand gun against the right side of Joanne's head.

"FBI, freeze right where you are," she commanded.

Joanne reacted with blinding speed and with one quick motion dropped her coat, moved Agent Davis' gun away from her head with her right arm and punched Agent Davis twice in the throat with the bottom handle of her gun.

Agent Davis' knees buckled and she fell to the floor, trying to breathe. Joanne quickly kicked Agent Davis in the face, breaking her nose and knocking her unconscious.

Joanne pointed her weapon at Loretta's head but before she could pull the trigger a voice suddenly yelled from across the room at the front entrance.

"FBI!" Agent Gregory shouted loudly as he reached for his service weapon.

Joanne quickly walked towards Agent Gregory, pointing her handgun with its maxim silencer attached, and fired two quick rounds into Agent Gregory's chest. He fell back against the front entrance door and slid slowly down onto the floor.

Joanne walked rapidly through the entrance doors, stepped over Agent Gregory's dead body, and walked out into the cold January night.

Four teenaged boys in high school jackets were purchasing tickets from Maxine as a black Cadillac suddenly pulled up with Bobby Collucci at the wheel.

"Get in!" he said.

Joanne opened the back door and jumped into the back seat.

The car quickly pulled away from the theater as snow began to fall harder.

"Where the hell were you?" she asked.

"I had to drive around the block when some flatfoot in a uniform told me I couldn't park where I was," said Bobby.

"Park? You weren't supposed to park!" she exclaimed. "You were supposed to drop me off, go once around the block. Three minutes forty-one seconds and I would have been right on the corner where I needed to be!"

"It started snowing," he added. "I thought I should stop and wait instead."

"I saw the snow. What I didn't see was you! You weren't there! You fucking moron!"

"Hey, I'm sorry," said Bobby. "That copper made me move."

"That wasn't what you were told to do!"

"Again," he said. "My apologies. Let's try and stay in the moment here. The fact is you're safe. Right? The car heater is working nicely. Going in that theater was a smart move on your part."

"It was the only move open to me and I had to shoot my way out of the god damn place no thanks to you!"

"I said I was sorry!"

"I'll be sure to tell the FBI that when they come crashing down my door to arrest me! Bobby said he was sorry, Mr. Hoover."

"Still," he added. "Like I said. Very smart on your part. And look what happened. Our timing was perfect after all."

"It was dumb fucking luck and nothing more. Pull over and check the front tire," she asked.

"Check the front tire?" he asked. "For what? There's nothing wrong with the front tire."

"I know that. Bobby."

"So why stop?"

136

"Because I'm going to change my clothes back here, moron, and I don't want to have to deal with you trying to get a free peep show or maybe strain your god damn neck trying to check me out in my underwear. You hear me?"

"I've seen plenty of women in their underwear," he said.

"Just do what I've asked!" she demanded. "Please!"

Do your job.

Drive the car.

Do whatever she asks.

"Yeah. Sure. Okay," Bobby said. "I hear you. Don't you think we should be putting some distance between us and this town right now?"

"No one saw me get in the car. We got time and I need to change. Now pull the damn car over without drawing any attention to yourself and get the hell out!"

"All right!" he barked.

Bobby turned at the next corner and pulled the car over about halfway up the tree lined block. Bobby got out of the car and walked around the front to the passenger side front tire and looked down at it.

Snow began to fall heavier.

A good minute and a half went by. Sirens began sounding in the distance.

"Hurry it up," Bobby said. "It's getting cold out here."

The rear right window slowly came down about five inches and Bobby leaned over to peer inside.

Joanne fired one shot into Bobby's face and he fell dead in the snow.

Joanne, now wearing the clothes from the other day, got out of the car, slid into the driver's seat and drove off into the night. Bobby lay dead in the snow with his eyes wide open and blood trickled from his face to the sidewalk. A woman walking her dog saw Bobby's body and began to scream.

Back at the Beacon more gunfire resounded through the theater as the film's action played out its own dramatic moments up on the big screen between Victor Mature and William Bendix.

A uniformed policeman, Officer Mike Reed and the ticket girl, Maxine, attended to Agent Davis as best they could. Agent Davis slowly came to and they helped her slowly to her feet.

"Are you okay?" asked Officer Reed. "Your nose looks broken."

"It is," she said. "Where's Cedric, the theater manager?"

"We were wondering that ourselves," said Maxine.

"Check the left side about halfway down. See if he's okay."

Officer Reed nodded, lit up his flashlight, and ran down the left aisle.

Agent Davis looked to the front door entrance and saw Agent Gregory lying on the floor.

"Oh no," she said quietly. "No!"

Agent Davis walked quickly to Gregory's body and knelt down close to him.

Tears flowed down Agent Davis' bloodied face as she wiped the melting snow water from his hair and gently closed his opened eyes with her right hand.

"I told you to stay in the apartment, Richard. I told you. Stay. In the apartment. Do not engage."

Special Agent Edwards came running in with three other agents behind him. Agent Davis looked up at Agent Edwards with tears streaming down her face. Agent Edwards looked at the dead body of Agent Gregory lying on the floor and shook his head in disbelief.

"What the hell is all this?" he asked.

"I told him," Agent Davis replied. "I told him to stay in the apartment and do not engage."

"The shooter did this?" asked Agent Edwards.

Agent Davis nodded yes and wiped the tears from her eyes.

Officer Reed returned and looked down at Agent Davis.

"Is Cedric okay?" she asked.

138

"He's dead," said Officer Reed.

Agent Davis sighed heavily, looked up at Agent Edwards, and wiped another tear from her face.

"I'm sorry boss," she said. "I am really sorry. I should have taken her down. The manager said he could bring her up to me."

"Stop it," said Agent Edwards. "You got caught off guard. It happens. We lose people. That happens too. If anyone is to blame here it's me. I put Agent Gregory here. Not you."

"I want to take full responsibility for this," Agent Davis said. This was my snafu, boss. Not yours. When you speak with Hoover you tell him it was me. Not you."

"This is not going to sit well with Hoover," said Agent Edwards. "I can tell you that. It's not going to sit well at all."

"Full responsibility," added Agent Davis. "That's how I'm going to write up in my report and I want you to make sure I take the hit on this. Agreed?"

"I'm taking the blame here."

"No," said Agent Davis. "Me and me alone. Promise me."

Agent Edwards sighed deeply.

"Please," she pleaded.

"All right," said Agent Edwards. "You need to get that nose of yours looked at right away."

"I will," she replied. "One other thing? I would like to be the one to speak with Agent Gregory's wife."

"That's not protocol and you know it."

"I know," she said. "If it wasn't for Agent Gregory coming in here like he did, it would be me lying here on this floor instead of him. The man saved my life. He's a hero and I want his wife to know that. To hear that. From me."

"Her name is Sarah," said Agent Edwards.

"I know," replied Agent Davis. "I know."

MAGENTA DAIRY

Agent Edwards nodded his agreement and began pacing the floor. Sirens sounded and four police cars and an ambulance arrived outside the theater.

CHAPTER TEN

Our small commando squad approached Verdun's compound under cover of darkness and we quietly parked our two vehicles behind some palm trees about two hundred yards from the main road. A light misty fog began to slowly drift across the area giving us even more cover as we shut off the headlights.

Everyone got out silently, checked their gear, and set their weapons for the attack. All the women wore black boots, slacks, tops, and black knitted caps.

We were armed and ready.

Liz looked down at her watch. Mandy looked through her binoculars and checked the grounds.

"What have we got, Mandy?" asked Liz.

"Quiet as an empty church," she replied.

"Jojo and your man Charlie should have been here by now," said Liz. "We've given them ample time. Something's not right."

We all looked towards the house but couldn't see anything through the fog except for some faint lighting coming from the windows.

"Do you see anyone or anything moving out there?" I asked.

"No movement that I can tell," said Mandy.

"Something's not right," said Patsy. "Jojo should have been here for at least the last twenty minutes or so."

Rustling footsteps sounded off in the distance.

"Hold up," I said. "Do you hear that? Someone's coming this way."

We crouched down taking cover and pointed our weapons.

Charlie suddenly appeared through the fog carrying Jojo over his right shoulder. His left hand was holding his side and you could tell he was bleeding. Charlie dropped Jojo on the ground directly in front of Liz.

"What the hell happened," asked Liz.

"This crazy bitch tried to stick me with her knife but I was too fast for her," announced Charlie. "We got to the shore, did our recon and were heading here to you and she suddenly turned on me. I had to put her in a choke hold and it knocked her out."

"Sissy!" barked Liz. "See to Charlie's wound."

"Yes ma'am," said Sissy.

"It's nothing," said Charlie. "She only grazed me with her blade. She must be working with Verdun in some way, shape, or form. We've already been to the house. Verdun and his men are nowhere to be seen."

"They've all left?" I asked.

"Looks that way," said Charlie.

"No boat at the dock?" asked Liz.

"No boat," said Charlie.

"Did you check the warehouse?" I asked.

Charlie shook his head no as Sissy patched up his wound with some bandage.

"No. After finding the house empty I thought we could all go check the warehouse. It's dark too and we noticed a big lock on the entrance garage."

"All right. You and I could go give it a once over and we can send these lovely ladies back home and out of harm's way."

"We're not going anywhere until this is all said and done," said Liz.

I nodded to Liz.

"I hear you, Liz," I replied and turned back to Charlie.

"You're certain Verdun and his boys are all in the wind?" I asked.

"Jojo said Verdun had a boat. A Steelcraft. It wasn't at the dock. The house looked as if they all left in a real hurry. Lights still on. Doors wide open. The warehouse is all dark and quiet."

"Let's go take a look," I said.

"Hold up, Mr. Atwater," said Liz. "Before we go, Jojo has some explaining to do first."

Liz lowered her weapon and walked to Jojo.

"Stand her up," said Liz.

Myrtle and Alice each grabbed one of Jojo's arms and stood her on her feet. Liz looked closely at Jojo and slapped her hard across the face.

Jojo slowly came to and opened her eyes.

"What the hell do you think you're doing Jojo?" asked Liz. "You tried to kill this man?"

"Yes I did," she answered. "And I'd do it again if I had the chance."

"Talk to me," demanded Liz. "Why are you trying to sabotage this operation? Trying to hurt us all like this?"

Jojo stood silent and spit on the ground.

"I'm not saying another word," said Jojo.

Liz stepped in closer to Jojo and stared hard into her eyes.

"You can talk to us now, Jojo or you can explain things to us with a heap of inflicted pain running throughout your body. Your choice. But one way or the other you are going to talk to us. So? What the hell is going on with you? Tell us the why? Have you been working with Verdun?"

Jojo hesitated to speak.

"I asked you a damn question!" barked Liz.

"Yes," she answered. "Verdun has been paying me for information. For months. Months! But I didn't do this for Verdun."

"Then for who?" Liz asked.

Jojo looked around at everyone and spit on the ground again.

"Truth be told, I did it for love," said Jojo.

"Love?" asked Liz.

"Yes. Real love. True love."

All the women began to groan loudly in unison.

"Jesus H. Christ Jojo," added Myrtle. "You turned on us and stabbed this man for that rich bitch?"

"She's not some tourist rich bitch," defended Jojo. "She's a woman of power! Beauty! She's a woman with a vision for the future! Not some down and out lesbo drinking her life away."

I thought of the picture hanging in Verdun's office and once again my head began to spin and pound and I knew in my gut what I was about to hear.

"Who the hell is she talking about?" I asked.

"Some little cunny Jojo fell in love with over one weekend months ago," said Liz.

"A little cunny?" I thought. "They have no idea."

"She came into the bar one Friday night throwing lots of money around. Took a sudden and special liking to this one."

"A sudden liking? You mean a sudden licking," said Crystal.

"Fuck you, Crystal," screamed Jojo and tried to lunge at her but Myrtle and Alice held her arms tightly.

"Loved her and left her," said Patsy. "Filled her head with a bunch of nonsense about taking her down to Mexico this summer. Getting her away from the Keys. Away from all of us. Living the good life with money to burn."

"I told you, girl," said Ronda. "We all told you! That little slit played you from moment one."

"You all can go fuck yourselves!" yelled Jojo. "Rachel loves me. You'll see."

There it was. The name I knew was coming at me once again.

I heard the name Rachel and that familiar explosion went off in my head a second time. The two bullet hole scars in my chest suddenly seemed to tighten and burn. I walked up to Jojo and got right in her face.

"This woman you're speaking of? Her name is Rachel?" I asked.

"That's right," said Jojo. "What's it to you anyway?"

"Let me tell you something, sister. This Rachel you're speaking so highly of? I'll bet you dollars to donuts she's not just rich. She's filthy rich. Right? Money in the millions."

"That's right," said Jojo. "She has millions. Millions and then some."

"And she's beautiful. Your Rachel is a real stunner. She's prime stock and a real knockout kind of woman. The kind of woman who makes heads turn when she walks into a room. Any room. Right?"

"Right again."

"Absolutely beautiful. Head to toe."

"Yes," agreed Jojo.

"I'll tell you something else, Jojo. I'll bet this rich and stunning Rachel looked deeply into your eyes, told you she loved you and only you, and then she promised you the world. Right? Also promised you unbelievable amounts of cash?"

"Yes. She did. And she meant it. Every word. Every dollar. I could tell. We had a special connection. A bond."

The other women groaned loudly again.

I locked eyes with Jojo and smiled.

"What did she want from you? Besides all your love and affection?"

"She asked me to recruit Liz and the rest of these girls."

"Recruit them? Recruit them for what?" I asked.

"I don't know exactly. She said she was going to need protection. She wanted women she could trust."

"And fuck," said Patsy.

Jojo turned and spoke directly to all the other girls.

"She was going to pay all of us huge salaries!" she announced. "Huge!"

"This woman of yours? This Rachel?" I asked. "Are you talking about Rachel Stone Barbieri? Is she your Rachel one and only?"

"What are you?" she asked. "Some kind of freaking psychic?"

"Answer the question," I said. "Rachel Stone Barbieri? Is that her name?"

"That's her," said Jojo. "You know her?"

"Yes. I do. She was crazy about me too. And about a dozen other men and women. She put two bullet holes in my chest and left me for dead. Rachel's a real peach. Your friends here are right about her. Rachel played you. Rachel Stone Barbieri plays everyone."

Jojo shook her head no.

"You're wrong. You're all wrong about her. Rachel Stone Barbieri is going to rule the world and nobody is going to stop her. Not ever. She's going to be more powerful than the ancient Romans or the Nazis could ever dream of."

"Where did she promise to take you in Mexico? Mexico City?" I asked.

"No. She said she had some new place she was building. On sixty acres. By the water."

"Where? By what water?" I asked.

Jojo stiffened up straight and looked away from me.

"I'm not saying another word about her," she said. "Not to you or to any of you! Fuck you!"

Liz stepped up, grabbed Jojo's right pinkie and snapped it back until it cracked at the knuckle.

"Ah!" screamed Jojo. "Jesus Christ Liz! What the hell are you doing to me?"

"I told you! Either talk now or talk to us through a lot of unnecessary pain."

"Fuck you, Liz!"

"Fuck me?" Liz fired back.

"That's right. Fuck you! Fuck all of you!" Jojo cried.

Liz grabbed Jojo's ring finger next to the broken pinkie and snapped that finger back to the knuckle. Jojo screamed in pain and Liz grabbed her middle finger.

"You tell this man what he wants to know or I will break every finger and every toe on your body and then I will start removing them all one by one with that knife you're so very fond of using!"

Jojo looked at her hand and her anger suddenly turned to fear.

"All right. All right. Stop. Don't hurt me anymore. Please? I'll tell you what you want to know."

"Where in Mexico?" asked Liz and grabbed the middle finger tighter.

"Cozumel!" she screamed. "She told me she was having her new place built somewhere in Cozumel."

I walked up to Liz and placed my hand on her shoulder.

"Hang tight here," I said. "I definitely want to ask her some more questions. Charlie and I will go check the warehouse. And for the record? I do like your style of interrogation."

Liz smiled and let go of Jojo.

"You haven't seen me really work," she said and punched Jojo square in the face and she dropped to her knees.

"You'll wait here?" I asked.

"Sure," said Liz. "We'll wait."

"No more questions or broken fingers for this one?" I asked.

"No more questions," said Liz. "We'll keep her here until you get back."

"Charlie and I shouldn't be too long. A half-hour, max."

"Take Patsy and Ronda with you. Just in case."

147

"Sounds good," I said and nodded my agreement. "You have that number for the Navy?"

"I got it," said Liz and turned to Ronda.

"Grab some bolt cutters, Ro. If we hear any shots we'll come running."

I pointed to the main house.

"Why don't you and the rest of the girls go up and check the house. Inside and out. Every floor. Top to bottom," I asked. "We hear any shots? We'll come running."

Liz smiled.

"We can do that," replied Liz.

I nodded my agreement to Liz once again and headed to the warehouse with Charlie, Patsy, and Ronda close behind.

As we walked through the mist Charlie quickly caught up and walked alongside me. I looked at him and laughed.

"What's that laugh all about?" he asked.

"So when were you going to tell me?" I asked.

"Tell you? Tell you what?" Charlie replied.

"That you've been playing me all along."

"What do you mean?" he asked.

"For one thing you're not a cab driver. A real cabbie would never have seen Jojo coming at him with her knife. The way you handled her tells me you've had training and lots of it."

"And you are a good detective."

"I have my days."

"You're right. I'm not a cabbie and I have had a lot of field training. First with the Marine Corps and then with the FBI."

"I should have known right off. I'll admit I didn't have a clue until tonight. You're good. You're very good."

"Thank you."

"Who sent you to me?" I asked.

"Special Agent Edwards. He told me to watch your back. He said you have a tendency to lose sight of your goal at times."

"My goals?"

"Yes."

"He said that, did he?"

"He did. He also said you were someone to be counted on when push goes to shove."

"Is Charlie your real name?"

"It is, only it's Agent Charlie Lindman with the FBI, Florida Field Division."

I shook Charlie's hand and we kept walking.

"Welcome to the fight. And thanks for having my back, Charlie."

"My pleasure. Can I still keep the fifty?" he asked.

"Did you really have an Aunt Millie and a friend down at the Coroner's office?" I asked.

"Yes," said Charlie. "I do."

"Then keep the fifty. Money well spent as far as I can tell."

Charlie nodded and smiled.

"Thanks, again," he said.

The warehouse sat about a hundred yards behind the house. It was a good twenty feet high with one large roll up metal door. The door was padlocked but Ronda quickly cut it open. Charlie rolled the entrance door up and we went inside.

Charlie found a light switch to the left and flicked it on but the place remained dark. Patsy handed me her flashlight and I scanned the room. The warehouse was empty except for one very old truck with a canvas back. Ronda checked out the truck with her flashlight.

"Six men in here, all dead" she announced. "They're all lying face down. Shot in the back."

I ran to the truck and shined in my light wondering if Verdun and his two goons, King and Kong were among the group.

Verdun wasn't and neither were his two goons.

"Verdun must be on that boat with his two body guards," I said.

"Ten bucks says he took a lot of cash with him too," said Ronda. "Guys like him always do. How much do you think he took?"

"A boat load for sure," I said and left it at that.

I also wondered if Verdun found the two million in cash locked in that trunk that Santoro spoke of.

Ronda looked up and pointed to an upstairs section that sat in the left end corner of the building.

"We got a second floor here, guys" she said.

"Patsy?" I asked. "Get back to Liz and tell her to put that call in to the Navy. The one she and I talked about."

"Yes sir," she answered and headed back to the house.

"Let's see what we got up there," I said and started for the stairs.

I went up the stairs first, followed by Charlie and Ronda. I opened the door slowly, walked to my left, and hit a light switch but again, no lights came on. Ronda took a few steps past me and stepped into the room, pointed her flashlight, and jumped back for a second when she saw what the light revealed.

"Oh my god!" she said. "Oh my god! Is that a human head?"

There was a decapitated head of an older woman sitting on a flat dusty desk facing nine metal cages on the floor. Each 3x6 cage held a woman, some naked, some half-dressed, but all appeared to be either dead or asleep.

There were sixteen empty cages on the opposite wall and the smell of feces and urine permeated the entire floor. We approached the cages slowly and Ronda noticed one girl move slightly.

"This one in here is alive!" she exclaimed and cut open the locked cage with her bolt cutter.

"See if you can get some light up here, Charlie," I said.

Charlie took out his lighter, lit it up, and walked away looking for a power source.

"Can I borrow that bolt cutter?" I asked.

Ronda nodded yes, handed me the tool, and I checked out the other cages one by one. It appeared the women had all been heavily sedated and simply left to die. I cut the first cage open and checked the half-naked woman's pulse. It was very faint but she was still alive.

"Charlie!" I cried out. "Go outside and fire some shots. These women up here are still alive and they need medical attention ASAP!"

"Yes sir!" responded Charlie and I heard him run quickly down the stairs.

A faint voice caught my ear.

"Help," the voice said. "Please? Help me."

I pointed the light in the far corner and saw a young woman wearing only panties and curled up in a fetal position. I ran to her, quickly popped the lock and pulled her out.

Three quick gun shots suddenly sounded and the young girl held onto me tightly.

"What was that?" she asked.

"They're only warning shots. It means help is on the way. You're going to be all right little lady."

"Thank you," she whispered. "I know the man who did this to us. He is an evil man and his name is Verdun. Luis Verdun."

"We know. He's gone now but we will find him."

"He's on his boat heading to Mexico. He has my mother with him."

"Your mother?" I asked again. "Is her name Louise?"

Bewildered, she looked up at me and smiled weakly.

"Yes," she said. "Verdun is obsessed with her."

"What's your name, young lady?" I asked.

"I'm Diana," she said.

"Diana Santoro?" I asked.

"Yes," she said. "I'm Diana Santoro. How do you know my name?"

Before I could answer she closed her eyes and drifted off into unconsciousness.

I held her close as Ronda checked the remaining cages. The results she found were not good.

Several hours passed, and the FBI and Miami State Police were on the scene with numerous ambulances administering medical attention.

Only four girls were found alive, one being Diana, and they were transported to the very hospital built by Louis Verdun eleven years ago.

Charlie had notified the FBI to come onto the property and take over the investigation into Louis Verdun's illegal enterprise of drugs and human trafficking.

I thanked Liz and her girls for all their help and support.

Jojo was taken into custody for attacking an FBI agent along with Mike Bass for questioning in regards to Luis Verdun and all of his operations.

Bass quickly made a deal and began squawking out information like a frightened little chicken.

Jojo told her attending doctor she had taken a nasty fall when asked about her broken fingers.

Liz discovered the Santoro trunk hidden up in the attic crawl space of the main house. When I opened it using the key he gave me, I discovered the two million in cash still untouched. I was certain it was Maria's last gesture to keep the trunk hidden and out of Verdun's grasp. Upon searching Verdun's bedroom, Charlie and I found the bogus property deed he had made with his name , which was luckily folded next to the real deed held by the late Maria Santoro for all those years.

Unfortunately the severed head we discovered was Maria's. The remainder of her body was never found.

I personally placed Diana's inheritance money and her deed to the Keys property in a private safety deposit box and brought the key and all the bank information to her in the hospital.

Diana, recovering nicely, stared down at the bank key in disbelief.

"This is mine?" she asked. "This is all mine?"

"All yours," I said. "Your father's last request. His final way of saying I love you."

"A very nice gift from someone I never really knew."

"He just wanted to make things right. For you and for your mother."

"No word on Verdun's whereabouts or my mother?"

"Not yet," I said and stood up beside her hospital bed. "We have authorities out searching for him and your mother. We'll find them."

"I hope so. Luis Verdun is insane. The longer he's around my mother the worse off she is going to be."

"You get well and stay strong. For you and for your mother."

"I'll try," she said.

"You take care, Diana. If you ever find yourself in trouble? Don't hesitate to call me."

I handed her my card and a single tear ran down her cheek.

"Thank you, Mr. Atwater," she said. "For everything. I'll keep your card close by."

"And I'll make sure you hear about your mother. Keep your hopes up. We'll find them. I promise you."

"Even if the news is bad. You'll tell me. Won't you?"

"Yes," I answered. "Good or bad I'll tell you."

"Thank you," she repeated and held back her tears.

"So long, kid," I said and walked away.

My work for Roberto Santoro was complete and there were only two things now left to do.

One was to find Luis Verdun and Louise and the other was to find Rachel Stone Barbieri and take down her operation once and for all.

I knew it was not going to be an easy task.

Rachel Stone Barbieri was becoming more powerful and making new contacts every day but I knew nothing would stop me or the entire FBI to finally catch this woman and prevent the evil she was bringing into the country. She was making heroin readily available in every major city in the United States and developing creative ways to smuggle it in.

A sudden new strength was building inside me and I knew in my heart I would use every ounce I had of that strength to stop her, Verdun, and anyone else we met along the way. This drug cancer was beginning to slither heavily into our midst and infect our new world culture and I hoped upon hope we could shut it down before it began destroying us all. I had seen first-hand too many of our boys coming back from the war and choosing drugs in an attempt to blot out their pain and their anguish over fighting in a world war.

A new war had surfaced and discovering who this new enemy was became as difficult as the fight itself.

Rachel Stone Barbieri was the one clear enemy we could define and she was at the head of this new war, living the good life with her millions somewhere in Cozumel. I knew nothing was going to stop Special Agent Edwards, Detective Blaine, and myself from finding her exact location and bring her back to the States, alive, and in handcuffs.

I didn't know how we would find her or how we would even bring her back but I knew one thing for certain.

We would find a way and make it happen.

No matter what.

I booked the first available flight back to Los Angeles and set up a meeting with Detective Blaine and Special Agent Edwards at my office so we could begin our next strategy concerning the capture of Magenta Dairy and the destruction of her entire operation.

CHAPTER ELEVEN

The dual sixty-two twenty engines of Louis Verdun's thirty-six foot Steelcraft cut through the water at top speed. Verdun knew he was pushing his boat too hard as he and his two henchmen, King and Kong, stood on the fly bridge staring out into the clear star-filled night. Time was pressing against Verdun and he wanted to reach the Mexican coast as quickly as possible and without incident. He had to travel light and fast and knew he was right in executing his remaining men.

Dead men tell no tales.

Verdun also knew he would have to quickly rid himself of King and Kong once they reached the Mexican coast.

One man.

One story.

He would give Louise a final chance to be his one true love or she would have to go too.

Verdun knew his southwest course would eventually bring him straight to Rachel Stone Barbieri's new compound in Cozumel. Once he arrived and told her of his problems in the Keys, he knew she would help him set up a whole new operation and make a new start.

He couldn't fathom that Rachel would say no and turn down his request for assistance.

Verdun had given Rachel safe harbor in the past when she was on the run and now it was her time to return the favor.

Verdun also knew he would have to twist some facts as to the how and the why he had to suddenly bolt from the Keys. He also hoped to make her realize he had no choice but to leave his own compound in the States and come to her like this on such short and unannounced notice.

"One man, this Patrick Miles Atwater, a nickel and dime gumshoe from Los Angeles, managed to turn my life upside down, and I intend to get my revenge and regain everything I have lost once I am back and settled in again," were the words he practiced over and over in his mind, readying himself for his initial conversation with Rachel in Cozumel.

One man.

One story.

Verdun convinced himself the one man story would sell. Rachel had her own one man story with J. Edgar Hoover and now he had his with this troublesome private eye, Patrick Miles Atwater.

Verdun's unannounced arrival in Cozumel and his story had the added bonus of the presence of Louise and the condition she was in. But that would only be a problem that needed a decent explanation if Louise promised him her heart again. Then he thought of another possible problem, even if she did say yes. That second thought had Verdun even more concerned.

Rachel liked women and although Louise was not some young female she was still an extremely attractive woman for her age, and if she and Rachel had an opportunity to speak alone together it might cause problems with Louise getting Rachel's full support.

As Verdun stood on the deck of the Steelcraft he began to think that his obsession with Louise may have to finally come to a close. If she refused to make one last choice in his favor in regards to his upcoming meeting with Rachel Stone Barbieri, well...

Verdun's henchmen, King and Kong, had urged Verdun to forget about Louise but Verdun would not listen to their suggestions or their protests. In his mind and in his way he loved Louise and told them both in no uncertain terms that he would win back her heart and she would once again be his woman like before.

His thoughts drew him back to his first meeting with Louise.

Luis Verdun met Louise and her daughter Diana nearly three years ago. Louise came to the Glass Palace looking for work and Luis was smitten by her almost immediately, giving her a job the very next evening serving cocktails. Two months passed, Luis asked her to dinner and she accepted. She had no idea who Luis Verdun really was or how extensive his illegal activities had spread through southern Florida.

Louise was attracted to Verdun at first and his demeanor with her led her to believe he was a successful businessman and underneath his tough exterior was a kind and compassionate man with a big heart.

Luis Verdun pretended to be exactly that.

At first.

Their courtship went on for several weeks with Luis always behaving like the perfect gentleman. He brought her flowers almost daily, gave her ample amounts of money to buy food and clothes for her daughter and for herself. Louise thought she had put the gangster life behind her after leaving Santoro, but had no idea she was stepping into an even bigger criminal enterprise by becoming involved with Luis Verdun.

Louise began asking the other girls at the Glass Slipper who this man Verdun was. When she discovered some of the evil things he was in control of, she told Luis about her life with Santoro and how she could never again fall for any man involved in any criminal activity.

Their short but torrid love affair quickly ended.

Louise quit her job and left the Glass Slipper.

Verdun was not happy with her departure but he accepted her decision.

At first.

He started dating numerous other women bestowing lavish gifts on all of them from expensive champagne to brand new cars but Verdun could not get Louise out of his mind.

Or back into his control and his bed.

Once Louise was completely free of Verdun, Willie "The Nose" Kendall tried to wine and dine her but Louise told Willie politely that would never happen.

Verdun began pushing for Louise to return to him but she was steadfast and refused his every gift. He offered to buy her a house, a trip to Paris, and even a small business of her own choosing, but all of Verdun's pleading fell on deaf ears.

One night Verdun got word of Willie Kendall's move on Louise and he finally went ballistic. King and Kong brought Louise against her will to a small beach house just outside of Miami where she found a naked and badly battered Willie nailed to a chair.

"Do you see this man?" asked Verdun. "He tried to kill me! Do you know why? Because he wants you for his own. As do I. Who do you choose? Tell me. Now. Tonight. I need to know where your heart lies?"

"Let Willie go, Luis!" she begged. "This is not right. Willie and I aren't what you are thinking. I'm not seeing anyone!"

"Don't lie to me, Louise," he demanded. "I know all about this man!"

"I'm not lying," she said. "And you are wrong about Willie!"

"Choose!" he repeated.

"I can't!" she cried. "I can't! This isn't right, Luis. Please? Don't make me do this."

"You must!" Verdun screamed. "Choose and I will let Willie go but you have to make your choice one way or the other! Now who will it be?"

Louise tried to calm herself and began taking deep breaths. She was beside herself with fear and anxiety and the only thing she desired was to have this nightmare called Luis Verdun to end.

"Tell him to go fuck himself, Louise!" shouted Willie.

"No one asked for your opinion, fool!" said Verdun and kicked Willie's chair back and down onto the floor.

"I choose Willie!" screamed Louise suddenly and started to cry.

Verdun walked quickly to Louise and stared hard at her face.

"What did you say?" asked Verdun in a quiet voice.

Louise, sobbing frightened tears, slowly looked up at Verdun and spoke in a quiet and calm voice.

"You asked me to choose. I choose Willie."

"You choose Willie?" he asked.

"Yes. I choose Willie. Now let him go. Like you said."

Verdun walked to Willie, pulled out a hand gun, and shot Willie once in the forehead, killing him instantly.

Louise screamed and Verdun slapped her so hard across her face she fell to the floor in a heap.

"If I can't have you? No man will ever have you. No man! Do you understand me? I am Luis Verdun! And you! Are my woman! Mine!"

Louise fought back her tears and wrapped her arms around herself.

"I said do you understand me?" he screamed.

"Yes!" she screamed. "Yes! I understand you!"

"You see how deep this love I have for you truly is? Yes? You see?"

"I see," she whimpered.

"Take her home and then take care of this mess."

King and Kong nodded and lifted Louise to her feet and took her out.

Days after Willie's death, Luis would have King and Kong bring her to his hotel suite where he would force Louise to strip naked and have sex but when he made love to her she showed no interest or emotion through the entire ordeal.

Again, Luis went ballistic and beat her.

Louise decided to get as far away from Luis as she could but before she and her daughter Diana could skip out, Verdun brought Willie's dead body to their small trailer in Coral Gables. He left the body there, hoping Louise or Diana would be pegged for Willie's demise, and took both women against their will to his compound in the Keys.

Luis placed Diana in one of his many cages, shot Diana up with heroin, and threatened to turn her out to clients for sex if Louise did not comply with everything he expected from her.

"Do you see what you have made me do?" said Luis.

Louise instantly conceded to anything Luis wanted from her as long as he promised to leave her daughter Diana alone. Luis agreed but purposely kept Diana out of sight to maintain his total control over Louise.

Louise became extremely worried about Diana and began arguing with Verdun to see her daughter.

Luis' answer was to beat Louise with a broken broomstick handle.

Word came down to Luis that Willie "The Nose" Kendall's body was discovered. Not knowing how much federal heat would be generated towards him, he told his two men to kill the hired bodyguards, take Louise and what money he had on hand, and race across the gulf to Rachel Stone Barbieri and the safety of Cozumel.

Naked and badly battered, Louise lay in her cabin on Luis' boat headed for Mexico with only one thought in her mind.

Luis Verdun must be destroyed before they reached Cozumel.

Louise rolled her head in a vain attempt to ease her pain and although her body ached, she knew Luis had not broken any part of her. Her mind was intact and her spirit kept her strong. She prayed to God for help and hoped for a miracle.

Footsteps suddenly sounded from outside her door and she quickly closed her eyes and pretended to be asleep.

Luis entered the cabin and closed the door with a loud bang.

He placed his handgun on the nightstand and removed his shoes, shirt, and pants.

"Louise?" he barked. "Wake up! I need you right now and then I need to get some much needed rest. Do you hear me? Louise? Wake up!"

Louise opened her eyes and slowly pulled back the covers on the bed and opened her arms and legs to welcome him into her.

"I'm here, my love," she lied.

"No," said Luis. "Turn over. On your stomach. I want you from behind."

Louise rolled over and Luis knelt down on the bed and pulled her hips up to him. He slapped his penis across her ass several times and entered her abruptly. As he drove himself into her, Louise's head and chin were pushed to the edge of the bed near the wall.

In the midst of all her pain and ordeal she suddenly realized her prayers had been answered.

The miracle she humbly prayed for quietly rolled into her view.

Louise looked down onto the cabin floor and saw a sharpened pencil rolling back and forth from the wall to the bedcover. It was covered with dust and most likely had been there for months.

Unnoticed.

Unseen.

Until now.

As Luis reached his climax and came inside her, Louise reached down and grabbed up the dusty pencil with her right hand.

Luis sat on the edge of the bed and pulled his underwear on.

A knock rapped loudly on the door.

"What is it?" Verdun asked.

"There is a boat approaching," said Kong from outside the cabin door.

"A boat? What kind of boat?" he asked.

"It's too dark to tell."

"I'll come topside. Give me a few minutes."

"Yes sir," said Kong and walked away.

"I need you to get dressed, Louise and wait here until I come and get you. Do you understand?"

Louise sat quietly on the bed and put the pencil in her left hand.

"Are you listening to me?" he asked without looking at her.

Louise came across the bed and leaned up behind him and lightly touched his shoulder.

"I hear you," she said. "Who would have a boat out here at this time?"

Luis stopped putting on his pants and tapped her right hand with his.

"Don't you worry my love. I will handle everything as I always do."

A sharpened pencil and now another boat approaches. This was Louise's only chance and she knew in her heart and mind it was the right time for her to act.

Louise raised her left arm and suddenly started stabbing Luis in his neck with the pencil, over and over again.

Once.

Twice.

Three times.

Again and again and again until she thought her arm would drop off from fatigue. Blood spurted a deep dark red everywhere as it poured from Luis' neck. She stopped as quickly as she began and stood up on the bed ready to kick him if necessary.

Luis managed to get to his feet and he turned and faced Louise. His eyes were wide open and he had a look of shock and disbelief as he held his neck with his right hand and tried to speak. The bleeding had been non-stop and he opened his mouth wide but no sound uttered from his throat except for the gurgling of the blood as it left his body.

Luis' blood had shot out over the bed, the wall, the lamp and nightstand and Louise's naked body as they stood facing each other. Luis turned to his right and attempted to reach for his handgun but suddenly lost consciousness and dropped to his knees, landing on the right side of his face as the upper half of his body fell onto the bed directly in front of Louise.

Louise held the pencil tightly in her left hand, slowly knelt down on the bed, and watched Luis bleed out until he took his final breath.

Louise stared at his body for a few moments and jammed the bloodied pencil deep into Verdun's left ear.

Louise slowly got to her feet and picked up Luis' handgun.

Bloodied and battered she kept the gun and after several deep breaths, casually and calmly opened the cabin door and headed topside.

King and Kong stood on the bridge. Kong was looking out to the left through binoculars still trying to identify the oncoming boat and King was manning the helm. Louise stepped out onto the deck, approached them, and stopped at the bottom of the four steps leading to the helm.

Kong put down his binoculars, mildly surprised at seeing Louise standing on the deck completely naked and covered in blood. He touched King's shoulder and King turned and
quickly shut down the engine.

"Jesus Christ!" King cried.

The boat rocked back and forth for a few moments of silence.

"What are you doing out here?" asked King.

"Where is Luis?" Kong asked and saw the gun in her hand.

Louise raised her arm, pointed the gun, and without saying a word fired all six shots into both men as they attempted to protect themselves. King fell from the helm, down onto the deck, and lay dead at her feet.

Kong, losing blood rapidly, jumped down onto the deck and grabbed Louise by her throat with one hand.

"You bitch! What have you done?"

Kong tried to squeeze her throat tighter but sensed he was losing too much blood and growing weaker. Louise stared into Kong's eyes, reached up, and began breaking Kong's fingers one by one until he no longer could grasp her neck. Louise stepped back and Kong fell face down, dead, onto the deck.

She stood breathing heavily and a spotlight suddenly shined down onto the deck and Louise heard a voice.

"This is Lieutenant David Hopkins of the United States Navy! Drop your weapon. We are coming aboard."

Louise loosely tossed the gun aside and dropped to her knees.

Her only thought was of her daughter Diana whom she hoped was still alive and well. Tears ran down her bloodied face as she began crying uncontrollably.

CHAPTER TWELVE

My flight back to Los Angeles gave me ample time to clear my head and prepare for what we needed to do in regards to Rachel Stone Barbieri AKA Magenta Dairy. I stepped out of the plane just around noon expecting to see Phil waiting for me. I was happily surprised to see Special Agent Edwards leaning against the flight entrance fence sporting a new hat, a new suit, and shiny new shoes.

"You're a sight for sore eyes," I said and shook his hand. "Nice suit. How was New Jersey? Any progress?"

"Some," he said. "Some good. Some not so good."

Agent Edwards' response made me want to begin asking questions immediately but I remained silent, knowing he would give me the entire run down before we left the airport. We both stood silently waiting for my luggage to arrive.

"Do you want a smoke?" he asked.

"I quit," I said.

"I started," he replied and lit one up with his lighter.

"How was Florida?" Agent Edwards asked.

"Thanks to your man, Charlie, things worked out okay on my end. For the most part."

"I was just looking out for you. One friend to another."

"I fully understand and I appreciated the help. I probably would have done the same for you. Or for Detective Blaine if situations were reversed. How is Blaine these days?"

"Eager to get back at it. He's currently on two weeks of vacation and putting in a new lawn. Doing it all by himself."

"Never figured him to have a green thumb," I said.

"He doesn't," said Agent Edwards.

The luggage arrived and Agent Edwards quickly took my bag and we walked to his Dodge parked in a no parking zone.

"A fancy new lighter, a brand new hat and suit and now this? You're turning into a real rebel these days," I said kiddingly. "Something tells me there has to be a new woman in your life. Is that what this new look is all about?"

Agent Edwards grinned broadly.

"Do you remember that cute waitress at the counter the first time you and I met?"

"I remember her," I said. "The little cutie giving you the eye in the coffee shop."

"We're seeing each other."

"Good for you," I said with a smile. "What's her name?"

"Debra. Debra Serrano."

"How long has this been going on?" I asked.

166

"Seven or eight months now. Lately we've been talking long distance on the phone since I was sent to New Jersey. We're having dinner tonight at her place. She rents a little guest house in Toluca Lake from some film producer."

"A film producer?" I asked.

"Some Russian guy named Val Newton. I only met him once. Seems to keep himself pretty busy. Always at the studio. Debs hardly ever sees him. She met Boris Karloff."

"Mr. Frankenstein himself? Did she get his autograph?"

"No. Debs didn't even know who he was. She's not a big movie fan."

"No Hollywood glitter and glamour in her eyes. She sounds like a down-to-earth, practical type girl. Perfect for a guy like you."

"She is a very practical young lady."

"I'll bet she likes the G-Men stories though. Right?" I asked with a grin.

"She does actually."

"Do you talk shop with her?" I asked.

"Never. I don't tell and Debs never asks."

"Debs?" I asked. "Sounds like you're getting serious with this girl."

"It's moving in that direction."

"Looking forward to meeting her," I said. "She seems to be rubbing off on you rather nicely."

Agent Edwards smiled, tossed my bag in the trunk, and we climbed into the Dodge.

"We have a lot of information to go over," he said with a serious tone. "A lot of information."

"Good information or bad information?" I asked.

"A little of both," he said.

"Tell me everything," I said.

Agent Edwards fired up the Dodge and pulled out of the airport.

"Are we going to your office or your apartment?" he asked.

"It's Friday," I said. "Phil will be manning the office. Let's go there first."

Agent Edwards headed onto the coast highway toward Santa Monica.

"I understand this Luis Verdun got away?" asked Agent Edwards.

"He did. The Navy is out looking for him. Charlie told me he would keep us updated," I said. "What have you got on Magenta? Anything?"

Agent Edwards opened a folder on the seat between us and handed me a photo.

"Who is this?" I asked.

"Her real name is Lindsey Kesset. She's an orphaned street kid from Johnstown, Pennsylvania. Both parents are deceased. She's an only child and has had some minor priors ever since she turned sixteen. Over the years this girl has been arrested for shoplifting from high- end stores, pretending to be Karen Highdreth, prostituting herself to lawyers as Barbara Sanger, running small time street cons as a Miss Eva Leyner, and her last arrest on record back in '47 was for drug possession. Marijuana. Two pounds! She called herself Joanne Parrish on that one and there's been an arrest warrant out for her for failure to appear ever since. The photo you're looking at was taken by Agent Richard Gregory. It was taken a few days ago, just before he died from gunshots Miss Parrish so kindly put into him. The blonde hair is a wig. She's actually a brunette."

"A brunette who killed a Federal agent?" I asked.

"No hesitation whatsoever. She put two shots in his chest and walked away."

"This kid has moved up. A real pro," I said.

"Definitely. Someone out there has taken her under their wing. Agent Davis and Agent Gregory were staking out this street level lowlife named Henry Long. He had ties to Ponce Delgado and threatened the Assistant DA of New Jersey's wife in regards to our other old friend, Rockwell, who is about to turn on Magenta any day now. This Joanne also shot and killed Henry and in the process of her escape also killed a theater

168

manager. Agent Davis attempted to apprehend her and she broke Agent Davis' nose before knocking her unconscious, and then killed Agent Gregory as he attempted to arrest her."

"Jesus Christ. Armed and extremely dangerous." I said.

"Extremely is right," added Agent Edwards.

"And now she's in the wind?" I asked. "Just like Verdun?"

"Yes, but before she skipped town she also killed a nephew of mobster Carmine Scarola."

"Jesus H. Christ! Her MO is beginning to sound very familiar to you know who?" I said.

"This one has Magenta written all over her."

"Yes. Something gets in your way you either offer to pay big money or just shoot to kill and move on. Who's this mob nephew?" I asked.

"His name is. Was. Bobby Collucci. He was Carmine's sister's kid. We found his body several blocks from Henry's place and we also found his car abandoned at the Newark airport. We managed to get some prints on this Joanne person from Bobby's car."

"Any leads on where she might be?" I asked and put the photo back in the folder.

"She left an expensive coat behind and we're trying to see if that can lead us anywhere. She had a silencer on her weapon."

"A silencer?" I repeated. "Most mob hits are extremely loud and very public. Makes any probable witnesses duck for cover."

"We think this hit was supposed to be short and swift but something went wrong and she ducked in the theater to try and stay hidden."

"Until this Bobby arrived?" I asked.

"Yes."

"You can run but you can't hide. Not with Agent Loretta Davis on your trail. This hitter has definitely stepped up from simple minor priors right to the big time. What's your take on this woman?"

"We think she was brought in specifically to take Henry Long out. We really don't know more than that but I have Agent Davis checking in with Carmine Scarola and hopefully he'll co-operate with us and possibly point us in her direction."

"A mobster and an FBI agent having a sit down conversation?" I asked.

"It's a new world out there," he said.

"I guess it's worth a shot," I said.

"Hoover felt so," added Agent Edwards.

"Ponce Delgado," I said. "Rockwell. This new shooter Joanne. And Verdun. It's simply mind blowing to me."

"How so?' Agent Edwards asked.

"They all have one person in common. One person connects them all together. Our favorite girl, Rachel Stone Barbieri. Her contacts and her reach is unbelievable."

"It is. Yes," said Agent Edwards. "Magenta is out there somewhere and I am not going to rest until we find her and shut her ass down completely."

A big smile crossed my face and Agent Edwards took notice.

"What is it?" he asked. "I've seen that smile before."

"I have some information for you."

"Good information or bad information?" he asked.

"Oh it's good. It's very good. It's so good your mind is going to explode."

What is it?" he asked.

"I know where Magenta Dairy is."

Agent Edwards suddenly pulled the Dodge to the side of the road, put it in park, and looked at me excitedly.

"You know where Magenta is and you didn't tell me when you got off the god damn plane?"

"You have always been the lead on this from day one. I thought my news could wait until I heard what you had to tell me."

Agent Edwards shook his head in disbelief.

"Where is she?" he asked.

"She's built some type of protective compound in Cozumel."

"A compound in Cozumel," Agent Edwards repeated. "Mexico?"

"It comes from a good source. An ex-lover of hers from Florida. Another person touched by Magenta's long armed reach."

"What's his name?" Agent Edwards asked.

"It's not a he. It's a she."

Agent Edwards nodded his head yes, knowing Rachel's tastes in sexual partners being both male and female.

"And you're positive this is a reliable source?" he asked.

"Most definitely. Yes. Agent Lindman has this woman in custody down in Florida and he's questioning her extensively. I'm surprised you didn't already know all this."

"I didn't."

"I think we should get someone down in Cozumel right away. We should start looking around for this place of hers and figure out how we can get in there, pull her the hell out, and get her back here in the States."

"I'll call Hoover as soon as we get to your office," said Agent Edwards. "This is awesome news! Mexico! Of course. It makes sense. She must be shifting her entire operation from the tunnels to the sea. We'll have to alert the Navy, the Coast Guard, and every port from Florida to Texas!"

"Too bad we're back fighting another war over in Korea right now," I said. "I'd personally ask Truman to declare war on Mexico and storm her beach tomorrow morning with every available soldier."

"We could ask him," added Agent Edwards. "Maybe he'll say yes?"

"We're not going to do that sitting here on the side of this road," I said. "Let's get moving!"

"Oh yeah, right. Right!"

"Kick this old Dodge into gear, Edwards, and let's get to it!" I said.

Agent Edwards grinned broadly and pulled back out onto the coast road. As we reached my office, Agent Edwards parked the car, shut off the engine and looked at me with concern.

"What is it?" I asked.

"There's something else I haven't told you."

171

"Your bad information?" I asked.

"Yes."

I could sense by his hesitation that it was really bad news. He took a deep breath and looked at me.

"Agent Correlli is dead," he said. "And his new partner. A young female. A new recruit. Only had a few months in the field."

My breathing intensified and my hands clenched into fists as I took in the news.

"This Joanne person?" I asked.

"No. Someone much worse. Whoever it is tortured them both before killing them. A local New Jersey Detective is working the case, a man named McCrory and he has agreed to keep us in the loop. This guy was a real pro and I doubt if McCrory will ever get a handle on this."

"How bad was it?"

"In a word? Horrific. There are no other words to describe what this animal did to them. They were both cut up badly and tortured mercilessly. That's all I want to say about it."

I took in the news of the torture as if I was just hit by a bus. We sat in the car staring ahead blankly for about two minutes without either of us uttering a word. I looked over at Agent Edwards.

"This has to be Magenta Dairy's doing too. She told us we were all dead men, including Agent Davis. Remember? Correlli and his partner's deaths and the manner of their deaths has to point back to her. It has to. Whoever this killer is? Has to be working on her orders. Has to be."

"Again," said Agent Edwards. "I agree. And you're right. Magenta has a very long reach. That is a major disadvantage for us."

"Do we have any leads on this monster?" I asked.

"Not as yet. He's smart and he's lethal. We all have to watch each other's backs very closely, twenty-four seven, until we catch this son of a bitch."

"Not only us," I said. "People close to us, too. Jesus Christ! Nobody's safe."

Agent Edwards nodded his agreement.

"Nobody," he repeated. "Maybe Rockwell's testimony will open up a few good leads and help us put a lid on her?"

"Let's hope so," I said. "Magenta has people on both sides of her all running scared. The good and the bad."

"She's not going to scare us off. Or take us out. Not us. Not now. Not ever!"

We stepped out of the car and went into my office.

I tried to change my somber mood as Phil jumped to her feet and gave both of us welcomed hugs. We cracked open a new bottle of Scotch and were sitting around my desk sharing information about my Florida trip and Agent Edwards' confrontation with the New Jersey Assistant DA when the office phone rang.

Phil answered it from my desk.

"Patrick Atwater's office," she said. She listened and looked at me. "It's some guy named Barney."

Phil handed me the phone.

"Yeah, Barney? What's up?"

I listened intently to Barney's news.

"Thanks Barney. I'll try and get up to see you and Betty and Jake in a couple of days. We'll talk more then."

I hung up the phone and Phil looked at me.

"What is it?" she asked.

"Roberto Santoro died this morning. Barney just got the news."

"Is there going to be a service of some kind?" Phil asked.

"No service. Cremation."

"A client of yours?" Agent Edwards asked.

"Yeah," I said. "He's the one who sent me to Florida looking for his daughter and his ex. Damn it! Now he'll never know how it all turned out."

We all sat silent for a moment.

"Santoro knows," said Phil.

"How can you say that?" I asked.

"Because of all the private dicks in this town Mr.. Santoro chose you," she said.

173

"He chose Patrick Atwater because the name is in the front of the listing."

'No!" exclaimed Phil. "This has nothing to do with some phone listing! Roberto Santoro chose you Patrick because he knew Patrick Miles Atwater was the right man for the job, you would come through for him, and you did. End of story."

"Maybe," I said.

"No maybe, Phil's right," added Agent Edwards. "If I needed a private eye you would be my first call."

"See," said Phil.

I raised my glass and smiled at Phil.

"Okay. To Roberto Santoro. May he rest in peace."

"Roberto Santoro," said Phil and we all touched glasses and sipped our Scotch.

"Oh crap, I need to call Hoover," said Agent Edwards.

"I'll go connect you," said Phil and walked out of my office.

"I'll give Detective Blaine a quick call and get him up to speed," I said.

"Good idea," added Agent Edwards.

I took another long hard swig of my Johnnie Walker and thought about Louise and Diana. And then my thoughts drifted to Agent Correlli and his murdered partner.

"What is it?" asked Agent Edwards.

"I thought we only had to chase down one person. Now we have three heartless bastards on our list. This never gets easier does it?"

"We'll get them," said Agent Edwards. "We'll get all of them."

"Hoover is on line two," yelled Phil from her desk.

Agent Edwards picked up the phone and I stepped out of the office to give him some privacy.

CHAPTER THIRTEEN

Assistant DA Jonathan Wainwright struggled with his new silk tie until Carole stepped behind him as she had so many times before and quickly made the perfect Windsor knot. He placed his hand on hers and stared at her in the mirror.

"You always get it right," he said.

"Not always," she replied. "But this one today looks perfect."

"It does," he replied. "Just like you. Perfect."

Carole looked away from his glance and he turned, put his hand gently on her cheek, and looked into her eyes.

"Ae you feeling any better, honey?" he asked.

Carole sighed heavily and smiled slightly, hoping he couldn't see the truth in her face. She wanted to scream what she was hiding from him, but knowing it would not have made a difference she ignored the feeling and lied.

"Now that Henry Long has been put down like the mad dog he was? Yes. I'm feeling much better," she replied and kissed his cheek. "I am feeling wonderful as a matter of fact."

"I am so glad to hear that," he said.

Carole suddenly held him close.

"Stay home today, Jonathan, and make love to me."

He held her tightly for a few moments then gently pulled away from her grasp and faced her.

"I would love to do exactly that, darling" he said. 'But I'm taking the very deposition today from the man your monster Henry warned us not to speak to."

"That man Rockwell?" she asked knowing full well who Rockwell was.

"Yes. Rockwell."

"Can't someone else in your office take his deposition?"

"It's my case honey. I have to be there. You know this."

Jonathan could see her disappointment and hugged her again.

"I know you of all people understand," he whispered.

She sighed heavily and looked at him.

"I do understand," she said. "I just don't like it."

Jonathan hugged her again but her mind was a thousand miles away. She did her best to hide her distant thoughts.

"Modarelli is the New Jersey D.A.," she added. "Why doesn't he or someone in his office deal with this Rockwell person? Let you stay home. Here. With me. Like this."

She snuggled up close to him and kissed him deeply.

"I want you all to myself today," she whispered. "Please?"

"Carole? Sweetheart? I love you but this is my case. My responsibility. I am that guy in Modarelli's office. We can get together tonight. I promise you. But the office is counting on me in regards to Rockwell and I have to go and I have to be there. I'm sorry."

"The wheels of justice must turn and turn," she said and straightened his tie one last time.

"Yes they must," he agreed and kissed her passionately.

"I'm sorry, Jonathan. I'm just being selfish this morning and I'm sorry."

Jonathan smiled at her, thinking she was just feeling left out. He thought he would surprise her with flowers when he returned from his day's work.

Carole didn't want flowers and she was not sorry. Inside she was a panicked mess and wanted desperately to share her thoughts with Jonathan but restrained herself from speaking. He looked into her eyes and smiled.

"It's all right, honey. We'll have tonight. I promise."

"I love you," she said.

"I love you, too."

"I'm sorry for letting what happened affect me so," she said. "I haven't been a very good wife to you these past few weeks."

"No apologies necessary. The important thing is we got past it all and now we are back on track. Yes?"

"Yes," she said. "Back on track."

"Remember this, honey. Good always triumphs over evil. And we are the good guys. Don't ever lose sight of that fact. You hear me?"

"I hear you," she replied and smiled a fake smile as he kissed her cheek.

"We have a lot of good people looking out for us."

"I know," she said.

"You'll be okay?" he asked.

"I'll be fine," she lied. "Don't forget this."

Carole grabbed his briefcase from the bedroom chair and handed it to him.

"Will you be coming home late?" she asked.

"No. Not today, darling. The deposition is at ten and when that's completed? I am coming right home to you my love. Straight home to you."

She smiled broadly finally getting the one piece of information she so desperately needed.

"I will make us a special dinner. A celebration dinner. My good guy making the bad guy sing. Isn't that what you call it?"

"Something like that. Yes."

He laughed and she knew she had weathered her internal storm and now there was only one more thing left to do.

"I have to run," he said.

"Okay," she said.

He smiled one last time and walked out of the bedroom. She followed him out but stopped at the top of the stairs, watching him walk out the front door. She sighed and stood there until she heard their car start up and drive away.

Carole turned, walked into the bedroom and sat on the bed near the phone. She took a long, deep breath and blew it out slowly. Carole took out a crumpled piece of
paper from under her pillow and opened it up. She picked up the phone, and dialed a number she read from the paper.

The phone rang five times before someone finally picked up and answered.

"Yes?" the voice asked.

"The deposition is at ten," she said and quickly hung up the phone.

Carole stared at the phone as if it had suddenly turned hot like molten steel. She caught a glimpse of herself in the bedroom mirror and the pangs of heavy guilt washed over her entire body.

Carole's body began to shake.

Tears started running down her cheeks as she sat there crying uncontrollably.

The monsters weren't gone.

A new monster had appeared. One her husband knew nothing about. This time it was a female voice with an eerie calm and a forceful manner.

Good once again had not triumphed or conquered evil as her husband so easily professed.

Not at all.

Evil was still extremely close by, still threatening her, and she was promised her secret betrayal would guarantee that her life and the life of her husband, Jonathan, would be spared this day.

This was what she was told and this is what she hoped to God this new monster's words would ring true for her and for her husband.

"Rockwell doesn't sing," she said aloud but in a subdued quiet voice. "Rockwell doesn't sing."

Carole tried to wipe away her tears but her guilt was too overwhelming and the tears would not stop no matter how hard she tried. She had never lied to her husband about anything but knew in her heart she would never admit the truth of this day to him or to anyone no matter what the outcome was going to be. Rockwell, a man she never met or even had a thought about, had truly become a matter of life and death for her and for her husband.

She was given a choice and she chose life and knew she would have to live with her decision, right or wrong, for the rest of her life. She gathered what strength she had left, tore up the piece of paper with the written phone number, walked to the bathroom and flushed the paper away.

Then she sat on the edge of the bathtub and wept once again.

Jonathan arrived at his office eager to work and began making certain everything was set in its proper order for the deposition. His secretary, a young brunette beauty named Molly Carter, came rushing into his office around 9:45 am.

"Rockwell is here," she said. "He's coming in from the parking lot under guard protection."

Jonathan walked to the window and looked down at the lot entrance.

Rockwell was wearing a dark blue suit and tie and his hands were handcuffed in front of his body. Four police officers escorted him across the lot and as they made the right turn towards the building entranceway Rockwell, a tall handsome black man, casually looked up, locked eyes with Jonathan, smiled, and raised his handcuffed hands to wave hello.

Molly joined Jonathan at the window and stared down at Rockwell.

"This is that guy who built all those tunnels for the Mexican drug dealers?" asked Molly.

"He's the guy," replied Jonathan.

"How many did he build?" she asked.

"Eleven," he said. "I'm pretty sure there are a lot more we don't know about yet and hopefully Mr. Rockwell will enlighten us with some of that information today."

"He looks more like a successful businessman than a drug dealer."

"Rockwell is a brilliant engineer. He lost his way but prison life has shown him the light. We're lucky to have him in our corner now instead of the opposition."

Jonathan and Molly smiled at each other and turned their attention back to Rockwell.

Jonathan's smile quickly turned to a look of horror as Rockwell's forehead suddenly exploded into numerous pieces of white skull and gray brain matter. Large volumes of his own blood poured from just above his eyes and sprayed the two officers in front of him before falling face down dead onto the pavement.

"No!" screamed Jonathan as he pressed against the glass. "No!!!"

"Oh, god!" Molly screamed in disbelief and looked away. "Oh my god!"

No gunshot was heard but Rockwell had clearly been hit from behind from a very high point across the street.

Jonathan actually saw the bullet exit Rockwell's skull and hit the pavement in front of him. Jonathan craned his neck and stared across the street but saw no gunman. There was one single window opened on the fourth floor of the office building across the street and Jonathan quickly surmised it must have been where the shot originated.

Jonathan opened the window and pointed over to the building across the street.

"The fourth floor window! On the left!" he screamed and two officers hustled across the street with their guns drawn.

Molly stood with her back against the wall, still screaming.

Jonathan picked up the phone and dialed the operator.

"This is Jonathan Wainwright with the District Attorney's office. We need an ambulance over here right now! A man has been shot outside the entrance area! Hurry please!"

Jonathan hung up the phone, walked over to Molly and held her until she calmed down and stopped screaming. Jonathan held her shoulders with his hands.

"I need you to stay focused, Molly," he said. "Can you do that for me?"

Molly's body would not stop shaking but she looked up into Jonathan's face and nodded yes.

"Good," said Jonathan. "Stay right here until I come back. All right?"

Again she nodded yes and Jonathan hurried down the stairs and out the entrance way until he reached Rockwell's dead body.

The two bloodied policemen were now joined by several other uniformed police as all hell seemed to break loose around the entire building. The street was quickly cordoned off and an ambulance arrived with its siren blaring. The police all drew their weapons and began searching for the shooter.

Their searches proved fruitless.

Whoever the shooter was got away cleanly without a clue or a trace of whom they might be or where they went.

Staring down at Rockwell's body, Jonathan Wainwright suddenly realized that a new wave of criminal had arrived on the scene.

These criminals were bolder.

They were smarter.

And they were extremely well organized and precise in their actions.

It dawned on Jonathan in that moment that a new tactic must be put into place if he was ever to fight injustice again in a court of law and actually win a conviction. The rules of engagement had changed dramatically and drastically.

His office now needed to become much tougher and bolder. His office also needed to become much stronger and smarter. His people, in order to win their fight now, needed to be able to fight fire with fire.

Any and all corruption within his walls would have to be located and stamped out completely. A new and stronger sense of trust would have to be established within house if these evil-doers were ever going to be stopped, prosecuted, and put away in prison.

The blatant and horrific daylight murder of his witness Rockwell shook Jonathan to his core.

His office clearly had become compromised in the worst way. Somehow the shooter knew where and when Rockwell was to arrive and Jonathan began to suspect everyone. He wondered who it was within the walls of his office that could have told them? Who could have betrayed his office like this?

"Who?" he kept asking himself over and over again. "Who was it?"

Jonathan never once suspected that the walls of betrayal were the walls of his own home where he and Carole were living their American dream.

CHAPTER FOURTEEN

Saturday morning I sorely wanted to stay in bed for an extra twenty minutes or so but several hard, loud. knocks at the front door of my apartment at the Sultan Arms jogged me out of my deep sleep and got me quickly to my feet.

I grabbed my .38 and walked cautiously to my front door, not knowing who or what to expect. I carefully opened my small metal peep hole and looked out only to see some gray clouds in the sky, the top of Agent Edwards new hat, and a donut sack he held up for me to see.

"I have breakfast and news," he said.

I opened the door and let him in.

"What is it?" I asked. "Don't tell me you've got some new leads already?"

"No. I have some news and thought you should hear it from me right away. Face to face."

"Why do I have the feeling I'm not going to like this news," I said and closed the door and locked it.

"Some good. Some bad news. The Navy found Verdun's boat."

"That's the good news. Where was it headed?"

"Mexico."

"And?" I asked

"And. Verdun is dead. Along with two of his men."

"King and Kong?"

"Unidentified at the moment but they were two big guys."

"Verdun and his guys are dead? That is good news. And Louise?" I asked half expecting the same reply.

"Louise Santoro is alive. Alive and well in spite of her ordeal with Verdun and she is back with her daughter in a new place in Florida until they figure out what they want to do with her new inheritance."

My heart pounded in my chest.

"That is great news!" I said. "Let me make us some coffee and you can give me all the details."

Agent Edwards held up the small bag I had noticed him carrying when he stepped inside.

"I brought donuts," he said.

"Even better!" I said. "I haven't been to the store yet. My kitchen is empty but I do have coffee."

Agent Edwards and I spent a good part of the morning sipping hot coffee and dunking our donuts. He told me every detail of how Louise had suffered at the hands of Verdun but finally finding the courage and strength to kill Verdun and his two goons.

The details of her experience on Verdun's Steelcraft was mind-numbing yet somewhat delightful to me at the same time.

"It was clearly a case of it being either her or them and no charges are being brought against her," said Agent Edwards.

"That is more good news. She is one tough cookie," I added. "Santoro told me Louise was a special kind of woman and he was right. You should have your gal, Debs, talk to her producer landlord. This Santoro story would make a good movie. Maybe get Bette Davis to play Louise?"

"You're the one with all the Hollywood connections. Not me. Bette would be a good choice though."

Agent Edwards took on a serious tone with a heavy sigh.

"I have more to tell you," said Agent Edwards and grabbed another donut.

"Ah yes," I said. "The bad news."

"I got the coroner's full report back this morning on Agent Correlli and his partner. They were both shot up with that same crap Rachel laid on you at her cabin up in Big Bear."

"Jesus Christ. That means they were both awake throughout their entire ordeal."

"I'm afraid so. Yes."

"This isn't just payback," I said. "This is evil payback. We have to find this son of a bitch before we nail Magenta. None of us or our friends are safe until we do! We have to get more men in the field. Men to keep watch on us and everyone close to us. Night and day until we get him! Jesus, Edwards, you have to call Hoover again and put this in action right away."

"I can't do that," he said.

His reply stunned me.

"Why the hell not?" I asked.

"Hoover's made some changes."

"Some changes? What are you talking about?" I asked feeling very confused. "What kind of changes?"

185

"After Truman's failed assassination attempt, the President thinks organized crime is now running rampant and in some way responsible for orchestrating that
operation," said Agent Edwards.

"Organized crime?" I asked. "Involved in killing the President of the United States?"

"That's his take on it."

"I thought it was two militant Puerto Rican boys?" I asked.

"That's what was reported in all the newspapers but they had help getting into the country, assistance in obtaining their weapons, and Truman wants Hoover to drop all his current drug investigations for now and concentrate solely on organized crime."

"But they are both related! No one is more organized in crime than Magenta Dairy for Christ's sake! She has a longer reach than any other organized crime syndicate could ever have! Hell, she's probably got half of them on her payroll as we speak! If we bring her in? She could give the President and Hoover all kinds of names and information. I know an expert down in Florida who will make her talk. Believe me! She'll have Magenta Dairy singing all kinds of songs to every department in the FBI."

"I'm sure your guy is very good and I agree with everything you are saying," said Agent Edwards. "But the President is adamant about this new direction."

"Adamant?" I asked.

"I'm afraid so," he added.

"Hoover cannot drop the ball on this, Edwards," I said. "You'll have to meet with him and convince Mr. G-Man he's going in the wrong direction."

"He hasn't dropped the ball entirely. He still wants you and Blaine on Magenta Dairy. You both can use any and all forensics offered by the FBI, but unfortunately you're on your own now in regards to taking down Magenta. Hoover's number one priority is the mob and that's the way of it."

"Magenta Dairy is bigger than the god damn mob! Her control stretches globally! Truman and Hoover should be able to see that! Shouldn't they?"

"Yes," replied Agent Edwards. "They should see that. Hoover sees that. But Truman wants Hoover to shift his entire approach to crime in America and Hoover has to do what the President orders him to do. It's politics and it's also a big part of Hoover's job."

"It's a dumb move," I said. "Hoover isn't chasing Machine Gun Kelly or Ma Barker like he did back in the thirties. This is a woman in total control of the drug trade that's pouring into this country! If that isn't organized crime then what the hell is?"

"Again. I agree, Patrick. You are right."

Agent Edwards sat silent and sipped his coffee. I stared at him knowing he had more bad news.

"But," I said and waited for his reply.

Agent Edwards put his coffee cup down and looked at me.

"But I have to do what I'm told, too. You and Blaine will just have to somehow work smarter."

"Why do you keep saying me and Blaine? Where are you in all of this?" I asked.

"I've been transferred."

"What? Transferred? This isn't bad news! That is insane!"

Agent Edwards took a deep calming breath and started over.

"I've been transferred," he repeated.

"To what?" I asked. "To where?"

"I'm assigned to begin work with Israel."

"Israel? Doing what?"

"There's an Israeli team searching out Nazis. I'm the FBI Agent placed in charge."

I couldn't believe what I was hearing.

"We are this close to finally nailing Magenta Dairy and Hoover is sending you off to Israel?"

"The Nazi hunters are in South America. Argentina. Brazil."

187

My head began to shake, not believing Agent Edwards' words.

"Nazi hunters? This is crazy. This is nuts! Who is going to watch your back in god damn South America?"

"I'll be well protected."

"What about your girl, Debs? You have to know Magenta will use her if they have to and with you in god knows where down in South America, they will use her!"

"I got Hoover to agree to a two man detail to watch over her. They will protect her and she'll be safe until I get back."

Again my head shook and my ears began to ring.

"A two man detail is not going to stop a man who can torture and murder two federal agents right under our nose! God damn it!"

"It's all he can do right now!" cried Agent Edwards.

"That is bullshit! You're telling me the FBI can only afford a lousy two man team to watch over the girlfriend of a decorated agent like yourself?"

"It isn't about affordability! It's about priorities!"

"What about Barney?' I asked. "What about Betty and Jake? Who's going to watch out for them? Their lives will be on the line in this too! Do they get a two man team to watch over them? Well? Do they?"

"Detective Blaine is taking care of them with some local LAPD uniforms," replied Agent Edwards. "They will keep a watchful eye and make sure they are all safe."

"Night and day?" I asked. "Because that is what it is going to take and you know it! Magenta has people everywhere!"

"And so will we!"

"No we won't!" I shouted.

I took a deep breath and calmed myself down.

"So now what? You're telling me that you are going to chase Nazis down in South America somewhere and Blaine and I are completely on our own?" I asked.

"For right now? Today? This moment? Yes!"

Again my head began to spin.

"This is nuts!" I said. "We can't possibly do all this on our own."

"There were only four of us in Aruba!" said Agent Edwards.

"Yes," I replied. "And only three of us came back alive! Magenta is bigger now! Stronger. She has us on our heels and you know it! You should have told Hoover you needed to stay with us! Stay in this until the very end instead of leaving us alone."

"You won't be alone. Besides Detective Blaine, you will have Agent Davis. She's been suspended for three months pending a full investigation into the death of Agent Gregory but she is going to work side by side with you and give you both all the support you'll need. I'm also sending out Agent Lindman to you. He's a great asset to any team! And the entire LAPD will be working for you on this."

"We still need you. Here. With us."

"I'm sorry, Patrick, but my hands are tied. When you nail these two killers Magenta has sent out after us and when you're ready to make your move and take Magenta down? I'll come back straight away and give you all the help you'll need. That is my promise to you."

"What about Hoover and the Nazi Hunters?"

"I said I promise and I mean that."

"I'm still Special Agent Atwater?" I asked. "Recognized G-Man by the FBI director himself?"

"Yes. You still have that status. For as long as it takes," he said. "Hoover's word. He knows you and Blaine will do what you need to do and get this done. And so do I."

A smile came across my face.

"Detective Blaine, Charlie, and Special Agent Loretta Davis?" I asked.

"All part of your team."

"And the LAPD?"

"Also in the mix. Yes."

"Who's my contact at the LAPD?"

"Some captain named Gibbons. Blaine says he's a good man."

"And this Gibbons knows what we are up against and that our number one priority is taking down Magenta Dairy and her killers for hire? Yes?"

"Yes. You will work as a four person team and you won't stop until we have Magenta in our sights and we take these other two monsters off the street. Hoover can go chase his mobsters, I'll hold the Israelis' hands while they chase the Nazis, and you and your team go catch the big fish, Magenta."

I put my donut down and offered my right hand.

"This is not going to feel right without you here with us," I said. "It's not going to feel right at all."

"My hands are tied but only for the moment. Nail these killers, Patrick and then we'll take down Magenta together. Just like we did before only this time she is not going to shake herself loose."

"I have your word on that?" I asked.

"Yes," he said. "You have my word."

Agent Edwards and I shook hands solidifying our new agreement.

"All right, we'll find them," I said. "We'll find all of them. That's my word on it."

Agent Edwards smiled but I could see in his face that Rachel Stone Barbieri was getting under his skin and he was not feeling confident in regards to her. I had enough confidence for the two of us and if this was the way things had to be for right now, then I convinced myself I would make it all work.

Somehow.

Some way.

My first order of business was to see Detective Blaine as soon as possible and my second order was to meet with the entire team and put a twenty-four-seven working plan into action until we started getting results.

I picked up the phone to call Detective Blaine when a loud boom suddenly resounded from above from a huge thunder blast.

"Holy crap!" said Agent Edwards. "Was that thunder? That had to be right over us!"

Agent Edwards got to his feet and looked out my kitchen window.

"Jesus! It's raining cats and dogs out there," he said. "This morning the damn sun was shining."

"It's a California rain and shouldn't last too long," I said. "It never does. "Pour yourself another cup of coffee and grab another donut, Nazi hunter."

Agent Edwards poured himself another cup as lightning streaked across the darkened sky. A few moments passed and another loud boom thundered above us.

"Wow!" I said. "Now that one was really loud too and pretty damn close."

"Does that mean something?" asked Agent Edwards as he peered out my kitchen window.

"I remember this kind of a storm back in '46. It rained and poured just like this for a week straight."

"California rain?" asked Agent Edwards.

"It's the west coast's version of winter," I said. "We'll weather the storm. We all will. Right?"

"I hope so," said Agent Edwards as he stared at the darkened clouds above. "I truly hope so."

CHAPTER FIFTEEN

The California rain did not stop.

It had not stopped for two days straight. It was a little after three-thirty in the morning and Detective Blaine's Van Nuys backyard was forming a small pool of water near his back fence resembling a miniature version of Lake Arrowhead. Detective Blaine had gotten up on this particular Saturday night, now turned to early Sunday morning, to use the bathroom and just happened to gaze out his bathroom window and saw what the rain was doing and what was now occurring in his yard.

"Son of a bitch," he said aloud, flushed the toilet and quickly washed his hands.

Detective Blaine walked to the kitchen back door, slipped on a pair of rubber boots, placed an old worn tennis hat on his head, and walked out into the rain still wearing his blue pajama bottoms and white tee shirt.

A long handled shovel leaned against the house alongside a metal rake and a dozen bags of lawn seed. Detective Blaine grabbed the shovel and walked to the rear of his yard. He stood there in the rain getting soaked and took a quick assessment of the pooling water.

Detective Blaine began to dig a small trench from the wooden fence to the rising lake and the water quickly drained back out into the alleyway behind the fence.

Satisfied with his brief feat of engineering, he plowed through the remaining mud and headed slowly back to the house.

Before he reached his back door a car pulled up in the alleyway behind his house, setting Detective Blaine's police instincts instantly into high gear. He stopped, turned, and wondered who could be driving around here at this time of night and in this kind of weather.

And most importantly, why?

Then he remembered his phone call warning from Patrick and Agent Edwards two days earlier concerning this unknown killer of Agent Correlli and his partner, and a shiver went down his spine. He thought of running into the house and getting his gun but convinced himself he was being overly paranoid and decided to stand his ground and observe this new arrival on the other side of his fence.

"Probably two young lovers needing a place to make out," he thought.

Whoever was in the vehicle shut off the engine and headlights and exited the car. Detective Blaine heard the one car door shut and focused his eyes through the rain and on the alleyway.

He stood in the rain and mud holding his shovel and the single alleyway street light shining from the rear of the house next door allowed just enough light to notice a pair of black leather gloved hands suddenly gripping the top of his wooden fence. Before he could yell out or utter a single word, he watched a tall older man prop himself up and leap over the fence into his muddied yard.

The man was Terrence Bruce.

Terrence was dressed all in black and Detective Blaine could tell straight away the man was in good physical condition just by the easy manner and speed he had scaled the fence.

Was this the man he had been warned about?

Terrence took a few steps but stopped dead in his tracks realizing that the man he had come to kill was not fast asleep in his bedroom as expected but for some odd reason was very wide awake and standing right in front of him in his rain-soaked backyard, armed with a shovel as if expecting someone to arrive.

The two men stood without a word facing each other for a few moments until Detective Blaine finally broke the silence.

"Can I help you with something, mac?" asked Detective Blaine.

Terrence quickly reached for his hand gun and Detective Blaine's police instincts once again kicked in and he rushed at Terrence. Terrence managed to get the gun out but as he attempted to point it and get off a quick shot, Detective Blaine had swung his shovel and knocked the gun from Terence's hand, dropping it into the mud.

Detective Blaine kept moving closer to Terrence. He swung his elbow into Terrence's face and tackled him to the wet and sloppy ground.

Terrence quickly grabbed hold of the shovel and the two men began rolling back and forth in the mud and the rain, each trying to gain the upper hand. Both men traded strong, powerful punches, with threatening blows to their bodies and faces but still holding onto the shovel. The two managed to get to their knees facing each other and struggling for ownership of the shovel. Detective Blaine held onto the shovel tightly when Terrence suddenly surprised Detective Blaine with a quick sudden head butt, knocking him down and onto his back.

Still holding the shovel, Detective Blaine landed into the rainwater and mud with a thud and a splash and he felt a strong numbing feeling in his face. Reaching up to touch his face, he realized Terrence's head butt had broken his nose and it was bleeding.

A lightning bolt seared across the sky and thunder boomed through the pouring rain.

Terrence quickly got to his feet and pulled a knife from a sheath attached to his ankle. Detective Blaine looked up, saw the knife glisten in the fleeting moment of the lightning flash, hauled himself to his feet and pointed the shovel at Terrence.

"If you think you're going to stick me with that thing, old man, then come ahead and take what you got coming," challenged Detective Blaine.

Terrence laughed to himself.

"You're being too kind, mate," said Terrence and took a step closer.

Detective Blaine waved Terrence in even closer.

"Come on, you old fuck!" said Detective Blaine as he wiped the blood from his eyes. "You want to do this? Then let's do this!"

The two men began to circle each other as thunder suddenly boomed again above them.

Terrence suddenly lunged at Detective Blaine and managed to cut his left thigh with his knife.

"When I'm through with you, Detective Blaine, you'll be nothing but a large pile of very small cut up pieces," announced Terrence.

Terrence lunged again but missed cutting Detective Blaine's face by inches.

"I don't think so," said Detective Blaine and waved the shovel back and forth. "Whoever hired an old Mick like you should have their head examined. You belong in a nursing home, grandpa."

"I'm going to cut out your heart, Blaine, and have it for me breakfast," said Terrence.

"Then you come and get it, old man!" taunted Detective Blaine. "You come and get it!"

Terrence smiled and kept circling but accidently stepped into the trench Detective Blaine had hastily dug, twisting his ankle and falling to one knee. Terrence looked down for an instant to see what caused the fall and Detective Blaine reacted instantly, hitting Terrence across the side of his head with the flat of the shovel and knocking him unconscious.

Terrence lay in the mud on his left side, out cold.

Detective Blaine quickly grabbed the knife and the gun and checked Terrence's pockets for any identification. A deep wound over Terrence's closed eyes oozed blood slowly out and over the mud covering his face.

"I'll be right back, tough guy," said Detective Blaine. "Oh, and you are under arrest for assaulting a police officer, you Irish prick. I'm calling this in and getting my cuffs."

Tired from the fight, breathing very hard, and bleeding from his pummeled face, broken nose, and wounded leg, Detective Blaine slowly limped back into the house.

Completely covered in mud, Detective Blaine, drenched from the rain, and still wearing his boots, picked up the kitchen phone and dialed the operator.

As the phone began to ring, Detective Blaine put the knife and the gun on his kitchen table and plopped himself down.

The operator's voice came on the line.

"Operator," she said.

"Give me the police. This is Detective Blaine, Van Nuys Division, Badge number three eighteen," he said and looked down at his wounded leg.

"Yes sir," said the operator.

The cut was deep and still bleeding.

Detective Blaine leaned over, grabbed a nearby kitchen towel, and wiped the mud away from the wound with one end of the towel while pressing the wound on his leg with the other end.

Another voice came on the line.

"Van Nuys Police Department," the voice said. "Sergeant Leyner here."

"Hey, Mason. This is Detective Blaine."

"Good evening, Detective."

"I need you to send a bus, a couple of uniforms, and whoever is on call at the Detective squad over here to my place asap."

"That would be Detective Franklin, sir."

"John's a good man," said Detective Blaine. "Put a rush on it. Will you?"

"Yes sir! Right away, sir. Are you all right over there?"

"I've been better but I am okay. Some old man just tried to stab me with his knife. I'm bleeding but I'm okay."

"Yes sir," said Officer Leyner. "We'll get right over to you. Is the old man who attacked you still there?"

"He's here but he's no longer a threat," said Detective Blaine and pressed harder on the wound. "Just get them all over here now. Okay?"

"Yes sir," said Leyner.

"Thank you."

Detective Blaine hung up the phone and finally felt he was catching his second wind.

Suddenly he heard a car attempting to start up.

Detective Blaine pressed on his wound, rose up out of his chair, grabbed a handgun from a kitchen drawer, turned on his back yard light, and looked out.

Rain still fell hard but the man lying unconscious in the mud was nowhere to be seen.

"God damn it!" screamed Detective Blaine.

He looked out through the rain, seeing headlights shining through his wooden fence from the car in the alley. He raced out with his gun in hand, running quickly as he could towards the fence.

Lightning streaked and thunder boomed as the rain became more intense.

Detective Blaine reached up and pulled down one wooden board from his fence, pointing his weapon through the empty space at the car in front of him.

"LAPD! Stop what you are doing!" he demanded. "Get out of your vehicle and raise your hands in the air!"

Detective Blaine stared at the car and realized the man wasn't there.

"Damn it," he cried.

Detective Blaine drew a deep breath and listened for a few moments. He pulled another board from his fence and leaned his head in.

"Run, you son of a bitch!" he cried. "You can run but you can't hide! Not from us! Not from the LAPD!"

Detective Blaine felt the pain from his broken nose and wiped some of the blood from his face.

"God damn it!" cried Detective Blaine again and made his way slowly back into the house.

He caught a glimpse of himself in the glass pane of his kitchen door and saw his swollen nose and face.

"Son of a bitch," said Detective Blaine aloud and turned towards the alleyway. "I should have hit you harder, you limey bastard!"

He sat back down at his kitchen table and tried to crack his nose back into place with his right hand but only made it worse.

"Son of a bitch!" he said again. "Son of a bitch!"

Detective Blaine picked up his phone and dialed Patrick's number.

Suddenly he heard a voice from behind him.

"Hello again, Bucko," the voice said.

Detective Blaine dropped the phone, quickly reached for his handgun and turned to fire. Terrence, also bloodied and covered in mud, stood behind him with a long sabre in his hands. Terrence stepped forward and stuck the sabre deep into Detective Blaine's chest, stopping him in mid-turn but he managed to fire off one round, missing Terrence's head by mere inches and slamming into the wall.

"You lose, Blaine," said Terrence.

Terrence leaned harder into the blade until it came out on the opposite side of Detective Blaine's body.

"How does that feel, eh?" asked Terrence. "This beauty is my special light cavalry sabre, mate. Designed by John Le Marchant and made back in 1796. A very expensive gift from an old friend. I use it a lot. It's also the tool I'm going to use to cut you up! Just like I said I would. Compliments of Rachel Stone Barbieri, Detective Blaine of the LAPD."

Detective Blaine struggled to speak and tried to breathe but his body refused to respond. He rolled his eyes back and his body slumped out of his chair and down onto the floor.

Terrence removed the sword and stared wide eyed down at Detective Blaine's dead body. Terrence raised the sabre above his head and started chopping up the body with several swings of the weapon. He suddenly stopped mid-swing as he heard Patrick's voice coming from the dropped phone.

"Blaine?" Patrick asked. "Are you there? Blaine? Pick up!"

Terrence picked up the phone and put it to his ear.

"Detective Blaine will not be taking any more phone calls," said Terrence.

Terrence dropped the phone, grabbed his knife and gun, and walked out the back door.

"Who is this?" asked Patrick yelling through the phone. "Blaine? Are you there? Talk to me! Blaine!"

Detective Blaine's blood slowly trickled down, covering the phone in red as it lay on the floor.

Outside, the sound of Terrence starting his car and slowly driving away echoed across the flooded back yard.

Police car sirens blared off in the distance.

Thunder boomed as the rain fell harder and harder.

CHAPTER SIXTEEN

The clouds seemed to be all locked in with no sign of escape in the California sky over Los Angeles and the steady rain had become non-stop for two more days. Mud slides and major flooding in the streets were the topics in all of the newspapers and the local television news channel, KTLA.

The untimely death of Detective Blaine was not.

His demise never even got a mention in the obituary columns. Any words in relation to the death of our friend was purposely being suppressed.

After one more day the rain finally stopped and Detective Blaine was quietly laid to rest next to his old partner, Detective Munoz. The entire funeral was done quickly and quietly. The Chief of Detectives, who also happened to be my LAPD liaison officer, Captain Don Gibbons, felt that Detective Blaine's manner of death would only panic the good people of his city if they knew some deranged person was in their midst, cutting up policemen with some type of long sword.

Agent Edwards and I totally disagreed with Captain Gibbons' decision and we let him know our feelings in no uncertain terms.

Captain Gibbons was not pleased and he refused to back down on his decision.

The good Captain did assure us the LAPD would do everything in their power to find this man and bring him to justice.

"This happened to one of our own in our city and we are going to keep a tight lid on this. We'll run this entire case as we see fit without outside interference from any federal government agency including the FBI," Captain Gibbons announced and politely dismissed us from his office.

Agent Edwards and I were devastated.

Our good friend was murdered and instead of a big funeral and an even bigger follow up news story about Detective Blaine's years with the police force and all he had accomplished, he was being treated like some unknown vagabond and given a small three sentence paragraph in the obituary page.

We were not pleased.

We were angry.

We wanted the public to know, and we wanted the press and the entire LAPD to get involved in assisting us in capturing this maniac.

Detective John Franklin and his new partner, Detective Don Budd, were assigned to the murder case. In spite of Captain Gibbons' orders to keep the FBI out of the case, we were told they would keep us in the loop as their investigation proceeded.

Our much needed extra protection provided by the LAPD for the people closest to us was suddenly dropped. Agent Edwards and I began to wonder whose side they were on and who it was that would even give an order like this?

We decided to bite our tongues, concentrate on the matters at hand, and not pursue the answer to that question until sometime far off in the future.

First things first was our priority.

I decided to hire some men on my own to keep our friends protected.

Agent Lindman and Special Agent Davis arrived in time for the funeral and joined Special Agent Edwards and myself along with Phil, Barney, Betty, and Jake. We all stood silently holding umbrellas as a light rain drizzled down on us and our murdered friend's coffin and we said our goodbyes.

Leaving the service with thoughts of the late Detective Munoz, I was surprised to see Mrs. Sara Munoz waiting for me by the back end of my Ford coupe. Phil and I approached her and with an angry look she stepped up to me and slapped me hard across my face.

"You promised me and my son, Roberto, you would stop this evil woman and now look at the results. Another good detective lies dead in the ground," she said. "A good man on the right side of the law! You and your federal agent friends are losing this war, Patrick Atwater."

"A battle, yes. Several battles in this war, Mrs. Munoz. And you are right. This woman does have our backs up against the wall right now. She does. But let me tell you this. In spite of all our current losses, we will prevail. That is my new promise to you and to Roberto. We will not stop and we will not rest until this war is won and she is stopped forever."

She reached out and tenderly touched my cheek.

"I am praying your words ring true, Mr. Atwater," she said. "For my husband, myself, my son, and now for Detective Blaine."

Mrs. Munoz nodded to Agent Edwards and walked to her car with her son Roberto sitting at the wheel.

"Who is that?" asked Phil as Mrs. Munoz and Roberto drove away.

"Sara Munoz," I replied. "Her late husband was Detective Munoz. He was shot and killed by Rachel Stone Barbieri when we were in Aruba attempting to arrest her. He was Detective Blaine's partner. The LAPD called them Holmes and Watson."

Everyone said their goodbyes while Phil and I decided to take the remainder of the day off and start fresh the next morning.

We got into my coupe and drove to an indoor shooting range in the valley. I wanted to be sure that Phil knew how to handle a weapon if the situation arose I told her what we were up against and how imperative it was now to be on the lookout for everything and anything.

Barney, Jake, and Betty were warned also.

"I'll be careful," Phil promised me.

I hoped she was right.

Phil was dead on right when she said she could shoot. Her scores were slightly better than mine and she promised not to tease me about it. We drove back to the office and I set a meeting with Agent Davis and Agent Lindman for the very next day.

Agent Edwards had to leave for his meeting with the Israelis.

I gave Phil the photo of Joanne taken by Agent Gregory, had a buzzer lock installed on the office entrance door, to the office, and gave her a walkie-talkie. I told Phil if she saw this Joanne or anyone appearing suspicious she should radio down to the private body guard I hired. He was a retired cop named Richard Barkley and a good man with a gun. He knew how to keep a watchful eye and at the same time not draw attention to himself. Barkley also had a brother-in-law named Monty Crow, also a retiree from the LAPD, and I placed him at my old booth number eight at Barney's By the Sea.

I didn't feel I was doing enough to protect the people close to me but it was all we could manage at the moment and I knew I had to live with that and hope it was enough.

Time would tell.

Special Agent Davis and Agent Lindman arrived in separate cars at the office precisely at nine the following morning. The first rays of sunshine burst through the clouds as the incessant rain had finally stopped. Agent Davis' face still wore the bruising from her encounter with Joanne but in spite of everything was in good spirits and eager to get to work. Agent Lindman lent a hand, carrying a box of photos given to Agent Davis by Agent Edwards the night before.

Phil had made a pot of fresh coffee and bought extra donuts, knowing our meeting would likely run late into the night.

She buzzed them inside.

"Good morning," Phil said. "Patrick's in his office waiting for you. Grab yourselves some donuts and I'll bring in some coffee."

"Thanks, Phil," said Agent Davis.

"I take mine black," said Agent Lindman.

"Me too," said Agent Davis.

I sat at my desk as we ate donuts and drank our coffee and then got down to business.

"Where did you want to start?" asked Agent Lindman.

"I wanted Van Nuys PD to do tire impressions on this killer's car but the rain washed all that away." I began. "We only have one slight lead on this guy."

"What's that?" asked Agent Davis.

"Just before Detective Blaine was killed he called me but before he could speak he dropped the phone as he was being murdered."

"You heard the entire attack?" asked Agent Lindman.

"Yes," I said. "As far as I could tell, the killer had an Irish accent. He called Detective Blaine by name and he also called him Bucko. He spoke about the weapon he used. It was some expensive sabre made just before the nineteenth century. Very old and very expensive."

"What else did the bastard say?" asked Agent Davis.

"He told Detective Blaine he lost. And then he said he was going to use the sabre to cut him up into little pieces, and then he proceeded to do so. Before he began he also told Detective Blaine it was compliments of Rachel Stone Barbieri."

Both Agent Davis and Agent Lindman gasped and sat silently for a few moments.

"Holy shit! This guy sounds demented," said Agent Lindman.

"He's demented alright," I said. "Which is why I asked you to bring these photos this morning."

I picked up the box, opened it, and dumped the four hundred some photos on the desk.

"These are all photos of the late Jonas Stone and his illustrious illegal career as the most successful man in global real estate."

"What are these photos going to tell us?" asked Agent Davis as she sipped her coffee.

"I think we should begin by looking into Magenta's father's life and career," I said.

"What's a dead man going to tell us?" asked Agent Lindman.

"Plenty if my hunch is right," I replied.

"How so?" asked Agent Davis.

"I think our killer might have done some similar work for Magenta's father back in the day. You can't run their kind of operation without making enemies or having to make certain people disappear and disappear in a way that doesn't point back to them. They say there's no honor amongst thieves but this family demands loyalty from the people they work with. This guy might just have been around for years. These old Stone family photographs you brought might show us who we're searching for. I know it's a stretch but if not these, the man is a ghost and we'll have to wait until he strikes again. I do not want that to be our only option."

In the morning light, I noticed the extent of Agent Davis' bruising in the morning light and she saw me staring.

"Are you in any pain?" I asked.

"Every day, all day," she responded. "The doctor told me it's going to take about six weeks before I feel like a human again."

"I can relate," I said and turned to Agent Lindman.

"And how is that knife wound of yours?" I asked.

"Healing nicely," he said.

"Did you glean anything of importance from that woman Jojo?"

"Other than how pretty Rachel's eyes are and how she sounds when she makes love? No. Liz and the other girls are itching to have you call them and let them go to war for us though."

"We just might need them," I added. "For now? Let's get to work. Shall we?"

The two agents and I began looking through the photographs.

There were over four hundred photos outlining Jonas Stone's life and career as one of the richest men of his day.

"If the son of a bitch is in here we will find him," said Agent Lindman.

We all knew this man was relentless and we agreed we wouldn't stop seeking him until we had him in custody.

Or in the morgue.

As night fell, Phil went home and we had Chinese food delivered. By ten o'clock there was nothing more we could do except try to plan our next move.

I stretched out on the office couch a little after one a.m. Agent Lindman kept watch on the front entrance while Agent Davis kept looking through the photographs. When they both began getting tired they took turns sleeping and keeping watch every two hours until the sun came up.

I made a fresh pot of coffee and Phil arrived a little after seven a.m. with ham and egg sandwiches and two dozen more donuts.

We decided to sift through the family photographs for a fifth time.

"Did you get any sleep?" I asked.

"I got enough," Agent Davis replied. "Let's keep looking."

About twenty minutes went by and Phil suddenly held up a photo of Jonas Stone and his wife on holiday in Spain dated 1938.

"I think I got him!" she shouted, spilling her coffee. "I mean I'm pretty sure this might be our guy."

While Phil grabbed a towel and wiped up the spilled coffee, I took the photo and stared at it closely.

"What makes you think this is our guy, Phil?" I asked.

Phil took the photo back and looked at it closer.

"Not the guys in the front of the shot. Look at the guy staring at the wall behind them," she said and handed it back to me.

Agent Davis glanced over at the photo.

"I remember seeing that photo," she said. "Jonas Stone with some Nazi higher up. Just before the war."

"Yes, I remember that one too," said Agent Lindman. "I think I do. I do. The wife is in the picture, too. Right?"

"Right," I agreed.

The photo showed Jonas Stone and his wife at one of their many socialite parties, dressed to the nines and sipping champagne with some Nazi uniformed German diplomat named Kyle Echardt. Two men standing in the background were listed as Stone's business associates. On the back of the photo were their written names.

Daniel Watson and Terrence Bruce.

"Do you see it?" Phil asked. "He's looking at it like it's Jane Russell in her underwear."

Agent Davis took the photo and stared at it.

"Holy shit! I completely did not see that at all. This guy definitely has that look on his face but that's not Jane Russell. Not by a mile."

"No, it's not," said Phil.

"It's a god damn sabre," said Agent Davis. "Hanging on the wall."

She studied the photo of Jonas Stone, his wife, and the Nazi diplomat, with two men in suits in the background.

One of them was looking up at a sabre hanging on the wall.

Agent Davis handed the photo to Agent Lindman, who looked at it closely.

"But is this the sabre?" asked Agent Lindman. "The same one that killed Blaine and Correlli and his partner? And is this Dan Watson or is it Terrence Bruce?"

"I'll call this in to FBI forensics and see what we can find out," I said. "Good eyes, Phil."

"Thanks," replied Phil.

"I'm sorry we didn't see it the first go round," said Agent Davis.

"That's because you people don't get your proper rest," said Phil. "And you don't eat proper meals either. Don't they teach you that stuff at the academy?"

"That's not important right now," I added. "If this is our guy then we now have both of our killers identified! That's the important thing. We got a name to a face. Phil?"

"I know," she said. "I'll get forensics on the horn."

"Thank you," I said.

Phil got up and went to her desk.

We all smiled excitedly at each other and sipped our coffees.

"I think we got our guy," I said.

Agent Davis and Agent Lindman nodded their agreement.

"Line two," Phil called from the other room.

I stared at the photo and picked up the phone.

CHAPTER SEVENTEEN

The Mexican courier, Alejandro Madrid, arrived at the large cast iron hacienda gate sixteen minutes after four p.m. He was over an hour late for his afternoon appointment but he knew his tardiness would be easily forgiven.

The people he met and dealt with on a weekly basis were always of a forgiving nature. They were always eager to please him, to make him as comfortable as possible, and would even bestow multiple favors on his behalf to assure he was always well cared for.

They always cared for Madrid and Madrid always took what was offered.

Alejandro Madrid was a political gate keeper.

He was the middle man, operating daily between big illegal money makers and even bigger men with political power. Secret deals were made and Alejandro Madrid was the secret voice between those deals.

Madrid, a thin bald-headed man of fifty-three dressed in a dark blue three-piece suit and tie, sported a pencil-thin moustache, and wore round rimmed glasses. Madrid had worked as a private courier for Mexican President Muchado for over twenty years but at this particular destination today he had been instructed to speak only English and to do everything that was asked of him with kindness and respect.

He sensed that this client was different than the rest and he was correct in his thinking.

Madrid sat in the back of the black Packard acting as if he was Mexican royalty visiting some European princess.

His years of loyal service to President Muchado made the special courier untouchable by every black market entrepreneur seeking the president's favor.

And there were many black market entrepreneurs operating in Mexico.

Some had been there for years.

This American woman was brand-new and clearly different from the rest because she had amassed immense wealth during her relatively young life and had now become the number one most powerful distributor in the newly organized drug trade.

Madrid knew he had nothing to fear from her.

The American woman needed Muchado's compliance and protection and she was willing to pay handsomely for their agreement as everyone else doing their business in Mexico had always done.

As long as you kept your agreements and made your payments, your business could thrive in Mexico. That was the rule happily extended from the government.

The word was if you could pay, you could stay.

This woman's business paid more than the rest.

Much more.

210

The woman's new compound was impressive by any standard and Madrid could tell upon arrival, seeing the thick steel gate guarding the entrance, that this was not the kind of woman to place demands on.

He was, after all, the eyes of the powers that be in Mexico and would make an accurate report to his President on every pro and con he encountered during this visit.

He knew there would be no extra perks at this hacienda. Not the kind of perks he had become accustomed to over the years with other black market entrepreneurs.

No sexual favors given here. Not from this woman.

This woman had more powerful friends around the globe than President Muchado could ever imagine. But President Muchado ran an entire country, and ran it with a strong hand. As long as payments were made, President Muchado agreed to give her the space she required to run her enterprise without fear of any repercussions from his camp.

At least not at the onset of their agreement.

There was, however, one small problem and Madrid kept thinking on how he should approach the subject with her. The black Packard's engine idled quietly as the tall armed guard stepped from his station house and motioned the young driver at the wheel, Bernardo, to roll down the car window.

"Mister Alejandro Madrid," Bernardo announced. "To see Mrs. Barbieri."

The guard looked in the back seat and Madrid nodded politely to him.

"You're very late, sir," said the guard. "I don't know if she is seeing any guests at this time."

"Totally my fault," said Madrid. "Please convey my humblest apologies to Senora Barbieri. We had a tire go flat about ten miles back. Bernardo? Show the man."

Bernardo smiled and nodded his agreement to the guard's face and held out his dirtied hands from changing the tire.

"I will tell her you have arrived," said the guard.

"Thank you, young man," said Madrid graciously.

The guard went back into his station and picked up the phone. A few moments passed and the guard stepped out as the gate slowly opened. The guard nodded, waved the car through, and Bernardo drove the Packard onto the grounds.

The driveway was long, curved slightly, and rambled up a small hill. Madrid began counting how many guards were actually present. These were little facts he knew would be written into his report. The main house was completely hidden behind a small forest of trees.

Madrid was impressed.

The Packard pulled up and another armed guard quickly opened the back door and stood at attention as if some Mexican General was about to step out.

Madrid slid out with an empty leather bag in his hand and walked up the eight steps to the front doors. Two more armed guards stood at the double doors. One guard opened the door and motioned Madrid to go inside.

Madrid nodded calmly and entered the house.

The double doors led into a fair sized entrance room with floor-to-ceiling windows on the left and right sides and several potted plants on either side. A stone wall directly in front of Madrid with a metal railing above the wall led to some open spaced area. A tall handsome black man dressed in an expensive black suit and tie looked down at Madrid from the railing above.

"Mister Madrid," he said. "Allow me to welcome you to Cozumel. I am Thomas."

"Gracias, Thomas," Madrid replied and quickly corrected himself. "I mean, thank you."

Thomas pushed a button on the railing and the stone wall in front of him suddenly parted like the Red Sea. A beautiful young Mexican woman in a black and white maid's outfit motioned Madrid inside from where she stood.

Madrid walked passed the stone wall and entered a large sun filled foyer with stairs going up both sides of the room, which led to a tiled veranda overlooking the Gulf of Mexico.

Rachel Stone Barbieri, dressed in a pale yellow pants suit, sat at a small white table with three leather chairs, sipping a large cold margarita.

Madrid and the maid walked up to Rachel.

"Mrs. Barbieri," said Madrid and clicked his heels and bowed slightly. "My apologies for my tardiness."

Rachel stood up and extended her hand.

"Apology accepted and hello Mr. Madrid," replied Rachel as they both shook hands and traded smiles. "I was told of your troubles with your car's tire."

"Travel has its displeasures at times," he said and counted another five armed guards off in the distance.

"Please be so kind to give your leather bag to my maid, Teresa. She will return it to you shortly. I promise. Would you like a cocktail? I am drinking a margarita."

"A margarita, yes, thank you," he said. "It has been a long drive."

As Rachel gestured to Thomas, Madrid was amazed at how attractive Barbieri appeared and tried very hard not to stare at her body.

"Please. Sit," she said and she and Madrid sat down across from each other.

Rachel stared at Madrid without saying a word. She leaned in and casually sipped her drink. Madrid shifted in his chair and waited for her to speak first. He noticed several pleasure boats down at her newly constructed dock with six more armed guards standing watch.

Rachel suddenly closed her eyes, leaned her head back, and took a deep breath.

Madrid took in the outline of her firm breasts, her long legs and flat stomach, and noticed his mouth suddenly watering like one of Pavlov's dogs.

Rachel opened her eyes and smiled at him.

"I love it here. I have found this country of yours to be extremely relaxing. Would you agree?"

"Yes," he quickly replied not knowing how to read what was really going on behind her beautiful face or what feminine charms were hidden beneath the outfit she was wearing.

Thomas brought Madrid his drink and placed it down in front of him.

"Thank you," said Madrid.

Madrid took a big sip and nodded.

"Excellent libation, Mrs. Barbieri. Thank you," he said, and smiled at Rachel as he felt his erection beginning to rise.

"How is your president these days?" she inquired, stirring her drink.

"The president is well," he said and took another sip. "Very kind of you to ask?"

Rachel could sense something was troubling Madrid and addressed it immediately.

"Is there a problem I should know about, Mr. Madrid?" she asked.

"A problem?" he replied.

"Yes. I am sensing there is something possibly troubling you? Or maybe troubling your President?"

He was impressed with how she so easily read what was behind his eyes. He realized he was sitting with a very intelligent and beautiful woman and decided to be completely honest and truthful with her.

There was no room for any political games or gain here. He also felt there was no need to discuss his now waning erection as he proceeded with the business at hand.

His stature as the gate keeper impelled him to try and test her one last time.

"A problem?" he pretended. "No, Mrs. Barbieri. There is no problem. Let me assure you."

Madrid took another sip and Rachel laughed. He knew she was catching him trying to be coy and left it at that.

"I know when there is something sitting on a man's mind, Senor Madrid. You are enjoying your cocktail but your eyes and your thoughts are elsewhere. Speak freely. Please? Perhaps I can be of some assistance in the matter?"

Madrid pushed his drink aside and looked directly at Rachel.

"You are a beautiful woman, senora."

"Thank you," she said.

"You also have a beautiful hacienda here. Stunningly beautiful. And? President Muchado is quite content with the arrangements you have made with him. Profoundly content."

Teresa walked up to Madrid carrying his leather bag now filled with cash, and placed it next to his chair.

"Thank you," he said as Teresa smiled and walked away.

"And?" Rachel pressed. "Or should I say but?"

Madrid sighed heavily.

"Come on, Madrid. Spit it out. Spit all of it out. Please? I know this is our first meeting but let's allow ourselves to be open and honest right from the start and into our future."

"All right," he said and went right to it. "Your presence here in Cozumel has all the locals talking."

"Talking? About what? Exactly? I have no problems with the locals here. No one outside of these walls knows my real business or why I am even here."

"They know a wealthy senora lives here and there is talk you are planning to build several hotels in this area."

"Yes. We have been discussing that possibility. That is true."

"And a hospital?"

"Yes."

"And a school?"

"Yes again."

"Word of your kindness and your generosity in this particular area has echoed all the way back to Mexico City. To the President himself and all of his political allies throughout Mexico."

"I would think that would be a good thing but your face is saying just the opposite."

"It is not your development here that is a concern. No. These things will create jobs for the locals. That is all well and good. It will also bring tourists. Another good aspect. Positive."

"But?" she asked.

"Do you know the name Ix Chel?" Madrid asked.

"Ix Chel?" she asked. "No. I do not."

"Ix Chel, according to the writings of Diego Duran back in 1579, said there was supposedly a Mayan goddess who once lived here in Cozumel. Right here. Where we now sit. A very popular Mayan goddess. The Mayans even built a temple to her."

"A temple? To this Ix Chel?" she asked.

"Yes. Ix Chel is the goddess of fertility."

Rachel laughed and almost spilled her drink.

"Fertility? I can assure you Senor Madrid, I am no goddess of fertility."

"Regardless, Senora Barbieri? The locals are a very superstitious group and they are all now saying you are this Ix Chel. You have somehow transformed yourself and have come back to your roots to bring wealth and prosperity to all who live here."

Rachel laughed again.

"This is the concern I see on your face? That I have become a goddess to the people of Cozumel?"

"No," said Madrid. "Ix Chel is also not our concern. It is all being spoken in whispers but it is still being spoken. Still being believed as truth. President Muchado felt you should be made aware of this growing superstition."

Rachel laughed again.

"I will try to live up to my goddess status as long as the locals do not attempt to get too close and discover what it is I really do for a living . I have agreed to maintain a low profile here in that regard and you can assure President Muchado and his political friends all across Mexico, I intend to keep that arrangement intact. If a hotel or two and a new hospital and a school is the opinion of the locals to be some Mayan prophecy of prosperity, then I will accept that role gladly. I still don't see how a hotel or a hospital could cause any unwanted concern."

"As I said that is not the concern, Senora. The concern is the Americans. One American in particular."

Rachel's face suddenly dropped her relaxed smile and her new look became serious.

"One Federal American?" she asked knowing full well who Madrid was speaking of.

"Yes, Senora," he replied.

"J Edgar Hoover," she said. "And his little ant army of special G-men agents?"

"Yes," said Madrid. "Mr. Hoover has sent a letter and has asked President Muchado personally to turn you over to the FBI."

"Turn me over? How does Hoover even know I'm here in Mexico?" she asked. "Did Muchado tell Hoover this?"

"No, Senora! No one has said a word. I swear to you!"

"Then how does Hoover know I am here in Mexico?" she asked.

It was Madrid's turn to smile.

"He does not know. Not for certain. We have discovered that Mr. Hoover has sent out many letters such as this to other countries around the globe in his search for you. His request is in the context of if. If President Muchado learns of your presence here in Mexico, Hoover has asked the President to turn you over to him immediately."

"If?" she asked.

"Yes. If."

"And how did the President respond to this if?"

Madrid smiled again and took a sip of his drink.

"President Muchado has no intention to dishonor the agreement you both have put in place. He told Hoover he would be happy to comply to such a request if your presence was ever discovered here in Mexico."

"If?" she asked again.

217

"Yes. If. The President also told Mr. Hoover he would send out his own agents to search for you. He even put myself in charge of this intense official government search that I am now completely responsible for. I even have access to as many soldiers I may require to detain you."

"How is that intense search going?" she asked with a slight grin as she sipped her drink.

Madrid sat up and looked around for a few moments.

"Not well. There has not been one sighting of you as yet. Not one."

"How unfortunate for Mr. Hoover," she said.

"Yes," he added and raised his glass to her and smiled. "To the unfortunate."

"To the unfortunate and bravo to President Muchado," Rachel replied. "Tell your President I appreciate his full support."

"I will tell him, senora," said Madrid and sipped his drink once again.

"President Muchado's' position in this matter is most appreciated. Hoover is nothing more than a mangy American mutt who likes to bark but he will never bite me or your President as long as I remain here in Cozumel and under his radar. Please let me know if Mr. Hoover persists in this manner and then your President's difficulties will become my difficulties and then I will make certain those particular difficulties disappear. Forever."

Madrid raised his glass again.

"Saluda to you, Senora Barbieri," he said.

"Saluda," she replied, clinking her glass to his and they both drained their glasses.

Rachel stood up and smiled down at Madrid.

"Our business of the day here is now complete. Please enjoy my money. I have other urgent matters needing my attention. Thomas will escort you out."

Thomas suddenly appeared and stood by Madrid's chair. Madrid stood up slowly and shook Rachel's hand.

"My thanks to President Muchado and to meeting you, sir," she said. "I have taken the liberty of replacing all four of your tires. And your spare. Drive safely, senor."

"Thank you," Madrid replied and watched Rachel turn and walk away.

Madrid licked his lips and sighed as he watched Rachel stroll across the patio and disappear into another section of the house. Madrid noticed Thomas standing to his left.

"Mrs. Barbieri is a very beautiful woman. Would you agree?"

Thomas ignored Madrid's response and nodded Madrid towards the entrance.

"This way, sir," said Thomas.

Madrid picked up his leather bag and followed Thomas across the patio leading back to the front entrance.

As Madrid reached the front door, two quick gunshots suddenly echoed across the patio. Madrid turned slightly, wondering if the shots were part of Rachel's urgent matters she had to attend to.

Madrid took a deep breath, nodded his thanks to Thomas, and stepped outside.

Bernardo sat waiting patiently in the Packard as Madrid got into the back seat and settled himself. Bernardo turned to Madrid with an excited look in his eyes.

"We have new tires," he announced.

"So I was told," Madrid replied.

"Well?" Bernardo asked.

"Well what?" asked Madrid as he glanced down at his watch.

"Is it her?" asked Bernardo.

Madrid did not understand Bernardo's question.

"What are you talking about?"

"Her. The Senora? Is she her?"

"Is she who?" Madrid responded.

Bernardo sighed heavily.

"Ix Chel?" Bernardo asked. "Is she Ix Chel? In the flesh?"

Madrid considered Bernardo's question for a few silent moments and pictured Rachel standing naked in front of him with a smoking pistol in her hand.

"Most definitely," said Madrid. "The Senora is most definitely Ix Chel. In the flesh."

"How do you know for certain?" asked Bernardo. "Did she do something magical to prove to you she is Ix Chel?"

Madrid thought of the two gunshots he heard.

"Beyond the tires being replaced?" Madrid asked.

"Yes. Beyond the tires. Of course."

"Then no. She did nothing magical except sit and share a margarita with me."

"Did it taste magical?"

"No."

"Then how do you know for certain?" Bernardo pressed.

"I know for certain that Senora Barbieri is Ix Chel in the flesh because she is beautiful as she is wise and she can bestow upon us much, much more than we could ever dream of bestowing on her. That is how I know."

Bernardo thought about Madrid's words for a few moments.

"And all that makes her a goddess?" Bernardo questioned. "A real life goddess?"

"Yes, Bernardo," replied Madrid growing tired of Bernardo's continued questions. "That is what makes her a real goddess. Rachel Stone Barbieri is a real life goddess living here in Cozumel."

Bernardo sighed in awe.

"And is this goddess as beautiful as she is powerful?" he asked.

Once again the naked picture of Rachel Stone Barbieri crossed Madrid's mind only this time she was lying down on a large round bed beckoning him to come to her.

"Si," Madrid said. "The Senora is as beautiful as she is powerful. Now drive the car, Bernardo. It is time to go. Enough of all your questions."

"Si, senor," said Bernardo.

Bernardo grinned like a schoolboy, started the engine, and drove away.

Madrid sighed heavily, moved the leather bag closer to him, leaned his head back, and watched in his mind as Rachel Stone Barbieri made passionate love to him.

Madrid also dreamed of how he would someday destroy this arrogant American woman and take her empire for his own.

CHAPTER EIGHTEEN

Thursday afternoon came and went and still we had no word from forensics. Agent Lindman and I stayed at my apartment while Agent Davis took Phil up on her invitation to stay at her new apartment in Burbank. I made sure Phil leased the apartment using a phony name to keep her protected and the rental manager, a no nonsense woman named Heather Delice, understood our situation and supported the ruse. Phil chose to be Terry Cormick to her neighbors. Agent Davis and I also gave her pointers on how to spot anyone tailing her and several ways of losing that tail.

I wanted Phil to feel safe and hopefully protected.

I put in a 5 p.m. call to Phil and she always told me she was fine and not to worry about her.

"My bodyguard, Rick, is on the job," she would say and then give me the office run down. "We had a few calls today. Two were wrong numbers, four were sales calls, and the other five were possible clients willing to wait until you return to the office on Monday. At least that's what I told them. They're mostly divorce cases wanting to know who's cheating with who? What should I tell them if they call back on Monday wanting to speak to you?"

"Take down as much information as they'll give you and tell them I'm tied up with a big case right now but I'll get back to them as soon as I can," I said.

"Patrick, that's like saying three weeks from never. Can't you chase Magenta and still take care of some of these clients? "

"Sorry, but no. I can't. We'll just have to wait and see how this all plays out, doll."

"You be careful out there," she said.

"You do the same and keep that heater I got you, close," I added and hung up the phone.

Three more weeks had passed and we hadn't gotten a break on Magenta Dairy or her hired killers. Agent Lindman had Chinese food delivered and as we sat down to some chicken chow mein, moo goo gai pan, several egg rolls and ice cold beers. The front doorbell rang. We instantly grabbed our hand guns and I pointed mine at the front door as Agent Lindman held his gun out in front of him and opened the door.

Special Agent Loretta Davis stood in her light blue wool suit and heels and slowly raised both her hands holding a bottle of Johnnie Walker Scotch and a folder in the other.

"Don't shoot," she said. "I bring good booze and good news."

We lowered our guns and she tilted her head and stared at us through a bandage heavily taped across her nose.

"What is this?" I asked. "Trying not to be recognized?"

"I saw my new doctor today," she said. "He had to reset my nose. Nice huh? Are you going to let me in?"

I backed up and Agent Davis stepped inside.

"Nice digs, Patrick. How much do they hit you up for here?"

"I pay forty-five a month."

"Not bad. Not bad at all. Hey, Charlie. How's Patrick's couch working out for you?"

"I've been on better but I got no complaints," said Agent Lindman. "What have you got for us?"

"First off, you, my handsome compadre, need an immediate shower. Trust me. A girl knows these things. I brought us some good Scotch and the intel on this Irish bastard in love with his sword. Ooh, I smell Chinese."

Agent Davis walked to the kitchen and began making herself a plate. I grabbed a third plate and another beer from my refrigerator and we all sat down at the table and started passing around the food cartons and silverware.

"Your female shooter has had a few aliases over the years," said Agent Lindman.

"She's definitely connected to Magenta." Agent Davis said and took a swig of her beer.

"That's our theory too," I said.

"No theory," added Agent Davis. "Fact. I have a lot to share. Terrence Bruce is the man we are looking for, boys. Bruce is also connected to Magenta. Surprised, right? Here. Read."

Agent Davis handed me the file folder and I looked through it.

"As you guys know, I had a sit down with Carmine Scarola and he finally came through with a little private phone call this morning."

"He called you at Phil's?" I asked.

"No," she replied. "I called his home early this morning and used my no nonsense federal voice. I stated who I was, promised him he wasn't being taped, and it must have worked because we talked for about fifteen minutes. Carmine is not happy with our Miss, who is she again?"

"Parrish." I said. "Joanne Parrish."

"Parrish," she repeated. "Right. She was definitely brought in for the hit on Henry Long with Carmine's assistance. Of course Mr. Scarola also swore to me he only provided transportation and was only taking orders from someone higher up in his little organization."

"Did he say who?" asked Agent Lindman.

"No, and I didn't ask. We all know Magenta is pulling the strings with this and taking out people left and right who might even whisper about her operation. Carmine did give me one good lead on Joanne Parrish and I want to follow up with it starting tomorrow unless we have other pressing business to attend to? Do we?"

"Are you following this lead up alone?" I asked and handed the folder over to Agent Lindman.

"I am. Yes. Carmine's deceased nephew picked Joanne up at some cabin in Pennsylvania. I want to fly out there and see what I can find."

"And what if you find her there?" asked Agent Lindman.

"I'm hoping she is there. I will confront her, break her nose and face, arrest her and then I will notify the local authorities."

"That's your plan?" asked Agent Lindman.

"I owe her that much," said Agent Davis.

"And if she resists this plan of yours?" I asked.

"Then I'll be calling the local coroner instead. Which is really what this broad deserves and you both know it."

Agent Davis took another swig of beer and grabbed another egg roll.

"This Terrence Bruce has been a busy man with a long career," said Agent Lindman.

"A very long career," added Agent Davis.

"Arrested nine times for questioning in regards to nine murders?" asked Agent Lindman as he read over the folder.

"Nine times over a twenty seven year period," said Agent Davis. "No convictions. Not a one."

"Who had such a concise file on this guy?" I asked.

"It's one of Hoover's private files. The files he keeps of all his rich and famous suspects plotting the demise of democracy. Hoover, I discovered, has files on everyone minutely famous or rich and the people that work with them." said Agent Davis. "And with this guy, Terrence? Every time the police began looking for the usual suspects they always grabbed him up and he always walked away scot free the very next day."

"How the hell does that happen?" I asked.

"Jonas Stone's solicitor and legal fixer." said Agent Lindman and handed me back the file.

"That's correct," added Agent Davis. "Same one. A guy named Haggis. Dix Haggis. Nine times. Four different European countries and Haggis amazingly shows up the very next morning and Terrence Bruce walks. Insufficient evidence in every case. Every case. And these are only the ones he actually got arrested on. Lord knows how many others there were where he actually did the deed and got away on his own. Probably fifty or more over the years."

"Well, he is not walking this time," I said. "This guy, Terrence. Your girl, Joanne. And Magenta. They are all going down. One way or another."

"I like the sound of that," said Agent Davis.

"Me too," I said. "And I like this new look on your face. It's almost tribal."

"I can break both your noses too if you'd like?" she asked kiddingly.

We all clinked our beer bottles and drank.

Agent Davis looked over at Agent Lindman.

"So Charlie? Are you going to take that shower now or what?" asked Agent Davis as she smiled at Agent Lindman.

"I guess I should," he replied. "I am smelling a bit ripe."

"You should," she replied. "Trust me."

"How about letting me tag along with you on this trip to the cabin in Pennsylvania? If we can get Miss Joanne Parrish out in the open I would happily assist you with that all important call to the local coroner."

"Sure, Charlie," she said. "You can tag along. What do you think, Patrick?"

"I think that's a good idea. Getting out in the field is always better than sitting tight waiting for intel. I'll go keep tabs on Agent Edwards' girl and see how all my other hired hands are faring until I hear back from you both."

Agent Davis reached out and touched Agent Lindman's arm.

"I'm only going to let you tag along, Charlie if you promise me, showers every day. Agreed?"

Agent Lindman looked down at Agent Davis' hand and patted it with his own.

"Agreed," he said and smiled. "I'm impressed that you can smell anything with all that nose gear you're sporting."

"It will be off soon," she said. "Go shower and pack. My bags are already set and loaded in the trunk."

"You are itching to get at this woman?" I said. "Aren't you?"

"Yes. The sooner the better,"

Agent Davis winked at Charlie and took another swig of her beer. Charlie left the table and headed to the bathroom for his much needed shower.

I could sense a sweet connection occurring between Charlie and Agent Davis and I enjoyed their new-found camaraderie. I knew they would have each other's backs once they did meet up with Joanne Paris.

She would not be an easy arrest by any means. The woman was well trained and, like Magenta, seemed to always be one or two steps ahead of everyone and everything.

I asked Phil to set up their flight tickets to Pennsylvania for the very next available flight, and decided to take a drive out to Toluca Lake the next morning to finally see Special Agent Edwards' girl, Debs.

I got up early, hit the local Texaco, and gassed up the coupe.

"That will be two dollars, Mac," the attendant said.

I paid the kid and headed out to the valley.

CHAPTER NINETEEN

Terrence drove his black Chevrolet up the canyon road looking for 1128 Utica Drive. His hands and face were splattered with blood and there were small pieces of Detective Blaine's flesh stuck in his hair and on his coat sleeves. His pants and shoes were also covered and there was a good amount of blood covering on car floor and spotting the front seat.

Luckily, the rain and the darkness of the night brought little attention to his present appearance.

The house was a small two bedroom tan colored stucco built in the late thirties and it sat rather high up from the road. There was a small wooden one car garage in the rear and the house itself sat in the center of the street surrounded by several large shade trees. Terrence drove up the steep driveway, got out of the car, and opened the garage door. He drove the car in quickly, grabbed two bags from the trunk, and closed up the car and the garage for the remainder of the night.

Lightning flashed and thunder boomed and Terrence caught his reflection in the large rear bedroom window.

He was beginning to feel slightly dizzy from the deep gash on the side of his head, courtesy of Detective Blaine's shovel, and his appearance in the glass surprised him as to how much wet mud and blood covered his clothes. He found the key to the back door hidden under the milk box and let himself in.

The house had been recently refurbished, professionally cleaned, and was sparsely furnished with just the bare necessities. There was one double bed with a single lamp and nightstand in the first bedroom which included a radio, and the second bedroom was completely empty. The living room had a small couch, two lamps and two end tables and a small coffee table. A good sized mirror hung behind the couch, giving the room a look larger than it actually was.

Terrence walked straight to the hallway bathroom and dropped his bags just outside the door. He stripped down naked and tossed all his bloodied clothes in the far end of the bathtub.

He took a long close look at his wounded head in the bathroom mirror and realized he was clearly going to need four or five stitches. He took a fast hot shower, wrapped his wet clothes in a large towel and tossed the heap onto the bathroom closet floor.

He took his suitcases to the first bedroom and laid out some fresh clothes, but decided to stay in just his underwear and t-shirt. He fashioned a cold compress using a hand towel from the bathroom and kept it pressed to his head as he slowly explored the rest of the house. He went to the kitchen and discovered the refrigerator was completely empty. He found a working phone in the living room sitting on the end table next to the couch.

He dialed the number Rachel asked him to memorize.

A man's voice picked up on the first ring.

"Hello?" the voice said.

Terrence waited briefly before he spoke.

"This is Terrence."

"What do you need?" the voice asked.

"I need my car to disappear. It's sitting in the garage and it's a bloody mess and I mean that literally. I will need a replacement vehicle straight away with current California tags, and I will require some stitches. Now. Tonight. I also need some food for the next few weeks. Nothing fancy. Basics really. Bread, eggs, milk, tea, and some fresh cold cuts and mustard. And bring me some good Irish whiskey, and some female companionship so I can lay low for a few weeks, heal and rest myself up, and then get back out on the road to finish what I need to finish."

"I understand. Is that everything?"

"For now? Yes. If I need anything else I will call again. This house will have to be thoroughly cleaned once I'm gone. There will be a substantial amount of garbage and collateral damage that will have to be picked up and processed."

The voice hesitated to speak for a few moments.

"I understand," replied the voice.

"Excellent," said Terrence.

"Do you have a vehicle preference?" the voice asked.

"No. It just has to be roomy and run well. Nothing fancy. But make certain the woman you send is a colored girl and make it plain to her she'll be spending some quality time here with me. Once she's here I will need her to remain here."

"Yes. I understand. Hold on," the voice said and Terrence checked the compress on his head.

The compress was working well but Terrence was still bleeding from the wound.

"Bloody hell," he said aloud and placed the compress back on his head.

A few minutes went by and the voice came back on the line.

"Are you there?" the voice asked.

"I'm here. And I'm still bleeding."

"I'm sending you a girl named Seedy," the voice said. "She'll bring you a new vehicle and come in your back door. Seedy can stitch you up, she can cook and feed you, and she will give you everything else you may require from her."

"Very good. How long will I have to wait?" Terrence asked.

"She'll be at your back door in two hours. We'll come and get the other car once you're out of there and back on the road. Anything else before we end this conversation?"

"No, that will suffice," Terrence replied. "And thank you."

The line went dead and Terrence hung up the phone.

Terrence went back to the bathroom, popped four aspirins and thought he would rest for the next two hours but decided instead to do a few lines of cocaine and wait for Seedy's arrival.

He placed his hand gun on the end table, took out the green folder and started looking through the photos. He stopped once he saw Agent Edwards' picture and took out the small photo of his girlfriend, Debra. He read her address and noticed she lived in Toluca Lake. He unfolded his street map of Los Angeles and marked the location.

"You are quite close by, lassie," he said aloud. "You shouldn't be too troublesome for Terrence the Bruce."

Terrence wrote the words collateral damage above Debra's face, put the map aside, spread out some lines of cocaine, and snorted one very long one.

"Ah," he cried and leaned his head back. "Much better, yes!"

He began studying the folder page by page.

Two hours passed and Terrence had finished his eleventh line when he heard a car coming up the driveway. He closed the folder, slid it under the couch, and grabbed his handgun.

Seedy walked in the house from the back door as he was told she would. She acted as if she was some long time roommate arriving from a late evening of shopping at the grocery store. Terrence leaned forward, took a quick glance at her, and put the handgun back on the end table.

He liked what he saw and licked his lips.

The girl was in her early twenties, thin and attractive, and wore skin tight blue jeans and penny loafers and a white long sleeved button down shirt. Her hair was a series of dark curls that hung down to about the middle of her neck and she sported a welcoming smile that instantly melted Terrence's heart and aroused his aging manhood.

She carried a grocery bag in each hand, the keys to a tan Pontiac now parked in front of the garage, and a large woven multi-colored bag over her left shoulder. She put the groceries and the car keys on the kitchen counter, casually stepped into the living room, and placed her bag on the large leather easy chair.

"Hello. I'm Seedy," she announced and gave Terrence a smile and a quick glance over. "What name should I call you?"

"You can call me Bruce," said Terrence.

"All right, Bruce," she said. "Let's take a look at that head of yours."

"Did you bring the whiskey?" he asked.

"If that's what you wanted then I'm sure it's in one of those two bags that were sitting in the back seat of the car. I brought the bags in. They're on the kitchen counter. Shall I pour you some?"

"Please," he begged. "You should put the food in the fridge, too."

"All right," she said.

Seedy went back into the kitchen and Terrence heard her putting away the food, opening the whiskey bottle, and pouring him a glass. She returned quickly and handed Terrence the glass.

"Thank you, love," he said and took a big gulp.

Seedy got up close to Terrence and checked his wound. She smelled of fresh jasmine but Terrence could only detect a hint of the sweet fragrance due to all the drugs he had packed up his nose.

"How much of that stuff have you had?" she asked.

"Just a few lines," he lied.

"You are going to need at least six stitches here as far as I can tell, Bruce. I don't have anything to numb this. Are you going to be able to deal with the pain?"

"I'll deal. I'm already quite numb, thank you."

Seedy chuckled and went over to her bag.

"I can see that," she said. "The whiskey will help with your pain too."

"Just stop this bloody bleeding. Please?"

"No problem, Bruce. Are you in any pain now?"

"Nothing I can't tolerate."

"I'll have you fixed up in no time."

Seedy began prepping everything she would need to stitch up Terrence's wound. After cutting back some of his hair and cleaning the wound she took her needle and looked at Terrence.

"Are you ready?" she asked.

"I was born ready, darling."

"Not darling," she corrected him. "Not love or sweet thing. My name is Seedy. I'll call you Bruce and you call me Seedy. All right?"

"All right," he replied. "Seedy it is. Why are you called that? What kind of a name is Seedy?"

Seedy began stitching and explained.

"My real name is Catherine Denice Smythe. CD Smythe. Those two initials became my new name. Seedy. And it just stuck."

"Now that you have explained yourself, I completely understand and I like the name," said Terrence. "How long have you been doing this kind of work?"

"Four years. I was planning to be a nurse. Maybe work the night shifts at some local hospital in Westwood but the money I make doing this kind of work is ten times better than any nursing job, it's all cash, I get to meet a lot of interesting people, and it's a lot more fun than all the constant updating information you have to deal with working at some hospital. Work like this also allows me to really unwind. I get to still do some nursing duties now and again. And let my hair down. If you know what I mean?"

"I do, Seedy. I do. You have to love the work you do."

"That's it in a nutshell. Love your work. Yes. Looks like your line of work has a few drawbacks."

"It does. At times."

"How did you get this gash in your skull?" she asked.

"A little altercation with a gentleman and his shovel that escalated rather quickly. I received this blow in the process of working out our differences."

"He hit you pretty damn hard."

"He did. Yes."

"Did you win the fight?" she asked.

"I did."

"And the other guy?" she asked. "Did you hurt him?"

"Let me just say he fared worse. A lot worse as it were."

"How are you faring? Are you okay with my stitching?"

"I'm doing fine, Seedy."

"It's pretty deep," she said.

"Are you from Los Angeles?" he asked.

"I am. I own a house in Compton."

"Do you have any children or someone special in your life?" Terrence asked.

"Nope. No kids. No boyfriend. I've been down that relationship road too many times. At the moment, Bruce, my one and only special person in my life right now is you. And only you."

"I like that," he said.

"That accent of yours tells me you're not from around here. Are you?"

"I am not. No."

"Where do you call home?" she asked.

"I live in London."

Seedy cut off her stitching and stepped back to look at her work.

"You're all set, Bruce. You can take those stitches out in about a week or so."

Terrence got up and checked the stitching in the mirror behind the couch.

"We're going to be spending some time here together, Seedy. You can remove the stitches when you feel it's time for them to come out. All right?"

"Okay," she said. Whatever you say? Whatever you want? Make sure you keep that area clean if I have to go out and get us some more whiskey or whatever."

"I will."

"Maybe you could wear a nice hat for a while."

"I don't like hats," he said

Terrence sat back down on the couch and took another swig of whiskey. He looked Seedy up and down and over and smiled.

"You are a very attractive woman, Seedy," he said.

"Do you want to eat something now or did you want to get right down to a tumble or two?"

"I could use a good shagging, Seedy, yes and then I need to get some much needed rest. We can eat some food later. Much later. Would you like some whiskey or maybe do a line or two of what I have here?"

"I don't drink alcohol."

Seedy smiled and looked down at Terrence's stash sitting on the coffee table.

"But I do enjoy a line or two, now and again."

"Wonderful!" he said and started preparing some more lines.

"That is a huge stash you have there," she said.

"It keeps me focused," he replied.

"Is that good stuff?" she asked.

"Oh yes, Seedy. This is top of the line," he said and laid out a few more lines from his stash. "It's uncut."

"Uncut?" she asked surprisingly. "I never had uncut before. Not ever."

"Then you , Seedy are in for a real treat. Enjoy."

Seedy leaned down and did two quick lines.

235

"Oh my, my! That is the top of the top of the line! If we are going to party, Bruce? Do you have any music in this place? I like music when I get down. If that's all right with you, that is?"

"Certainly. I like music. I think there's a radio in the back bedroom," said Terrence.

"I'll go grab it, Bruce and we'll get your party started."

"Excellent," he replied.

Seedy went in the bedroom and brought the radio back to the living room. She plugged it in across the room and searched for a station. She finally found a station playing "I Get Ideas" sung by Tony Martin.

Seedy stepped out of her shoes and began slowly removing her clothes. Terrence wet his lips as he watched her undress.

"Before I forget, the keys to your Pontiac are on the kitchen counter. The car is real nice and it's all gassed up. Should I make you a sandwich?"

"You can do that later, Seedy," Terrence replied. "Much later."

"Do you like Tony Martin, Bruce?" she asked and casually stepped out of her jeans.

"Not especially," he replied and ran his hand down one of her legs.

"I think his voice is very sexy. For a white guy."

Terrence slipped out of his underwear revealing his large erection.

"Do you think you can put up with me, Seedy?" he asked.

She nodded and flashed another warm smile.

"I can put up if you can keep up," she said. "You are in really good shape."

"For an old man. Is that it?"

"You don't look old to me. No sir. Not in the least."

Seedy brushed a bit of his hair back behind his ear and stroked his erection.

"Thank you, Seedy. You're very sweet."

"Thank you. Where do you want me?" she asked.

"Come and lay down right here," he said and patted the couch with his right hand.

Seedy removed her underwear, walked over to the sofa completely naked, and laid down. Her breasts were firm and her nipples had become rock hard. Her vagina was completely shaved clean as were her long smooth copper colored legs.

"Like this?" she asked and tilted her head back.

"Yes. Perfect," he said.

Terrence smiled, licked his lips, and tapped out two lines of cocaine onto Seedy's bare flat stomach. Terrence leaned down and quickly snorted both lines deeply up his nose.

"Can I try a little more of that?" she asked.

"Most certainly my sweet," said Terrence. "Excuse me. My apologies. Most certainly, Seedy."

Seedy smiled.

"Let's give this a go. Shall we?" he asked.

Terrence took a pinch from his stash and placed it neatly onto the tip of his large erection and pointed it at her face.

"There you go Seedy," he said. "Have a bit of a go at that."

"I will," she said.

She rolled her naked body closer to the edge of the sofa and snorted the drug cleanly from his manhood.

"How is that, then?" he asked.

"It's very good, Bruce," she replied. "Woah! It's more than good. Uncut is really outstanding."

"As I am also. What do you think about my little fellow here?" he asked "The one now staring you so lovingly in your eyes?"

"That is no little fellow, Bruce, as I'm sure you have been told many times," she said.

"I have. Yes. More times than I can remember. Shall we make our get together a memorable one?" he asked.

"I can do that, Bruce," she said. "I can do that."

Seedy sat up on the sofa and took him deeply into her mouth.

Terrence reached out and gently rubbed her vagina with his right hand and Seedy moaned slightly in response to his welcomed touch.

"That's very good, Seedy," he said. "Very good indeed. Just like that. Yes."

Terrence and Seedy both sat in silence for several moments enjoying each other's bodies. Terrence began to suddenly moan deeply and he arched his back and exploded wildly into her mouth.

"Oh yes, Seedy," he said in a voice no louder than a whisper. "Yes."

Terrence sat back and took several deep breaths. Seedy ran her fingers lightly across his upper thigh.

"Was that memorable enough," she asked.

"That was fine, Seedy. Most fine."

"Can we do a bit more of that powder, Bruce?" she asked and spread her legs out invitingly.

"A capital idea, Seedy," he replied and did another quick line of cocaine. "A capital idea."

Terrence set up another line and looked at Seedy. She smiled up at him, leaned over, and snorted the entire line.

Seedy and Terrence spent the next three weeks having sex over and over, stopping every now and then only to do more lines or make something to eat. They did this day and night until Terrence's private stash of cocaine, several bottles of Irish whiskey, and every morsel of food were almost completely gone. Spent and tired, they would wind up going to the back bedroom, sleeping in each other's arms until the morning sun lifted their long nights into even longer days.

Terrence became totally enamored with Seedy and although she was enjoying herself with this total stranger as she was told to do, there was something about him that struck her as being a bit off.

A bit odd.

Strange.

It wasn't that he was older. Or had an Irish accent. Or wasn't an American. Or wasn't an excellent lover.

It was his silent behavior that made her shudder.

The first night they lay together in bed she asked him what kind of work he did. He just smiled at her and said it was not to be a topic of conversation. They talked about history and politics and music but as the days became weeks she began to sense him distancing himself from her more and more when it came to having an actual conversation.

In the three weeks she was there he made no phone calls. Not a one. He received no phone calls and had no visitors. And even after Seedy removed his stitches he refused to go outside for a walk, bask in the California sunshine, or take her to an early movie in town.

Seedy began to feel there was an unspoken danger about this man, as if he might be hiding from someone.

Or worse.

Her experience with her "Johns" as they were called, usually lasted an hour or two and sometimes a long weekend. Bruce was different than most. His sexual appetite was insatiable and she had never spent this much time with any "John."

Not like this.

There was something in his eyes whenever he looked at her. She always managed to smile and hide her true thoughts and feelings about him but she was beginning to feel extremely anxious and wasn't sure why. She thought it just might be the drugs making her feel this paranoid around Bruce but there was real distance in his eyes that she couldn't quite explain or put her finger on.

Seedy felt this fear of Bruce growing stronger every day and didn't know what to do about it until one morning after an exceptionally long night of love-making she got the answer she was seeking.

Seedy was the first to rise and went straight to the bathroom and plopped herself down on the toilet to pee. The cool tiles of the bathroom floor felt good on the soles of her bare feet. She flushed the toilet and as she washed her hands at the sink she looked at herself in the mirror.

"You are a sight for sore eyes, party girl, and you better start wearing hats this early in the morning before you go scaring people," she said to herself aloud as she tried to fluff out her matted hair.

She decided to take a quick shower but caught an odor of something foul and opened the small closet door next to the tub. Seedy held her breath in horror when she saw Terrence's clothes lying on the floor in a heap all wrinkled, crumpled, still damp and covered in dried blood.

She stared down at the clothes and a sudden fear shot through her body wondering what this man, Bruce, was really all about, and what kind of person did you have to be to get your clothes looking the way these did. This amount of blood was not from some deep cut on his head. There was blood and also small pieces of human flesh rotting on the closet floor.

She backed up slowly from the closet and caught a glimpse of herself in the bathroom mirror, jumping as if someone else had just entered the room. Her breathing became accelerated and her hands started to sweat. She dropped to her knees in front of the toilet bowl and began to dry heave until what little was in her stomach burst from her throat and into the bowl.

She stood up quickly and washed her face with warm water and rinsed out her mouth.

Seedy crept back into the living room trying to be as quiet as she could. As she bent down to retrieve her underwear, she noticed a green folder lying under the couch. She reached down, took the folder, placed it on the couch, and opened it up.

She saw the photos.

She read the names.

She read all the addresses with notes on who was known to be a friend, a close relative living nearby. Terrence had written small notations on Agent Correlli and Detective Blaine's photos. Deceased is what he had written along with the date and time. She saw his note above Debra's face.

Collateral damage.

Seedy realized she had been spending all this time with a hired killer.

A high-end pro.

Highly organized and extremely well connected.

She had heard stories of this type of particular gun for hire.

Seedy knew that these kind of pros do not like witnesses.

Any witnesses.

Ever.

She closed the folder, quickly gathered up her large bag, her shoes, and all her clothes and although she was still buck naked, went out the back door quietly and started walking quickly down the driveway.

Fortunately for Seedy the street was quiet except for some morning chirping of birds and a lone dog's barking coming from somewhere further up the hill.

Seedy ducked behind some bushes and in spite of her hands shaking furiously managed to get her shoes and clothes on and thought about goings back to steal the car keys. She quickly changed her mind and began walking swiftly down the hill into Hollywood looking back every now and then to see if she was being followed.

Seedy knew she was breaking the underground code of rules by leaving this man she was hired to be with, but Bruce wasn't your average man on the run or some easy trick simply looking for a good time party girl.

This man was that different breed.

Much different.

She probably would never be called to work the underground circuit again and told herself she would change her phone number when she got back to the little house her late mother left her and start looking for other employment the first thing tomorrow morning. She had but one calming thought rolling through her brain over and over again.

Especially after seeing those bloodied clothes and smelling the rotting flesh.

The thought pushed her forward down the hill faster and faster.

One step and then another. Over and over again.

She was alive and she was going to stay that way for as long as she could and never go back to this way of life or deal with people like Bruce ever again. She looked back over her shoulder several more times until she finally left the neighborhood and reached the main road that ran up the hill from Hollywood.

CHAPTER TWENTY

It was just after nine in the morning as I headed up Laurel Canyon Boulevard on my way to meet Debra Serrano. I promised Agent Edwards I would do everything in my power to stay in touch with her and keep her as safe as I possibly could. Phil dropped Agent Davis and Charlie at the airport for their flight to Pennsylvania, I grabbed a quick coffee to go, and headed up the hill.

It felt good to be back on my home turf once again in spite of all the threat and death being thrown at us by Magenta Dairy. The gods were on our side now and I was going to do whatever it took to keep the gods on our team and guide us to our final outcome.

I had to suddenly jam on my brakes as I approached the first stop light in the canyon. The light was green and in my favor but a tall young colored girl in jeans and a white blouse ran against the light to cross the

242

street to the little convenience store and if I hadn't swerved to the left, I would have hit her for sure.

My coffee flew to the passenger side door and the entire contents covered the floor.

The young girl put up her hand to me as her "I'm sorry" apology and I just shook my head at her and took a deep breath, thanking my lucky stars there were no other cars coming my way from any direction. The girl appeared rattled, as though she was dealing with some unfortunate circumstance in her life and the last thing she needed was yours truly stepping out of my car and reading her the riot act about the benefits of road safety. I turned my wheel, continued up the hill, but kept observing the troubled girl in my rearview mirror.

I could see she realized the store wasn't open yet and she continued to move swiftly down the hill.

I thought to turn my car around and offer her a lift but figured she might think I had other plans after stepping out in front of me the way she did. I took another deep breath, put the troubled girl out of my mind and headed to Toluca Lake.

I wondered if Debra Serrano knew how lucky she was to be living in the first bedroom community of Los Angeles, as Toluca Lake was known, and surrounded by some of Hollywood's most celebrated entertainers. People like Hope and Crosby called Toluca Lake their home as well as WC Fields, Bette Davis, Richard Arlen, and America's number one female aviator Amelia Earhart, until her untimely mysterious disappearance back in 1937.

I had never heard of Debra's landlord, the producer Val Newton, but figured he must be making decent money in the film industry to afford a house with a guest house in Toluca Lake. I hoped I could make his acquaintance at the same time meeting with the woman that now owned Special Agent Edward's heart.

I arrived at the house which sat back about fifty feet from the street. A gray four-door Cadillac was parked in front of the two car garage and I decided to pull into the red bricked driveway and park alongside it. The house was an all-white Spanish style one story with a red tiled roof, a well-manicured lawn, and looked like it was built in the twenties. I stepped out of the coupe and heard music coming from the back yard. The music was slow and mellow sounding and I guessed it to be some piece by Mozart or Beethoven but I wasn't really sure.

I walked around the back and saw the small guest house sitting adjacent to the swimming pool. It had a red wooden front door and half of the building was covered in green ivy. Under the large wooden patio covering, I saw a man sitting on one of the five lounge chairs, making notes on a legal pad. He was a stocky man wearing shorts and a light pink polo shirt. He had brown curly hair and thick hairy arms and my arrival didn't seem to bother him in the least.

"Are you Atwater?" he asked.

"I am," I replied and walked up and offered my hand.

"I'm Val Newton," he said. "You're here to see Debra?"

"Yes," I said.

"She just ran out to the store to get a few things and told me she'd be right back. Would you like a cup of coffee?"

"Sure."

I noticed an electric coffee pot sitting on the small bar behind him.

"Help yourself," he offered and went back to his pad.

I poured myself a cup of joe and noticed several small bottles of prescription medicine setting next to his chair with a tall glass and a half-empty pitcher of water.

"Come and sit," he said.

I sat in the chair next to his and noticed a paleness to his face and skin. This was not a well man. He addressed his condition straight away.

"I had a heart attack several months back and now I'm dealing with god damn gall stones. I look like shit and I feel like shit."

He grabbed a cigarette from his shorts pocket and lit it up with a gold lighter.

"My doctor told me to quit these things but it's not the cigarettes that are killing me. It's this god damn movie business."

244

You're a producer, right?" I asked.

"I was a few years back. Did a couple of films with Karloff that were mildly successful. Bedlam, The Body Snatchers. My big claim to fame was Cat People."

"I saw that picture. I liked it."

"Thank you. These days I'm a producer's assistant. I'm working on a new film at Columbia called My Six Convicts. Stanley Kramer is producing. Written by Donald Powell Wilson. The storyline is supposed to be based on fact but I'm sure Kramer will change that all around. Nothing's sacred in this town except box office profits. I heard you did some work for Quentin Thayer?"

"I did."

"A real shame what happened to him. All those women coming and going you just knew one day he'd find one that was a bit off the mark. A nice man. A good actor."

"Yes he was," I added.

It was obvious Mr. Newton had bought the phony story printed in the papers of Quentin's demise and I for one was not about to enlighten him on what had really happened.

I took another gulp of my coffee and heard a car pull up the drive.

"That's probably Debra now," said Newton and took another drag on his cigarette before putting it out in the ash tray.

A few moments went by but Debra did not come in the back where we were sitting.

"That's odd," said Newton and his front doorbell rang.

"Would you like me to answer that door for you?" I asked.

"I'll get it. It's probably someone from the studio with more script changes."

Newton got up and walked inside. I took another sip of my coffee and glanced over at the screenplay sitting on his chair. I was about to pick it up and read the first page when I heard Newton arguing with someone. I couldn't make out what they were saying but I could tell the conversation was becoming more and more heated. I stood up and looked through the patio French doors and saw a tall older man suddenly grab Newton by the throat and push him against the wall of his foyer.

I opened the doors and rushed into the house.

The older man was choking Newton with his left hand as he pressed him hard against the wall. Newton flailed at the man with his arms but couldn't break the hold he had him in.

"Hey!" I yelled, taking the man totally by surprise just slightly enough to loosen the hold he had on Newton's throat. Newton pushed his weight forward and grabbed the man with both arms and pushed him against the front door frame.

It was in that moment I realized the man I was looking at was Terrence Bruce.

I rushed towards them but Terrence quickly pushed Newton into me and ran out the front door.

"Are you all right?" I asked Newton.

Newton tried to speak and suddenly grabbed at his chest. His eyes widened and his knees buckled and his body slowly dropped to the floor. I reached out and laid him gently onto the carpeted floor as Bruce ran to his car. I stood up and took a quick glance out the window and saw a tan Pontiac try to pass by a dark blue Chevy coming up the drive. I caught the first few numbers of the license plate, 1F47, as the Pontiac scraped its rear left fender with the Chevy's and then sped away.

"I can't breathe," said Newton. "I can't breathe!"

"Hold on," I said. "I'll get you some help!"

Debra walked in the opened front door.

"Who was that maniac in the driveway? He scraped my car and just drove away!" she said and saw Newton and me laying on the floor. "Oh my god!"

"Call an ambulance," I said. "I think it's his heart."

Several minutes turned into several hours as Debra and I sat in the waiting room at Cedars Sinai Hospital awaiting word on Newton's condition. Boris Karloff and Stanley Kramer both arrived within minutes of each other and were speaking with the floor nurse as the doctor on call, a tall white haired gentleman, Dr. Barry Polster, walked up to Debra.

"I'm sorry, Miss Serrano, but Mr. Newton expired a few moments ago."

"Died?" she asked. "He was only forty-six?"

Doctor Polster put his hand on Debra's shoulder.

"He was not a well man. This episode was his third heart attack in these past few months and unfortunately the damage was beyond repair. I am very sorry for your loss. I understand Mr. Lawton was a cousin of yours?"

"Yes," said Debra. "My mother's cousin actually."

"Nurse Marsh will have some papers for you to sign and a few standard questions if you are up to doing that at this time?"

"Yes. Of course," she said.

Doctor Polster nodded with a reassuring smile, turned, and walked away.

Karloff walked up to Debra.

"My sincerest condolences, young lady," he said. "Val was a good man and a close friend of mine. He will be sorely missed."

"Thank you," said Debra.

Karloff looked at me and extended his hand.

"Are you a family friend?" he asked.

"A friend of Debra's," I replied.

"Boris Karloff," he said.

"Patrick Atwater," I responded.

Karloff gave me a quick hand shake, a solemn nod, and left the hospital. The young producer Stanley Kramer also gave his condolences and told Debra the studio would be paying all the funeral expenses. The police had been called in and I gave a brief statement to the local investigating detective, a balding Italian man, Detective Mike Muto. I told Detective Muto about the tan Pontiac arriving at the house, the scraped fender, and a loose description of the man Newton tangled with but I held back the intel on the license numbers I had seen and the fact that I knew the bastard's name and who he was working for.

Our team was going to track down and arrest Terrence Bruce.

It was not going to be some random detective from the LAPD who just happened to be on call the day Terrence Bruce decided to pay Debra a visit.

Not if I could help it.

"Is there anything else you can tell me, Mr. Atwater?" Detective Muto asked. "Anything at all?"

"Afraid not, pal," I said, and drove Debra back to her house.

I explained everything to Debra so she could understand the seriousness of the situation we were dealing with. I asked if she had some other relatives she could stay with until we got our hands firmly on Terrence Bruce and Joanne Parrish. She had recently quit her job at Walgreen's and was doing behind the scenes work at the studio for Newton and Kramer and making good money. She realized the possible danger she was now in and decided to go up to San Francisco and stay with her best friend, Janine Bivona, until she heard back from us.

I cleared her sudden absence with Kramer and his production company and also got permission from Debra to place someone in Val Newton's house in case this man Bruce returned to Toluca Lake to finish whatever it was he had in mind.

I could see the fear now settling in Debra's eyes.

Debra never realized what Agent Edwards and the FBI had to deal with on a daily basis and I could tell she was not only fearful but was becoming worried for his safety and for mine.

I was concerned about hers.

"I never go to funerals," Debra said. "They make me feel afraid for some reason. But after hearing what you just told me I am really feeling frightened. For myself and for everyone in this country. Who are these people? How can they be so sadistic and cruel?"

I assured her we had the man power to stop this threat and she seemed to calm down some. I also assured her that Agent Edwards would be getting in touch with her very soon. That made her feel a bit more at ease.

After a few more reassuring conversations, she packed and I was finally able to put her on the first bus headed north.

I decided to put myself in harm's way and stay on the grounds until Agent Davis and Agent Lindman returned from Pennsylvania.

I parked my coupe in the garage at the Toluca Lake house but purposely left the garage door open so that anyone coming up the drive would know I was here. I walked through the entire house checking out every room and locking every window and door except for the French doors leading out to the pool area. I hoped Terrence Bruce would make one more trip back to Toluca Lake.

If he did come?

Me and my .38 would be waiting for him.

And I wouldn't need any hand cuffs.

Not this time around.

I sat alone in Debra's guest house living room, in the dark, looking out at the pool and waiting. I ran several scenarios through my head trying to think of how Terrence might approach the house and how I would react in turn. I knew I would have the element of surprise in my favor and also knew the next time Terrence Bruce and I met face to face, one of us would never see another sunrise.

TWENTY ONE

The state prison guard waited patiently for the clock on the wall to strike the four o'clock a.m. hour so he could do his third and final check of all the prisoners locked up for the night in cell block nine.

Cell block nine had been his assignment for the last eleven years since becoming a prison guard and he had always worked the eleven p.m. to seven a.m. shift without one single incident. Other cell blocks had the usual daily fist fights, the occasional suicidal hanging, or a shanking of an inmate who, for whatever reason, had it coming to him.

But not in cell block nine.

Cell block nine was different from all the rest.

Completely different as far as a regular prison was structured.

Inmates learned upon arrival that if you were lucky enough to be placed into cell block Nine, then you were expected to carry yourself in a certain well-behaved manner at all times and without question. If you did what was asked of you and never showed any signs of resistance to any of the prison guards on duty, then your time spent at cell block nine would be something you would be talking about to your grandchildren's grandchildren in the years to come.

This was conveyed to each new inmate arriving into cell block nine by the only black prison guard in the entire New York prison system.

The prison guard's name was "Big" Harold Hoffer, a mountain of a man with strong arms, large powerful hands, kind brown eyes, and a smile as perfect and white as any man could ever wish for.

Anyone coming into the system and trying to act tough or do their time with a bad attitude towards "Big" Harold Hoffer, other guards, or other inmates, was transferred to another cell block immediately without question or any possibility of returning to cell block nine, even if they suddenly realized their mistake and changed their demeanor for the better. There were no special transfer papers written up or any requests of transfers ever noted. The prisoner who didn't abide by "Big" Harold's rules was removed immediately without question and never to return. Even if the prisoner was able to complain to the warden himself, his pleas would fall onto deaf ears.

Prisoners got one chance in cell block nine and one chance only.

Every prisoner wanted to do their time in cell block nine.

"Big" Harold owned and operated cell block nine without question and the warden, a hard task master of a man in his early fifties named Anthony Dowdell, was always one of the first to tell state officials that his prison was totally under his control. In reality, Warden Dowdell was taking heavy monthly payments from the privileged few doing their time in cell block nine.

Every prison guard knew what Dowdell's system was about and that cell block nine was "Big" Harold's domain, completely off limits to any outsiders' prying eyes or any investigations as to what may or may not be transpiring there.

The wealthiest criminals were always sent to cell clock nine first and these same criminals were highly rewarded for their monthly cash payments to "Big" Harold and to the warden with an endless supply of cigarette cartons, Havana cigars, name brand alcohol, drugs, privately cooked meals, and beautiful women willing to service their every need. Most importantly they received outside information on the status of their own criminal organizations.

The perks were the absolute best but all the perks came at a price.

Cell block nine always had the richest prisoners doing their time and for the past several months had been hosting two of the wealthiest men to ever rest heads in cell block nine.

The two men were Ponce Delgado and his right hand man, Rockwell.

The guards kiddingly called them Robinson Crusoe and his man, Friday.

Delgado paid three times the normally charged fees to guarantee his and Rockwell's safety and comfort and "Big" Harold made certain that Delgado got everything he asked for and then some.

Delgado's lawyer, one of the best criminal attorneys in the country, a man named Dix Haggis, told Delgado it would only be a matter of a few more weeks before he and Rockwell were officially released and all charges against them dropped due to the FBI making false statements and planting evidence in the state's case against him.

Rockwell did not like prison life and never trusted Delgado no matter how many times he tried to reassure Rockwell that he would be safe doing his time.

"Haggis will get us out," Delgado would say. "He can pull many strings."

Rockwell didn't trust Haggis either. He quickly made other plans, deciding to turn on Delgado and sing to the first DA who would listen and offer him a deal.

Jonathan Wainwright listened and a deal was made.

Delgado had heard about the untimely shooting death of Wainwright's star witness, Rockwell, and was now concerned for his own safety once he was released. Delgado stood in his darkened cell with his pants and underwear down by his ankles as an attractive female hooker was secreted in to service him while he waited for any additional outside word from "Big" Harold Hoffer on his release.

Delgado leaned back against his bunk and drew in a heavy breath as he suddenly climaxed into the young hooker's mouth.

"Did I do okay?" she asked.

"You did just fine," said Delgado as he pulled up his pants and sat on his bunk. "What's your name, girl?"

"I'm Marcie. Marcie Rubin."

"Marcie Rubin?" he repeated. "What kind of name is that?"

"It's my name. My friends call me M."

"Is that a German name?" he asked.

"No. It's a Jewish name. I'm a Jewish girl."

"You're a little kike?" he asked.

"I don't like that term," she said.

"But that's what you are. Right? A little Jew kike. Hitler must have somehow missed you when he was lighting up all those ovens and fake showers during the war."

"That's an awful thing to say," she said.

"Hey, it's history. All you Jews are safe now. Nothing to worry about. Right?"

"I guess."

"Guess or not, I'm still going to call you my little kike. Don't take it personal."

Delgado looked at her and laughed.

"You're getting paid for this. Aren't you?" he asked. "Paid pretty damn good, too. Right?"

"The money's good."

"Then I can call you whatever I want to call you."

Delgado reached down and grabbed the back of her hair.

"And I can do to you whatever I want to do to you! Jew or not!"

"Please don't hurt me. My name is Marcie. You should call me by my real name. Marcie."

"I'm calling you my little kike," said Delgado. "And I'll make damn sure every other inmate you ever come see in here from now on will call you that too. My. Little. Kike."

Marcie placed her hand on Delgado's knee and smiled.

"Okay, if that's what you want?" she replied. "I'll get used to it."

Delgado let go of her hair.

"Damn right you will! And don't sweat it none my little kike. I'm not going to hurt you."

"Do you want me to stay the night? I was told I could get more money if I stayed the night. That is if you want me to?"

Delgado stared down at her and smiled.

"Yeah," Delgado said. "Take off that phony prison uniform and jump in my bunk. I have to talk some business right now with "Big" Harold."

"Okay," she said with a big smile and began removing her clothes, folding them neatly onto the empty bunk above Delgado's.

"Big" Harold quietly strolled down the cell block carrying a freshly laundered prison uniform and cap under his arm and stopped in front of Delgado's cell.

"Everything okay in here?" asked "Big" Harold.

"Everything is good in here," said Delgado. "It is very good. This broad could suck the chrome off a Cadillac."

"Enjoying Miss Marcie then?" Harold asked.

"You mean my little kike?" asked Delgado. "She's a very talented woman. For a Jew. And yes. Thank you "Big" Harold. We are having a very good time."

"Will the young lady be staying the evening?"

"Most definitely," said Delgado.

"Big" Harold handed Delgado the folded uniform and cap through the bars.

"She should put this on in the morning when I take her out of here."

"I know the drill," said Delgado and handed the folded clothes to Marcie.

Marcie smiled as she stood naked in the jail cell. She waved at "Big" Harold as she took the clothes from Delgado, placed them on the floor and climbed into his bunk.

"So tell me, "Big" Harold, what's the word on me walking out of here?" he asked. "Is that going to happen and when?"

"Big" Harold looked up and down the cell block and leaned in closer to Delgado and smiled.

"You must have something good with a grin like that," said Delgado.

"I do," said "Big" Harold.

"Tell me," said Delgado.

"I was told you'll be out of here by tomorrow afternoon. All charges dropped," said "Big" Harold.

"This is true?" Delgado asked.

"Yes," replied "Big" Harold.

Delgado sighed with relief.

"I have your word on this?" asked Delgado.

"You have my word."

"What about Hoover and that little piss-ant, Edwards," asked Delgado. "They'll never stop looking for me."

"Yes they will. You are going to disappear and by the time they even hear you're out you'll be on a private plane to Columbia. Your safety has been guaranteed."

A broad smile rose on Delgado's face.

"This is very good news, my friend. Very good news."

"I thought it might make you smile," said "Big" Harold.

"This is all reliable information? You are certain about tomorrow? Not some other day?"

"It's reliable. I just received a phone call from your lawyer, Mr. Haggis himself, confirming everything. You, my friend, are good to go."

"Did they find that shooter who took out Rockwell?"

"Big" Harold looked down the cell corridor once more.

"No. Not yet."

"I know who took him out."

"I heard it was Barbieri who had Rockwell put down," said "Big" Harold.

`"It was her all right. She's making some kind of move. I need to know if her plans are going to include me or not."

"I don't know the answer to that, my friend," said "Big" Harold.

Delgado looked "Big" Harold in the eye.

"There would be a very large payout to you, "Big" Harold, if you could find out where Barbieri is these days?" asked Delgado. "I have some close personal friends back in Columbia who want to meet with her. Privately. And soon. Very soon."

"How much money are you offering?" asked "Big" Harold.

"Fifteen thousand," said Delgado. "Cash."

"Big" Harold smiled .

"The word on the street is she is in Cozumel now but I don't know that for sure. If she is she is still distributing your product line. And must be doing very well."

"That bitch owes me," said Delgado. "She owes me a lot."

"You two will work things out."

"She's free. I'm still stuck in here. I need to know what she is doing and what is happening with our business. I have been totally in the dark with her. I need to know where she is in Cozumel."

"You'll know soon enough," said "Big" Harold.

"Barbieri has me worried. No one seems to know what she is really doing or who she is really working with these days. This is information I need to know. And I need to know as quickly as possible."

256

"Haggis also had some other good news," whispered "Big" Harold.

"Other good news? I'm listening," said Delgado.

"Haggis said to keep calm and stay relaxed. He said Barbieri knows you of all people have always been loyal and you have nothing to fear from her. He also told me that Rockwell was just something she had to deal with."

"Big" Harold's assurances sounded all well and good to Delgado until Harold mentioned Barbieri and Rockwell's demise.

"I don't believe that for a second," said Delgado. "Rachel Stone Barbieri is only loyal to one person and that's herself."

"Why would you say that?" asked "Big" Harold.

"She got out. Why are the rest of us still rotting away in here? Explain that."

"These things take time," said "Big" Harold. "You're getting out of here tomorrow."

"Loyalty and trust in this business is extremely hard to find," said Delgado. "Especially with a woman like Barbieri. Rockwell was an impatient fool. I am not."

"Big" Harold looked down the corridor once again.

"Oh hell. Somebody's coming this way," he whispered and looked at Delgado.

"Who is it?" asked Delgado.

Delgado tried to look down the corridor from his cell.

"Is it Haggis?"

"No," said "Big" Harold. "It's death."

Suddenly Delgado's body stiffened and his eyes opened wide as Marcie, still naked, drove an ice pick deep into the back of Delgado's head. She pulled out the pick and Delgado fell dead onto the cold floor.

"Big" Harold looked down the quiet corridor then looked at Marcie and smiled.

"Nicely done," "Big" Harold said.

"Thank you," she replied.

"Put him next to his bed, put on those fresh prison clothes I gave you, and I'll come and get you both in three minutes," said "Big" Harold. He looked down the dark quiet cell block one more time. "Quickly, hand over the pick."

Marcie handed "Big" Harold the pick. He wrapped it up in a paper bag and stuffed it in his shirt.

"Three minutes, M," repeated "Big" Harold. "Don't make me wait for you like last time."

"Is it the laundry truck again?" she asked.

"Yes," said "Big" Harold. "It's the laundry truck again and if that driver, Ziggy, starts pushing you for another freebie? I want to hear about it."

"He's going to push, Harold, Ziggy always does but this time you will hear about it. Believe me."

"Get dressed, M and when I get you your money? You go someplace and you disappear. You hear me?"

"I hear you," she replied.

"This never happened. You were never here. And you sure as hell never heard of Ponce Delgado."

"Who?" she asked and smiled over at "Big" Harold.

"I'm going for the cart. Three minutes. Move that pretty little ass."

"Love you too," Marcie said.

"You did good, M. You did real good."

"Thank you again," she said.

"Big" Harold smiled and walked away.

Marcie reached down and dragged Delgado's body to his bunk. She placed Delgado next to his bed, leaned down and spit into his dead face.

"Fuck you, Mr. Delgado. You didn't see that coming now, did you?"

Marcie grabbed the folded uniform and got quickly dressed.

"In three days, your little kike will be on a beach in the Bahamas" she said aloud. "You however will be in some stinking land fill upstate right alongside Ziggy asshole if he doesn't behave himself today."

The bars to the cell suddenly slid open and "Big" Harold wheeled in a large laundry cart and heaved Delgado's body in along with all the bedding. Marcie placed the blanket over Delgado and looked at "Big" Harold.

"Big" Harold turned and extended his arm to Marcie.

"You're carriage awaits my lady."

"Thank you, sir," Marcie replied, took "Big" Harold's arm and stepped into the cart.

"No noise and no movement. You got it?" asked "Big Harold.

"This ain't my first rodeo," Marcie replied. "I know the drill."

"Big" Harold covered Marcie with the other blanket and bedding and wheeled the cart slowly down the corridor.

"I'll meet you and Ziggy when I get off shift. I'll have your money."

"Thanks, "Big" Harold," she said. "Same place as before? Right?"

"Yes. Same spot."

The bars to Delgado's cell slowly closed.

Rachel Stone Barbieri's reach had stretched out once again.

Out with the old.

In with the new.

CHAPTER TWENTY TWO

I sat in Debra's house in total darkness until the sun came up. I heard a few cars pass by throughout the night but other than that there was no activity whatsoever.

No Terrence.

I decided to abandon my sitting in Debs' house for the day and see if Phil had gotten me any information on the partial license plate I managed to see. By noon she had given me a lead on three possible owners with that plate number. The first one was up in San Francisco and Phil asked the local police there to check it out. The plate belonged to a brand new Cadillac owned by a female lawyer named Heather Starr.

Strike one.

The second lead was somewhat local down in Manhattan Beach and the tags were owned by a tall Italian woman named Linda Distefano who ran her own restaurant with her husband Lorenzo. I checked that one out myself with no luck.

Strike two.

They say the third time is a charm and my last lead brought me to a small house in Burbank owned by an old silent screen actress named Shelby Graham who claimed to have had an affair with Charlie Chaplin back in the day.

When I arrived at the house and there was an old dusty gray Plymouth sitting in the driveway, I knew I had hit pay dirt. The rear license plate was missing. I stepped up to the front door and rang the bell.

Miss Graham was dressed quite nicely and I showed her my PI identification. It appeared she could barely read it but she was gracious and asked me in anyway.

I asked about her missing license plate and she had no idea it was even missing. She offered me a cup of coffee, and she got on the horn and called her niece, Missy Panasci, who arrived in a matter of minutes.

"You'll have to excuse my aunt," Missy said in confidence. "Her mind is not as sharp as it used to be and as the days go by she seems to be getting worse instead of better."

"I understand," I replied and Miss Graham proceeded to tell me all about Chaplin and her career in the flickers, as she called them.

I spent about another fifteen minutes with the two ladies, getting an education on the early days of the motion picture business, kindly thanked them for all their help, and left Burbank with the exact plate number which was 1F4770. I had Phil notify the LAPD to be on the lookout for the plate last seen on a brand new tan Pontiac along with the description of Terrence Bruce. I figured if Bruce was coming for Debs to get to Agent Edwards, then he would surely be coming for Phil or possibly Betty, Jake, or Barney at the restaurant if he was looking to get to me.

I decided to draw Bruce out and give him every opportunity to find me and kill me.

I drove out to Barney's and parked the coupe close to the road so anyone driving by would know I was there. I also told my man Monty to drive out to Toluca Lake and sit watch at Debs' place as I took over my usual spot in the rear booth at Barney's. I explained my plan to Barney and he welcomed the chance to empty his shotgun into Mr. Bruce if he dared to take one step in his establishment. Jake and Betty also understood my present situation but I could sense they were a bit uncomfortable knowing there was still some hired killer roaming Los Angeles with murder on his mind. I thought their attitude was a bit odd and wondered why but as soon as I sat down in my booth I got my answer.

"We're pregnant," said Betty, as she and Jake sat across from me grinning from ear to ear.

"Pregnant? That's wonderful news," I said. "Congratulations."

"Thanks, mate," said Jake.

"How far along are you?" I asked.

"Four months," said Betty. "We haven't picked out any names as yet but we would like you to be godfather to our baby."

"Godfather?" I asked. "Thank you. I would be honored to do that. Does that involve any diaper changing?"

"It might," said Jake. "Every now and again. Is that going to be a deal breaker?"

"Absolutely not," I said. "I know I'm asking a lot from you both right now but I don't know what else I can do. I want all of you to be safe but I need to get this guy to show himself. If you have any other suggestions, I'm open."

"We'll be fine," said Betty. "Jake and I are going to Australia to meet his family."

"I think we'll be quite safe down under," said Jake.

"Australia? Are you leaving tonight?" I asked.

"No," said Betty. "Another month or so at the least. We've been saving up for it."

"How much do you need?" I asked.

"You've spent enough money on us, Patrick giving us the honeymoon and all," said Jake. "And Barney helped us get into our new house. We'll get to Australia on our own."

"Okay. I hear what you're saying but hear me out on this. You're right. You'll both be safe down under as you call it and I'll be able to do what I need to do with you both on the next ship or flight leaving for where exactly?"

"Bairnsdale," added Barney standing at the bar wiping glasses.

"Okay. But this needs to happen right away. As soon as possible. No waiting for another month. And this isn't a gift. I'll have Phil get you all squared away, I'll pay for it all now and when you get back you can pay me back with interest if that's what you want but let me do this and let me do this right now. Today. Please?"

"We wanted to take a cruise," said Betty.

"If that's all right with you?" Jake asked.

"A cruise it is," I said. "It's perfect. The salt air. The gentle rocking of the sea. I love it! Let me call Phil and make this happen for you both. Please? Okay?"

Betty looked at Jake and he nodded yes.

"Okay," said Betty. 'We'll do as you've asked."

"Great!" I said and shook Jake's hand. "Let me call Phil right now."

I went to the phone booth and called Phil. A few hours passed and she had Jake and Betty booked for Bairnsdale in one week's time. I stayed for the dinner rush at Barney's that night keeping a sharp eye on everyone coming in and out of the front door and finally followed Betty and Jake to their new house on Mulholland.

I told them I was not going to let them out of my sight until they were both safely on the ship and heading out across the South Pacific.

263

I made certain the house was locked up tight for the evening and got some much needed shut eye sleeping in their spare bedroom as Betty and Jake began packing for their cruise to down under.

I didn't like the fact that we had to wait an entire week but I hoped someone might find the stolen plates on the tan Pontiac and grab Terrence Bruce off the streets of Los Angeles.

It was a long shot but it was the only shot I had going for me.

CHAPTER TWENTY THREE

Special Agent Davis and Agent Lindman flew to the Johnstown Airport in an eight passenger shuttle flight from Pittsburgh. They had been flying in and out of several airports as they traveled across the country and were the only passengers on the last flight except for two elderly women who were returning to their old home town to ride the town's Incline Plane one more time. Both women appeared highly curious as to how Agent Davis broke her nose but were polite enough not to ask, and neither agent offered any explanation.

They wished the ladies well and rented a car. The sun had set once they got into the nearby vicinity, and they began looking in the dark for the three boulders sitting on the main road described to them by Carmine Scarola.

"We're almost nine miles out of town and all I've seen are two deer and the moonlight," said Agent Lindman.

"Three boulders," said Agent Davis. "Three boulders that are obvious and easy to see was what I was told."

The rental car came over a slight hill and headed around a slight curve.

"There's three boulders," said Charlie, and drove slowly past them. "Do you think that was it?"

"It's the only three we've seen so far like that," said Agent Davis. "It's got to be it. Pull over."

A small clearing sat about ninety feet across from the entrance and Charlie pulled in and stopped the car. He shut off the engine as he and Agent Davis turned and stared back at the roadway entrance to the cabin.

"What do you think?" asked Agent Lindman.

"Lots of trees," said Agent Davis. "Would be great cover for us if it was July instead of March."

"We'll leave the car here and go in tonight," said Charlie. "The darkness will be our cover. There's a full moon up there and we have a fairly clear night. What could be better?"

"Knowing Joanne Paris is in there all alone, unarmed, and hopefully unconscious."

"Now you're just wishful thinking," said Charlie.

"A girl can dream," she added. "Those old ladies on the flight were very nice. I don't think I'd want to ride on some incline plane that was built sixty years ago. Sounds dangerous."

Before Charlie could respond, a car came down the highway.

"Car coming!" said Agent Davis and suddenly leaned over and kissed Charlie.

The car passed and Agent Davis leaned back in her seat.

"What did you do that for?" he asked.

"I didn't want us to be seen gawking at the road. Someone drives by and sees two people necking they don't give it a second thought."

"Really?" he asked. "You really believe that?"

"Yes," she replied. "I do."

"I don't remember learning that piece of information back at the academy," said Charlie.

"You must have slept through that class," added Agent Davis.

"Car!" cried Charlie and leaned over and kissed Agent Davis again.

Agent Davis pulled away slowly but stayed close to Charlie's face.

"There wasn't any car coming. You did that on purpose," she said.

Charlie grinned broadly.

"Guilty. I saw an opportunity, Agent Davis, and I took it."

"Did you learn that at the academy?" she asked. "Calling an improper advance on a girl an opportunity?"

"No," he said. "And I apologize. I'm sorry."

"Apology accepted. You are a fairly good kisser, Agent Lindman."

"Am I?" he asked.

"Fair. Yes."

"Thank you," he said. "I'll assume you must have had a lot of practice at kissing being you're such an expert judge of what's fair, good. Or even great."

Agent Davis grinned.

"I've had my fair share," she replied. "If you don't mind, Agent Lindman? I'd like to try that again. Maybe in the process you could boost your status from fair to maybe good? Or maybe better?"

"One more time?" he asked. "Really? You're serious?"

"I'm serious," she said. "It's been a long time since I've felt being close to someone."

"Me too," said Charlie.

Charlie slid in closer to Agent Davis and kissed her deeply.

"Aren't there rules in the FBI about this kind of interactive behavior between agents?" he asked.

"I'm sure there are but right now we are under the cover of darkness, we're both single adults, and what Hoover doesn't know about how we are feeling won't hurt him," she said with a smile. "Besides? This is a dangerous mission. We don't know what to expect. What we might encounter? Or if we will even survive the night in the process of our duties."

"What about Joanne Parrish?" Charlie asked.

"We'll wait one hour, as you suggested, set up a take-down strategy, and then we will go in and arrest the little bitch."

"Sounds good to me," said Charlie and gently kissed Agent Davis again. "Truth be told, I liked you, Special Agent Davis, the first time I laid eyes on you."

"You did?"

"Yes. I did."

"Seriously?" she asked.

"Truth be told? Yes. Seriously."

"That's funny, Agent Lindman because I felt the same way about you," she added.

"Really?" he asked.

"Yes, really," she said and kissed him again.

"You can call me Charlie," he said.

"You can call me Special Agent Davis," she said and laughed.

Agent Lindman and Agent Davis smiled at each other and fell back onto the front seat, locked in each other's arms.

CHAPTER TWENTY FOUR

Monty Crow had been watching the pool area from Debs' living room window for over nine hours straight. Day turned into night and he thought he would wait one more hour and then call Patrick and give him his report on what he did or didn't see.

There wasn't much to tell.

He heard loud music playing from several houses down and figured it to be some sort of family celebration. He tapped his foot to the beat of Gene Krupa's drums and for a brief moment pretended it was he pounding on the skins for Glenn Miller and his orchestra. His musical fantasy came to a sudden halt as a car came driving up to the house. Applause and laughter echoed from the party house down the way as Monty sat up straight holding his .45 and staring out from the darkened room.

Several minutes passed.

Monty could see the headlights still shining across the front lawn and could hear the car's engine still idling. He took a deep breath and decided to call Patrick.

Monty quietly picked up the receiver and dialed.

I picked up on the fourth ring.

"Atwater here," I said.

"It's Monty," he whispered. "A car just pulled up the drive and it's been sitting out front for the past few minutes."

"What's the make?" I asked.

"Can't tell from this position," whispered Monty. "What do you want me to do?"

"Hang tight until I get there. If it's our guy? Shoot first and we can ask the proper questions later. But for the time being hold your position. I'm on my way. I'm leaving right now."

"Roger that," Monty whispered and quietly hung up the phone.

Monty stood up slowly, walked to the far end of the window and tried to see the car sitting out front. He could only hear the engine running and see flashes of light from the headlights. He checked his hand gun and pulled back a part of the curtain to check the front of the house.

A single gunshot rang out, piercing the front living room glass and entering Monty's chest very close to his heart. The shot pushed him back, knocking him to the floor. He laid on the floor trying to breathe and the pain in his chest made his mind spin in a thousand directions.

He heard footsteps walking across the pool deck and he felt around in the dark for his gun. He couldn't locate it and as the pain began to increase, he struggled to stay conscious. Someone grabbed his arms and dragged him to the back bedroom.

Monty tried to see who it was but the room was too dark. He knew it had to be a man.

A strong man.

A woman would have much difficulty dragging him so easily to the back bedroom.

Monty's breathing came in short bursts and the pain seemed to lessen somewhat. As he opened his mouth for more air, a piece of paper was stuffed into his mouth, making it more difficult to breathe. A single lamp came on and Monty looked to his right, trying to see who was in the room with him, but as he heard the man leave he passed out.

I told Barney to keep a sharp eye out until I got back and left the restaurant. I jumped into the coupe, and sped towards Toluca Lake as fast as I could without drawing any speeding tickets. I hoped upon hope that the car in Debs' and Verdun's drive was that of an impatient Terrence Bruce, and with Monty's help we would end this hired threat once and for all.

I knew once I arrived I had to approach the house with extreme caution. Terrence Bruce was a consummate pro and not some hop-headed gangster I should take lightly. I had the element of surprise in my favor and the additional help of Monty at Terrence's back and myself covering the front. The night traffic heading into the valley was almost non-existent and I arrived at the house in record time.

I shut off my headlights and parked the coupe a few houses down from Verdun's driveway. I grabbed my .38 and walked cautiously towards the house.

The entire place was dark and there was no sign of any vehicle in the driveway, running or not. I walked slowly and quietly up the drive making certain not to step on anything that would give away my position. I reached the house, stood in the darkened silence, and listened for any movement or sound.

I went to the front door and tried turning the knob.

The door was locked.

I walked a few feet heading for the back yard and stopped once again to listen.

A slight breeze blew through the palm trees above but the rest of the grounds were dead silent. I reached the pool area and noticed that the glass door to Debs' living room was wide open with a small lamp shining from the rear bedroom. I quickly surveyed the entire area, stepped cautiously past the opened door and entered the dimly lit living room.

I saw the bullet hole in the glass and Monty's handgun laying on the floor. As my eyes became adjusted to the darkness I noticed a large blood smear on the floor leading to the back bedroom.

I pointed my .38, walked down the short hallway, and stepped into the bedroom.

Monty was lying on the bedroom floor bleeding from a gunshot wound to his chest. He was barely alive and struggling to breathe. I quickly cleared the rest of the house and ran to the phone.

The line had been cut and the phone was dead.

"Damn it," I said and grabbed a kitchen towel. I went back to the bedroom and pressed it onto Monty's wound.

"Hold this on there, pal, as best you can!"

Monty opened his eyes and tried to speak but words would not come out.

"Hang in there, Monty. I'm going to get my car and drive you to the hospital! I'll be right back!"

I raced down the driveway as fast as my legs would take me, got to the coupe, threw it into gear and drove up the driveway. I ran back into the bedroom but I was too late. The wound in Monty's chest was a fatal one and he bled out and died on the bedroom floor.

His eyes and mouth were wide open.

I dropped to my knees in front of my dead friend and checked his neck for a pulse even though I could see poor Monty was gone. I reached out and gently closed my friend's eyes and noticed something stuck in his mouth.

I reached in and pulled out a folded piece of paper.

I unfolded the paper and brought it over to the lamp.

"Hello Patrick," the note read. "Violets are blue, roses are red, all of your friends, and then you, will be dead." It was signed "T" in one large letter.

Panic rushed through my body and one word came bursting out of my mouth.

"Betty," I cried and ran out of the house.

CHAPTER TWENTY FIVE

The evening dinner rush at Barneys By the Sea had gone very well and Betty sat at the bar drinking iced tea and counting out her tips for the evening. Jake stepped out from the kitchen, poured himself a cold beer from the tap, and sat down beside her.

"How did we do tonight, love?" asked Jake.

"It doesn't really matter now. Does it?" she asked.

"I'm just curious," he replied.

Betty grinned and finished counting.

"We made thirty-eight dollars tonight, honey" she said and leaned over and kissed Jake lightly.

"How much of that would you have added to our Aussie fund?" Jake asked.

"I would have put in twenty-five. And we should keep our Aussie fund money separate so we can pay Patrick back in a timely manner. Agreed?"

"Agreed. Are you sure we don't need some of the money for other things?" he asked.

"We're good," she said. "Put this money away and don't think about it."

"Yes, love."

She held out the money and Jake took it.

"I can't believe in a week's time you and I will be sailing off and sipping cold Fosters in Bairnsdale before we can say I kissed a kangaroo."

Barney stepped out from the kitchen carrying three bottles of Vodka.

"Did you lock the front door, Betty?" Barney asked.

"The front door is locked, Barney," she replied.

"Where's our bodyguard?" asked Barney.

"Monty called Patrick to meet him over at that girlfriend of Agent Edwards' house," said Betty.

"What's that all about?" asked Barney. "He was very vague about it with me."

"We're not sure either," said Betty.

"All we know is Patrick is switching places with Monty until Betty and I are safely on our way." said Jake.

"I'll hold this fort down with my shotgun until he gets back," said Barney. "That limey bastard comes near us I'll take his damn head off with one shot."

Barney looked behind the bar but didn't see the gun.

"Where's my damn shotgun?" he asked.

"I hung it in the kitchen," said Jake. "I wanted it where I could see it."

"I want it where we all can see it. Put it back where she belongs. Right here," he pointed. "As always."

"Yes sir," said Jake and headed to the kitchen.

"Where the hell is Bairnsdale exactly?" asked Barney and began replacing his liquor supply behind the bar.

"It's just south of Melbourne, Barney," said Betty. "It's Jake's home town."

Jake returned and replaced the shotgun under the bar.

"The gun is back," said Jake.

"Thank you, Jake," said Barney and drew a deep sigh.

"What is it now, mate," asked Jake.

"I don't know what I'm going to do with you two gone for a whole two weeks," said Barney.

"Don't start your whining again, old man," said Jake. "It's only two weeks. Michael Stewart will be coming over from the Beverly to handle your kitchen orders like the expert chef he is."

"A cook with two first names? He sounds totally incompetent. And who are you calling an old man?"

"Should I have said old bastard?" Jake replied.

"Absolutely, Jacko," said Barney.

Barney smiled , poured himself a beer from the tap and offered up his glass for an evening toast.

"To another fine night at Barney's By the Sea."

Jake and Betty raised their glasses and clinked them with Barney's.

"I am going to miss you two," said Barney and took a swig from his glass.

"We'll miss you too, Barney but I've already got the new girl, Cher Silvers is her name, knowing full well how you like your tables run and your tickets written," added Betty. "Cher will do just fine and you'll survive until we get back."

276

"I'm sure Cher is good. I'm sure she's very good but she's not you, Betty. With you gone I think I'll need two more waitresses in here for sure. Business is beginning to pick up and you're just the best damn waitress ever! I'm going to need more help! I know it."

"No you won't, Barney," Jake added. "Cher and Michael can hold their own. And like my Betty says, you will survive."

"Who's going to watch that new place of yours while you're both down under sipping that rot gut Fosters beer and kissing kangaroos?"

Jake smiled and shook his head at Barney's little Australian dig.

"Barney?" said Betty. "You told us you would keep an eye on the place while we were gone! Take the mail. Stock our fridge with Jake's favorite beer. Put the crib together."

"Did I?" joked Barney.

"Yes you did!" said Betty.

"Was I drunk at the time?"

"It's hard to tell with him, honey," said Jake. "He might have been drunk when he made all those promises."

"Don't fret, Betty. I'll keep my one good eye on the place and make certain it's safe and sound until you both return. I won't read your mail either and I may put a bottle or two in your fridge. Whatever is not selling well here. I don't know diddly about any crib construction but I'm sure after a few beers I'll figure it out. "

"Thank you," Betty replied. "Whatever you want to do will be fine with us. Right honey?"

"Absolutely," said Jake.

A loud knock on the front door suddenly echoed across the bar.

"Are you expecting someone, Barney?" asked Jake.

"No," he answered and looked at the clock on the wall. "It's too early for my cab ride."

Jake stepped up and put his hands on the shotgun.

"Maybe it's Patrick back already," said Betty and walked to the door.

"Betty hold up!" warned Barney.

Betty paid no attention to Barney's warning and kept walking.

"Keep your hands on that shotgun," said Barney.

"Don't worry. I will," said Jake and stared at the door.

Terrence Bruce stood at the front door sporting a gray moustache and goatee, gray hair, and thick black rimmed glasses. He peered in and smiled a friendly grin through the glass.

"I'm sorry, sir," said Betty. "We are closed for the night."

"Closed?" he asked using a faked French accent. "I was hoping I could get a quick night cap before heading back to my hotel," said Terrence. "Oui?"

Betty turned to Barney.

"It's some Frenchie and he wants a night cap," she said.

"Do you know him, Betty?" asked Jake.

"Never saw him before," she said. "He's not the cab driver either."

"It's too far past the hour, Barney," said Jake as he held the shotgun out of sight behind the bar.

"Shall I let him in?" asked Betty. "He's wearing a suit and tie. Got a nice French accent. Probably some kind of salesman, most likely."

Barney thought for a few moments.

"One drink will only lead to two and besides the register is already closed. Tell him we're sorry but he will have to come back another time."

Betty turned back to Terrence.

"I'm sorry, sir. You'll have to come back another time."

"Tres bien," said Terrence. "Another time it will have to be. Au revoir."

"Good night," said Betty and walked back to the bar. "He seemed like a nice man."

"It's one thing if you know the man but letting strangers in after-hours is never a good thing," said Barney. "Especially with all this business with poor Detective Blaine and Patrick and his bodyguards. You can't tell who might be knocking on your door."

"Barney's right," said Jake. "We have to be careful. Like Patrick said."

"Oh my god," said Betty. "You don't think that could have been the man Patrick is looking for?"

Outside Terrence walked back to the parking lot, got into his tan Pontiac, and took out a new vial of cocaine. He poured out two long lines onto a small mirror, chopped the mixture with the side of a match book cover and bent down, snorted both lines quickly, and then rested his head back in the seat. He closed his eyes for a few moments, then opened them and stared over at Betty's Hudson.

It was the only car still in the parking lot.

Terrence started up the engine and drove away.

Jake came running out carrying the shotgun but only got a glimpse of Terrence's car as it drove away. Jake turned around and went back inside.

About fifteen minutes passed and a yellow cab pulled in and parked with the engine running.

The cab was Barney's ride home, a standard practice of the one-eyed owner.

Jake and Betty left the restaurant and Betty waved to the cab driver before walking to the Hudson. Barney stepped out, locked the front door and got in the cab.

"Good evening, Harry," said Barney.

"Good evening, Barney," said Harry. "Nice night."

"One of the better ones I must say," said Barney.

Jake got behind the wheel of the Hudson and Betty waved a quick goodbye to Barney as the yellow cab drove off into the night.

Betty snuggled up close to Jake as the big Hudson headed north on Sunset into Hollywood.

The road was long and curving but Betty and Jake always used their drive home time to talk about their work day at Barney's, unwind somewhat, and discuss together what they were looking to do in the future.

Barney helped them put a down payment on a small two bedroom house up in the Hollywood hills on Mulholland Drive. The house was built back in the 20's and needed some refurbishing inside and out. Two of

Barney's regular customers, long time construction workers Vincent and Dominick, gave Jake a helping hand and got the place up to snuff in no time.

The house sat far off the main road and the backyard had a beautiful view of the LA skyline and the valley below.

It was the perfect house for Betty and Jake and they seemed to grow closer with each passing day.

"My feet are killing me, honey" said Betty as they headed up Coldwater to the house.

"Take your shoes off, woman," said Jake.

"I can wait until we're home. Would you rub them for me before we go to bed?" she asked.

"I will rub every inch of you, darling," added Jake.

"Is that a promise?"

"Absolutely."

Jake and Betty arrived at home just after midnight, parking the Hudson just outside the back door leading to their dining room and kitchen.

Jake shut off the engine and looked at Betty.

"What?" she asked.

"We don't have to go on this trip if you're not up for it," Jake said.

"I want to go," Betty said. "I am up for it."

"I know you are. But what about the baby?" he asked.

Jake placed his hand lovingly on Betty's stomach.

"I'm only four months, Jake and I'll be fine. We will all be fine. Walking around is good for pregnant women."

"Are you sure? If anything happened to this little one because of all the travel I could never forgive myself."

"Don't worry, honey. Besides, this baby wants to be where you grew up just as much as I do. We are going and it will be wonderful. And when she's ten years old we will go back again to Bairnsdale and you can show her all the things she missed on this first trip."

"She?" he asked.

"Yes. She," Betty repeated.

"I think you are mistaken, Mrs. Farnswell. Come this July we are having a baby boy."

"Really?" she asked. "You know this as a fact?"

"No. I don't care what we have. I will love it, boy or girl."

"Maybe we'll have both?"

"Twins?"

"That would be a surprise,"

"It would. Do twins run in your family?" she asked.

"No."

"Not mine either."

Jake and Betty smiled at each other.

"I love you," Betty said.

"I love you too," said Jake.

Jake leaned in and kissed Betty deeply. Betty responded in turn and gently grabbed his face with her two hands.

"I don't know a damn thing about being a mother or a parent," said Betty.

Jake raised two fingers in the air.

"That makes two of us," said Jake. "Who does, anyway? My mum didn't know and my dad still doesn't know. We'll do just fine. I'm certain of it. Scared or not we'll get through it and we'll get through it together."

Betty smiled and kissed Jake.

"Let's go in and I'll get to those feet and ankles of yours," said Jake."

"Sounds wonderful," she added.

Jake and Betty got out of the car and went into the house. Betty entered first and when she turned on the light switch the kitchen light did not come on. Betty tried the switch several times as Jake walked by her.

"Something is wrong with this light switch, honey."

"The bulb must have blown out," Jake said. "I'll turn on the living room lamp."

"All right. I'm going to get out of these shoes."

Betty sat down in one of the four kitchen chairs in the darkened room and took off her shoes. She began rubbing her feet and realized Jake had not turned on the light. She turned and looked towards the living room.

"Jake? Jake, honey? What are you doing in there?"

An eerie silence filled the room.

"If you are trying to scare me, Jake Farnsworth it is working. Please stop your fooling around and turn on the light so we can go to bed. Please?"

The house remained dark and quiet and the silence grew heavier.

"Jake?"

Betty waited in the dark for a few more moments and started to become a bit irritated with his childishness.

"Jake! Seriously! What are you doing, honey? Please answer me."

Betty was not having his little joke. She stood up and walked slowly and carefully into the living room, feeling her way through the darkness as she navigated past the furniture. She got to the lamp and turned the switch but nothing happened.

"This is not funny, Jake Farnswell. Not funny at all."

Betty checked the bulb and realized it had somehow become loosened.

"This bulb is just loose," she announced and tightened the bulb in and turned the switch.

She felt something wet on her arm and noticed there was fresh blood running down her arm to her hand. She glanced to her left and saw Jake's bloodied body sitting on the left side of the couch.

He was dead.

His throat had been slashed wide open, and large amounts of his blood glistened down his body onto the couch and had puddled on the floor.

"Ahhhhhhh!!!" Betty screamed and her body began to shake and tremble uncontrollably. "Oh god! Oh my god! Oh Jake! My god! Jake!"

She looked down and saw more of Jake's blood splattered everywhere and slowly started to back up. Sheer terror raced through her entire body. Betty turned quickly towards the kitchen door and began to run but was suddenly violently stopped. She felt a sudden cold pain deep in her stomach.

Betty looked down and realized she had run into a long sharp knife held by Terrence.

He stood in the darkened kitchen completely naked and covered with blood spatter.

"Good evening, Betty," he said and tilted his head slightly. "I'm Terrence. It appears you have had an unfortunate accident involving my sabre. As did your man Jake."

Betty could see her shoes lying on the kitchen floor.

Betty looked up slowly at Terrence and realized she was looking at the same man she had seen earlier at Barney's.

The French man asking for the nightcap.

The man Jake chased after with Barney's shotgun but couldn't catch in time.

Now he stood in their home speaking with an Irish accent. The monster had finally come and there was no escape. It was the monster Patrick warned her about and now he had taken her Jake's life, and now he was taking hers. And her unborn child's.

"You?!" she whispered.

Betty tried to breathe but her lungs would not fill with air. She felt the tip of the knife scraping at her spine and instinctively placed her two hands down on her stomach next to the blade, hoping to somehow protect the life inside her from this evil horror standing in front of her.

Betty wanted to fight back and save her life. Bring back Jake and save her baby too but she knew her life was quickly coming to an end.

A quiet peace drifted through her body and she felt a single tear run down her cheek as she stood in the semi-darkness, realizing her life and that of her unborn child was slowly bleeding out of her, and her own death was now a few short moments away.

Terrence grabbed Betty by her right shoulder and slowly removed the sabre.

"Rachel Stone Barbieri sends her condolences," he said. "Patrick Miles Atwater will be joining you both very soon. I can guarantee you that."

As Terrence held Betty against the counter, she stood silently terrified and watched as her own blood began to cover Terrence's hand, arms, and face, while he ran the sabre across her chest and continued slicing at her until he slashed her throat.

Betty's hands clenched into fists, her knees buckled, and she dropped to the floor, unable to scream or speak. Her last dying thought was of faraway Bairnsdale, picturing herself, Jake, and their baby lying there on a warm Australian beach together.

Betty closed her eyes, took her last breath, and was gone.

Terrence got down on one knee and began cutting into her neck and removing her head with his sabre.

Betty, her unborn child, and her loving husband Jake were no more. Their lives snuffed out and their bodies butchered as requested by Rachel Stone Barbieri.

Collateral damage.

Terrence knew these three particular deaths would set Patrick into a mental tailspin that would give Terrence the edge to catch Patrick off guard when the time came to kill him.

Graphic and personal.

Terrence stood up and calmly placed Betty's head on the kitchen counter.

Terrence, breathing very hard, took the sabre and walked to the bathroom.

Terrence took a hot shower washing every trace of Jake and Betty's blood from his body and his sabre. He shut off the water, toweled himself and his weapon dry, and walked into the bedroom. Another black suit and tie were laid out neatly on their bed along with his shoes, socks and underwear and he quickly dressed.

He stepped out into the living room with the sabre wrapped in a large brown towel. He started walking towards the front door and stopped himself. He raised one hand and looked at the floor.

"I'm sorry," he said. "I completely forgot. Do either one of you know the meaning of Magenta? Yes? No? Maybe?"

Terrence waited for the response which never came.

"Betty? Can you hear me, love?" he said.

Betty and Jake's lifeless eyes stared out in silence.

"I didn't think so," he said, leaned over, and shut off the living room light. "I'll be saying good night, then."

Terrence walked out the front door, wiping the doorknobs inside and out with the end of the towel.

He looked up at the evening sky and took a deep breath. The neighborhood was dark and quiet. He heard a dog barking off in the distance and walked casually and quietly the two short blocks to where he had parked the Pontiac.

He got to the car and opened the trunk. He opened a large leather bag filled with other tools of his trade and gently placed the sabre and towel on top and closed the bag. He shut the trunk quietly, got in the car, and took out his vial.

Terrence did another line of cocaine and began to laugh.

"Can't wait until I see you again, Mr. Atwater," he quoted. "I really cannot wait!"

Terrence rolled his head and neck until he felt it crack and started the engine.

The engine sputtered but didn't kick in.

He turned the key a second time and pumped the gas a bit harder and the engine sputtered but still would not engage.

Terrence sat back and took a deep breath and heard a car approaching. He stretched his head to the right and saw Patrick's Ford coupe driving quickly to Jake and Betty's house.

"Mr. Atwater," he said aloud. "I will let fate decide if you live or die tonight."

Terrence sat waiting patiently as Patrick drove the Ford coupe to the front of the house. Patrick quickly jumped out of the car and ran straight to the front door.

With gun in hand, Patrick reared back and kicked in the front door and ran into the house.

A light came on in the living room and from Terrence's positon, he could look up the hill and tell Patrick had entered the house.

A few more moments of silence passed. Terrence listened intently.

Patrick's sudden horrified and heartbroken screams echoed loudly across the entire valley.

"There you are, my bucko," Terrence said aloud. "I hope you enjoy the little gift from me to you."

Terrence laughed to himself.

"And now we'll let your fate speak," he announced.

Terrence looked around, rolled his neck a second time, and turned the key.

"What's it to be?" he asked.

The engine finally kicked in and came to life. He gassed the engine and patted the dashboard.

"Ah, Mr. Atwater!" he cried. "The fates have spoken and you'll live another day! Maybe even two."

Terrence began to laugh harder, threw the engine into gear, and drove off into the night.

CHAPTER TWENTY SIX

Special Agent Davis and Agent Lindman checked their weapons and decided to approach the cabin from two sides. Agent Davis would approach from the south and enter the front door, Agent Lindman would take the north side, and enter through the rear.

"Are you ready to do this?" asked Agent Davis.

"I'm ready," replied Agent Lindman. "Three shots means all clear and our target is down."

"Agreed," added Agent Davis.

Each walked to the three boulders with shotguns in hand, stepping into the woods and taking their chosen positions.

A car came down the highway, turned right and entered the roadway to the cabin. As the car passed Agent Lindman's position, he walked quickly across the roadway and found Agent Davis ducked down behind a tree.

"Did you make the vehicle?" he asked.

"It was a dark blue Chevy," she said. "I couldn't catch the plate."

"Me neither," said Agent Lindman.

"Did you see the driver?" she asked. "Or any passengers?"

"No. It came in too quickly," replied Agent Lindman. "I was doing my best to stay out of sight."

"Me too," she added.

"Any guesses as to who it might be?" he asked.

Agent Davis grinned.

"Let's hope it's her and Magenta," said Agent Davis.

"That would be sweet," said Agent Lindman. "But could we get that lucky?"

"I don't think so," she replied.

"Should we call in some assistance?" he asked. "Get the locals involved now?"

"No. For all we know they could be in Magenta's pocket. We're here now. We're well armed. Someone is definitely in the cabin. The law is on our side here, too. Let's go make an arrest."

Agent Lindman smiled.

"Okay, but let's change our approach. Let's go in slow and quiet like and go in together, side by side, until we can see what we got."

"That works for me," she replied. "Let's move."

Agent Lindman nodded and the two approached the cabin slowly, quietly, and cautiously.

The dark blue Chevy was parked in front of the house and a tall, good looking man, missing his pinkie and ring finger on his left hand, got out carrying a single grocery bag. He didn't bother to knock or ring the bell, he simply walked inside and shut the door.

"Is that you, Benny?" a voice yelled out from up the stairs.

"It's me, baby" said Benny as he walked into the kitchen.

Benny began removing the groceries. He had purchased everything he needed to prepare a simple Italian dinner of meatballs and spaghetti. He started getting out the necessary pans and utensils as Joanne Parrish entered the room dressed in jeans, boots, and a sweater, and grabbed him around the waist.

"You were gone forever, Benny," she said and he turned and faced her.

"I was only gone for two hours," he said. "I had to put Carmine on the train."

"Two hours felt like two days," she said, and kissed him deeply.

"Did Carmine pay you everything he said he would?"

"He did. And thank you for all your assistance."

"I like the way you say thank you," he said and kissed her again.

"For a guy with only eight fingers you do all right."

"I only do what is needed to be done."

"Yes you do, baby," she purred. "Yes you do."

"So? All this drama over Bobby's death is now officially done and forgotten between you and Carmine? Right?" he asked.

"Yes," she said. "No more hard feelings. It was only business. The air has been cleared thanks to you intervening, and Carmine said he would be in touch with Rachel with some more contracts in the near future. Big name contracts. Thank you, thank you, thank you again for speaking on my behalf."

"You are a special kind of woman," Benny said and kissed Joanne again. "And now that we've had a chance to spend some real time together, I think the future is looking brighter for the both of us."

"I feel that way too," she said and kissed him again. "Can I help you cook our dinner?"

"You can chop some onions but they have to be cut very thin. Very. Very thin. It adds a real special flavor to the meatballs," he said.

"I would love to chop some onions for your meatballs, mister."

"I'll go down to the wine cellar and get us a nice bottle of wine," he offered.

"Perfect," she replied and took out the cutting board and began chopping onions.

"I think we should go down to Cozumel and see Rachel's new place," she announced.

"Sounds good," yelled Benny from the wine cellar.

"We could have a really good time down there. The three of us," she said.

Benny walked into the kitchen holding a gun with a silencer and fired one round into the back of Joanne's head. Her blood and brains splattered across the kitchen wall and covered most of the side window and her body dropped to the floor.

"That's for Bobby Collucci, you piece of shit. No hard feelings. It was only business."

Benny walked up closer, pointed his gun down, and fired another round into her head. He turned and walked up the stairs.

Benny found the cash bag given to her by Carmine Scarola, put on his coat, placed the gun in the bag, carried it down the stairs and left the cabin leaving the door wide open.

Benny got into the Chevy, turned it around, and drove out to the highway.

Agent Davis and Agent Lindman emerged from the woods onto the roadway but were unable to see the license plate or who was in the car.

"Was it her?" Agent Davis asked.

"Couldn't tell," Agent Lindman replied.

"Let's do this," said Agent Davis.

Agent Davis and Agent Lindman pointed their shotguns and approached the front door. Agent Davis nodded to Agent Lindman and they rushed inside.

Agent Lindman went up the stairs quickly with his gun pointed as Agent Davis swept through the downstairs area.

A few moments passed and Agent Lindman came down the stairs to find Agent Davis in the kitchen.

"Jesus Christ!" uttered Agent Lindman. "Is it her?"

"It's her," said Agent Davis. "She took two to the back of the head."

"Mob hit," he said and took a closer look at the body on the floor.

"That would be my guess," said Agent Davis. "No one upstairs?"

"All clear," said Agent Lindman.

"This has to be payback for Bobby Collucci," said Agent Davis. "Carmine's nephew."

"This is not going to sit well with Rachel Stone Barbieri," said Agent Lindman. "That's for damn sure. She's going to consider this an act of war."

"Going to war with the mob ain't easy," Agent Davis said.

"She'll need more than a few good hitmen," said Agent Lindman.

"Maybe Rachel's next on the hit parade list?" suggested Agent Davis.

"That would upset me greatly," said Agent Lindman.

"That would upset all of us greatly," she added. "Let's do a complete search of the house and the grounds and then call in the local authorities and the local press. Maybe we'll get lucky and this little story will go national. Put a few names out there as possible connections to this hit,
even though I'm sure they're all doing their damn best to remain anonymous."

"Sounds good to me," said Agent Lindman. "I'll start with the upstairs."

Agent Davis nodded her agreement.

"I'll cover this floor," she added. "But first I'm going to put in a call to Patrick. Let him know we got our girl."

"Somebody did," said Agent Lindman and walked away.

Agent Davis looked at Joanne's body and picked up the kitchen phone.

CHAPTER TWENTY SEVEN

Rachel, wrapped in a silk robe, had just finished her morning breakfast of huevos rancheros and two cups of hot black coffee when the vomiting suddenly began. Every time she thought the eruptive situation inside her had passed she would experience another wave of sickness building inside her and have to run once again to the toilet and eject more of her stomach contents.

Rachel spent the remainder of the morning running back and forth from her bedroom to the bathroom toilet, vomiting consistently, when a knock on the bedroom door caught her attention.

"Who is it?" she cried.

"It's Thomas, Miss Barbieri."

"What do you want, Thomas? Can't it wait?"

"A courier has arrived with a message," he said calmly.

"A courier?" she asked.

Rachel sighed heavily and wiped her mouth with the back of her hand.

"Give me a moment," she said, and slowly got to her feet.

Rachel looked at herself in the mirror, then washed her face and hands with hot water and soap. She noticed some vomit on the lapel and right sleeve of her robe and tried to wash the spots out. She rubbed the robe with a towel, put the towel over her shoulder, and opened the bathroom door.

Thomas stood with a small envelope in his hand.

"Where's the cook?" she asked.

"She has gone home for the day," Thomas answered.

Rachel took the envelope and stared up at him.

"I want you to send someone to her house right now, and bring her back here, to me."

"Yes, Miss Barbieri."

"And call for a doctor. I think the damn cook has tried to poison me. Go!"

Thomas turned and walked away as Rachel headed back to the toilet and vomited again.

"My god! What the hell has she done with me?" she said aloud.

Rachel sat down on the tile floor and tried to catch her breath. She took several deep breaths, calming her somewhat, and opened the courier's note. Rachel read the note, crumpled it in her hand, and tossed it on the floor.

"Rotten sons of bitches!" she said aloud. She leaned back against the tiled wall and hugged herself.

"I'll make them pay for this, Joanne! I'll make them all pay for this!"

Tears ran down Rachel's cheeks. She quickly wiped them away and slowly got to her feet. She took a deep breath, walked into her bedroom, and picked up her phone.

"Get me Carmine Scarola immediately. Thank you."

Rachel saw a glass snow globe of New York City sitting on her dresser. She picked it up and tossed it hard against the wall, smashing it into pieces. She removed her robe, dropped it on the floor, and walked back naked to the bathroom. She turned on her shower and stepped under the hot steaming water.

"Sons of bitches!" she screamed.

Rachel stepped out of the shower and wrapped a towel around her head and chest as her phone rang. She marched to the phone and picked it up.

"Hello, Carmine. I thought we had a deal?" she asked.

"We did have a deal," he replied. "What is wrong?"

"What is wrong?" she screamed. "What is fucking wrong!?? Is that how you are going to play this now?"

"I don't know what you are talking about or why you are so upset?" he answered.

"Joanne Paris! She's dead. Someone put two bullets into the back of her head!"

"When did this happen?" Carmine asked, doing his best to sound uninvolved.

"Last night, you son of a bitch! We had an understanding! A trust! Your nephew gets popped because he didn't do as he was instructed and now you take issue with me over it? With me? This is not acceptable, Carmine, and there will be consequences. Major consequences! If you think for one second..."

The phone line suddenly went dead, stopping Rachel mid-sentence.

Rachel stared into the phone, shocked with his bravado.

"You lying son of a bitch! You think you have the balls to go up against me? I will have your balls on a silver platter and feed them to my dogs!"

Rachel slammed the phone down hard three times before leaving it in its cradle. She paced back and forth for several moments then quickly walked into her large closet, picked out an outfit of black slacks and a black sweater and got dressed.

A good twenty minutes passed and as Rachel sat in front of her mirror finishing her hair and makeup, Thomas entered with the cook. Her name was Camille Vazanno, an attractive older Mexican woman with a kind smile and long black hair.

"Here is the cook, Miss Barbieri, as requested," said Thomas.

Rachel stood up and faced the woman.

"What is your name?" Rachel asked.

"I am Camille," she answered.

"Who put you up to this?" Rachel asked.

Camille glanced at Thomas with a confused look.

"Don't look at him!" Rachel cried. "Look at me! Answer my question!"

"I was hired by Thomas to be your cook. I don't understand what it is you are asking of me?" Camille replied.

"I have been throwing up all morning, Camille, after eating a breakfast you prepared for me! Why is that? Are you trying to poison me? Did someone ask you to poison me?"

"No! I could never do such a thing! It was not my huevos rancheros, Senora Barbieri."

"No?" she asked. "How can you be so sure?"

"Because if you got sick like you say? Then it was the coffee," she replied. "Not the eggs. The coffee."

"You put poison in my coffee?!!!"

"No, senora! No! It is not poison that made you sick."

"I am not following!"

Camille looked over at Thomas again and sighed.

"What?!!" screamed Rachel.

"It is the water, senora."

"The water?" Rachel repeated.

"Si. Si, senora. You are new to this area. Everyone coming here for the first time gets sick with our drinking water. Some get better but some do not. I am told you are a powerful woman, Senora Barbieri. Some say you are Ix Chel. You can use your powers to cleanse our water. Make it safe for everyone to drink. Yes?"

Rachel looked at Thomas.

"Is what she said true? Do people get sick drinking the water here?"

"I did," said Thomas. "When I first arrived I got very sick. So did the house maid, Teresa, and several of the guards."

Rachel turned back to Camille.

"So the water in the coffee is what made me ill?" she asked. "That's what you're saying to me?"

"Si, Senora. No one told me to poison you. I could never do such a thing. I love to cook. To make people feel good eating what I prepare. I love working here. Working for you. I would never do anything to jeopardize my position here. Never."

Rachel stared hard at Camille and pondered her words for a few moments.

"I'm going to have bottled water brought in here and I want you to use it every time you need water. Even if it's to wash your hands. Do you understand?"

"Si, Senora," said Camille.

"I have plans to build a school and a hospital here. And several hotels. I am going to have someone look into this tainted water situation and we will find a solution. I can promise you that. We can't have the people living and working here or any tourists coming in to Cozumel in the near future getting themselves ill over drinking water. Right?"

A smile crossed Camille's face.

"Right! Yes! Thank you, Senora Barbieri. Thank you."

"Have someone drive Camille home," said Rachel.

"Yes, Miss Barbieri," said Thomas and walked Camille out.

"Thomas?" said Rachel calling him back into the room.

"Yes?" he asked.

"Order bottled water immediately and if I ever get sick like this again I want that bitch to disappear. Do you understand?"

"Yes, Miss Barbieri. I understand."

"Good. Get me Dix Haggis on the phone."

"Right away," said Thomas. "Will you still be seeing the doctor?"

"Yes. When he arrives send him in here. And I want you to get me three dogs. Three big dogs."

"Dogs?" asked Thomas. "What kind of dogs?"

"I don't know. Just as long as they're big and will do as I ask."

"I will see what I can do."

"Thank you, Thomas."

Thomas nodded and left the room. Rachel walked to the mirror and brushed her short blonde hair.

"Are you Ix Chel?" she asked herself. "Superstitious nonsense."

Rachel's phone suddenly rang and she picked it up immediately.

"Hello Dix. We have a situation to discuss. How soon can you get down here?"

Rachel listened and played with her hair as she stared into the mirror.

"Good," she said and hung up the phone.

Rachel's house cook, Camille, was dropped off at the modest one bedroom home she shared with her younger cousin, Evalina. Camille smiled as she watched the car drive away and was greeted at the front door by her cousin.

"Well? What happened?" asked Evalina.

"We didn't use enough," Camille replied and went inside.

"She's still alive?"

"Yes" said Camille. "All that powder did was make her throw up."

"Throw up? Madre de Dios! Did she accuse you? Is that why she sent a car for you?"

"Of course she accused me."

Evalina grabbed Camille by the arms and began looking for signs of bruising.

"But you're not hurt? She didn't punish you somehow?"

Camille laughed lightly.

"No," said Camille. "She accused me. Yes. But I used the water story."

"The water story? Madre Dios! And it worked?" asked Evalina.

"Luckily for me it did but whatever it was that Madrid gave you was definitely not potent enough. Or maybe the hot water in the coffee did something to it. I don't know. All I know is she's still alive and so am I."

Camille sat down and removed her shoes and rubbed her feet.

"We'll try more next time," Evalina added. "Something a lot stronger. Madrid will keep his promise to us. You'll see."

"He better!" Camille said. "Rachel Stone Barbieri is no Ix Chel. She is moving huge amounts of product now, shipping it all to god knows where! She is nothing more than a wealthy gringa who sells drugs to the world. If I fail again she will kill me, Evalina. That's who that woman is. She is evil."

"We will stop her and Madrid will make us both rich. As he promised."

"Madrid is a coward."

He will still make us rich," said Evalina.

"I hope you are right, cousin. This type of power turns good people into bad people. Very bad people. Barbieri and Madrid both scare me. And they should both scare you, too. We have to be smart before we become rich. And careful. Very careful."

Evalina stood for a moment taking in Camille's words and then reached for a bottle on the fireplace mantel. She poured two small glasses of tequila.

"We will bide our time for now and when Barbieri dies, we will come out of this as wealthy women. Rich and happy, cousin. And we will be able to go anywhere in this world we choose. Anywhere. Madrid can do as he pleases and so will we. Mark my words. Rich and happy. That is our destiny here."

Evalina handed Camille a glass.

MAGENTA DAIRY

"Here," Evalina said. "Drink. To our future."
"To our future," repeated Camille. "If we both live long enough."
They sipped from their glasses and drank to their future.

CHAPTER TWENTY EIGHT

Phil was finished for the day at the office and she skipped to the luncheonette across the street to get a burger and fries to go. She slyly nodded to my undercover man, Rick Barkley, who was sitting in the rear booth drinking his coffee while trying to keep a watchful eye out for any glimpse of Terrence Bruce or his tan Pontiac.

An entire week had passed.

Betty and Jake's murders had become front page news in just about every newspaper in southern California. Barney had closed the restaurant indefinitely and he and I and Phil saw to it that Betty and Jake and their

300

unborn child were cremated, which was their wish. All three of us had sat in Barney's by the Sea in booth number eight hoping Terrence Bruce would come for any one of us.

We were armed, we were angry, and we were ready for a fight.

We drank to the memory of our murdered friends. We laughed, sharing stories from days past, and we cried together off and on for four days and four nights straight.

Barney was completely devastated but was glad to have Phil and me staying with him as he struggled to deal with such a horrific loss.

We all felt the loss deeply, but Barney used beer after beer to try to cope with his grief and make some sense of it all.

He couldn't, and the beers didn't help, but it did give Barney some much needed moments of rest as the days and nights wore on.

Phil was heartbroken too, which through the week turned into anger, and she vowed to shoot Terrence Bruce on sight no matter how or where that might occur.

Barney and I did not disagree with her.

I put on a good front the first day after the murders, trying to hold everything together and find the strength to be the voice of reason and compassion even if it was just for Phil and for Barney alone.

I kept blaming myself over and over again for not doing a better job of protecting Betty and Jake.

My thoughts kept returning to things I could have done or should have done but all the "even ifs" and the "I should haves" in the world wasn't going to change what had happened.

That was my biggest struggle.

Betty and Jake were gone forever and there was nothing I could do about that.

Not ever.

The second day I lost all control and every ounce of my deep sadness poured out from my guilt ridden soul, washed with endless tears and unbelievable grief.

Jake and I had become great friends but Betty had always been my closest friend, my best friend, and always had my back even when she felt I was doing the wrong thing.

Betty was my rock.

Terrence Bruce and Rachel Stone Barbieri took Betty and Jake away from me in a foul and senseless killing and I was going to be the one to make them both pay dearly for their actions.

My deep sadness for the murders of Detective Munoz and Detective Blaine and now Betty and Jake and their unborn child became an outrageous boiling anger which quickly escalated until it manifested into an acute hatred I had never experienced before in my entire life.

As the sad week came to a close I focused all that hatred in one direction, aimed straight at this unfeeling, cold blooded killer for hire named Terrence Bruce, the man who had snuffed out our best friends' lives forever.

"An eye for an eye," I said as I slowly sipped my third Scotch. "That's how it's going to be. There isn't going to be any arrest with this monster. Or with Rachel Stone Barbieri. I'll promise you that."

As Friday came I put Barney up at the Roosevelt Hotel under the false name Thomas Leonardis, with a cover that he was a screenwriter hired to write a project for Paramount Pictures and was not to be disturbed. I knew the desk man at the Roosevelt, a brave ex GI named Ronald Bull, a man we nicknamed Bulldog back in our war days. I met Bulldog in Berlin while I was on special detail with Patton. There were only four of us Marines rolling with Patton's army back then and Bulldog was our commanding officer.

"Anyone comes in asking for me, Phil, or Barney you get me on the horn right away. You hear me?" I asked.

"Will do," said Bulldog.

I left my card and a photo of Terrence Bruce and told Bulldog this guy Bruce might change his appearance to throw people off but he would still have to ask for our names and that would be the giveaway to make the phone call.

"Don't worry, Patrick," he said. "I got this."

I jumped in the coupe and headed for the office.

Meanwhile, Phil had grabbed her dinner to go, climbed up the stairs to the office and reached the front door. She noticed a light coming from my office and, dropping the burger to the floor, quickly pulled out the pistol I gave her that was now stuffed in her handbag. Phil took a deep breath, tested the doorknob, and discovered the office door was unlocked.

Phil opened the door quietly and nervously stepped inside, pointing her weapon and darting her eyes from side to side looking for anyone who might be hiding inside.

She moved silently across the main floor, passed by her desk and made her way slowly to my office. Still pointing her weapon, she stepped inside and prepared to fire.

Suddenly, she felt cold steel pressed against the back of her neck and heard a voice.

"I'll take that gun, sweetheart," the voice said.

Phil froze, began to sob and shake, and held out her weapon to be taken.

"On second thought, I'd like a hot cup of joe and a few bites of whatever it is you left out there on the entrance floor," I said as I leaned back against the doorway.

Phil turned and punched me on the shoulder as she wiped her tears.

"What is wrong with you?" she screamed.

"Me?" I asked. "What is wrong with you? What have I been telling you? What made you think you could do a sweep through here? Alone? And face off with somebody like that? Just because you're a good shot and you have a gun in your hand doesn't make you Dick Tracy or Sam Spade. You're more like Spade's partner, Miles Archer."

"He's the partner who got killed. Right?" she asked.

"Right. Just like Terrence Bruce would have done to you right now if it was him up here waiting for you instead of me. I'm sorry for scaring you, Phil but this guy is a real pro and I needed to teach you a lesson. If

303

you see something wrong you go get Richard up here and you call me or the police right away! Understood, Annie Oakley?"

"Understood," she said.

"Good. Go get your dinner and go home. And watch your back and keep watching your back every second until we get this guy. Okay?"

"Okay," she said.

The office phone rang and Phil picked it up.

"Patrick Atwater's office," she said.

Phil listened intently for a few moments.

"Hold on, please," she said and put the call on hold.

"It's some woman named C.D. Smythe. She says she knows where Terrence Bruce is."

"Lock the front door and patch me through," I said and ran to my office and picked up the phone.

"Line two," yelled Phil.

"This is Atwater," I said.

"My name is Seedy Smythe," the woman said. "I read in the papers about that couple that was murdered up off Mullholland. I spent some time with the guy I think did those people in."

"Why do you think that, Miss Smythe?" I asked and wrote her name down.

"The guy I was with had a folder. A green folder. I read it. All of it. The folder had names and addresses and photos of people. Those two people that got killed? I saw their pictures in that folder. When he was sleeping. That's why I'm pretty sure this guy is the one that done it. His name is Bruce. He never told me his last name."

"How did you meet this guy?" I asked.

"I work for a law firm, Russeau, Dietz, Haggis, and Moore over on Wilshire."

"Are you a lawyer?"

"No sir."

"What is it you do for this law firm?"

"Whatever they ask me to do," she replied. "Usually I just have to spend some time with whoever needs their time spent, if you catch my drift?"

I understood completely and hearing the name Haggis confirmed everything for me.

"I'm a nurse, Mr. Atwater. Sometimes these people they send me to? They need that kind of servicing also."

"Like removing bullets and stitching guys up?" I asked.

"Yes," she said. "This guy had a nasty gash on his head. I fixed him up. Took six stitches. Spent almost three weeks with that freak and his crazy habits. When I found the folder and saw what was in it I got out of there as fast as I could."

"You said you saw their names and their pictures?" I asked. "You're certain it was them?"

"Yes," she answered. "I saw them and I'm certain. Quite certain."

"Why haven't you called the police?"

"The police could arrest me too if they wanted to. I'm not going to jail for that freako."

"Why are you calling me?"

"I'm calling you, Mr. Atwater, because I saw your picture in that folder too. And your secretary's picture. Phil. Right? A pretty young white girl? Drives a Hudson? You drive a coupe. A Ford coupe."

"Do you know where this guy is now? This guy Bruce?"

"Yes," she said. "I know where he is. I know exactly where he's staying."

"What's the address?" I asked and grabbed a pen.

A few moments of silence passed. I waited for her to speak and then realized what her silence was all about.

I didn't have long to wait.

"What's in it for me?" she asked.

"What do you want?"

305

"What does anybody want, Mr. Atwater? Money. And lots of it. I ran out on that freak because he scared me. I won't ever get paid for that time. I need some cash now and I need it today."

"How much do you want?" I asked.

"The police are offering a five hundred dollar reward for any information leading to his arrest. If you want this guy then I want double that amount. You hear me? Double. For what I had to do for that guy believe me I earned that kind of cash. I did."

"All right," I said. "I'll bring you half now and once I have Bruce I'll give you the rest. Fair enough?"

"Fair enough," she said.

"Do we have a deal, Miss Smythe?" I asked.

A few more moments of silence hung on the line.

"Okay, Mr. Atwater," she replied. "We have a deal."

"Great! What's your address?" I asked.

"I'm staying at my brother's house right now until I know this guy is off the streets for good. My brother sells used cars in Compton. Here's his home address."

Seedy no sooner gave me the address when her phone line suddenly went dead.

"Miss Smythe? Seedy? Are you there?"

I hung up the phone and had Phil quickly put five hundred dollars from the Santoro file into an envelope and I headed out to Compton. Seedy sounded legitimately scared over the phone and her quick hang up concerned me greatly. My gut told me she was on the level about Bruce. I didn't suspect she was just some street whore secretly working with Bruce and now making an attempt to lure me into some trap so Terrence could kill me.

It didn't matter much to me which way my trip to Compton was going to play out.

Not today.

Not tonight.

Special Agent Davis and Agent Lindman were in the air flying back to Los Angeles and Special Agent Edwards was still somewhere in South America, all of them much too far away to present any assistance to me or my situation.

I was totally on my own and drove rapidly to Compton to check it all out no matter what the truth of our conversation might be.

All I kept telling myself was that I finally had what sounded like a solid lead on Mr. Terrence Bruce the monster, and I was going to follow it up no matter what, where, or how it led me.

My gut also told me if this was the day Terrence Bruce and I were finally going to meet face to face, then only one of us would be going home shortly thereafter.

I checked my .38 and stepped on the gas.

CHAPTER TWENTY NINE

Alejandro Madrid and Dix Haggis sat next to one another in the rear seat of Madrid's black Packard as the car slowly headed up the hill to Rachel's compound.

"I appreciate you picking me up at the airport," said Dix.

"I was happy to offer you the ride," replied Madrid. "Mrs. Barbieri has been very generous since arriving here in Mexico and giving you passage to her compound is the least I could do in return."

"It's appreciated," said Dix and stared out the window. "This is a beautiful country you have here."

"Beautiful, yes, but very poor," added Madrid. "Still very backward when compared to the rest of the world."

"Change for the better is always a slow process," said Haggis. "I understand construction has already begun on several hotels and a hospital here in Cozumel."

"Yes," replied Madrid. "And a baseball field for the children. Mexican children love your American baseball. Baseball allows our little ones to dream of one day playing in the World Series."

"Maybe people like you and me and Mrs. Barbieri can make that happen one day."

"I would love to see nothing more," Madrid lied and wondered if this lawyer, Dix Haggis, had ever spent any nights with Rachel Stone Barbieri.

Haggis was tall, a few years younger than Madrid, and he had a flair about him that Madrid thought Rachel might find attractive. He put his thoughts away as the car approached the well-protected compound gate.

The driver, Bernardo, pulled up to the gate and lowered his window as the guard stepped up holding a brand new M3 machine gun.

"Mr. Madrid and Mr. Haggis to see Mrs. Barbieri," said Bernardo.

The guard peered in the rear of the vehicle and waved them through as the wide gate opened.

Haggis was impressed at how well protected Rachel was at her compound. Every guard was well armed with M3s and they all appeared quite focused as they held their individual and numerous positions around the entire grounds.

"A person would need an Army to take this place," Haggis said.

"He most certainly would," agreed Madrid.

The two men walked side by side into the front entrance where they were warmly greeted by Thomas.

"Hello Senor Madrid," Thomas said. "Mr. Haggis, a pleasure meeting you, sir."

"Likewise, Thomas," said Haggis and they shook hands.

The men were escorted to the outdoor patio where a table was set with various Mexican dishes, some diced chicken and pork, beans and rice, freshly made tortillas, and several lobsters and giant shrimp.

"Would you care for a cocktail?" Thomas asked.

"What is Mrs. Barbieri drinking?" asked Haggis.

"Margarita rocks with a splash of Grand Marnier is her drink of the day," said Thomas.

"I'll have the same," said Haggis.

"Make that two," replied Madrid.

Thomas nodded and gestured toward the table.

"Help yourselves to some food, gentlemen," offered Thomas. "Mrs. Barbieri will be joining you shortly."

"Thank you," said Madrid as he stepped to the table and fixed himself a plate.

Haggis took a look around and noticed several yachts out in the small cove. One boat was docked at the pier and four men were loading eight pallets of fresh fish onto its deck. Haggis smiled, knowing full well what lay beneath those fish, well hidden from prying eyes.

"Those are expensive loads of fish," said Madrid. "Dead fish that will never see the market place or a wealthy man's plate."

"The cost of doing business," said Haggis.

Thomas brought the drinks and placed them on their table.

"Dix," said Rachel as she walked up to greet him, drying her dyed blonde hair and wearing leather sandals and a pale yellow bathing suit. Two large German Shepherd dogs trotted alongside her.

Dix gave Rachel a hug and a kiss and Madrid pretended not to notice as he grabbed another piece of shrimp and sipped his margarita.

Hello, Mr. Madrid," she said. "So nice to see you again."

"Very nice seeing you, Mrs. Barbieri."

Madrid looked at Barbieri from her head to her toes. The angle of the sun beaming down on her yellow suit made her appear naked as she stood next to Haggis. Madrid licked his lips and could tell Barbieri could sense what he was thinking.

Madrid tried to deflate his wanton looks.

"My compliments to your chef and to your bartender," said Madrid and raised his glass to her. "The food is quite exceptional."

"Thank you," she replied. "And thank you for meeting Dix at the airport."

"Your thanks is not necessary," he added. "The pleasure was all mine."

Rachel grabbed two pieces of pork from the table and tossed the meat to the dogs. The dogs devoured the pork quickly and obediently sat down.

"These are the new men in my life," she said. "Caesar and Napoleon."

"They are beautiful animals," said Dix.

"How was the flight in?" she asked.

Uneventful," said Dix. "Senor Madrid was kind enough to offer me a ride from the airport."

"I told him you were coming and I knew he was arriving today also."

Thomas brought Rachel her drink and handed it to her.

"Thank you, Thomas. Please tell Maria that Mr. Madrid is here."

"Yes, madam," said Thomas and walked away.

Rachel sat down at the table next to Madrid and stole a shrimp from his plate.

"These are good," she said and smiled.

Dix sat down next to Rachel and sipped his drink. Rachel stared at Madrid.

"You have that look in your eye again, Mr. Madrid," said Rachel.

"What look is that," he asked.

"You like the food. And the drink. And the way I wear this bathing suit. But your face, once again, and your eyes are telling me you have come here with some news. And this news is not good news."

"You are very astute, Mrs. Barbieri," he replied. "My compliments once again."

Madrid smiled and sipped his drink.

"You are speaking of our mutual friends now sitting in Havana?" she asked.

"Yes," said Madrid. "My President wants your guarantee they will not become a problem."

Madrid knew he had to pick and choose his words carefully.

"Please let me assure you and your President that nothing will ever become a problem as long as I am here in Cozumel honoring our agreement."

"These men are not to be trusted, Mrs. Barbieri. My President worries when our friends in Havana make certain decisions without first consulting with us."

"You can trust me, Senor Madrid, when I tell you that no decisions will ever be made without my knowledge or my consent."

"You are in control? Yes?" he asked.

"As always," said Rachel and sipped her drink.

Thomas and Maria stepped out on the patio. Maria carried a brown leather bag and handed it to Madrid.

"Gracias, Senorita," said Madrid and quickly corrected himself. "I mean thank you, Miss."

"Tell your President he has nothing to worry from our friends in Havana or his friend here in Cozumel. Construction has begun. Business is good. And together we will all profit and grow. Thomas will show you to your car."

Haggis quickly stood up and offered his hand.

"A pleasure meeting and talking with you, Senor Madrid," said Haggis.

Madrid rose slowly, glanced at the two dogs watching his every move, and shook hands with Haggis.

"Enjoy your stay in Cozumel," said Madrid.

"I fully intend to," said Haggis and smiled at Rachel.

"Until next time, Miss Barbieri," added Madrid and followed Thomas out carrying the brown leather bag. Maria nodded and walked away.

"Interesting man," said Haggis.

"Madrid is a pig and a fool," said Rachel. "How is it he knows anything about our friends in Havana?"

"They obviously contacted him or President Muchado," said Haggis.

"Exactly," said Rachel. "If they want to cozy up to the mob then they will both see where that will get them. And see it very soon. I am not waiting on this, Dix. They want a war with me then I am going to give it to them. In spades."

"Where do you want to start?" he asked.

"Right at the source."

"Carmine Scarola?"

"Yes," she replied. "He and his small-minded friends think they can fuck with me? We'll show them all who they are fucking with and they won't have a clue as to who is doing what or when. Did you make the list as I requested?"

Dix took out an envelope, opened it, and placed a single page in front of Rachel.

"These are the names of all five New York families, their under bosses, and their street soldiers," said Dix. "Who should we hit after Carmine?"

Rachel pointed at several names as she spoke.

"Here. Here. And then this one here. That should put it all into motion. No collateral damage. That's critical. Absolutely none. Understood?"

"Completely," said Dix, finishing his drink and using a pen made some notes on the page.

"Thomas?" yelled Rachel.

Thomas stepped out onto the patio.

"Yes, madam?" he asked.

"We would like two more margaritas, please."

"Yes madam," said Thomas and walked away.

Rachel rubbed her foot on Dix's leg and smiled.

"I've missed you," she said.

Dix returned her smile with one of his own, put the pen down, and kissed her hand.

CHAPTER THIRTY

I found the house easily and decided to park around the corner instead of right in front. The house had a detached garage and the driveway sat on the side street. I parked the coupe and waited. The corner street light illuminated most of the house and the rest of the street was dark and empty.

It was also quiet.

An unsettling quiet.

I got out of the car, crossed the street, and walked up the driveway.

The garage doors had several small windows so I peeked in and noticed it was completely empty except for an old rusted bicycle with bent handlebars and two flat tires. I walked up to the back door with my .38 behind me and gave the door my best police type knock.

I waited a few moments but there was no answer.

I gave the driveway a quick looksee and tried the door. It was unlocked.

I pointed my .38 and stepped inside.

The kitchen was small and everything seemed to be neat, clean, and undisturbed. I walked through the dining area and stepped into the living room. It too was empty and I moved slowly down the hallway. I clicked on the light and checked the bathroom. I shut off the light and moved to the next room, a small bedroom.

There was no closet and the room was empty.

I continued down the hallway and entered the master bedroom.

I clicked on the light and what I saw made me gasp.

A black woman who I assumed was Seedy, was lying naked and face down on the bed in a pool of her own blood. Her clothes, shoes, and underwear had been tossed about the room. I stepped in cautiously and took a closer look at her.

Someone had cut her throat from ear to ear.

My mind flashed back to my near accident on Laurel Canyon and realized that this was the same girl I had almost hit with my car.

I quickly checked the small bathroom, and satisfied the house was empty, put my gun away.

I checked the girl's pulse, hoping there might be some signs of life but I couldn't find one. The blood was fresh and her body was still warm, telling me this must have happened right after her phone call to me.

I picked up the phone and called the police. I told them who I was and what I had found and was told they would send someone out.

I stepped out on the back step and took a moment to calm myself.

Terrence Bruce was once again two steps ahead of me and now, because of me, another innocent life had been taken.

I sat there wondering what I could possibly do next to find Terrence Bruce and end all this killing, when a cream-colored Cadillac pulled into the driveway. I stood up to greet the black man at the wheel.

The man was Seedy's brother.

I told him who I was and why I had come to see his sister. I told him not to enter but he was adamant about it and made his way inside.

"Oh sweet baby, Seedy!" he cried as he stood in the doorway.

"Your house is a crime scene now and we need to step outside," I told him.

We went outside and waited for the police. He was clearly upset and saddened by the sight of his dead sister, but stayed calm and composed.

"I knew this was going to happen to her one day," he said. "She wouldn't listen to me. I told her time and time again to get out of the life she was living. Even told her I'd help her get back on her feet. Live like normal folks. But she always said no. And now this. My sister was a nurse. She could have done some good in her life. Helped people! Now she'll never help another soul. Never. Do you know who did this to her?"

"I'm pretty certain it was the last man she had been with," I said.

"That freako guy named Bruce?" he asked. "The one with the dented head and the folder full of pictures of people he killed or was going to kill?"

"Your sister told you about Bruce?" I asked.

"She told me everything about that no good bastard! Some crazed Irishman from London."

"Yes! That's him," I said. "Do you know where he might be?"

"Damn right, I do," he said. "After Seedy ran out on that crazy blow freak I had my man John Joseph put a tail on him."

"John Joseph?" I asked.

"He's an ex-cop from Chicago. My cousin. Came out here to sell some of his police stories to the moving pictures people. He told me this Bruce drives a tan Pontiac but the plates on it are fake. That shit is against the law!"

"Where is Bruce now? Right now?" I asked.

"He's holed up in Studio City right off Ventura. Some empty house for sale on Woodbridge. The place has a Stone Realty sign right in the front yard. Nice ranch type."

He reached in his pocket and took out a small note pad and started flipping pages.

"Here it is," he said. "One five nine oh five Woodbridge. John Joseph is up there right now keeping eyes on him."

He tore out the page and handed it to me.

"You'll find John Joseph sitting in a dark green 1948 Chevrolet. You show John Joseph this and he'll help you take that son of a bitch down! Hell! He'll even help you kill the rotten bastard if that's what you have to do? My cousin knows how to do stuff like that. Believe me. He has put down quite a few bad boys in his day."

I took the page, read the address, and put it in my pocket.

"Thank you. I think we should wait for the police," I said.

"Wait for the police? This ain't Beverly Hills, Atwater. This is Compton. The police ain't gonna be here for at least another hour."

"An hour?" I asked. "This is a homicide."

"Don't matter. Not to them. It's how it is over here. One hour. Believe me. Maybe two. You jump in that car of yours and go get this bastard. I'll deal with the police. And I won't say a word about anything else until I hear from you. Agreed?"

He stuck out his hand and smiled.

"Agreed," I said and shook his hand. "Tell them I had to go check a lead and I'll come back in a couple of hours max. Okay?"

"Okay," he replied. "That motherfucker needs to disappear for what he did to my sister and before he goes hurting anybody else. Black or white. Do you need a piece?"

"No," I said. "I'm covered."

We shook hands again and I handed him the envelope meant for Seedy.

"What's this?" he asked.

"Your sister and I had a deal," I said. "She had some pertinent information I desperately needed and I was willing to pay her for it. That's only half of it as we agreed. I'll bring you the rest after my conversation with Mr. Bruce. My word on it."

A tear fell from his right eye and he nodded at me.

"I'm happy to hear my sister did some good in this world."

"What's your name?" I asked.

"Smythe," he answered. "Donald Smythe. My friends call me Smitty."

"I will get back to you, Smitty," I said. "I'm sorry about your sister. I think she was going to turn her life around like you had asked. That envelope was going to be her new start."

"Do you really think so?" he asked.

"Yes," I replied. "I really do."

"Thank you, Mr. Atwater."

I nodded to Smitty, hopped in the coupe, and headed for the valley.

I didn't know if my words about Seedy were true or not but I hoped that's how Smitty would always think of his sister in the future.

Traffic was light and I came up Tujunga Boulevard and made a quick turn onto Woodbridge Avenue. I drove up the quiet neighborhood street very slowly and saw John Joseph's dark green Chevy parked under some trees. I parked near the corner by a mailbox, shut off my engine and my headlights, and stepped out onto the street.

There was an eerie, calm, quiet all around me, the kind of quiet you experience just before an oncoming storm.

I approached John Joseph's car slowly and could see it was empty. The driver side window was down and there were a dozen or more crushed out cigarette butts beginning to pile up on the road next to the front tire. I looked in the car. The keys were in the ignition and there were several empty bottles of beer sitting on the passenger seat. I was about to turn away when I noticed something glistening on the seat near the empty bottles. I reached in and touched it with my index finger and realized it was blood.

Fresh blood.

"Had Terrence discovered he was being followed," I thought to myself. "If so, has he killed John Joseph or did Terrence knock the poor man unconscious and take him into the house for questioning?"

I took out my handkerchief and quickly wiped the blood from my hand.

I turned towards the house and saw the Stone Realty sign sitting in the front yard about three houses down. I took a deep breath, pulled out my .38, crossed the street and headed to the house.

It was a two story home with a brick archway set over the driveway which led to a wooden garage near the back. The entire house was dark and from my angle appeared empty. I walked quietly around to the back and noticed a candle flickering from a window upstairs.

"Someone was up there," I thought to myself.

I went to the side door of the garage and peeked through the glass pane.

Terrence's tan Pontiac had been backed in telling me there was a ninety-nine per cent chance he was inside the house and just might be waiting for someone to come looking for John Joseph.

I thought of Betty and Jake, their unborn child, my good friend Detective Blaine, and Agent Edward's girlfriend's relative, the sad writer producer, all dead and gone forever and all because of some hired monster now just a few feet away from me. I took another deep breath, walked up the rear porch steps, and tried the back door.

It was open.

I entered the house as quietly as I could and stood in the kitchen until my eyes adjusted to the darkness.

I walked through the empty kitchen, pointing my gun and listening for any kind of movement or sound. I cautiously entered the hallway leading to the front door and the upstairs and kept moving forward. I peered into the living room. There wasn't a stick of furniture to be seen.

I walked to the bottom of the stairs and heard my first sound.

It was water running.

I leaned against the wall and listened. It was shower water coming from the upstairs bathroom.

"Was Terrence purposely running the water hoping to lull me into dropping my guard and my gun," I thought.

I held that thought as a possibility and took three steps up.

The shower water sound suddenly stopped. I froze and kept my .38 pointed at the top of the stairs. Someone was definitely in the bathroom.

Footsteps sounded from the bathroom, down the upper hall, and headed to the rear bedroom where I had seen the candle burning from the window. I wondered if John Joseph was lying dead up there somewhere or maybe his body had been stuffed in the trunk of his car.

I cursed myself for not checking John Joseph's car more carefully.

I took another deep breath, blew it out slowly, and headed up the stairs, knowing full well what I was about to face.

I thought of Betty and moved faster.

I reached the top of the stairs and could hear movement in the back bedroom. I leaned my back against the wall and pointed my .38.

A good two minutes passed and suddenly the candle light went out and the house became completely dark. I quickly shut my eyes for a few seconds, hoping to adjust my sight to the upstairs darkness. I opened my eyes and a sudden burst of wind rattled the house and somehow parted the overcast clouds and a bright ray of moonlight lit up the hallway.

The gods were on my side.

Terrence Bruce casually stepped out of the bedroom wearing a black suit and tie and carrying two suitcases.

Terrence saw me standing against the wall pointing my .38 and he stopped dead in his tracks.

"Well now," he said calmly without batting an eye. "Mr. Atwater, I presume. Good evening to you, sir."

"Put the bags down, Terrence, and get on your knees," I said.

"If I must?" he said.

"You must," I said, trying to imitate his Irish accent. "Do it!"

"Yes sir," he replied.

He put the two bags down onto the floor and dropped to his knees.

"Now put your hands on top of your head and interlace your fingers."

"Yes sir," he complied again and put his hands on his head.

"Where's John Joseph?" I asked.

"Who?" he asked.

"You know who," I said.

"I will assume you are referring to the dark burly gentleman in the green Chevrolet," he said.

"I am."

"I'll have you know he's alive and tightly tied up in the trunk of his car. For now. Does he work for you? Is that how you found me?"

"No. He was working for Seedy, the girl you murdered tonight."

"Ah, yes. Seedy. I liked her. I did. In my way. She was an excellent nurse. A very attractive, comforting, companion. Until something frightened the poor lass and she ran off. She unfortunately became an annoying and difficult loose end, as they say."

"Is that what all these people you've killed are to you? Annoying loose ends?"

He looked at me and smiled.

"We're all loose ends, laddie. And we all must do what we are paid to do."

"Your killing days have come to an end, pal." I said.

Terrence laughed and his tone suddenly went from light to cold and dark.

"Is that what you think, Mr. Atwater?"

"It's what I know, pal," I replied.

He stared hard into my eyes and I could see his wheels turning, wondering how he could possibly kill me in the next few moments.

"Rachel was right, Mr. Atwater," he said. "You are such a little man. Little in thought. Little in life. Little in your view of this world. The real world."

"Say what you want. I'm not the one on my knees with my hands on my head and a gun in my face."

"Well said, Mr. Atwater. Well said. This isn't the first time I've had a gun pointed at me. You are a smart gumshoe, I'll give you that. Your arrival here tonight was highly unexpected on my part. Looks like you got me. You did. That's true. You found me and you caught me quite flat footed. Fair and square. Call in the police. I'm assuming they are on their way. Call Mr. Hoover himself and the entire FBI if you must. Arrest me, sir. Please? By all means! Put the cuffs on me and take me away. Do your sworn duty as a good upstanding private eye or a brave little G-Man or whoever you think you truly represent nowadays doing what it is you do. You have me, sir. Dead to rights. Take me in. Put me in irons."

"You're going to get the chair for what you've done."

His tone became light once again.

"Oh no, Mr. Atwater. Not the chair! Heaven forbid."

"You think this is funny?" I asked.

His tone jumped back to serious and cold.

"Funny sir? I will tell you the truth. It's downright hysterical. You'll see. The police will arrive. They will arrest me. They will lock me up tonight. Yes they will. And you, sir, you can write all those horrible things I've done to all those special people you were so close to, you can write all their names down on your official private eye report but come the morning, laddie? Come the morning? I'll be a free man. And people like yourself? The little people of this world will be spending the remainder of their pathetic little lives wondering how in this world can something like that happen with such a terrible monster of a man like myself? You'll wonder the longest, Mr. Atwater. Terrence Bruce, locked up on multiple murder charges and yet, somehow, someway, did not do one day convicted behind bars. Not one day, laddie! Not a one!"

"You're absolutely right about that, pal," I said.

His eyes widened and his mouth opened in mock surprise.

"Glad to see you're finally seeing the light, Mr. Atwater. This is how things really are you see in this new world of ours. The real world. And the real people who actually make all the decisions for the small wee folk like yourself."

"Drop your weapon," I said.

"Excuse me?" he asked.

"I said. Drop your weapon."

"I don't have a weapon, sir. Unless you're considering these two suitcases of mine lethal weapons?"

"I think I will, sir. Yes. I will."

"Their contents may hold something lethal," he said. "Especially this one here on my left."

He looked down at the suitcase to his left and smiled at me.

I instantly thought of Betty. And Jake. The baby. Detective Blaine. The hairs stood up on the back of my neck and I spread my feet out and looked at Terrence with unbridled hate in my eyes.

"Stop or I'll shoot!" I said.

"Stop what?" he asked seemingly confused for the moment. "You're not making any...

Before Terrence could utter another word I fired one round and shot the son of a bitch square in his forehead just above his left eye.

He stared at me with this stunned bewildered look on his face as parts of the back of his head sprayed the door and wall behind him. His eyes rolled back and he fell face down onto the floor. I took out my partially bloodied handkerchief and used it to open one of the suitcases.

Terrence's fancy sabre was sitting right on top wrapped in a brown towel.

Betty's towel.

It was one of the towels belonging to the set I gave her as a small housewarming gift.

Using the handkerchief I picked up the sword and pressed Terrence's dead hand around the handle and dropped both to the hallway floor. I closed the suitcase and placed them both at the head of the stairs.

I walked down the stairs and thought about Betty again.

I stopped at the bottom step, sat down, and cried my eyes out.

"I am so sorry, Betty," I cried out. "So sorry."

I sat for a good four minutes letting every tear flow out of me until I thought I heard her voice.

"Patrick?" the voice asked.

I wiped my eyes and saw Phil through the glass in the front door staring at me. I got to my feet and opened the door.

It was Phil's voice I heard and she stood in front of me holding her gun.

"I heard the shot and saw you sitting there," she said. "I asked one of the neighbors across the street to call the police. They're on their way. Are you all right?"

"I am. You were following me?" I asked.

"Me and your man, Barkley," she said and pointed to him standing at the curb.

Barkley smiled and waved at me.

"Is he dead?" she asked.

"Yes. He came at me. With that sword of his."

Phil could see in my eyes I wasn't telling the entire story as it had played out. I was alive. Terrence Bruce was dead and gone and that was all that mattered.

To me.

And to her.

"You didn't have any choice but to shoot him. Did you?"

"No," I said. "I didn't. It was him or me."

"Yes," she agreed and smiled at me. "I understand completely."

"Good," I said.

"Where's Smitty's cousin?" she asked. "Is he all right?"

"Hopefully he's tied up and alive in the trunk of his car. The keys are in the ignition."

Phil turned to Barkley.

"He's in the trunk," she said.

Barkley walked over to the car, grabbed the keys, and got John Joseph untied and out of the trunk. He was bruised but alive and well.

I sat down on the front steps. Phil sat down next to me.

"Two down and one more to go," Phil said. "Right boss? One more and we can get back to normal business hours."

"Maybe for you," I replied. "Normal business hours for me are twenty-four seven. Always have been when I'm working a case."

"And you're really good at it, boss," she added. "Really good."

"Thanks," I said.

We both sat in silence waiting for the police to arrive.

"I could use a drink," she said.

"Me too," I replied.

"A double," she added.

"Sounds good," I replied and wiped another tear from my eye.

"Are you going to be okay?" she asked.

"No," I said. "But I will be. In time. Maybe. Maybe not."

Phil sighed and leaned on my shoulder.

Police sirens sounded off in the distance and several neighbors began coming out to the street.

CHAPTER THIRTY ONE

It was April Fool's Day but what transpired in New York City on this night was not going to be any laughing matter. The small Italian restaurant, Asiago's, was exceptionally busy for a late Sunday night in Manhattan and Carmine Scarola sat with his new girlfriend, Madelyn, sipping Champagne and waiting for their dinner to arrive.

Madelyn was visibly upset with Carmine. He had promised to take her to California for a screen test at a major studio but had to cancel their flight for this evening because of some special business meeting Carmine needed to attend and to be available at midnight in Brooklyn.

This was what he was told on the phone by the dock union rep, Pete Malloy.

"Someone's skimming our funds, Carmine," he said. "The Don heard it was you. You need to come in and explain yourself."

Carmine would never skim funds and knew the charge against him was bogus but when the Don asks for you? You go. No questions asked.

He cancelled the flight to California and the dinner at Asiago's was his way of apologizing.

"How's the Champagne, Maddie?" he asked.

"It's fine," she replied coldly.

"Hey? What's the matter with you? Do you know how hard it is to get a table in this joint? Even on a Sunday night? Most people wait months to dine at Asiago's."

"I don't want Asiago's, Carmine. You promised me Hollywood. That's what I wanted and you promised me!"

The waiter came with their two plates of veal saltimbocca and set them down.

"Is there anything else you need, sir?" the waiter asked.

"Some more bread," said Carmine.

"Yes sir. I'll bring it right out. Enjoy your dinner."

The waiter left and Carmine began to dig into his food. Madelyn sipped her Champagne and ignored Carmine as best she could.

"What's the matter with you? You're not going to eat?" he asked.

"I'm not hungry!" she replied rather loudly.

"Keep your voice down and don't embarrass me in here, Maddie. This meeting I got tomorrow? I have to be there. It's business and it's important."

"So is a promise, Carmine," she snapped back.

"Baby, I'm sorry. I'll get you another audition after tonight. Now, please? Eat your food and behave yourself."

"Drop dead, Carmine!" she said and poured her Champagne over her plate of food.

Two men dressed as waiters suddenly approached Carmine's table, pulled out handguns and fired four shots each into Carmine's face and chest. Carmine fell back against the leather booth and Maddie began screaming as loud as her shattered nerves would allow. Other people in the restaurant were screaming and ducking for cover.

The two waiters ran out the front door to an idling black Cadillac which sped away.

Downtown in the Village, Frank "The Gorilla" Vesta left his favorite whore house with his two nephews but before they reached their waiting limo a single shooter stepped out from the alleyway with two handguns blazing, killing all three men.

By the time the sun rose in Manhattan the next morning, Pasquale Vetano, a rising lieutenant in one of the five mob families and his young son, Michael, were both shot to death sitting in their family car after seeing a movie. Two mob lawyers, Johnny "Rockets" Provono and "Tiny" Tommy Tesca were shot and killed entering an elevator at a swanky hotel in mid-town.

In a short four hour time period, a supposed beef over stolen money escalated to a bigger beef over territory which then escalated a third time to a complete power struggle within all five mob families doing their business in the city. Everyone connected to organized crime had suddenly declared war on each other, "Going to the mattresses," as they all attempted to figure out what was happening within the ranks.

Only two people knew what was really happening in New York and those two people were Dix Haggis and Rachel Stone Barbieri. Haggis had called her from his home in Long Island as he sipped his morning coffee.

"It's April," he said. "We should be expecting a lot of rain in the next few weeks."

That was all he said and he hung up the phone.

Rachel lay naked on her massage table and smiled, knowing her plan had been put into action successfully. She hoped the mobsters in New York all killed each other instead of putting down their weapons and seeking a peaceful settlement to this all-out war of ghosts they now found themselves engaged in.

"Thomas?" she asked. "I would like a pitcher of mimosas brought out to the veranda please. I feel like celebrating this morning."

"Good news?" Thomas asked.

"Yes, Thomas. Very good news."

Thomas walked away as Rachel enjoyed her massage by the young and attractive masseuse, Christina.

"You have very beautiful skin, senorita" Christina said. "The gods have smiled greatly upon you."

"Yes they have," said Rachel. "Yes they have."

Rachel reached out and stroked Christina's leg.

"The gods have been generous to you, too," said Rachel. Your skin is very soft. Very supple."

"Thank you, senorita," said Christine and smiled as their eyes met.

Thomas walked across the patio carrying the pitcher of mimosas on a silver tray. Rachel sat up, covered herself with a sheet and poured herself a drink.

"What's your name," Rachel asked.

"Christina," the young masseuse replied.

"You are a very attractive young lady."

"Thank you," Christina said.

"You're very good with those hands of yours. Can I call you Christy?"

"Yes," Christina said.

"Would you like to have a drink with me, Christy?" she asked.

"Yes, thank you," said Christina.

"We will need another glass, Thomas," said Rachel and handed Christina her drink.

Thomas nodded and left again. Rachel rolled her neck and took in the warm tropical air.

"Go ahead," said Rachel. "You don't have to wait for me. Enjoy."

"Thank you," Christina said and sipped the drink.

Christina suddenly dropped her glass and it shattered on the tiled flooring. She grabbed at her throat and began choking. Rachel reached out as Christina's knees buckled and she fell to the ground.

"Thomas!" cried Rachel.

Thomas came running and Christina began foaming at her mouth as her body shook and she struggled to breathe.

"What is it?" asked Thomas.

"Something was in the mimosa," said Rachel. "Call the doctor!"

Thomas picked up the phone plugged in at Rachel's patio table and began dialing.

Christine looked up at Rachel and stopped breathing.

She stopped moving.

Foam slowly rolled out of the side of her mouth.

"Thomas, wait!" said Rachel. "It's too late. She's gone. My god, this poor girl is dead."

Thomas hung up the phone, knelt down and searched for a pulse. He got close to her face and smelled her opened mouth.

"I smell almonds," said Thomas. "That means cyanide. This girl has been poisoned."

Thomas turned and looked up at Rachel. Rachel put on her robe and placed the sheet over Christine's dead body.

"Who made the pitcher?" Rachel asked.

"Camille," said Thomas. "The cook."

"Give me your gun," Rachel requested.

"My gun?" Thomas asked.

"Yes," she responded. "Your gun. Now. Please?"

Thomas stood up, opened his jacket and removed his pistol from its holster.

"Thank you," she said.

Rachel took the gun and walked across the patio and into the house.

Camille was busily whipping some flour and eggs with a large wooden spoon as Rachel entered the kitchen with Thomas right behind

331

her. Camille's calm demeanor turned to sheer panic as her eyes widened and watched Rachel walking towards her pointing the pistol in her direction.

"Que paseo, senora?" said Camille and dropped the spoon onto the counter.

Rachel fired five quick shots into Camille's chest pushing her back against the oven. Camille fell to the floor, gasping for breath. Rachel straddled Camille's body and pointed the gun at Camille's face.

"Who told you to kill me?" she asked.

Camille's fingers twitched and her throat made a gurgling sound as her blood ran from her mouth to the floor.

Rachel pointed the gun closer and fired one more shot into Camille's face.

Camille's body went limp and more of her blood began to slowly cover a large area of the floor.

Rachel stepped away from the body and calmly handed Thomas his gun.

"Have someone take Christy's body to her family. Tell them she was poisoned by this crazy bitch cook. I want to have a huge funeral for her. I'll pay all expenses. Flowers, church, coffin. The biggest and the best. I also want the local press to cover it."

"The press," Thomas repeated. "Do you think that's wise. Putting your picture in the newspapers?"

"Just do it, Thomas. I'll worry about any photos."

Thomas nodded.

"And Camille?" he asked.

"Call the local police and have them dispose of her."

Rachel walked to one of the kitchen drawers and took out a large knife and tossed it to the floor next to Camille' body.

"Tell the police she attacked me after killing Christy and I had to shoot her in self-defense. Luckily you were standing close enough to me so I could grab your gun. Pay them well for their services. And for their full co-operation in the matter."

"Yes, Mrs. Barbieri," he replied.

"Put the word out for another cook and make sure whoever it is? Knows what just happened here. Understood?"

"Yes, Mrs. Barbieri," Thomas said. "Understood."

"I'm known here as Ix Chel," said Rachel. "The goddess of fertility. I'm also going to be the goddess of justice. Ix Chel sees a wrong and she makes it right. She makes it right on her own terms and by her own hand. No one is going to defeat Ix Chel. These people down here want a god damn goddess in their midst then I'm sure as hell going to give them one."

"Yes, Mrs. Barbieri," said Thomas.

"There's a coup going on here, Thomas. A god damn coup. Somebody down here wants me gone and wants me dead in the process. I need to know who the hell is behind it and I need to know by the end of the day. Does this Camille have any family here?"

"She lives with a cousin," said Thomas. "A younger woman named Evalina."

"Take some men and do what you need to do to get the truth out of her and when you do? Kill her slowly and burn her house down to the ground. Down to the ground."

"Yes, Mrs. Barbieri."

"And tell all the guards to stay alert. High alert. Anyone starts fucking with our shipments I want to hear about it immediately! Who? Where? And when?"

Thomas nodded once again and picked up the house phone.

Rachel walked to her bathroom, turned on her shower, removed her blood stained robe, and stepped under the water. She knew it was too soon for the New York mob to turn their suspicions onto her. This attempt on her life had to be someone here in Mexico and someone powerful enough to believe they could go against her.

Someone greedy enough to think they could win.

Only one name entered her mind.

Rachel immediately shut off the water and stared at the wet tile on the wall.

"Alejandro Madrid," she said out loud in a soft tone. "You greedy, slick, dumb, son of a bitch."

She took a deep breath and turned the water back on.

She knew she was in trouble.

Madrid had the entire Mexican Army at his command. If he came at her now with seasoned troops she couldn't fight that kind of battle for long.

He would win and she would lose.

And she would be killed.

Terrence Bruce's warning had come true.

His words, "Trust no one," echoed through her mind.

Rachel screamed and pounded the wet tile with her fists.

CHAPTER THIRTY TWO

Phil drove out to Compton and paid Smitty the balance of the money promised to Seedy and the LAPD gave me a free pass in the shooting death of Terrence Bruce.

Self-defense in the apprehension of a suspect was the final call.

It was the right call as far as I was concerned. A monster like Bruce did not deserve any trial. We all knew he would have walked if his case ever even went that far and we all knew it never would. He said he would never do a day in prison and I was more than happy to assist him in keeping his word.

I owed his death to Betty. And to Jake. And their unborn child.

Rachel Stone Barbieri considers herself to be at war with us then war is what she was going to get.

No prisoners.

Two down and one more to go.

The press ran the story with a picture on page three of yours truly and the six uniformed policemen who arrived on scene that night. The bigwigs at the LAPD added their comments of how I was supposedly working my case with their assistance and I didn't argue the facts.

Terrence Bruce was dead and gone and that was all that really mattered to me.

Smitty's cousin had his statement taken but no one took his picture. He did manage to plug Smitty's used car dealership in the process. I never heard if the plug gave Smitty any extra car sales.

I gave the press the names of everyone Terrence Bruce murdered and spelled the names all out so there would be no mistakes in the story. Every name was listed but Seedy Smythe's name was not.

Seedy was listed as a young girl from Compton.

I was offered a glossy copy of my news photo but I refused it.

Barney reopened his restaurant and hired a new cook, John Dazzo, a top notch chef who arrived straight from Italy. Dazzo changed up the menu to Barney's liking and his new waitress, Cher, did her best to try and fill the void left by the sad absence of Jake and Betty. Barney got back to his blue towel and tending the bar but kept his shotgun close at hand. I could still see the heavy loss in his eyes and every so often he would suddenly burst into uncontrollable tears.

We both did.

Barney and I planned on taking a trip to Jake's hometown in Bairnsdale once our team completed our final take down.

I set up my apartment at the Arms with all the intel I could get my hands on in regards to Cozumel and after four days the place began to look like a military command post. Agent Edwards would have been proud of me.

336

Agent Lindman managed to get some aerial photographs of Rachel's compound through his connections with the Navy and Agent Davis kept us in the loop with the FBI's forensics team. Days and nights passed and the three of us went over numerous ideas on how we might approach her compound, apprehend her, and return her to the States.

It was an enormous undertaking but we were determined to come up with a workable plan now that we knew exactly where she was.

"A frontal attack is completely off the table," said Agent Davis. "Unless we had a small army leading our assault. And? There are way too many well-armed guards covering the grounds for us to sneak in under the cover of darkness and grab her up. Even if we could come up with some kind of explosive diversion, Barbieri would still be tightly protected and not one of us would be able to get close to her."

"Give me a rifle and a scope and I'll get a bullet close to her," said Agent Lindman.

"That's not going to work even if that was our only choice," I said. "You won't be able to get that close to take the proper shot. Her death is not our goal."

"Killing her might be our only choice," Agent Lindman added.

"Patrick's right. You'll never get the shot," said Agent Davis. "It's physically impossible.

She pointed to the aerial photos.

"Look," she said. "The house is too high up on this rise and it's covered with trees. You could sit anywhere out there for weeks and never see her."

"We've spent too much time on this already," Agent Lindman added and looked at me. "Let's just ask the Navy to blow her and her place off the map. We can tell Mexico it was an accident and we are really sorry."

"That's not going to happen and you know it," I said. "We are not going to kill her. We are going to kidnap her. Kidnap her and bring her back here. Our terms now. Not hers."

"Who wants a beer?" asked Agent Davis.

Agent Lindman and I both stared at my board and raised our hands. Agent Davis grabbed three beers from my refrigerator, opened them with my church key and handed them out to us. Agent Davis took a big swig and stared at the board.

"Holy crap," she said.

"You see a way in?" I asked.

"I think so," she said.

Agent Lindman and I put our beers down and stared at her.

"What?" I asked. "Tell us."

"We need an inside man," she said. "Or woman. Someone that works there at the compound. A cook. A guard. Someone we can trust."

"Okay," I said. "We bribe a guard or some Mexican pool boy. So what? What does that get us?"

"The inside man tells Rachel he or she has suddenly come down with some rare disease or some type of fever."

"A fever?" asked Agent Lindman.

"Maybe. Whatever it is? It's highly contagious."

"That would definitely create a little panic amongst the troops," said Agent Lindman. "I like it so far."

"Then we send in a doctor. Our doctor. He examines her. He tells her she is fine but discovers something else. Some flaw in her heart."

"Yeah. It's black," I added.

"The flaw is fatal if she isn't operated on within the next few days and only six doctors in the world can do this type of heart surgery. Our doctor calls New York or Paris or somewhere and sets an appointment for her. He tells her he can get her to this doctor and he can also guarantee her safety. She travels on a private plane or a private boat thinking she's going somewhere for surgery, only we're the ones waiting for her when she arrives."

"I get it. We make her come to us," I said.

"Yes!" said Agent Davis and sipped her beer. "What do you think?"

"I like the concept of bringing her to us but getting an inside man is going to be difficult," I said. "If he or she isn't convincing enough it could cost them their life."

"The doctor too," said Agent Lindman.

Three beers later we began to write out everything we could possibly think of in order to pull off the kidnapping of the century and what might go wrong in the process. As the night got later, we came to the conclusion it wasn't going to work. The idea itself was sound, coerce Barbieri to come to us, but the execution of the plan would take an enormous amount of time and money if we were to do it correctly and be successful.

We finally agreed to scrap the doctor and the inside man approach and decided one of us would go for some much needed food. We threw down odd man out and Agent Davis lost. She was headed to the door when my phone rang.

"It's eleven-thirty at night," said Agent Lindman. "You having a late date we don't know about?"

I picked up the phone.

"Hello?" I said.

The voice on the other line was Diana Santoro. She had just received an odd phone call from Rachel Stone Barbieri. She related word for word her entire conversation with Barbieri and then I hung up the phone.

"What is it?" asked Agent Davis.

A big grin crossed my face.

"That was Diana Santoro," I said. "Rachel Stone Barbieri is having major problems at her new digs in Cozumel and she's reaching out to Louis Verdun for help. Barbieri dialed the only number she had for Verdun and that phone number is still active and sitting right next to Diana Santoro's new bed in Florida."

"Verdun is dead," said Agent Lindman.

"Yes!" I said with a smile. "But Rachel Stone Barbieri thinks he's alive."

"How can that be?" asked Agent Davis. "I thought this broad had eyes and ears everywhere."

"Everywhere but Florida," I added.

All three of us laughed and there was a loud knock at the door. We all drew our weapons quickly and I stepped up to my little peep window and cautiously opened it. I put my gun away, took a step back and flung open the door.

Agent Edwards stood in my doorway wearing a dark suit and tie, holding a small suitcase in one hand, and a bottle of Argentine wine in the other.

"Magenta Dairy, I presume?" he asked with a grin and stepped inside.

CHAPTER THIRTY THREE

Rachel Stone Barbieri paced her bedroom for hours. Her anxiety level was going through the roof and no matter how much she drank, ate, or smoked, her nerves would not settle down to a semblance of normalcy. She had been betrayed and now her plans in Cozumel were moving rapidly in the wrong direction and she began doubting her every thought about how to proceed.

She grabbed a bottle of tequila, made herself a roast beef sandwich and went out to the patio to think.

The hired guards around the grounds were also becoming anxious as they scanned their perimeters, not knowing exactly what it was they should be looking for. These men were well paid to provide protection for Rachel and her enterprise, but they would be no match for an army of seasoned troops.

Rachel knew she was about to be at the mercy of the entire Mexican government and waited for word from her spy in Mexico City as to the growing situation.

Would President Muchado condone her latest actions or would he strike up his army and go against her? She needed that information quickly so she would know how to proceed.

She took a deep breath, tried to relax, and hoped she might somehow negotiate her fading position if the opportunity arose.

Rachel sat patiently on the patio next to Thomas, eating her large roast beef sandwich as she waited for the highly anticipated phone calls from Luis Verdun and from her spy in Mexico City.

"Why hasn't Luis called me?" she asked.

"What were you told by the woman on the phone?" Thomas asked.

"She said Luis was driving down to the Keys from the Glass Palace with two of his men. I've been waiting over three hours. He should have called me by now."

"Do you know this woman?" he asked. "Maybe she was lying to you."

"Luis always has women around him. Women he controls through fear and intimidation. Whoever the woman was knows full well never to lie about Luis and his whereabouts. A lie, even a small one, would cost any of his women their life."

"Maybe he hasn't left the Palace yet. Would you like me to put in a call over there?"

"No," Rachel replied. "I don't want to tie up this line in case he does call or I hear from Mexico City."

"Very well," said Thomas.

Rachel took another bite of her sandwich as Thomas poured two large shots of tequila from the bottle sitting on the table. Thomas slid one of the shots to Rachel and she quickly gulped it down.

"Another please?" she asked.

"Are you sure?" he asked.

"Yes, please," she replied. "I need it. And I can handle it."

Thomas poured another shot and slid it to her.

"You were right about Madrid," Thomas said. "He is planning a move on you according to the cook's cousin, Evalina. Just before she expired."

"He promised those stupid women money. Money I am certain would have never been paid. His type of man never speaks the truth. But Evalina did. Didn't she?"

"Yes she did," said Thomas.

"If Camille or even Evalina had come to me first, told me what Madrid was planning, they would both still be alive and I would have rewarded them handsomely for their loyalty. Given them anything they desired."

Rachel shook her head and drank the tequila.

"Again," she said.

Thomas poured again.

"How many fingers did it take?" Rachel asked.

"None. I told Evalina exactly what happened to Camille and that I would begin my questions to her by first removing one of her eyes."

"That was a good start," Rachel replied.

"As I placed the silver spoon near her face she screamed out, began crying like a little lost child, and quickly begged me to stop and told me everything we needed to know."

"I knew she would."

"Why did you change your mind about torching her house?" Thomas asked.

"It's near the beach. I may have to use that house if I have to leave Cozumel quickly."

Rachel smiled and threw some pieces of her roast beef sandwich to her dogs. The dogs chewed up the pieces quickly and sat attentively at her feet. Rachel smiled and rubbed the dogs' head and ears.

"Have you decided what you are going to do with Madrid?"

Rachel looked at her watch and laughed.

"Senor Alejandro Madrid should be joining the late Camille and her talkative cousin Evalina within the hour. Greedy bastards like Madrid must be removed and removed quickly. I have no choice in that matter. It's business and anything less would be a clear show of weakness. I can't have that. Not now. Especially now. Even with Muchado looming over my head."

"Removing Madrid is the right call. I'm just sorry you didn't ask me to handle it for you. I never liked the man."

"If I sent you? Madrid would become suspicious immediately. Nervous."

"If I may ask? Who did you send?"

"His driver. Bernardo. He has been under my employ long before I came to Cozumel or even before I spoke to Muchado and made our deal."

Thomas nodded and lifted his glass.

"Saluda, Senora Barbieri."

Rachel smiled, raised her glass, and clinked with Thomas.

"To stupid women and stupid men. And stupid me."

"Kill them all," added Thomas.

"If I could?" she asked. "I would. But killing disloyal people is not the problem."

"How so?" he asked.

Rachel downed her drink and slid the glass to Thomas.

"Again," she asked.

Thomas poured another. Rachel drank it down.

"Greed is my problem, Thomas. Greed. My father, his entire life, always worked with people who had a strong sense of family loyalty and honor. These men could be taken at their word. They were trusted. They were always loyal. Like yourself. My father made those men rich. Made them wealthy men. Extremely wealthy men."

Rachel grabbed the tequila bottle and poured her own drink.

"Our enterprise runs on loyalty and trust. If someone got in the way of our business we used fear and that fear was successful. But now? Everything is changed. People are no longer afraid. They have replaced that inner fear with greed. Greed is the new order. When greed sets in and the money people were making with my father suddenly was not enough? They wanted more. And then they wanted control. It was greed that killed my father. I won't let that happen to me. My problem right now is how the Mexican President is going to take the news of Madrid's sudden passing. We have a deal in place and Muchado is being paid very well for his part. If this situation is not to his liking and he decides to break his promise to me and attack me here? I will be unable to stop him. We have good protection but we don't have the necessary fire power."

"You could kill Muchado too," said Thomas.

"I could. Yes. Killing any man is not difficult even if that man happens to be a president of a country. I could kill Muchado tomorrow but then someone else will take his place. And when that person sees what we do here and how much money is actually being made?"

"The greed factor?" asked Thomas.

"Yes," she replied. "The greed factor. It has become my one true enemy, Thomas."

"Then you need to have your own country," he said.

"I thought I did here in Cozumel. I should have known better and prepared this new move much more efficiently. Now a man like Luis Verdun? Like yourself? Honorable men. Loyal. Luis does not have the greed factor. Not with me or my family. He has always been our loyal friend. Someone to be counted on when you need a helping hand."

"Can Luis help you?" asked Thomas.

"I am hoping so," she replied and pointed at his empty shot glass.

Thomas filled his glass and drank it down. Rachel poured two more.

The white phone rang.

Rachel picked it up on the first ring.

"Yes?" she asked.

"This is the operator and I have your party," the voice said. "Please hold."

Rachel looked at Thomas.

"It's him. It's Verdun. It has to be."

Another voice came on the line.

"Mrs. Barbieri?" the voice asked.

Rachel knew immediately it wasn't Verdun's voice.

"This is Rachel Barbieri. Who am I speaking with?"

"I am called the Butler. I work for Luis Verdun. You and I met at the grand opening of the Glass Palace. Luis cut the large blue ribbon and we all drank to his success."

"I remember you. The bald gentleman."

""Yes."

"Where's Luis?" she asked. "It's imperative I speak with him immediately."

"Unfortunately, Mrs. Barbieri. Luis Verdun has been in a car accident and is in surgery at a Miami hospital."

"Is he all right?" she asked.

"He will be. Both of his legs were broken. Shattered actually. He told me to ask you what it is you require?"

Rachel sat for a few moments in silence and gathered her thoughts.

"Tell him I may have to leave Cozumel. If he could send his boat? He knows the boat I am speaking of. Please have him call me as soon as he can."

"I will tell him," the Butler said.

"Thank you," she replied.

There was a brief silence on the phone line.

"Are you there?" she asked.

"Yes. I could have the boat in your harbor and at your dock by Friday night at the latest," he said."

346

"Friday night? That would be good," Rachel said. "Please? Do that. It would be most helpful right now and most appreciated."

"Consider it done. I will give Luis your message."

"Thank you, Butler," she said.

"Thank you, Mrs. Barbieri."

The phone line went dead.

Rachel hung up the phone and looked at Thomas.

"Luis has been in a car accident. He's hurt his legs. They have him in surgery right now but he'll call me soon."

"He's sending the boat?" Thomas asked.

"Yes. It will be here by Friday. I am going to pack some things. If Muchado decides to come at me I'll have to move quickly."

"I understand. What can I do for you now?" he asked.

"Check with all the guards. Go to each and every one of them and explain the situation. If an army is what we will have to face then I don't want the men to die trying to protect me. It would be futile. Hopefully I will receive word and there will be time for them all to escape before anyone reaches the gate. Tell them they will all be paid well for their loyalty and service. Assure them of that."

"Yes, Mrs. Barbieri," said Thomas. "Will you need protection on Verdun's boat? I would be honored to stay at your side."

"Thank you, Thomas but I will be well protected with Luis. And I must do this alone."

Rachel took a piece of paper from her pocket and handed it to Thomas.

"Tomorrow morning I want you to take Maria and go to that address."

Thomas looked at the paper.

"Nogales?"

"Yes. I have friends there. You and Maria will be well compensated for your service and I will call you both personally when I know the details of what my future holds. There is a yellow Cadillac in the garage. It is yours."

"If Muchado still honors your agreement? What then?"

"I will stay and be Ix Chel. But that is doubtful. Our next big shipment comes in two weeks. I don't think I will be here by that time."

"The greed factor?"

"Yes," she replied.

Thomas nodded and walked away. Rachel grabbed the bottle of tequila and walked off the patio and headed down to the beach to her storage warehouse. The building sat back from the water about fifty feet and had direct access to the long wooden pier that ran a good three hundred feet out to the harbor.

Two armed guards stood at the ready. Rachel approached and they stood at attention.

"Relax, gentlemen," she said. "I am expecting a boat to arrive this coming Friday night. It is an important boat. You will allow this boat to come to the dock and you will let me know the moment it arrives. If I get on the boat? If I leave this harbor? I want you both to take what product you can personally carry out of here and then I am ordering you to set fire to this entire building. Do you understand?"

The two men appeared perplexed at her request but nodded yes.

"Si senora," they said in unison.

"Do not fail me. Your failure in this matter will have consequences."

"We will not fail you," said one guard.

"Good," she replied and handed over the Tequila bottle. "Tonight? This is for you. Enjoy."

Rachel turned and walked back to the main house.

The two guards watched her walk away and smiled as they looked at each other.

"She wants us to burn five hundred kilos?" a guard asked. "That's crazy talk."

The second guard looked to make certain Rachel was gone and out of hearing distance.

"Four hundred if we start moving them now," replied the other guard.

"To where?" he asked.

"We can bury them a mile down the beach. Over that rise. Away from the tides."

The two guards smiled again, put down their weapons and the Tequila, and went inside the warehouse.

CHAPTER THIRTY FOUR

I hung up the phone and beamed at Agent Edwards.

"Well?" he asked.

"She bought it," I said and took a deep breath. "She really bought it!"

Agent Edwards handed me a beer and we couldn't stop grinning.

"You are a god damn genius!" I said.

"Phase one completed," said Agent Edwards and looked at his watch. "Agent Davis and Agent Lindman should be here any minute and we will be airborne by morning! Airborne!"

"I thought for sure she was going to recognize my voice somehow," I said and took a big swig.

"I was standing right here and I didn't recognize that voice you were using. I told you it was good. It was god damn perfect! Thank god for the telephone. A great invention."

Agent Edwards sipped his beer and dropped himself down on the sofa.

"Thank god for you and your ingenious brain. It is an excellent plan," I said. "I never would have thought of doing this in a million years."

"It is good," said Agent Edwards. "Isn't it?"

"It's perfect. It's deserved on so many counts, too. So many levels. It's the right thing to do."

"I agree," said Agent Edwards.

"On one hand there is complete satisfaction for me and for Phil, I'm sure, and for Agent Davis and Agent Lindman. And on the other hand it's also a nice swan song for you, too, my friend. After everything we have been through? This? This puts the proper stamp on it all."

"You don't think we're stepping over the line a little bit? Working outside the letter of the law?" asked Agent Edwards.

"Of course we are. But it's justice," I said. "That's all that matters now. Justice for everyone she and her old man stepped on and snuffed out over the years. All those lives they have ruined pushing that poison."

"You're right. It is justice. Well-deserved justice."

"Yes it is," I added. "Hoover pulling you out of South America was perfect too! You can be here with us? You bringing us this brilliant plan?"

"It's all I thought about while I was down there."

"Where is he sending you?"

"New York City," said Agent Edwards. "Hoover is still chasing hoodlums out there and he wants me on his special task force based in Manhattan."

"You're done chasing Nazis in Argentina?" I asked.

"The Jews didn't want me down there anyway. They didn't want any Americans looking over their shoulders. I felt like a third wheel down there. A federal baby sitter."

"What about Debs?" I asked.

"Ah, Debs," he said.

Agent Edwards reached in his pocket, took out a small ring case and opened it up. He held out a large two carat diamond set in white gold. I took a closer look at it and whistled.

"Very nice. Have you asked her yet?"

"No. Not yet, but I'm flying out to San Francisco as soon as this business in Jersey is finalized."

Agent Edwards put the ring away and sighed.

"I really love her and she really loves me."

"Where would you two call home?" I asked.

"My position in New York is going to be a permanent one until I retire. No more hopping from state to state or country to country. I put a down payment on a three bedroom house in Montclair, New Jersey. Nice place to raise a family and I can ride into the city on the train every day."

"It sounds like you got this whole marriage thing worked out," I said.

"I hope so. Will you be my best man, Patrick?"

"I would be honored, my friend. Honored."

We no sooner clinked our beer bottles when Agent Davis and Agent Lindman walked in my front door.

"Did you get it?" Agent Edwards asked as he jumped to his feet.

Agent Davis opened a folder she was carrying and took out several pieces of paper all clipped together.

"Here's Doctor Belafsky's signature on all the necessary papers. I think there's six total."

Agent Edwards began checking every paper.

"Seven," said Agent Edwards. "Where's Roberto's compliance?"

Agent Davis took out another sheet of paper.

"Right here and with Roberto's signature," said Agent Davis. "I take it the phone call ruse was a success?"

"She bought it hook, line, and sinker," I said.

"So now we can say the butler did it?" asked Agent Lindman.

"He made it happen that's for sure," said Agent Edwards. "We still have a lot of work to do. Where is the driver's license and the birth certificate?"

Agent Davis reached in her folder again.

"Here. And here," she replied and handed Agent Edwards the two items he requested.

Agent Edwards looked the items over.

"These are perfect," he said. "Where did you...?"

Agent Lindman held up his hand and cut Agent Edwards off mid-question.

"Don't ask. If you don't know you can't tell. But they are perfect? Aren't they."

"Yes they are," he said as he showed them to me. I nodded my agreement.

"Let's order in some food. We can sit down and go over the game plan one last time and then tomorrow morning everything is a go."

"Sounds like a plan," I said and handed beers to Agent Davis and Agent Lindman.

"Wait," said Agent Davis.

What?" asked Agent Edwards.

"I want to hear all about Patrick's phone call."

"Why?" I asked.

"I want to convince myself that Rachel Stone Barbieri really did buy your butler routine and she's not turning this whole thing around and playing all of us."

"She makes good sense," said Agent Lindman. "If we are being played we'll be sitting right in the middle of a huge shit storm."

"Let's talk this all out," said Agent Edwards.

MAGENTA DAIRY

The room became eerily quiet as we all sat down at my kitchen table and considered our options.

CHAPTER THIRTY FIVE

The death of Alejandro Madrid enraged President Muchado and every one of his political associates. Madrid's naked body was discovered in an open field just outside of Mexico City.

There was one wound.

A single gunshot to the head.

The body had been there for several days. His black Packard and his driver, Bernardo, were nowhere to be found. An intense search was ordered to locate the car and Bernardo but after three days of searching with no leads or results, it was concluded that poor Bernardo must have met the same fate as Madrid and whoever was responsible did not want his body or the car found.

Several suspects were considered but Muchado knew of Madrid's intentions to take over the new enterprise at Cozumel and placed his childhood friend, Captain Sandoval, in charge of the investigation and the recourse. It was Muchado who got Sandoval sent back to Mexico with the promise that Sandoval would stand trial and be sent to prison.

That didn't happen.

Sandoval's charges were immediately dropped upon his arrival back to Mexico and the only punishment he received was a promotion to the rank of General and presented a nice home on the Mexican coast of Baja.

General Sandoval was beside himself with this golden opportunity to supposedly close down Barbieri's operations and rid Mexico of all illegal drug trade. The newspapers praised General Sandoval as Mexico's newest hero, taking his troops across the land and ending the sale and distribution of illegal drugs forever.

Nothing could be further from the truth.

General Sandoval's orders were to arrest Rachel Stone Barbieri and close down her operations immediately. Early Friday morning, General Sandoval and his troops entered Cozumel amidst much fanfare with Sandoval standing in an open jeep as he was driven through the small town and approached the front gate of her compound.

The gate was unlocked and as the troops moved in they discovered the entire compound was vacant except for two German shepherd dogs sunning themselves on the wide patio attached to the house.

Rachel Stone Barbieri and her entire staff were nowhere to be found.

By the end of the day, Captain Sandoval announced to the press that the illegal drug trade in Mexico had been completely closed down, and also announced his forthcoming retirement. He sent most of his troops back to Mexico City except for a small contingency of trusted soldiers needed to watch over the front gate, the main house, and the beach front warehouse, which still held three hundred kilos of prime heroin and uncut cocaine.

That evening, Captain Sandoval sat out on the patio feeding the dogs a share of a huge steak he discovered in the kitchen. He found three bottles of Champagne and, after chilling one for over an hour, popped the cork, and poured himself a large glass of bubbly.

He raised his glass with a huge grin on his face.

"To you, Ix Chel, for your house, your food, and this expensive Champagne," he said and laughed to himself. "I am going to love it here."

Sandoval downed several large gulps of bubbly and before he placed the glass back on the table began to choke. He reached at his throat with both hands and attempted to stand and call for a guard but the liquid made him unable to speak.

Unable to breathe.

Sandoval stiffened and fell to the patio. Dead by his own hand, sipping from a corked and wrapped unopened bottle of Champagne properly chilled but somehow laced with cyanide.

Soldiers had been ordered not to disturb Sandoval until the morning.

His orders.

There was only one guard down by the warehouse. He looked at his watch. The time was 11:30 p.m. A slight mist had come in off the water and he squinted his eyes through the fog as Rachel Stone Barbieri and her two guards approached from his left.

Rachel wore white slacks, a black turtleneck sweater and carried a large black tote bag on her shoulder. The guards carried suitcases in both their hands.

"Good evening, Jorge," she said.

"Ola Senora Barbieri," Jorge responded.

Rachel reached in her tote and took out an envelope.

"Fifty thousand American," she said. "As promised."

Jorge took the envelope and stuffed it in his shirt.

"Do you really have to leave us, Ix Chel?" he asked.

357

"Yes," she replied. "I must go but Ix Chel will never leave you or the people of Cozumel."

Jorge grabbed Rachel's hand and kissed it.

"You know what to do?" she asked.

Jorge nodded.

"Si. I will know what to do and what to say when the time comes."

Rachel smiled and the sound of a boat's engine was heard off in the distance.

"That time is here and now, Jorge. Remember to go when you see the flames. Not the smoke."

Jorge nodded and went up the trail to the house. Rachel and her two guards walked out onto the pier carrying the four suitcases. The guard put the suitcases down on the pier.

"Goodbye, gentlemen," she said and shook their hands.

The two guards looked out at the approaching boat.

"I'll be all right," she said. "You two go on, now. You have much work to do."

The two guards nodded and walked back to the warehouse. Luis Verdun's thirty-six foot Steelcraft glided slowly aside the dock with all lights off and a tall man wearing a wool cap and a pea coat leapt to the pier holding a rope, tying off the boat after it came to a stop.

"Rachel Stone Barbieri?" the man asked.

"I am Rachel," she answered.

The man smiled and extended his hand.

"Derrick Thomas at your service, Mrs. Barbieri."

Rachel shook his hand and Derrick looked down at the four suitcases.

"These ladies are traveling with you as well?" he asked.

"Yes," she replied.

Derrick quickly grabbed the suitcases and put them on the boat. He jumped back down and looked at her.

"If I may?" he asked.

Rachel nodded and Derrick lifted her aboard as well. Derrick jumped on board and looked her over.

"What's our destination?" he asked.

"Havana, Cuba," she replied.

"Let me put these down in your state room and we'll get underway."

The warehouse on the beach suddenly began to burn furiously.

"Oh my god!" said Derrick. "What is that?"

"That is another time. Another time going up in smoke," she said and sighed deeply.

"Did you want to ride up on the fly bridge with me or do you want to remain down below?" he asked.

"For now? I would like to watch that fire burn as we head out to sea."

"Certainly," he said.

Derrick took two trips and put the suitcases down below as Rachel stepping up on the fly Bridge, stared out at the raging fire. Derrick untied the rope, joining her on the fly bridge, and started the engine. The Steelcraft motored out slowly across the harbor and picked up speed as it headed out to sea.

"I've seen enough," Rachel said. "I'm going below."

"First door on your right," said Derrick.

Rachel stepped down onto the deck and went below. She opened the door to her right and stepped inside the dark room.

The door quickly shut behind her and the room lights came on.

Special Agent Davis stood behind Rachel at the door and Special Agent Edwards and Patrick Miles Atwater sat on two leather chairs facing her.

"Good evening Mrs. Barbieri," said Patrick. "Welcome aboard."

CHAPTER THIRTY SIX

The ambulance parked across the street from the front entrance as requested. Agent Lindman sat at the wheel and Agent Davis sat on the passenger side, dressed in a freshly laundered nurse's uniform and coat and Agent Lindman wore the white uniform of a hospital attendant.

The game was afoot, as Sir Arthur Conan Doyle would say in his tales of Sherlock Holmes and his man, Doctor Watson.

Both agents stared at the aged building as they waited.

"Can that be right?" Agent Lindman asked.

"What's that?" she asked in return.

"That stone reads 1876," he said.

"That's when it was originally built," she replied. "It was supposed to hold 350 people. Now it has more than nine times that amount."

"Nine times," he repeated. "Wow. That's going to be close quarters."

"Yes it is," she replied.

"How come the upper floors are different than the rest of the building?" he asked.

"Fire," she said. "Back in 1930. Some kind of faulty wiring."

"That could be dangerous. Faulty wiring in an old facility like this. The whole damn place could go up."

"It could," she replied.

Agent Davis and Agent Lindman both smiled.

"You look very cute in your nurse's outfit," Agent Lindman said. "Maybe we should play doctor later."

"I'll take your temperature and give you a physical when we get back to the hotel."

A big grin crossed Agent Lindman's face.

"I will hold you to that," he said.

Agent Davis looked Agent Lindman over.

"What?" he asked.

"I don't know which I like better. You as this hospital aide in white or that sexy sea captain in that pea coat of yours?"

Agent Lindman smiled.

"I'll be whatever you want me to be," he replied.

Agent Davis smiled, sighed heavily, and a concerned look crossed her face.

"We're doing the right thing here. Aren't we?" she asked.

"We all agreed. It's much deserved. She's not your average criminal. Don't forget that."

"I won't," she replied. "I won't."

The old building sat on three hundred acres and was filling up at an alarming rate. Every year more and more people were brought in and housed indefinitely. Adequate staffing was difficult not only to find but to keep. This fact forced the institution to hire on able bodied men and women with much less training as compared to the earlier periods of operation.

This had all been explained to us as Special Agent Edwards and I sat across the desk of the admissions officer, Doctor Donald Swarm. He removed his reading glasses, closed the folder we had handed him, and smiled .

"How long has Mrs. Munoz been in her present state?" he asked.

"Almost three years now," lied Agent Edwards. "Ever since her husband was brutally murdered."

"Most tragic events do foster this type of behavior," said Doctor Swarm.

"You've seen this kind of behavior before?" I asked.

"Oh yes," said Doctor Swarm. "Numerous times. Many patients here have taken on multiple personalities once there has been that initial mental break. It's so difficult to pinpoint and even more difficult to return the patient to their normal selves. Doctor Belafsky has done the right thing by bringing Mrs. Munoz here. This personality she harbors is clearly escalating to a highly unsettling level where in my personal opinion may manifest to where she will become a danger, not only to herself, but to others."

"We all felt that, too, Doctor," said Agent Edwards. "Having her here? Under your care? Is best."

"I agree and thank you for your vote of confidence," said Doctor Swarm. "We will see to it she gets the proper care she requires."

A light knock sounded on the office door and a tall woman in a white nurses' uniform entered holding a clip board.

"Gentlemen? This is Sara Units, our ward supervisor."

Sara nodded at us and got right to the matter at hand.

362

"Mrs. Munoz has been photographed and placed in room fourteen in ward six. She is still sedated and unresponsive but should become fairly lucid within the hour."

"Excellent," said Doctor Swarm. "We will know better how to accommodate her as these initial weeks pass."

"I need your signature on this, Doctor Swarm," she said.

Doctor Swarm quickly signed the form.

"Gentlemen," she said and left the room.

"Our business at hand is now complete. Do you have any questions? Concerns?" asked Doctor Swarm.

"If Mrs. Munoz becomes a problem your staff cannot handle please inform me immediately," said Agent Edwards. "I promised her son, Roberto."

Agent Edwards handed Doctor Swarm his new card and phone number. The doctor took it and nodded.

"Of course," said Doctor Swarm. "I understand completely."

"Could I see her before we go." I asked.

"Certainly," replied the Doctor.

We rose out of our chairs and Doctor Swarm led us down a back stairway leading to ward six.

There were numerous women wandering aimlessly through the hall. One was completely naked and quickly taken to a room by two large attendants wearing white uniforms. Another woman, about eight months pregnant, sat on a cot in the hall rubbing her stomach and wearing a torn blue hospital gown.

"Can't run, got to fly away," the woman kept repeating over and over in a soft voice as she stared at the ceiling.

Doctor Swarm and the floor staff totally ignored the woman.

Here we are, gentlemen," he said and unlocked the door with his pass key.

Agent Edwards and Doctor Swarm waited in the hallway and I went in the room.

Wearing a plain blue cotton dress and white slippers, Rachel Stone Barbieri sat in a wooden chair next to her single bed, staring out the window. She appeared relaxed and enjoying the sun on her face.

Anyone seeing her like this would think she had gone completely mad but I knew better.

Our entire team did.

I grabbed the chair and turned her around slowly so she could look into my eyes. I smiled at her and spoke in a soft low tone.

"I know you can hear me and I know you won't be able to move a muscle or speak for a while. I wanted to come and say goodbye properly."

Her eyes began to blink, telling me she was understanding every word I said.

"I'm taking a long trip across the ocean to spread the ashes of my friends. My dead friends. The friends of mine that were murdered on your orders. Orders that you will never be able to give again. To anyone. You? Your drug enterprise? And all your power and control? Are all gone. Blown away forever. Like smoke from a burnt out candle."

I looked around the room and stared back into her eyes. They began to blink faster and her breathing became elevated.

I smiled broadly.

"This place is going to be your new home from now on, Rachel. This little room with a view is going to be your new operational headquarters. And no matter what you may plot or plan, think or say? You are going to remain in here until the day you die."

Some women screaming at the top of their lungs suddenly echoed down the hall.

"Killing you or locking you up in some federal prison is too good of a punishment for a person of your caliber. This is where you need to be. This is where you will remain."

Rachel's eyes began to blink furiously and I knew my words had hit her hard.

I stood up and wanted to slap her face as hard as I could but I took in a deep breath and bent down close to her ear and whispered.

"You take care Rachel Stone Barbieri," I said. "You take care."

I took another deep breath and watched her eyes blinking and her body twitching. I turned to leave and Rachel suddenly reached out and grabbed my arm.

"Where's my money you evil son of a bitch?" she asked barely able to move her mouth.

I looked down at her and smiled.

"Your money is safe and it's going to pay for your room and board until you cease to exist. That's where your money is."

I removed her grasp and looked her in the eye.

"And you, Rachel Stone Barbieri, are the only evil son of a bitch in this room."

I turned, walked out of the room, and shut the door behind me.

Doctor Swarm locked the door.

"Everything satisfactory?" he asked.

"Yes and thank you, Doctor," I said and shook his hand. "Saying goodbye meant a lot to me. Take good care of her."

"Don't worry" he replied. "We will take good care of her from here on in."

Doctor Swarm walked us out of the ward and left us standing at the elevator.

Agent Edwards and I smiled at each other.

"This place is perfect," said Agent Edwards. "I hope she out-lives us all."

"One can only hope," I replied and the elevator doors opened and we stepped inside.

We exited the building, walked down the steps, taking in the warmth of the morning sun and breathing in the crisp clean winter air.

We stood on the sidewalk and looked around.

"Are you all right with this?" Agent Edwards asked.

"I'm good," I said. "You?"

"Absolutely," he replied. "Beautiful day. Isn't it?"

"Damn near perfect," I said.

"Jonathan Wainwright called me. Wants to run for Governor. Asked me to see about getting an endorsement from J. Edgar."

"Are you going to do it?" I asked.

"I told him I'd think about it."

A women inside the building suddenly screamed at the top of her lungs.

"Do you think that was her?" he asked.

"I hope so," I said. "I really do hope so."

Agent Edwards and I smiled and walked across the street.